STRAIGHT *Forward*

MARTIN PARNELL

Copyright © 2022 by Martin Parnell. All rights reserved.

This book or parts thereof may not be reproduced in any form, stored in any retrieval system, or transmitted in any form by any means—electronic, mechanical, photocopy, recording, or otherwise—without prior written permission of the author, except as provided by United States of America copyright law.

This is a work of fiction. Unless otherwise indicated, all the names, characters, businesses, places, events and incidents in this book are either the product of the author's imagination or used in a fictitious manner. Any resemblance to actual persons, living or dead, or actual events is purely coincidental.

All trademarks, product names, logos, company names, and brands are the property of their respective owners in the United States and/or other countries. All trademarks, product names, logos, company names, and brands used in this book are for identification purposes only. Use of these trademarks, product names, logos, company names, and brands does not imply endorsement. The author and publisher are not associated with any product or vendor in this book.

ISBN: 979-8-9857066-9-7
Library of Congress Control Number: 2022915207

Cover Models: Wyatt, James
Illustration by: Tim Bergmann (Bergmann Graphics)
Design by: Cassie Caldwell (Caldwell Design)
Legal Services: Ted Roe (Veritas Business Law)
Editor: Kristen Hall-Geisler (Indigo Editing, Design and More)
Author Advice: Ali Shaw (Indigo Editing, Design and More)
Publication Management: Vinnie Kinsella (Indigo Editing, Design and More)
Digital Marketing: Rachel Hutchings (Books Forward)

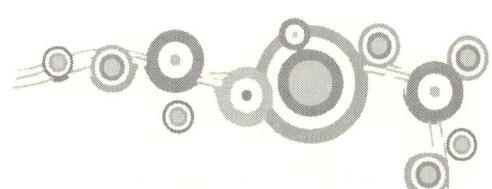

*To Wyatt
with thanks for the
beautiful friendship you inspired*

*Shoutout to Delta Airlines
for randomly seating us together,
which is how we met.
And from that chance meeting,
we have become such good friends.
Doesn't the universe work in wonderful ways?*

P.S.: Wyatt is the cowboy on the cover!

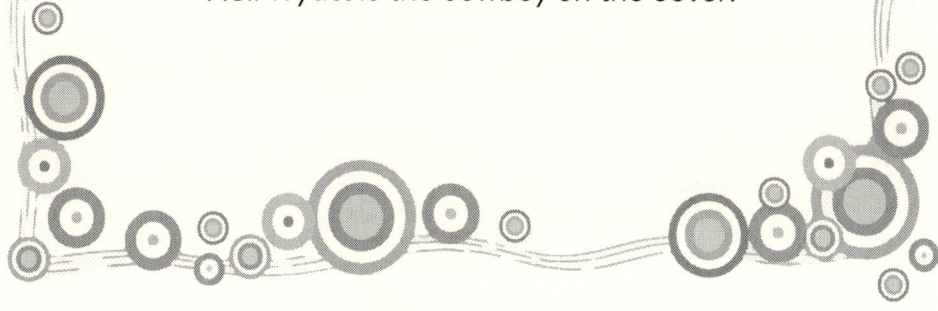

Contents

Helluva Way To Meet A New Neighbor 1
Machiavellian Intrigue 14
Revelations 26
Routines And Receptacles 36
Ballbusting And Smartassery 45
The Bros And The Ladies 50
Coach Ty 68
My Team Is Hot 73
Boys And Basketball And Bromancing 77
Makeover 93
As Simple As That 108
Two Things I Learned 117
No Biz Like Showbiz 121
A Better Understanding 125
Such A Nice Thing To Do 147
Pool Party (Guest Appearance By Dr. Ruth Martin) 181
What Happens In Vegas 194
Exquisite Torture 207
Only The Best For Martin 225
Go Big Or Go Home 232
Advice To The Lovelorn
  (Guest Appearance By Dear Abby Martin) 236
Touché 244
Nightmare 248
The King Holds Audiences 274
Isn't That Love? 281
Naughty Nurse 287
Planting Seeds (Guest Appearance By Gardener Martin) 295
The Beautiful Heart Of A Beautiful Man 302
Kid In The Candy Store 308
Yay Team 311
Well Deserved 318
Breaking News 330
The Door 339
A Note From The Author 345

Helluva Way To Meet A New Neighbor

"The door is open!"

Gossiping on the phone with my friend Amy, I noticed with great excitement that my new neighbor's back door was wide open. He and I were renting brand new adjoining townhouses with shared deck, pool, and backyard. I was more than eager to meet him.

"Should I go introduce myself? The owner says I'll like him. I'm really curious...I am not being nosy! I came out to water plants on the deck...No, I'm not drowning the plants just so I can wait out here...Well, he was supposed to show up midday yesterday, but he got delayed. So the owner came over to let the movers in...He arrived late last night. I wonder what he's like."

I heard a sudden clatter and a shout through his door.

"Goddammit!" A Southern accent. "Shit piss motherfucker hell god*dam*mit!"

"Are you all right?" I called out to him.

"I need ya, buddy. Damn, I made a mess. Could you come help me?"

"Gotta go, Amy. He needs my help. Call you later."

I stepped into his house and came to a dead halt.

A vision.

1

A gloriously handsome, masculine vision. Tall, fit, longish dirty blond hair, perfection.

This was the new neighbor? OMG!

Ladder and paint paraphernalia indicated the vision had been painting. The problem: the vision had a gallon of paint spilled all down his front, completely drenching his t-shirt, shorts, legs, and feet. Sopping. The face and hair had only a few splatters.

He smiled at me.

Dazzling!

"Helluva way to meet a new neighbor. I'm Ty."

"Martin."

"Had the paint can on the ladder for a second, and I bumped it. Stupid. Hell and damnation!"

"Don't move or you'll get paint all over everything. Wait one second, and I'll be right back. Whatever you do, don't move."

I rushed back to my place and got paper towels, scissors, and a roll of plastic garbage bags. When I returned, he was ruefully looking around at the mess he had made. The tarp had wet paint all over it, but fortunately not much had gotten on the hardwood floor. I kicked off my flip-flops and put a few garbage bags down on top of the splattered tarp so I wouldn't step on the wet paint.

"We'll get you to the bathroom to clean up. But you can't drip or track paint everywhere. Those clothes are so drenched they're completely ruined, and if you try to pull your shirt off, you'll get it all over and make more of a mess. So I'm going to cut your t-shirt away."

"No use cryin' over spilled paint, isn't that how the sayin' goes?" he joked.

The sound of his Southern accent and whiskey-baritone voice...what was that song about black velvet and a slow Southern style?

Get ahold of yourself, Martin.

"I'll cut the back of the shirt from waist to neck, and you slide it off slowly onto the tarp. Lean down so it doesn't splat when you drop it."

When he stood upright and revealed his beautiful chest with fine blond hairs, it was all I could do to not reach out and touch. Sigh. Perfect.

"Okay, now slide your shorts down without splatting."

"Gotta warn ya, when I wear gym shorts, I go commando."

Commando? That means...

An unwritten law of the universe says that gay men will somehow manage to see their straight friends naked. And I always seek to abide by that law! But usually not within five minutes of meeting someone.

"No problem. Let's get you out of this mess."

He carefully slid his shorts down and stepped out of them.

And THAT was just as perfect as the rest of him. The backside was a delight too. If this was a comic book, there would be a speech balloon above my head saying "GULP!" I hoped I wasn't too obvious, but who could help looking?

Holding his arms wide, he boasted, "With all this paint on me, I'm like a work of art."

"If we displayed you next to the Mona Lisa, we'd know why she was smiling."

Uh-oh. Was that too flirtatious?

He smirked and winked at me. *Oh man.*

"Here, use these paper towels to wipe off as much paint as you can." While he was cleaning up, *that* was bouncing a little bit. Mesmerizing.

Careful.

I put down a line of garbage bags as a path to the downstairs bathroom so he wouldn't drip paint or make footprints on the floor.

"Go shower. There's a little paint in your hair, so shampoo too."

While he was showering, I was efficient as always and cleaned up the mess, setting everything back up, ready for him to finish painting. I looked around his living room. Packing boxes and furniture were stacked away from the walls. A cereal box on the counter was the only item in the kitchen. I peeked in the refrigerator. A carton of milk and a six-pack of beer. Maybe he stopped at an all-night convenience store just before he arrived.

Our mirror-image townhouses were well designed and quite spacious. The first floor featured an open living room with kitchen and dining area, guestroom, full bathroom, laundry room, and storage. Upstairs had a master bedroom, another full bathroom, and two other rooms that could be guestrooms or den or office. Just as we did in the back, we shared the front porch, driveway, and small lawn.

He returned from the shower wearing a towel. Magnificent. He said, "Buddy, you didn't have to clean all that up. Thank ya kindly." He came quite close and said, "Did I get all the paint outta my hair?"

Helluva Way to Meet A New Neighbor

I was a mere few inches from him. He smelled soapy clean and manly. My pheromones were going berserk!

"All good. You're almost finished painting. When it's done, please come over and join me for lunch."

"Buddy, you don't have to do that."

"Oh, please. I love to cook. Cooking is my passion! And it's no fun to cook for just myself. You can be my very first guest, and I can show off." Using my intuitive sixth sense of food, I ventured, "I think you might like Tex-Mex?"

"Love Tex-Mex! Well, all right, if you're sure."

I said in a teasing but hopefully not too flirtatious tone, "The work of art—yourself—should continue painting, and when one masterpiece finishes the other, lunch will be served." *That definitely was too flirtatious.*

"Thanks for rescuin' me from the disaster, buddy."

I went out, turning back to smile and wave. He was regarding me curiously.

I went into a frenzy of preparation. I threw together a Mexican taco lasagna and put it in the oven. I made guacamole with my secret ingredient—not telling!—and tossed a salad.

And all the while, I was obsessing. Did I come on too strong? I was obvious, wasn't I? Surely he figured out I'm gay? And if he did figure it out, would he be okay with it or become distant? Was he freaking out? Currently the person freaking out was me!

The owner had told me, "My niece works for the city, and she said a new colleague was coming from Oklahoma and needed a place to rent. So I got on Skype with the fellow, and we made an agreement. He's a pretty decent guy; I can see you two getting along. I kinda think you'll like him."

I kinda think you'll like him.

Understatement. Of. The. Year.

Ty knocked on the back door and said, "Lunch ready? You sure this is all right?"

"Come in, Ty. Welcome!"

He was wearing a fresh t-shirt, shorts, and baseball cap this time. "Dang, your place is all set up."

"I did move in a week earlier than you did. Sit. I have guacamole and chips to start. Would you like a Corona?"

And so we began the journey of our friendship.

Ty radiated charisma and Southern-style charm. He smiled easily, his accent was delightful, and he called me buddy or pal every other sentence. We chitchatted in a friendly manner, enjoying our casual talk.

"Best guac I ever had. What smells so good?"

I served the Mexican taco lasagna and salad, and he attacked it with great gusto. He was a robust, muscular man, and if all he had eaten was a bowl of cereal this morning, he must have been starving!

"Fantastic," he said between bites.

"Have some more," I said, shoveling another huge slab of lasagna and more salad without waiting for a yes. I relaxed a bit as we talked. All was going well. He didn't seem to be freaking out.

I asked, "Is Ty a nickname? Is it short for something?"

Helluva Way to Meet A New Neighbor

"Take a guess. You'll never get it, not in a million years."

"Tyler...Tyson...Tyrone...Tiger with a y, Tiberius with a y?"

"I'm not named after a person."

"Not a person? Hmm...Typhoon?" I joked.

"You tryin' to say I'm a blustery windbag? Laugh it up, buddy." He had a big smile, enjoying keeping me in suspense. "It's a product."

"A product...Tylenol! Hey, when you meet a girl, you could tell her you're personally available to relieve stress headaches. Twice a day, morning and evening."

"Just one laugh riot, buddy, gettin' funnier by the minute." He looked like he was having fun, but I had a thought.

"Are you sensitive about your name? You don't have to tell me."

"No, you're gettin' closer. My mama liked usin' family names. She named my oldest brother after my dad. For my second and third brothers, she used combinations of my granddads' names. By the time I came along, she'd run outta family names for boys. She decided to be creative. When she found out if I was a boy, she'd name me after the first thing she saw. Can ya guess?"

"Give me a hint."

"Mama was pregnant and sittin' in the doctor's office waitin' for him to come back with the result."

"She saw a medical poster about...Typhoid! Oh wait, that's not a product."

He laughed and said, "Now who would name a kid Typhoid?"

"Typhoid Mary's parents?"

7

"Ya got me there. Give ya another hint: when the doctor came in to say it's a boy, she was doin' a crossword puzzle and holdin' a pencil."

I couldn't figure it out.

"So I'm named after a yellow number-two pencil. You know, like ya used in grade school." He slapped his leg and laughed. "Nobody ever gets it. My name is..." He grinned. "Dixon Ticonderoga Fields."

I burst out laughing and said, "That is so marvelous!"

"My mama, the creative baby-name lady."

"Why Ty? Why not Dix?"

"Yeah, right. Can you imagine goin' through my whole life with all those jokes about pencil dicks?"

That certainly does not apply in Ty's case—uh, pencil case!

"So Ty I am. You got another beer?"

Going to the refrigerator, I said, "Well, she could have been in the bathroom. And then we'd be calling you Prince."

"What?"

"Prince Charmin."

He laughed and threw me that dazzling smile.

He was a Prince Charming all right. Heart be still!

"You worked so fast," said Ty when I showed him how I had set up my house.

Ours was a unique rental situation. The owner had been my consulting client, and I became interested when he told me he had brand new adjoining townhouses needing renters.

"There's a problem, though," the owner said. "The townhouses aren't quite finished. I have this other development I'm working on. It has a strict timeline, and I incur a huge penalty if I don't meet the deadline. I need every one of my workers from all my projects right now at the development. So either I finish the townhouses later, or I make a deal with the new renter." He made an unbeatable offer. The rent was an under-market price, I think because he liked me. "If I give you three months rent free, would you finish painting the second coat on the walls, and take care of the final cleanup, the landscaping, and the filling of the pool with startup maintenance? I'll make the same deal to the neighbor, and you guys can split the cost of the landscaping and pool preparation."

The neighbor being the man from Oklahoma. Who he thought I might like.

I explained to Ty, "I had help setting up. My close friend Amy is a costume designer at a professional theatre, and she organized some scenery guys who take on extra jobs. It went really fast to have them paint and help with the furniture, worth every cent."

"I like these colors you're usin'. Your house feels all warm and cozy. My house is just plain ol' white."

"I picked the pale yellow, and the scenery guys helped me pick the amber and pearl gray trim and accent colors. If you want help, we can arrange for them to come by."

During our tour I especially made it a point to show him my well-stocked pantry, refrigerator, and freezer. I said, "I can make a midnight snack or prepare a banquet at a moment's notice." I had a plan in mind.

StraightForward

I asked Ty about his job.

"I work for the city of LA in a special department, same thing I did in Oklahoma City. But I had a colleague there I did not get along with. At all. Bad situation. When this job came up, I figured I could make lemonade outta lemons. I applied for the transfer and got it."

He seemed uninterested in talking about his work; he was vague on the details. I wondered if it was a boring job with not much to tell. A city job, maybe there was no excitement to be had.

Mine was not a boring job, at least to me. I told Ty, "I'm a consultant. I call myself the Consultant Who Finds Solutions. I have a reputation for solving problems, and now most jobs come through personal referrals. I help corporations, small businesses, all sorts of other organizations. I work almost exclusively online."

After the tour he said, "Martin, thanks for this mighty fine lunch. 'Preciate you helpin' me out, pal."

"Anytime."

He asked me to arrange to have the scenery guys help him the next day if they could.

My mind was whirling with ideas. Plans were hatching, the plot was thickening—whatever cliché you can come up with, that was about to happen.

If only I haven't blown it. Will he freak out when he finds out I'm gay?

I saw him again in the afternoon. He knocked on my door and asked if I would help him move the sofa out of the way so he could get to a stack of boxes. Of course I helped and offered further, but he declined.

Later he knocked again. He was shirtless, wearing his towel and a cowboy hat. One would think it an odd combination, but on him it looked *so sexy.*

"What's with the cowboy hat?" I asked.

"I'm just a country cowboy, born and bred. And here I am in the big city."

"Watch out for them city slickers," I said. *Namely yours truly.*

"Buddy, I hope you don't mind about this. I wanna go for a swim and lay out by the pool. Back in Oklahoma, I always used to go skinny-dippin' in the creek. The neighbors can't see us, and if it's just you and me around, would you mind if I went skinny-dippin' here? And I don't like tan lines. Like farmer tans or trucker tans. Hate that. Can I lay out buck nekkid? You already saw the goods this mornin', and I guess it didn't offend you. Would it bother you if I did that?"

Let me think. Would it bother me if he was flaunting his magnificent manliness? Would it bother me if I could perv and see him out the windows? As for the goods, as he called it, would it bother me to feast my eyes on them again? Would it bother me if I was driven to complete distraction by the sight of such a fabulous specimen of manhood? The only botheration would be me holding myself back from throwing myself at him. OMGissimo!

I breezily replied, in as nonchalant a tone as I could manage, "Oh, no bother at all."

"Yeah, I figure it's somebody's birthday somewhere, I'm wearin' my birthday suit in their honor."

And I was about to get the birthday present. "Put on sunscreen."

I had to restrain myself from going out there. I bided my time, though I did perv through the windows. More than once. Well, more than twenty-five times.

As there was no deck furniture yet, he was laying on his towel by the pool, tanning, with his cowboy hat over his eyes. The goods were certainly living up to their name. How nice that the universe contrived to have a somewhat exhibitionist man and a somewhat shameless voyeur as neighbors.

I brought out a tall glass of freshly squeezed lemonade with just the right amount of sugar, tinkling with ice cubes. "Here you go. When I have lemons, I make actual lemonade," I said with a smile.

"Hey buddy, you don't have to wait on me." He took a big swig. "Mmm, that hits the spot."

Time for step one of the plan. I decided to be bold. No tiptoeing. "How do you like your steak?"

"What?"

"Rare, medium, or well-done?"

"I know whatcha mean. But what do you mean?"

"For dinner tonight. Seven o'clock if that's okay?"

"Buddy, you don't have to do that. I was gonna call out for pizza. I was gonna ask if you wanted some."

He was going to ask *me*. "Ty, I told you. I love to cook. And it's exciting to have someone around because cooking for just myself is a drag. I have been itching for the chance to show off."

"You already did with lunch. It was dang wonderful."

"Please have dinner with me tonight. We can do pizza tomorrow if you want," giving him a chance to pay it back then. And it did guarantee another time to see him. "Nice, thick juicy steak cooked to perfection? Baked potato with all the fixings? Cole slaw? Peach pie for dessert?"

He groaned in appreciation. "I can't turn down an offer like that. That would be right nice."

"So what about the steak?"

"Medium-rare."

The rare meat I really was interested in was so close it was giving me the willies. So to speak. I had to force myself to not stare. Was it depraved to fantasize about putting suntan lotion all over that incredible body?

Get a grip, Martin. "See you at seven."

StraightForward

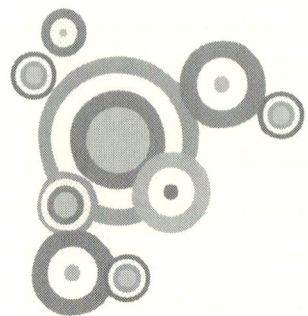

Machiavellian Intrigue

He stepped out his door right on time. He was in jeans, cowboy hat, cowboy shirt, and boots this time. And did they look good on him—hot hot hot!

I had set up a portable table and chairs out on the deck. I didn't set it up like a romantic candlelit dinner, I'm not stupid. But I did lay a tablecloth and make everything look nice. For appetizers we had cheesy pesto bread and stuffed mushrooms. I offered a selection of drinks, but he chose Corona again. I prepared a huge steak with black pepper sauce—flawlessly, if do I say so myself—and the baked potato was plump and fluffy. Sour cream, chives, butter, bacon bits, all ready to pile on. I plied him with food, heaping extra cole slaw.

The way to a man's heart...

Again he attacked everything like he was a starveling. Big appetite. To go along with big other things.

Down, Martin. Down!

We had a delightful conversation. I learned a lot about his family, about life on the farm. His father had passed away; he was close to his mother and three brothers, who were all married with kids.

"My brothers are hogtied by their wives, but I'm a free man. Ya know, if there's one thing I'll miss about Oklahoma, it's the kids."

"The kids?"

"My nieces and nephews. I always especially enjoy bein' around them. I'm their playful Uncle Ty. Whenever we had family get-togethers, I was always in charge of the kids."

Ty and kids? Now that was rather interesting. I couldn't quite picture it, but he seemed to be genuine about missing them.

As was evident when he said, "Goddammit, buddy, I already miss my nieces and nephews. Just a minute, I gotta call 'em right now."

And he did just that, teasing and joking with the kids. Even though I could only hear his side of the conversation, it was apparent they adored their Uncle Ty, because they didn't want to hang up. Another intriguing facet of this vibrant man.

After his calls ended, I had to find out more. "Clearly you miss the kids. Is there a girlfriend you'll be missing?"

"Only one? Buddy, there's a lotta girls who'll miss *me*. I have many, many girlfriends, Martin. You know, the one-night kind. I'm not lettin' a gal tie me down."

"So you're single."

"And willin'! I can't wait to meet me some big-city gals."

"Do you have a type? Let me guess your requirements." I joked, "Female? Breathing? Has always been female?"

He laughed and said, "I'm a little choosier than that. I like 'em busty and lusty. And I'm partial to blondes."

It popped out of my mouth without thinking. "I'm sure all the buxom blonde nymphomaniacs will be delighted to meet a handsome studly cowboy like you."

Yikes!

He smiled, and I hurriedly went on, "And are you really a cowboy? Did you ride the range or something?"

"We have a farm, so I'm not really truly a cowboy. My daddy raised some cattle, so we did have to round 'em up. But I like ridin' a horse, and I love rodeo. And if it matters, the Dallas Cowboys are my favorite team."

"So you like," making a wild guess about the team, "football?" Apparently I was right, as he smiled. "Did you play?"

"I did in high school. Also played basketball and baseball. Played basketball in college too. I've always been a good athlete. I'm hopin' I can find somethin' sporty here in LA."

The Consultant Who Finds Solutions could help with that.

Ty said, "Your turn. What's your story?"

"Martin Parnell has a story? If there is one, it's a sad saga of the small-town boy going to the big city. I'm from an O state too. I grew up in 'Stagnantville', Ohio, where the favorite spectator sport is watching grass grow."

"Sounds like some towns in Oklahoma."

"I went to 'Cesspool High School' and graduated 'sewer' cum laude." I wasn't sure whether Ty would get my sarcastic humor, but he obligingly laughed. "The second the diploma was in my hand, I walked out of the auditorium and into the night, never to look back."

"It couldn'ta been that bad?"

"I attended The Ohio State University, which was more fun than my hometown but still had an Ohio attitude. So once I got my degree in business management, I came straight to LA."

"How'd ya learn to cook like this?"

"When I was a kid, I spent summers with my grandmother. She taught me how to cook basic things. And in high school and college, I got a summer job with a caterer, and the chefs taught me the more complicated stuff." I smiled as I remembered how they had pseudo-adopted me when they saw how hard I worked and how much potential I had. "I just like to have fun cooking. It's relaxation for me."

"Ya still got family back there in Ohio?"

"No. My parents are no longer alive, and I don't have any siblings. I inherited the houses from my grandmother and my parents, and because I never want to go back, I sold both houses and invested. That's my nest egg."

"How come you never want to go back?"

"That's a long story, Ty. Growing up in Ohio was not much fun. California is where I belong."

Time to get on with my plan. Considering the sexual thoughts running through my head when I looked at him, it rightly should be called a sordid plan. But actually it was a good idea.

"Enough of ancient history. Ty, I'd like to discuss a proposal with you. You already know I love to cook. It's my passion."

"You're talented in the kitchen, buddy."

I was nervous whether he would like my plan, so I tiptoed this time. "And, forgive me, I get the impression that the kitchen is not your priority."

By now he had had several beers and was pretty relaxed. He gave me a mischievous look. "The bedroom is my priority, buddy. That's where I'm talented. Passion aplenty there." He winked at me and looked to see how I would react to his playfulness.

I could be playful Martin right back. "Oh, I see. The big-city girls should run for their lives. That rascally cowboy will steal their virtue!"

"No virgins left in LA," he said, holding up his fingers like a scout.

"So I should expect a parade of virgin sacrifices coming through your door? Will I find naked women lolling around the pool, like you're a sultan with a harem? Should I buy stock in a condom company because sales will skyrocket?"

"If you're gonna do that, tell 'em to up their XXL production."

OMG!

He grinned, and I think he was having fun with me. I was having fun teasing him right back. "And when women come around at three a.m. pounding on your door, and you have someone else in your bedroom already there, and then they start catfighting with each other, and the cops show up, and they arrest all of you, and handcuff you without any clothes on, and I have to come bail you out, and the newspapers offer me a lot of money, and the headlines say 'Neighbor Tells All About Next Door Love Lair,' that's what I should expect?"

"Sounds good to me!" he said, and we laughed. "Except it might be two someone elses already there." And he winked.

"Oh, I see. Mister Stamina," I said leadingly.

"Like a piston in a factory," he answered equally leadingly.

OM—! Stop right there. If I think OMG one more time, I'll have to enroll in seventh grade as a middle school girl.

"So what's this proposal?" he asked, changing the subject back.

Still fearful of coming on too strong, I tiptoed again. "I get the impression you might not like cooking."

"I can boil water. Ice cubes are my specialty," he joked. "Toast is a challenge, but I manage."

Time to be bold. Nothing ventured nothing gained. "So my proposal is this. Why don't you let me regularly make dinner for the two of us? I can have so much more fun cooking, and you can get a good meal. If you're busy or have to go out, or me the same thing, we just tell each other. Sometimes if you feel like pizza, we can do that."

"But you can't pay for all that food."

"We agree that you give me money, or we could go shopping together."

He appeared to be seriously considering the idea.

"You can make your own breakfast, and you'll do lunch at work. But dinner should be more than just pizza or a tasteless microwave abomination every single night. Wasn't this so much better than that?" I made a gesture to indicate the meal he had just inhaled. He gave a smile and a nod.

"Buddy, I'd be a downright fool to turn down a deal like that from a cookin' wonder like you. It's a bargain. Only if you're sure. And if you get tired of it, just say so."

"Let's go shopping tomorrow, and I'll show you where Ralphs is. But it has to be in the afternoon. I made a phone call, and the scenery guys can come help you in the morning. Nine o'clock okay?"

"That's great, pal."

He helped me clean up, and on the way out the door he said, "Buddy, I'm a hugger. I always gotta hug my friends. Thanks for a great meal and a great evenin'. See ya tomorrow!" He gave me an expansive hug. "Night, Martin," and he went back to his house.

I stood there in a complete fluster from being hugged. And then I rushed inside and got on the phone with Amy. I babbled on and on about Ty.

She said, "Martin, you're like a schoolgirl. I've never heard you so giddy about someone."

"He's wonderful!"

"I'm glad he's turning out to be a good neighbor."

And do I have a Good Neighbor Policy. "Wait till you meet him!"

"Martin?"

"Yes?"

"He's straight, isn't he?"

She wouldn't like this. "Yes," I finally admitted.

"Martin, we've been through this before. You shouldn't fall for a straight guy. No matter how wonderful he is. You know what that leads to. He gets uncomfortable, and you'll get hurt. I think you'd better back off and just say an occasional 'Hi neighbor' and leave it at that."

"Nothing will happen like that."

"Martin, it's not a good idea. Unrequited love sucks."

"Like when you had the hots for that actor, and he turned out to be married and oh by the way secretly gay? Like that?"

"I could go all day without being reminded of that. All year. All my life. Eternity."

"Ty is so dynamic, so charismatic. You'll see. You'll think he should go onstage at the theatre."

"Are you listening, or are you being a willful brat who should be spanked and sent to your room? Do you need to stand in a corner and wear a dunce cap?"

If Amy knew I'd already fed him two meals, seen him naked not once but twice—well, if you don't count the twenty-five pervs—and made a nightly dinner plan, she would give me permanent detention.

"It will be fine." I had diabolically intrigued so that I would get to see him frequently. And have so much more fun cooking, that was absolutely true too. Clearly, I am the heir-apparent of Machiavelli!

The next day, I was up early, and I put two signs on the front porch. One sign said Love Lair with an arrow pointing left to Ty's side. The other one said Neighbor Who Tells All with an arrow pointing to mine.

Ty laughed when he saw them. He made me take them down, but he kept the Love Lair sign and put it in his hallway pointing to his bedroom.

The guys showed up, and they spent the morning shifting furniture and helping with further painting. They encouraged him to have a nice blue in his bedroom even if the rest of the interior painting was white. He liked that as it reminded him of his bedroom back in Oklahoma. When I looked later, his place was sparsely furnished, masculine, classic. The bed in his master bedroom was enormous. Room for plenty of action there, I could certainly see.

In the several family photos displayed, Ty clearly resembled his father, and the brothers were all handsome men. His mother seemed like a strong woman. Well, you'd have to be strong to raise four boisterous sons on an Oklahoma farm. He also had photos and a few trophies from his athletic endeavors.

We went on our shopping expedition, buying tons of groceries. At the garden center we bought deck furniture together.

We had pizza in the evening as promised, sitting in his newly organized living room, which still smelled of fresh paint. We were getting along so well, easily conversing on all sorts of topics: hobbies, friends, travel goals.

I asked him more about his work, and he brushed it aside. He said it was unexciting, a lot of research. "My unit...uh... department looks at boring things like traffic and certain population demographics and stuff." I figured I would find out more about his work as time went along.

On the phone every night to Amy, I bubbled with enthusiasm about Ty. She admonished me and said she hoped she wouldn't have to pick up the pieces when I imploded. I assured her that no such thing would happen, that Ty and I were becoming good friends.

The owner called me to see how things were going. I told him everything was done with painting, landscaping, and the pool, and that Ty had reimbursed me for his portion. He asked how I was getting along with him. He would not be into Amy-style babble about Ty's masculine delights, so I simply answered, "He's a great guy."

"I talked to Ty just now. He told me he hit the jackpot with you."

Really?

"Glad you guys are getting along. I was pretty sure you would."

The jackpot? I won the lottery!

The next day he came over to talk about our shared area. I liked how industriously he was organizing his house—thank goodness he was not a slob. And while he was finishing the touchup painting, I almost hoped for another disaster just for the excitement.

"Would ya mind if I set up a movable basketball hoop in the driveway?"

"Of course not. As long as you don't expect me to play basketball with you."

"Yeah, I gotta find me a team or a club."

I could help him with that.

Then something came to mind. I had had a fantastically successful project for a CEO in Irvine who gave me a huge bonus for my work. He also told me he had a connection to the Lakers and a VIP box. And if I ever needed... "Ty, speaking of basketball reminded me. I've got access to a VIP box to see the Lakers. Would that interest you?"

"Hot damn! You bet!"

"I'll get in touch with my friend." Now would be the time to call in the offer from the grateful CEO.

Ty started getting acquainted with the neighborhood. He had a pickup that he had driven from Oklahoma.

I asked, "So back home, did your pickup have a rifle on a gunrack behind your head?"

He retorted, "You're makin' me out to be a redneck. No sir, I did not have a gunrack." Flexing, he added, "I do own these two guns here." *Is it wicked that I want to squeeze those boulder biceps?*

He loved his pickup and, as I would learn, frequently liked to wash it in the driveway. He went shirtless and wore these tight gym shorts that would get wet and cling. I quite liked pickup wash day. And he was such a good neighbor, he washed my car as well when it needed it.

As I was also a good neighbor and good Samaritan (never mind my ulterior motives), I offered to help a few times. I took the hose and somehow I 'accidentally' got him all wet just to see the sight. He chased me around the pickup, trying to retaliate, which was fun.

A woman who lived across the street always seemed to do yardwork when it was pickup wash day. And some teenage girls from down the block decided that was the time to walk their dogs. I was not the only voyeur in the neighborhood!

Ty often swam in the pool and suntanned. And yes he was "buck nekkid," and yes I admired. However, I had acquired a conscience and would not be such a voyeur. I reduced the perving from twenty-five to twenty-four times. A noble sacrifice on my part.

I was treasuring our dinner and evening conversations. He stayed longer every time, and I could feel a warm regard growing between us. True, he didn't know anybody else yet in LA, so I was his one friend option for right now until he made more. But I did feel we could have a potentially wonderful friendship.

And all the time I obsessed with worries about how he was feeling. Surely he's figured out I'm gay? How would he feel about that? Straight guys are sometimes afraid to be friends with a gay man because other straight friends will think he's gay by association. And gay men might be afraid to become friends with a straight man for fear of rejection.

Did I go too overboard with the dinners? Had I made too many flirtatious remarks? Had he noticed my perving? Surely he knew I liked what I saw? What if he decides to pull back and be merely a "hi neighbor" like Amy said? Was I coming on too strong?

Even as I stressed and obsessed, our journey of getting to know each other moved along. We shared opinions on politics, religion, history, money, movies, music, sports. Yes, I can talk about sports if I have to, mostly by never saying anything and letting the other person talk.

However, he always glossed over the topic of work. Well, I would find out more in time.

And he hadn't yet asked me if I had a girlfriend. Did this mean he thought I might have a boyfriend but didn't want to bring it up? Was he waiting for me to say something?

I hashed some of this out on the phone with Amy. How often does it happen that straight women have a gay best friend and vice versa?

But can a straight country cowboy and an effervescent gay man become good friends?

What are the odds?

Revelations

Not long after Ty had moved in, Amy brought her little nephew Tommy over in the late afternoon. She needed my help to babysit for a short time.

"Martin, thanks a lot for taking over at short notice. I have his backpack, and there's a sandwich in it."

"A sandwich? Oh, please. I'll take very good care of Tommy."

We heard a knock on the back door. Ty stuck his head in. "Hey, buddy." He saw Amy. "Oh, didn't know ya had company." Then he spotted Tommy hovering near Amy. He rushed over and squatted down to his level. "Hey little buddy! What's your name?"

"Tommy."

"Hey Tommy, what's happenin'!" Ty fist-bumped the wide-eyed little boy, who giggled a bit.

Ty stood up. "Who's this?"

Amy knew all about Ty from my nightly swoon calls. This was the first time they'd met. She was giving him a close look.

"This is my friend Amy, the costume designer. Amy, my neighbor Ty." I explained, "She has an emergency down at the theatre and needs me to babysit her nephew Tommy for a little while."

Amy further explained, "My sister Anne has an extra meeting at work, and her regular babysitter couldn't stay late. I promised to help out, but now this emergency came up, and I have to deal with it."

I added, "Anne's husband is in the military and is deployed at the moment."

Ty dropped right back down. "Hey Tommy, your daddy's a soldier! That's cool, huh?" And fist-bumped him again. More giggles.

Ty stood up and regarded Amy. He walked all the way around her in a fairly brash manner, thoroughly checking her out. People usually immediately notice Amy's exquisite cheekbones and cupid-bow lips. If she were wearing a bonnet, she could have been a demure model on the cover of a Jane Austen novel. However, Jane would have thought Amy most indecorous and unsuitable because her spitfire eyes—I think Amy's most attractive feature—were far from demure.

Ty finished his brazen inspection and said in his cheekiest tone, "Costume designer, huh?" Uh-oh. I could see the playful look in his eye and I knew he was about to tease Amy. His mischief-making commenced. "This clown day at the theatre? The circus come to town?"

"What?"

"Your outfit." Not ogling her curves as I had supposed, but her clothes.

"What about my outfit?" Amy snapped.

Uh-oh. Dudgeon level about to be raised to high. Umbrage about to be taken. I knew he was teasing, but she didn't know that. And she was not one to let it slide. Ty was about to discover that Amy's personality matched her eyes and her outfit. Not demure!

I was accustomed to Amy's over-the-top style. This time she was wearing leopard-print leggings, red strappy high heels, a bright yellow blouse tied at the midriff, giant hoop earrings, bright-red lipstick, and she had a leopard-print bandanna tying her rich auburn hair up. Auburn this week anyway. Her cat-eye rhinestone sunglasses were perched on her head. I had to admit she was...colorful, to say the least.

"That outfit is somethin' else. I need my safety goggles to look at that."

Amy was fuming and snarked at him, "Some of us have something called style. Which you clearly are not acquainted with."

Ty grinned. He seemed to be enjoying this repartee. "What kinda emergency does a theatre have anyway? Someone swiped the eyeliner? The leading man forgot his sock to stuff in his tights? Someone pitched a hissy fit and slapped somebody and everybody's goin' around tellin' everybody else they're not speakin' to each other?"

"The leading lady's finale dress has a small rip in it."

"Lawdy, bring it up to DEFCON ONE this very second! Evacuate the city!"

"She's in hysterics because it's a big moment in the show, and the costume is quite important. It helps her stop the show."

"Can'tcha just stick a safety pin in?"

Amy glared at him. "A safety pin is for amateurs. Apparently I have much higher standards than you. It's a fine, expensive fabric and needs an expert to fix it. Me."

Revelations

"La-di-da. Well, the Bible says ya reap what ya sow, and Amy says ya sew what ya rip." I laughed at his play on words.

Amy wouldn't give him so much as a smile. She turned to Tommy. "Your backpack has your drawing pad and pencils. And your swimsuit in case Martin will let you wade in the pool. I'll be back when I've fixed Natasha's dress."

Ty was grinning again. "Tell Natasha to come back with you when the show's over. I'll give her a real showstopper. She won't find an amateur here. Only the highest standard." Amy looked affronted. Ty winked at me and then gave his full attention to the little boy looking up at him with wonder. "Hey Tommy, drawin' is awesome, but the sun is still out and I think a big boy like you should be playin' basketball."

Tommy's eyes grew big. "Basketball?"

"You bet. Hop on and let's go." Ty bent down, and Tommy jumped up piggyback. "Giddy up!" Ty started galloping toward the door, and Tommy squealed with glee.

Amy stared after him and looked back at me. Her eyes held bloody murder. "How can you put up with that?"

It was a side of Ty I had never expected. With two fist bumps and a giddy up, Ty had taken over as babysitter, conquering the heart of a little boy named Tommy in five minutes flat.

Look how fast he had conquered the heart of a big boy named Martin.

Amy returned later in the evening. When I answered the door, she came in saying, "Sorry it took so long, Martin."

I said, "Shhh." I pointed to Tommy snuggling in the crook of Ty's arm, both asleep on the couch. It was charming and utterly adorable. I took a photo.

"We were watching a movie, but they nodded off."

Amy stared at them for a moment, looked at me, and then back again. Even she would have to admit it was endearing. She put her hands on her hips and said, "Huh."

"He's been nothing less than phenomenal with Tommy. I had no idea. It's been a revelation. I'm still agog."

"Who would have thought? Look at that. Like two little boys all tuckered out after playing all day."

Without opening his eyes, Ty said, "Big where it counts, babe." He opened his eyes and laughed at her indignant look. Tommy started waking up and yawning, but when he spotted Amy, he jumped up excited and ran to her.

"Auntie Amy, Auntie Amy, it was so much fun! Uncle Ty and I played basketball, and then we played frisbee, and then we went swimming, and Uncle Ty taught me how to do a cannonball, and then Uncle Martin made pisketti with meatballs, and we had ice cream with sprinkles, and then we watched *Toy Story*, and it was so much fun!"

I had originally planned to make moussaka for dinner, but changed it to kid-friendly spaghetti when Amy had called.

"Amazing how you could watch the movie with your eyes closed. And, um, pisketti and meatballs sounds yummy. Let's get ready to go." She looked at us. "*Uncle* Martin? *Uncle* Ty?"

I said, "Tommy's been a wonderful guest."

Amy reminded him, "What do you say, Tommy?"

He came over, solemnly shook our hands, and said, "Thank you, Uncle Martin and Uncle Ty."

Ty bent down and said, "You are one righteous dude, Tommy. You like to draw? Will you draw a picture of me? I think Auntie Amy would love to have a picture of me." He grinned saucily at her.

Amy said, "Yeah, I could use a new dartboard cover."

"Can I have a big hug, Tommy?" Ty held out his arms, and Tommy leaped into them, holding on tight with his sweet little red-cheeked face beside Ty's sunburned stubble.

Amy said, "Thanks, Martin." And a bit grudgingly to Ty, "Thank you."

"You're welcome, Bozo the Clown." He grinned and winked again at me. "Let's take you to the car, Tommy." Ty carried him out. Amy collected the backpack and followed, turning back at the door. She looked like she was about to say something, then shook her head like she couldn't find the words and walked out.

When Ty came back in, I said, "Thank you, Ty. You were a rockstar with Tommy. How come you're so great with little kids?"

"I love kids! My brothers' kids, my friends' kids, any kids! I'm just a big kid at heart. I love bein' fun Uncle Ty."

"You're way more than fun. Tommy was in heaven."

"That Amy, she's a real ballbuster, isn't she?"

"She's strong-minded, if that's what you mean. You were giving her a little grief. Why?"

"She loved it."

"I think you pissed her off."

"I know she loved it. That kinda ballbustin' woman wants to keep control of everything, but she secretly loves it when a guy gives her shit. The more shit, the better. She tried to keep up with me. Next time she sees me, she'll be gunnin' for me. And I'll give it back to her twice over."

"That's an interesting theory. Maybe you should go on Dr. Phil."

"I'm tellin' ya."

I looked a bit skeptical. "If you say so, Ty."

"I know so. I know so much more about women than you do, Martin. You get along with 'em, but I know 'em. I know what makes 'em tick, I know how they think, I know how to get 'em into a dither, I know how to make their heads spin, I know how to entice 'em directly into my bed."

Oh. Maybe now was the time to face the topic I had been stressing about. I asked carefully, "What makes you think I don't know anything about women?"

"Martin, come on. I got eyes. Just cuz I'm a country cowboy doesn't mean I don't know the ways of the world. I know you're gay. I knew it from the get-go."

He'd known all along! I had been holding my breath, and I huffed it out.

"What? Were you worried about that? I may be from Oklahoma, but I'm not an ignorant redneck bigot, Martin. Y'are what y'are. My mama taught me that everybody is a child of God and should be accepted exactly the way they are. I don't give a goddamn rat's ass that you're gay. No big deal."

"You knew when we met?"

"The paint disaster where ya rescued me and ya had to cut off my clothes? Your eyes were poppin', takin' a nice long look at my nice long dick like ya couldn't believe it." I blushed as he continued, "Not that I blame ya. It's a five-star dick." He looked at me mischievously. "Maybe I should say eight-and-a-half star dick."

You can predict what I'm thinking. It starts with O and ends with G.

He gave me a direct look. "Just to be clear we're on the same page. That you're not imaginin' things? Ya do know I'm straight?"

I mimicked him. "Ty, come on. I may be a naive small town boy from Ohio, but I got eyes too. You're straight as a laser beam. As a road in Nebraska. Around you, rulers and arrows feel like spirals."

"Martin, I like pussy. A helluva lot. If you like dick instead, so the fuck what. The most important thing is a person's heart. And you got a real big heart. I knew that the first time we met too." He hugged me and said, "Night, Martin."

As he went out the back door, I stood there. And like Amy, I felt like I wanted to say something, but I couldn't put it into words.

One revelation after another.

The next afternoon, Amy's sister Anne called. She asked if Ty would be around and wondered if she could come by. She said Tommy insisted he wanted to ask us something. I shouted at Ty and asked if he could come over.

When Anne arrived, Tommy came bounding in.

"Uncle Ty!"

"Buddy!" Ty picked him and whirled him around, Tommy laughing and shrieking. He threw him up and caught him and then hugged him.

Anne was just as agog as Amy and I had been. I said, "Anne, this is my neighbor Ty." He could see that Anne resembled Amy. Her face had the same lovely cheekbones, but her hair was a sedate honey brown and her California casual blouse and shorts were the antithesis of Amy's eye-catching garb.

"Thank you both so much for babysitting last night. Tommy has been talking nonstop all day, Uncle Ty this, Uncle Ty that. So I wanted to meet the famous Uncle Ty." She smiled. "Well. I see why now."

Yet another new fan!

I wondered if Ty would treat Anne like a ballbuster too. But he was totally respectful as he set Tommy down and, ruffling his hair, said, "You have a wonderful son."

"My husband Josh won't be back for another month, and I think Tommy has been a little starved for some male attention."

I said, "And Ty has been starved for kid attention. He misses his nieces and nephews."

"Tommy has something he'd like to ask you."

"Uncle Martin and Uncle Ty? Next week is my birfday on Saturday. Will you come to my birfday party? We'll have a trampoline and a bouncy castle and everything!"

I looked at Ty, and he immediately said, "We would love to come to your party, big guy. Right, Martin?" I nodded, not surprised at all that Ty would welcome an opportunity to substitute these kids for the nieces and nephews he missed so much.

Tommy shyly said, "Uncle Ty, I drew you a picture." Anne handed over a drawing of Ty. A little lopsided, but he had caught the brilliant smile.

"Buddy, this is awesome, thank ya so much." Handing the drawing to me, he said to Tommy, "Betcha if ya run, I can catch ya!"

"No you can't!" he shrieked as Ty growled and reached for him.

"I will!" And he started chasing Tommy around the room and out the door, Tommy laughing hysterically and Ty saying "I'll gitcha!"

Anne and I laughed, and she said, "Some of his friends from school and their parents will come. Amy will be there too. We'll have a few refreshments, and I'll buy a cake."

"You certainly will not. I'll bake the cake, Anne."

"Really? Oh, Martin, that's fantastic. Yours will be a hundred times better than a store-bought cake. Well, we have to go. Thank you again for last night. You were a lifesaver."

When Ty came back in after they left, I said, "You were nice to Anne. Why did you treat Amy so much differently?"

"I'm tellin' ya, Martin. I know women. Anne is sweet. Amy's a ballbuster. Anne needs sweet talk, and Amy needs a smart mouth."

"Amy will be at the party next week."

"You just wait and see. I'm gonna be the biggest smartass ya ever saw. She'll love it. And y'all will tell me I'm right."

I printed a copy of the adorable photo of him and Tommy snuggling asleep on the couch. A few days later, I noticed that the photo and drawing were prominently displayed on his refrigerator.

Adorable, indeed.

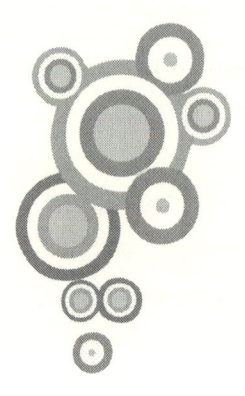

Routines And Receptacles

As we awaited Tommy's party where Ty planned to be a smartass, our lives had begun to take on a routine. Ty made his own breakfast and went to work. I worked from home as always. After work, he would cannonball into the pool for a swim, always skinny-dipping. Yes, always aware of that going on. I am an extremely perv-ceptive—oops, perceptive—neighbor!

Most evenings I would make dinner, and he never tired of my culinary creations. He always wanted seconds and thirds. I learned to feed a hungry man, that's for sure. I joked I could work for the army as I was cooking for the eating equivalent of one next door. Sometimes he would stay past dinner and we would visit, watch TV, just hang out. I loved that.

I know he appreciated our deal, and I had ever so much more fun cooking for two. I actually felt I was getting the better end of the deal because I got to spend quality time with him. I happily came to the realization he was enjoying our time together too. We were on the road to becoming good friends.

On one occasion, he insisted we go out to dinner so I could take a break. We went to a greasy spoon diner he had found. He wanted to have old-fashioned chicken-fried steak with mashed potatoes and gravy. I could have made it better, but this was his chance to do something for me. Besides, I always looked forward to the homemade pie in a diner.

When we walked in, he spotted four attractive women seated at a table. He said loudly to get their attention, "Hey, this must be Beautiful Ladies Night at the diner. Glad we came."

I whispered, "Or it's Big Flirt Cowboy night."

They had taken instant notice of the handsome cowboy. As we passed, he tipped his hat, flashed his dazzling smile and said, "Howdy, ladies."

They looked surprised and delighted. A brave one said, "Howdy, cowboy. And sidekick." At least I managed to not be completely invisible.

We moved on to our Formica table with red booth banquettes. Classic old-fashioned napkin holders, red and yellow ketchup and mustard squeeze bottles, sugar shakers with a cracker inside to absorb moisture, and round-topped salt and pepper shakers had a 1950s time warp feel. I looked back to see four heads close together as they giggled and reacted to Ty. As we sat he said, "Buddy, it never hurts to make a woman feel beautiful. Don't cost nothin', and they like it."

"I think we've reached the part where the rascally cowboy is conquering the big-city girls?"

"You'll see. One'll come over here to say hi 'bout the time they sling the grub on the table."

Ty caught the eye of other diners and nodded or said howdy if they were near enough. He took the place over as if it was his fiefdom.

"Now I can see Mister Charisma in action. Is this where you like to meet women?"

"Most of the time in a bar, but sometimes in places like this. I like gals who aren't all fancified, and if they like a diner, I'm halfway to likin' them."

Ty sat facing me, so I was the one who could see the women. They were playing rock paper scissors. And sure enough, as our platters arrived, the brave woman—whose rock apparently bested all presumptuous scissors—came over. Ty immediately stood up.

"Hello, darlin'. I'm Ty. This is Martin."

"Hi. I'm Leanne. We wonder if you would join me and my girlfriends for dessert. Our treat."

"Be delighted, sugar."

She handed him a piece of paper. "This is my phone number. Maybe we could meet for dinner here one night?"

"That'd be the highlight of my week, darlin'. I'll be over right after I wolf down this steak."

She wasted no time reporting to her girlfriends about his exciting acceptance.

"Ty, you are the most shameless flirt I've ever seen."

"Don't get nowhere hidin' in a corner."

When we finished our entrée, I declined to go to their table with him. "Ty, it's the handsome cowboy whose attention they want. Go over and give them a thrill. I'll have my pie and text Amy."

"Well, if you're sure."

Big Flirt Cowboy rolled up his sleeves to better show off his arms, unbuttoned another button on his cowboy shirt, and brashly and confidently swaggered over to their table. When he got there, he must have said something to the women, because they waved at me.

The waitress, a tough old gal named Betty—doesn't every diner have a waitress named Betty?—came over to take my order. She had bright-red lips, dangly earrings, and a wad of bubble gum being chewed like cud. Classic.

I said, "I've been deserted for dessert."

"Yeah, Ty comes in here reg'lar, mostly for just coffee and pie. Never fails. Some gal always gets the giggles." She regarded me, one hand on a hip. "You his boyfriend? Didn't think he swung both ways."

"No, he's a one-way swinger. Well, you know what I mean. I'm his neighbor. We're good friends."

"That so? Guess he's not a redneck after all. I'll getcha some fresh coffee, coming right up."

I enjoyed my pecan pie and daydreamed about being Ty's boyfriend. I kind of liked the idea that people might think that. If nothing else, it made me look like I had good taste in men. Never mind what they might think of his taste!

I shouldn't put myself down. I'm not six-foot-three and movie-star handsome like Ty, but I'm not Quasimodo, either. I'm a few inches under six feet, neither buff nor skinny, simply in reasonable shape for a man in his thirties. I've been told I have a sweet smile and sincere gray eyes. Apparently I have a demeanor that makes people feel comfortable talking to me. However, on the issue of who Ty might be coupled with, I supposed most people would expect such a gorgeous man to attract someone as fabulous as himself.

After their dessert, when we were on the way out, Ty winked at the ladies and said, "See all y'all next time it's Beautiful Ladies Night."

In his pickup I asked, "Is there any woman in the world who would resist you?"

"Haven't met one yet."

And why would they?

One more element to effectively describe the routine. How shall I put this? Enthralling, titillating, enrapturing, captivating, stimulating, compelling, gratifying, consuming…

Present participles be damned. I'm referring to his sex life!

Not long after he had moved in, he started going out after dinner if he didn't stay to visit with me. He was acquainting himself with every bar in the Valley, I think. And soon enough, a parade of women began visiting at night. I sometimes caught a glimpse, and they uniformly seemed to be blonde and curvaceous.

I often left my window open at night to get a cool breeze. I didn't like to have air conditioning on all the time. And it turned out Ty left his window open too. And some sort of acoustic circumstance led to me overhearing…things.

The first time it happened, I was startled and wondered what I was hearing. Oh—bedsprings and cries of rapture. Either he was extremely good in bed or she was a marvelous actress faking it like Meg Ryan in that funny movie scene. And he was indefatigable. A piston in a factory was right!

Routines And Receptacles

Their escapade carried on...and on...and on. And finally things, well, climaxed. And I thought okay, done. But no. Fifteen minutes later, it started all over. And finally that was done. At last I could sleep. But an hour later, it all began again. I had to admire his prowess, and I could appreciate that the lucky lady had a delightful if exhausting experience.

Of course I could have closed my window, and most times did. But other times, I was a voyeur with my ears and imagined.

What if it was me in there? What if he was in my bed? Or we were by the pool? On the sofa? Against the wall? On the floor? On the table? In the shower?

But I forced myself to stop and close the window. Those reveries would get me nowhere.

I understood Ty. I was completely aware that he had a strong sex drive, the libido of a man in his prime. He actively pursued women, cheerfully admitted to being a womanizer, and clearly stated he wasn't interested in anything beyond one-night stands. Casual sex and that's it. He was unapologetic. "I make no promises. I tell 'em right off the bat I'm not ever gonna be Mister Right. For one night only, I'm Mister Right Now. I want a good time, they want a good time. No one's forcin' anybody. Take it and then leave it."

They took it all right.

However, one woman wasn't going to leave it. She wanted more. She kept texting him and begging to see him again. She sent nude photos. He showed me some of the messages: "We're meant for each other." "I want your cock." "Let's make babies together." And the photos were highly explicit and in closeup.

She began stalking him. He thought he spotted her following him in her car. Notes appeared under his windshield wiper. Then one evening I noticed a car parked on the street. A blonde woman inside kept staring at our townhouses. Ty was not yet home from work.

I texted Ty: "I think that stalker woman is here. Sitting in a car waiting for you."

Ty: "Five minutes away."

He zoomed up in his pickup and blocked her car on the street. A neighbor's parked car was too close for her to back up, so she couldn't drive away. I wasn't able to see very well what was going on because his pickup blocked my view. He got out and it looked like he was showing her something. A minute later, he moved his pickup into the driveway, and she drove away, peeling out.

He said, "We won't be seein' her again." But he didn't explain further.

What did he show her?

Never short of an opinion, I naturally had to comment on his nocturnal endeavors.

"Receptacles."

"What?"

"Those women you bring into your Love Lair. Receptacles."

"What in the hell are you talkin' about?"

"They're nothing but a receptacle for your body fluids."

He laughed then said, "Always safe, buddy. And they're not complainin', that's for damn sure. For your information, there are other ways for a gal to reach a happy endin' without Old Faithful shootin'." He waved a finger and showed his tongue.

"I'm sure you could write new chapters for the Kama Sutra."

"Everybody leaves happy, pal. Satisfaction guaranteed, one hundred percent."

"I don't know why I'm talking to you about your women. I drive a stick."

Usually the women did not spend the night. I think he made clear the night was over and it was time to go. However, one Saturday morning I was having breakfast on the deck and a woman wearing his t-shirt over her panties stepped out.

"Hello," she said brightly.

"Good morning. Where's Ty?"

"He's still sleeping. He had to...work late."

"I'm sure he found this particular late work satisfying. Would you like some coffee? How about a freshly baked pastry?" I introduced myself.

"Martin. He talked about you. I'm Colleen."

I learned she worked in a pharmacy and had met him at a bar in Thousand Oaks. After some idle chitchat, she gave me a look over her coffee cup and asked forthrightly, "Is it hard for a gay guy to have such a hot neighbor?"

"He's a great neighbor. A really good guy and a super friend."

"That's exactly what he said about you. I guess you guys are handling your different lifestyles well. But come on, he's not hard to look at. You've got a lot to appreciate there. Isn't he a temptation?"

"Was he tempting for you at the bar?"

"His name should be Devil in a Cowboy Hat. He tips that hat, looks at you with those bedroom eyes with the pretty eyelashes, flashes that wicked smile, and you're on the road to bad girl hell. Heaven by the end though. I thought every other woman there was going to murder me when he put his arm around me at the bar, whispered in my ear, and we walked out together."

I acknowledged, "He is definitely not hard to look at."

"You're crushing, right?"

"Are you crushing?"

"Let me ask you something. Am I the only woman who's been here?" I hedged and she said, "I didn't think so. I'm one of a long line of all-too-eager women, no doubt. It's no use to even try for more than what I've gotten. That cowboy can't be fenced in."

She looked at the pool sparkling in the morning light. "You meet a charming guy, you spend the best night you've ever had in bed, and poof. It's over and you can't get it back again. He moves on to the next one and you're left aching for what could have been. Am I crushing?" She brushed the back of her hand at her eye. "Hell."

I sat quietly. She gave me a wistful smile and said, "I'll get my clothes and head out. Thanks for the coffee and pastry. You're a nice guy, Martin. I hope he doesn't break your heart like he does the rest of us."

Ballbusting And Smartassery

Ty outdid himself with full cowboy getup for Tommy's birthday party. He looked good! My cake was a triumph, if I do say so myself. I had made an enormous T. Rex, green and complete with candy claws and teeth. Sure to please a bunch of little kids.

"I got me a plan, Martin. At the party, I'm gonna entertain all the kids for a while so Anne and the other parents can take a little break. It'll be just like our family get-togethers back home when I'd take care of the kids. God damn, I'm missin' my nieces and nephews." And once again, he had to call them right then and there.

When we got to the party, streamers and balloons decorated the backyard by the pool. Tommy was beside himself and dragged Ty by the hand to meet his little friends. "This is my cowboy Uncle Ty!" and it took all of a minute for the kids to be crawling all over Ty and trying on his hat and asking where his pistols were and was his horse parked outside.

I chatted with the various parents who were there. A few of the dads had hottie dad-bods, so I was enjoying myself. I liked it even better when they took their shirts off to swim in the pool with the kids.

I heard Ty asking Tommy, "Where's your Auntie Amy?"

Anne answered, "She's coming. She has a little surprise for the kids."

Ty gave me a look and wink, and I knew he was planning devilry.

Ty was as good as his word. He was in his element entertaining the kids, taking off his boots and bouncing in the bouncy castle and jumping on the trampoline. The kids took turns piggybacking for giddy up, and he had desperate shootouts using a set of squirt guns Anne brought out. He was the good guy, and the kids were desperadoes, and when they got shot—that is, squirted—they died a dramatic death by falling in the pool. They wanted to have shootouts over and over, and he was so patient. I know all the parents appreciated their break from kid duty.

When Amy arrived, she was in a classic circus clown outfit with fright wig, red nose, and polka-dot costume. Ty came right over as soon as he saw her and said, "It's Bozo the Clown! You're gettin' better as a costume designer, it only took you two tries to get it right."

Amy turned to me. "I had to think of something that would appeal to little kids. I put myself into the mind of an eight-year-old, and I decided Ty would like it." She turned to him. "Plus I didn't want you to be the only clown at the party." Taking a whoopee cushion out of her bag, she made an enormous fart sound at him. Then went over to the kids.

With a knowing smile he said, "Told ya she'd be gunnin' for me. Hold your hats and hallelujah!"

Amy did some simple clown tricks with handkerchiefs and juggling, and the kids fell apart with the whoopee cushion antics. Later when we did gifts and sang "Happy Birthday," the parents were effusive about my cake creation. I gave Tommy a huge drawing pad and a big box of markers. Ty gave him a mini cowboy hat and a sheriff's badge.

As the party was ending, Tommy came over to sit on Ty's lap.

"Isn't this when we're s'posed to spank ya eight times?"

Tommy loudly protested and said his friends already had.

Ty raised his voice. "I see your Auntie Amy over there. I think she's the one who oughta be spanked." Amy heard us and came over to glare at Ty with her arms crossed. Ty whispered to me, "And I know she'd like it."

He turned back to Tommy. "Hey buddy, I see ya had some girls here at your party. Are they your girlfriends?"

"Ewwwww. I don't have a girlfriend!"

"Yeah, they have girl cooties, don't they? Later when you're grown up, you'll decide it'll be fun to catch 'em."

"Do you have a girlfriend, Uncle Ty?"

"I got so many I can't count 'em!"

Amy said, "Uncle Ty has trouble with things like counting. Plus no woman could stand him for that long anyway."

"I'm just too much for 'em in the—" and here he gave a lascivious wink, "—pistol-packin' department. Too hot to handle. I think Auntie Amy is scared of pistols."

"Do you have a pistol, Uncle Ty?"

Amy said, "Oh he has one. A derringer. So much a part of Ty, it does his thinking for him."

"What's a derringer, Auntie Amy?"

"A miniature version of the real thing. Not very scary at all."

"You got no idea, Bozo," said Ty. "We could have target practice, and then we'll see who gets scared."

"Too bad I'll never know."

Tommy saw a friend getting ready to leave and jumped off Ty's lap to run over to say goodbye.

Ty slapped his knee and said, "Wanna take his place?"

Amy turned to me and said, "You'd better get some medical attention for Ty. His jockstrap is too tight, and it's cutting off the circulation to his brain."

"Too tight for a reason, babe. You got anything in that clown bag o' tricks to relieve the pressure?" Amy honked her Harpo Marx horn at him, and Ty came right back with, "Is that you tryin' to say you're horny?"

She whoopee-cushioned him again and went off to the backyard gate to say goodbye to the parents.

Ty said, "She's like a long-tailed cat in a room fulla rockers. She's lovin' it."

Later, Anne called to thank me for the cake and gifts. She said Tommy wanted to wear his cowboy hat to bed, and she had to force him to put it on the pillow beside him. Anne commented, "I think Ty had more fun than the kids. All the parents loved that he kept the kids busy. But Amy was mad at him about something. She was cussing like a sailor."

"What did she say?"

"Oh, I'm kind of embarrassed to repeat it. She said 'I want to take those shitkicker boots and kick that shit-eating grin off his shit-sorry face.' Sorry. That's her language."

"Whoa. Amy at her most delicate."

"I said if she didn't want to see him again to tell you. And she said 'Oh no, I have to get revenge.'"

"It's nothing serious. They have fun pushing each other's buttons."

Anne sighed. "And my sister has plenty of buttons to push, that's for sure."

"That she does."

Later in the month, Anne's husband Josh returned from deployment and wanted to meet the famous Uncle Ty. We drove over to say hi. Josh was a tall, broad-chested man with a short military haircut and a masculine bearing. He and Ty greeted each other on the porch with a fist bump, hand-slap, and fist-clasp handshake, a bro thing I'd never learned how to do.

Josh said, "Thanks for being around, man. Anne told me you made things a little easier for Tommy. I appreciate it."

Ty said a little wistfully, "If I had a kid, I'd want him to be just like Tommy."

We enjoyed a nice visit with Josh and Anne. Tommy was more than delighted to have his parents and his 'uncles' lavishing attention.

On the way home after our visit I asked, "Would you like to have kids, Ty?"

"Yep! But not right now. Not ready for that."

I eyed him and said, "You've been with so many women, you probably have children all over the place, you just don't know. You're like a sperm bank paying out dividends."

"God damn, I hope I don't have any little Ty Juniors runnin' around. It wouldn't be for lack of tryin', buddy!"

Oy vey!

StraightForward

The Bros And The Ladies

Amy was throwing a party. She called to invite me, and I asked, "Can I bring Ty?"

Amy was silent. She finally said, "If you must."

"Shall I bring some appetizers?"

"Yes, please." And then with what I thought was a stifled laugh, she said, "Actually, it's a good idea to bring Ty. I have some friends he should meet."

"Will Kyle be there with his sporty friends?"

"Yes."

Kyle was Amy's jock friend from university. I had seen him a few times when Amy had get-togethers, and I had met his friend Jackson once.

Embarking on a Make Ty Welcome Project, I wanted to help him find sporty friends and places he could play basketball and football. Amy's party was a good chance for Ty to meet Kyle and the other sporty guys. Maybe he could fit into their group.

Little did I know when Amy said 'some friends', she was referring to a lot different group of friends!

We arrived at the party bringing artichoke dip and crackers, Italian meatballs with several dips, and potato croquettes. I nearly needed an armed guard to keep Ty from eating everything before the party.

We greeted Amy who was wearing an unusual faux-leather dress featuring three dozen multicolored, variably sized zippers. I complimented her. "Amy, that dress looks fantastic on you. So stylish." She twirled to show it off.

Ty had his own fashion review as well. "Every time I see ya, y'all're wearin' some kinda ding-dong getup."

"Says the man wearing a cowboy hat in a living room in California."

"That dress has more zippers than a Saturday night whore."

"Oh?" said Amy in a tone that should have made Ty run for his life. "Do you have something to tell us about how you spend your Saturday nights?"

"No sir, I don't pay to play. If anything, they'd wanna pay me."

"Pay you to go away."

"Dang! The costume designer forgot the most important zipper—the one for your lips."

I interrupted before World War III started. "Are Kyle and his friends here?"

"They are, on the patio." Amy smiled like she had a secret. "And by the way, Ty, there are some ladies here dying to meet you." Uh-oh. Amy had a little gleam in her eye, something was up. "Have fun," she sang out as she turned to greet another arriving guest.

We first went to the dining room to set down the appetizers, and a statuesque beauty turned around at our approach. It was Natasha from the theatre. Was this who Amy had meant?

Taking one look at Ty, she said, "Well! The party has started!" Natasha wore a clingy hostess pajama outfit, cinched with a rhinestone belt matched by chandelier rhinestone earrings. Her elaborate eye makeup verged on Liz-Taylor-as-Cleopatra style. Being a diva with no hindrance whatsoever on her expressions, her blatant down-and-up appraisal was aimed for the third balcony in a three-thousand-seat theatre.

I introduced them. "This is my neighbor Ty. Natasha is the leading actress at the theatre, a gifted performer."

He gave her an equally frank appraisal, appreciating where the clingy outfit clung. "Natasha? The finale dress gal? Be happy to lend a hand if you got any other dresses you wanna have ripped."

Favoring him with a brilliant showbiz smile and a seductive look that would send nosebleed row into palpitations, she purred, "I'd welcome your hand—or anything else—you choose to offer. Whenever the occasion—or anything else—arises."

"Somethin' may be arisin' this moment," as he hitched up his jeans.

One guess which woman Ty would end up with tonight.

"Hey buddy, where can I get me a beer?"

"Just go through that door to the kitchen. I'll be right there, I need to rearrange these dishes on the table."

I finished a few moments later and was at the door of the kitchen when I heard "Are you lookin' at my butt? Stop!"

"Why stop a good thing? Mm mm *mmm*, those jeans are doing a fine job of showcasing your ass...ets."

The Bros And The Ladies

I should have known Amy had something up her sleeve to get back at Ty. She had invited her outrageous drag queen friends! And Ty was the cowboy fly who had just walked into the drag spider's parlor!

I peeked in the door. Yep, as Ty would say. Miss Vanessa, the one who had spoken, was an extravaganza in lamé. Along with Miss Jenn, Miss Penelope, and Miss Doretha in full regalia, they were looking at Ty—by the refrigerator in his cowboy hat, shirt, boots, and showcasing jeans—with undisguised interest.

"Honey," chimed in Miss Doretha, "if you don't want us to admire the posterior delights, turn around so we can study the battle of the bulge."

"Oh sugar," said Miss Vanessa when Ty had turned around. "You're looking at me like I'm a pair of headlights. Don't worry, we know you're straight. We admire your straightliness. Your straightimity. Your straightosity."

"Are y'all makin' funna me?"

Miss Jenn gave a little screech. "He said y'all!"

"All y'all are makin' fun o' me."

Four drag queens screamed in delight and clapped. "All y'all!"

Ty warily said, "I came in to get a beer."

"A beer?" said Miss Penelope. "That's a sissy drink if there ever was one. Why is a stud like you drinking piss like that?"

"What in the hell?"

I could imagine Ty had never heard *that* from his Oklahoma buddies.

"You need to try a Miss Penelope Special. That's a drink with balls. I'll whip one up right now."

53

As Miss Penelope busied herself at the counter, Miss Doretha vamped her way closer. "So, cowboy. What horse did you ride in on? Who brought you here?"

Time to make my appearance and rescue Ty before the ladies figuratively tied him down and had their way with him. Literally was entirely a possibility. I popped into the kitchen and said, "I did. Ty is my neighbor."

"This is the famous neighbor? Cowboy, Martin did not do you justice *at all*."

I turned to Ty to fess up. I had to admit he was looking a bit like a deer about to be run over. "I've been telling everyone about you." I gave Miss Doretha a look of death, but she breezily said, "Martin was like the Town Crier shouting about this hot guy who moved in next door and who was so charming—"

"And Ty does not need to hear you flap your lips." Introducing them each by name, I finished with, "These are Amy's good friends. Ladies, Ty."

I recalled that Amy had told me the drag queens dressed in themes. Tonight's theme seemed to be jewel-tone lamé: Miss Vanessa wore amethyst purple, Miss Jenn was in ruby red, Miss Penelope shone in sapphire blue, and Miss Doretha radiated glamour in emerald green. Joan Crawford shoulder pads added to the chic, and they tottered in their matching high heels. I wondered, what do drag queens do if they have big feet? They must special order the shoes.

"Howdy...ladies?"

Miss Doretha said, "Not sure if we're ladies?. We are *most* ladylike. Except Miss Jenn, she's sluttier than a rabbit on steroids."

"Witch! You're jealous because I have so many devoted admirers, unlike you. Pay no attention to her, you divine Greek god. I am every inch a lady."

Ty floundered, "Every inch? But don't you…ladies have…you know…"

Miss Jenn was amused. "Do we have dicks? I'll show you mine if you show me yours."

Ty turned bright red and said, "No thanks."

"Don't be shy, sweetie. The evidence suggests yours is a sight to behold!"

Ty was wide-eyed, probably searching for a way to escape.

Miss Penelope flounced over. "And here is Miss Penelope's Special. A real man's drink. Oh go on, it won't turn you gay. We told you, we know you're straight."

He accepted it somewhat reluctantly and took a sip. "Hey," he said. "That's pretty dang good."

"Watch out, cowboy. It tastes good but it is *lethal*. Two of those will make you think we're real girls!"

Miss Vanessa cattily said, "Listen here, barmaid. No amount of alcohol will ever make us believe your falsies are anything but overambitious foam."

"Strumpet!"

Ty put the drink down. "Are you trying to get me drunk?"

Miss Vanessa said, "Oh honey, the headlights are off. Miss Penelope has very few standards—"

"Twat!"

"—but one of them is to not take advantage of drunk cute cowboys. No matter how sexy they look in their jeans."

Apparently whenever one of them got insulted, the target shot back with some sort of derogatory word in return. I soon learned they never repeated themselves.

I rescued him. "Don't worry, Ty, no one is going to take advantage of you. Miss Penelope's Special is a good drink. You can have one, but not two. Let's go to the patio. I want you to meet Kyle and Jackson."

"Oh them," said Miss Jenn. "That Kyle has a treasure chest. As in a slab of pectoral perfection. And that Jackson has outstanding cheeks."

Miss Doretha said, "They'll bore you with football scores."

Miss Vanessa asked, "What's wrong with football?"

Ty turned to Miss Vanessa in surprise. "You like football?"

"Sugar, I am in favor of any sport that features tight ends."

"Oh."

"I'll bet you played football."

"I was quarterback."

"Of course you were. And a million cheerleaders had a crush on you, and all the while you had your hands up the center's ass! Ooo, football players are just so latent, slapping each other on the ass all the time." Ty barely had time to be shocked before she asked, "What's your team?"

"Dallas Cowboys, 'course."

"You've got to be kidding. The sum total of their ball coordination skills involves scratching their nuts!"

"Hey! Them's fightin' words!"

"I am entitled to my well-informed opinion, sugar, which is that their cheerleaders have better moves than they do!"

"And my better-informed opinion says yours is a crock!"

"Should they be taking this outside?" asked Miss Penelope of the others.

"No!" hollered Miss Doretha. "That would put him in serious danger."

"Y'all think *I'd* be in danger?" asked Ty incredulously.

"Yes, because Miss Vanessa might break a nail!"

"And then you'd have to change your name," said Miss Penelope, "and go into witness protection. Fear her vicious revenge if such a thing ever happens."

Ty laughed and said, "I'm not ready to deal with a terrifyin' threat like that. We'll just wait till the next championship and then we'll see."

Miss Vanessa, ignoring all the comments, blithely informed him, "I like the Green Bay Packers myself."

Leered Miss Jenn, "On account of what they're packing no doubt."

Miss Vanessa declared, "Girlfriend, I'd give my left Tina Turner wig for a free pass to the locker room."

Ty asked, "Isn't the sayin' you'd give your left testicle?"

Miss Jenn explained, "You have to put the value in context, hot stuff."

"Testicles have their uses," said Miss Doretha, "especially when they're attached to something big and bold."

"But there are some things worth far more," stated Miss Penelope. "Tina Turner is incredibly awesome! A good Tina wig is priceless beyond compare, so much more valuable."

"Oh," said Ty. "Well, my left testicle is awesome too." At which the ladies giggled.

Time to move. "Come on Ty, let's go."

Taking his glass and looking relieved, Ty said, "Thanks for the drink, Penelope."

"*Miss* Penelope."

"Ooo, call her Miss Ross."

"Hag!"

"Miss Penelope. Nice to meet all y'all." Screams and claps.

"Cowboy, the pleasure is ours. Don't be a stranger, come back and talk to us when you get bored with those divine men. We promise we won't bite. Much. In fact, bring them with you. They could be dumb as a post, but they aren't hard to look at."

"Sorry about that," I said, leading him toward the patio. "I should have warned you Amy has some unusual friends."

"They are a little over the top."

"A little?"

"Okay, a lot. But kinda funny too. I've never been around a..."

"Drag queen."

"Drag queen before. Are they gettin' rid of their dicks?" He looked a bit green at the thought.

"I don't think so."

"They sure wear a lotta makeup. And big hair."

"Well, they do have to disguise their five o'clock shadow. And maybe they're Texas girls at heart."

On Amy's patio, Kyle and Jackson were chatting with a massive bodybuilder guy. Kyle had short black hair, piercing blue eyes, and eyebrows that made him look a little threatening. And indeed, along with impossibly wide shoulders, he had the gloriously prominent pectoral perfection Miss Jenn had mentioned. Jackson was a leaner surfer-dude type with curly blond hair, baby-blue eyes, and rosy cherubic cheeks. Both extremely good-looking.

"Hey Kyle, hey Jackson."

"Hi, Martin. This is our friend Declan, but we call him Deck."

I shook Deck's hand. The other guys were quite fit, but he was swole to be sure. He would be scary to meet in a dark alley, as in running into him would result in hitting the deck in more ways than one. But I would soon find he was a sweetie and a bit shy. He had a gorgeous Mediterranean look, and I later learned that he was half-Irish, half-Lebanese, his name coming from his mom's Irish roots.

"And this is my friend Ty."

"The cowboy neighbor," commented Kyle as they shook hands all around. Then he said in a not particularly friendly fashion—maybe a bro-challenge fashion—"We've heard about you." Ty sharply looked at him, reacting to the somewhat blunt tone.

Jackson blurted, "You seem to be on Amy's hit list."

"Amy," said Ty in a bro-challenge tone matching Kyle's, "is pitchin' a hissy cuz I won't let her walk all over me like other men do. I talk back."

"Ty has this interesting theory," I said. "He thinks Amy secretly likes it when men challenge her. And we all know 'pitching a hissy' is her favorite sport anyway." Jackson and Deck laughed, agreeing.

Kyle was coolly assessing Ty as we spoke. He nodded and said, "I think you just might be right." He smiled and continued in a more pleasant tone, "I've known Amy a long time. A challenge will do her good. Keeps her on her toes."

Kyle gave a friendly nod to Ty, who nodded in return. In some sort of bro fashion I didn't entirely get, it seemed to me Ty just got accepted into their fraternity.

I changed the subject. "If Ty looks a little shell-shocked, it's because he just met Miss Vanessa and her brood."

"Damn. Did they try to flirt with you?" asked Kyle.

Ty said, "I guess so. Do they flirt with all y'all?"

"They make jokes and say shit we don't get. There's one who makes some killer drinks."

I teased, "Miss Vanessa nearly broke a nail arguing with Ty about football teams."

Ty shook his head. "God damn, never thought a drag lady knew anything about sports."

I continued mischievously, "Miss Jenn says Jackson has outstanding cheeks."

Jackson shrugged. "What can I say? I have the face of a model."

I had to correct him. "They weren't talking about your face."

Jackson beautifully blushed while Kyle razzed, "Butt cheeks, man. They like your ass!"

Putting my Make Ty Welcome Project into action, I turned to Deck and said, "Obviously you work out a lot. Do you go to the same gym as Kyle and Jackson?"

Jackson said, "He's the biggest guy there, one of the trainers."

"Ty is new to town and doesn't know places to go yet. Would you guys show him your gym, maybe get him started?"

"Sure. Ty, want to go tomorrow?" asked Deck.

"Thank ya kindly, buddy, that'd be great. You guys play any hoop lately?"

I decided to go back to hear what the ladies had to say, which was probably more interesting than hoop stories. "I need a drink. Be right back."

When I returned to the kitchen, Miss Doretha exclaimed, "You selfish bitch, Martin, you've been holding out on us. That cowboy is sexy as hell. He has a package I want to unwrap with my teeth!"

"Delusionetta, dream on," scoffed Miss Vanessa.

"Wench!"

They so loved to insult each other. I asked, "Any more drinks available?"

Miss Jenn attacked. "Martin, we should slap you silly for not bringing that hunk around sooner. Didn't anyone teach you in kindergarten to share with your friends?"

"Ty is a nice guy, isn't he?"

"He is *fine*! I'd like to be stuck on Brokeback Mountain with him. What's his story?"

"He moved in next door, and we get along really great. He's from Oklahoma—"

"Where the wind comes sweeping down the plain. Never mind that—we want to know some gossip. Does he have a girlfriend?"

Miss Vanessa grimaced a little. "Did we scare him?"

Miss Doretha butted in, "Who cares about that? Get to the good stuff. How many inches?"

"No. Only at first. You'll have to ask him."

"A hunk like that doesn't have a girlfriend?"

"Well, he has a lot of girlfriends. For one night. You know. He's pretty independent."

"Whatever you do, bring him back in here. He's a lot more fun to look at than these rejects from the old bag factory."

I left them to enjoy bickering with each other and returned to the guys and their hoop conversation. They clearly were bonding, lots of sports talk. Very bro-ey, if that's a word. Bro-ish? Bro-esque? That doesn't sound quite right for these guys. Bro-ey it is.

I was pleased they were getting along so well. I hoped they would hang out with Ty; he needed more friends here in LA, and they seemed just the right type.

Kyle said, "Hey, Martin got one of those killer drinks. Let's go get one. What's her name? Penelope?"

"*Miss* Penelope," corrected Ty. *Well. Ty seems to have learned his lesson about drag queens.* Then he added, "But I think we're s'posed to call her Miss Ross." *Maybe not.*

We trooped back to the kitchen, where the ladies greeted us with great enthusiasm. They were suitably impressed meeting Declan, and Miss Vanessa said, "Ooo, I love bodybuilders. You could press my bench anytime."

"He's more likely," Miss Jenn pointedly said, "to mistake you for a dumbbell. We can change your name to Dumbbellina."

"Skank!"

Miss Jenn turned and, batting her huge false eyelashes, said, "Jackson, how are those beautiful cheeks?"

Jackson just grinned and said, "Everything they're cracked up to be." The ladies and I whooped in surprise, but it took the other guys a few seconds before they got the ass crack reference.

Kyle said, "Hey Miss Ross, can I have one of your Specials?"

The ladies burst into laughter. "Miss Penelope will do, Kyle." She made gallons of drinks, and Ty and the bros soon were howling at the outrageous remarks from the drag queens, the lethalness of the Specials helping the relaxation factor a lot. So relaxed that Miss Vanessa somehow convinced Deck to hike up his shirt so she could count his abs.

Miss Vanessa: "Ooo, I need my calculator to count so many of these abalicious yummies. One two three four five...oops, I lost track. I'll have to use the braille system."

Miss Penelope: "They didn't invent that for you to grope every man in sight, Miss Touchy-Feely."

Miss Vanessa: "Sow!"

Miss Jenn: "Oh, Jackson, I know all your tricks about how you meet women. You hang out in the supermarket produce section looking all bewildered and helpless trying to choose melons. Some hot babe with her own personal melon display comes along to offer assistance, and next thing you know, you're in bed squeezing her cantaloupes. Like this!" Grabbing his hands, Miss Jenn put them firmly on her boobs, flung out her own arms, started flailing with ecstasy, and shouted, "Oh Jackson, honeydew me!"

Well, that brought all conversation to a halt. *Jackson blushes so fetchingly, even when tomato red.*

The mortified Jackson said, "Miss Jenn was talking about how to squeeze melons?"

Miss Vanessa said, "Don't use those grotesquely misshapen lumps as examples of anything but wrinkly old gourds."

"Ox!"

Miss Penelope: "Unless you're getting off on some kind of warped thrill, Jackson, you can let go now."

Jackson abruptly brought his hands back as if he had touched a hot stove while we all laughed.

"Oh, that was exhilarating!" said Miss Jenn as she fanned herself.

Miss Doretha fixated on Ty, determined to find out more about his physical attributes. I vaguely recalled that Amy had told me she was a research librarian. For Ty, she had an outlandish method of inquiry.

"Cowboy, I have an ongoing research project where I compare a particular male anatomy to common household implements. Would your particular male anatomy be a screwdriver? A chisel? A turkey baster? A rolling pin?"

He thought for a moment. "Does batterin' ram count?... Miss Doretha, are you all right? You better set a spell."

My facial expressions are usually a closed book, but the Special had its lethal effect on me too. In an unguarded moment, the book was opened to Chapter Twelve: Dreamy Eyes as I, too, fixated. Then I noticed Kyle was watching me watching Ty. He smiled, glanced from me to Ty and back again, and raised his eyebrows meaningfully. I hurriedly looked away in a fluster over being caught.

A little later, I was listening to the bros and the drag queens in their various conversations. Kyle, who had a job dealing with investments, was discussing the stock market with Miss Penelope, who I gathered worked in a bank.

Ty and Deck were talking—well, arguing—about sports with Miss Vanessa. Hopefully Miss Vanessa would not break a nail. However, I believe she worked in some sort of salon or spa, so any such crisis could be easily solved. The subject moved on to bodybuilding, and it turned out that Miss Doretha had researched nutrition at one time. She joined in, giving Deck some pointers about a shredding diet.

Miss Jenn was giving Jackson ideas about how to style his hair and what color looked best on him. "You need to look spiffy when you greet clients at your mortgage office." I learned she worked at a fabric store, and I discovered she was the one who designed all the flamboyant outfits for the ladies.

Though I was nominally part of Kyle and Miss Penelope's conversation, I paid far more attention to eavesdropping when Miss Jenn and Jackson got onto the topic of Jackson's girlfriends. When Miss Jenn responded with salacious descriptions of her nocturnal endeavors, I found her kind of bulls and bears far more entertaining than the stock market kind!

Who knew that straight bros and drag queens had so much in common? Sports and diet and fashion and business and the bedroom. Maybe Miss Penelope should market her Specials as a social device.

After copious farewells and bicep clutches and flamboyant air kisses from the drag queens, Ty and I went into the living room. Amy turned toward us and said with a tease in her voice, "Well, Ty. Make some new friends? Get any phone numbers from some lovely new ladies?"

"Nice try. You wanted to get me all discombobulated with the drag queens. Do ya see me runnin' outta here yellin' mercy me? I'm not afraid of those drag ladies. If there's anything here to send me runnin', it's a scary clown dressed in a ziplock bag."

"Ty met Kyle and the bros. They're taking him to the gym tomorrow."

"Gotta look good for the ladies," said Ty. "Well, the ladies who *are* ladies."

"Try to exercise what's between your ears instead of between your legs!" she snarled as she huffed away.

Ty said, "I got that little raccoon up a tree, and she has no idea what to do. She's lovin' it!"

"If you say so."

Ty spotted Natasha impudently observing him from the corner and said, "Buddy, if you don't mind, I'll catch a ride home with someone else. I got some business to take care of. Show business."

The next day, Ty came yawning into my kitchen and said, "You got any coffee ready? I might not make it to the gym today. I already had the workout of my life."

"I see. Natasha is your personal trainer now?"

He looked at me, amused. "You figured it out? I gotta tell ya, she put on quite a performance. By the end, though, she gave *me* a standin' ovation. We had a coupla encores too."

I laughed. He was so matter of fact. I actually loved it when he told me about his escapades. That is, sexcapades.

"Wooee, she has a healthy pair'a lungs. I think the whole neighborhood heard her. That girl's a screamer."

No need to tell me that. I was forced to close my window *and* put in earplugs.

"But I had somethin' handy to use as a pacifier. I can handle a diva all right."

"Manhandle, you mean."

Ty did go to the gym and seemed to be bonding well with the guys. I congratulated myself on how successfully the Make Ty Welcome Project had started, thanks to the friends.

Natasha, diva extraordinaire, had certainly played her part.

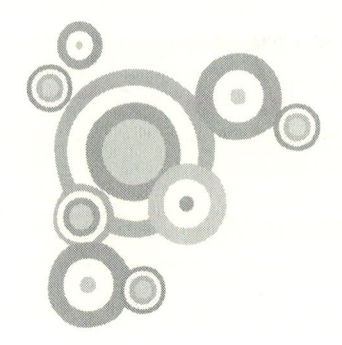

Coach Ty

Time for step two of the Make Ty Welcome Project.

Because Ty liked basketball so much and I had seen how amazing he was with kids, I had a talk with the director of a local youth club. The club had been my client at one time, asking for my consultation on restructuring their mission. I had offered cogent advice and arranged video conferences with other youth organization leaders to discuss successful ideas.

The club served at-risk teens from the area, trying to keep them off the streets and busy with healthier activities. The youth director had a thriving basketball program going, with youth teams meeting every night of the week. I wondered if he needed help. I told the director about Ty, his basketball skills, and the fact he was so remarkable with young people.

"Most of our teams are doing well," said the youth club director. "But we've got a particularly difficult group on Tuesday night. We can't seem to keep a coach going with them. Would your guy be willing to try?" I said I was sure Ty would give it a go. "All right, I'll be happy to give him a chance. I won't hold it against him if it doesn't work out."

Coach Ty

Ty was excited for Tuesday night. When we arrived, a group of teenage boys was warming up in the gym. Multiracial—Hispanic, black, white, Asian. They looked like tough street kids to me.

The director introduced Ty, and he began. I was at the door with the director to watch. Ty had barely started by saying he had played basketball in high school and college when one of the boys said, "What's that matter to us, cracker?"

"Did I really hear that? Did somebody just call me a cracker?"

The director and I looked at each other. I was surprised that a tough LA teen would know that "cracker" was a derogatory term for an uneducated poor white southerner.

"Not brave enough to step forward?"

The boys shuffled around, but no one said anything.

"I came here expectin' to play basketball with a group of young *men*. If you don't have the balls to say somethin' to someone's face, you don't have the balls to be on a team."

The boys shuffled some more, and one scowling boy stepped forward.

"I said it."

"So. What's your name?"

"Darius," he spat out.

"Well, Darius. Just cuz I talk like I'm from Oklahoma doesn't mean I'm an ignorant redneck. My mama taught me that everybody should be accepted for exactly what they are. And I'm not a cracker. And I'd prefer not to accept any of you as an asshole. I'd appreciate it if you'd accept me exactly as I am—a good guy wantin' to play basketball with some other good players." He looked directly at Darius. "Are ya good players? Show me what ya got!"

He threw out the ball, and they began. At one point, Darius haphazardly barreled through a group of players but failed the layup shot.

Ty said, "Hey, good drive, man. Maybe try somethin' like this?"

They set up the same play and with some fancy fakeouts, Ty neatly sidestepped them and reached the basket but didn't shoot. They looked impressed with how quickly he had gotten past the defense, but they tried not to show it. I wondered why he didn't take the shot as he could have easily made the two points.

He threw the basketball to Darius and said, "Your turn. I know ya got it in ya, man."

Darius made a similar pattern of fakeouts and successfully made the basket.

Ty shouted, "Great shot! That's the way, Darius!"

They played a scrimmage game. He encouraged and suggested and often said, "Good job!" and "That's it!" At one point a player made a completely blatant foul, and he blew the whistle.

"Now there's only one damn thing I ask, and I'm askin' for good sportsmanship. That was not cool, my man. You're better than that."

The boy said, "Yes, sir."

The game continued, and it seemed Ty was pushing them. The director said, "He's working them a lot harder than they're used to."

At the end Ty high-fived every one of them, saying thank you. Darius was the last in line and when they high-fived, he said "See you next week, Coach Ty!"

The director turned to me and said, "Coach Ty. That's great. Those boys called the last coach Blubberbutt and ran all over him. Please tell Ty we look forward to seeing him every Tuesday."

On the way home, I asked Ty why he hadn't taken that shot when he was demonstrating.

"It's not about me showin' how good I am. It's about lettin' that kid push himself and succeed. Let him be the star."

"But he was the one who challenged you."

"He's a boy in a man's body. He's testin' boundaries. I don't wanna show him up; I want him to succeed. So I let him be the one to make that shot. Deep down, like everybody else, he wants somebody to see he's good. Natasha over at the theatre wants applause, Darius wants his coach to tell him great job. Next week, I'll make him captain."

And because deep down like everybody else, coaches want somebody to see they're good..."The coach brings out the best. You're just as great with teenagers as you are with young kids. Brilliant work, Coach Ty."

He beamed in delight at my praise.

During the next several weeks, I went a few times to see how things were going. He had begun whipping them into shape. There were games coming up against other teams, and I could see they would be ready.

StraightForward

The boys had noticed me each time and finally I heard one of them ask Ty, "Who's that gay guy? Why's he here?" The boy didn't sound mean or offensive, just asking.

"Did I hear what I think I just heard? That's my super-good friend Martin. He's the reason I'm here at the club, as a matter of fact. And so what if he's gay? If you have a problem with him bein' gay, then you have a problem with me. In here we accept everybody for what they are. Black, white, brown, fat, thin, young, old, rich, poor, straight, gay, whatever. What I won't accept is an asshole. Ya got that?"

"Yes, Coach!" they shouted.

He brought me over to meet the guys, and after that, whenever I showed up, they hardly paid attention to me. Sometimes they would wave hello.

My Team Is Hot

The youth club director told me about an adult touch football league. Ty had been a quarterback, and I thought he might enjoy this. I called Kyle, Jackson, and Deck to see if they would join, and they had a few other friends to include as well. Step three began.

The touch football team league, overseen by Coach Jones, met on Saturday mornings at a large complex with several fields. The director had told Coach Jones that I was the one who organized the group, so I went along to introduce myself and the guys.

Coach Jones said, "Good to have you. You'll need a team name and matching shirts and shorts for when we have games."

"I'll deal with all that," I said.

"You guys take field number four against that group there."

I had to tease a little bit. "Coach Jones, do you have an oxygen tank on standby? These guys used to play football, but it's been years since high school, they're way out of shape geezers. They wheeze when they have to raise a beer glass. Do you think it will be safe?"

The guys were laughing. Of course Coach Jones could see they were exceptionally fit from the gym, but he teased right back. "I get it. The only pushups they do are when they push themselves up off the couch. We'll get them up to par, I promise. Okay guys, hit the field."

He wasn't really their coach; he managed the field and organized the rotation and competitions. He did insist that every team do some warm-ups and stretching and drills before they played.

All of the guys on our team had actually played football in school except Kyle, who had been a swimmer. He did fine, however. As I watched them play, even I could see they soon picked up old familiar rhythms and worked well together. Ty was the quarterback, like he had been in high school. Gosh, he was good. If he had been the quarterback in my 'Cesspool High School,' I'm sure I would have had a massive crush then too.

I noticed Ty sometimes checked to see if I was watching him. Was he trying to show off for me? I had some idea that in many situations, Ty would look to see my reaction. I obliged by cheering him on and applauding. At the end of their first game, the team won by one point.

"On a roll," I announced when they came over to me. "Championship straight ahead."

"How'd I do?" asked Ty.

"You are a fantastic quarterback. If Miss Vanessa were here, she'd be your number two fan."

"Who's number one?"

"Me of course!" Which put a pleased smile on his face.

My Team is Hot

I would sometimes come by on Saturdays to watch. The other teams got used to me being there. One time my guys played a gay team. My guys were great when they met these opponents, not treating them any differently from the other teams, and I was proud of them. One of the gay players said to me, "Your team is hot. You go, girl!"

For a team name, I suggested The Bros, which is what I always called them anyway. I had t-shirts made showing a bro fist bump. They were having a wonderful time every Saturday morning. Touch football was a great idea for Ty and all of them.

The Consultant Who Finds Solutions did it again!

Our routine changed a bit. Now Ty was eager for Tuesday evening youth club basketball and Saturday morning touch football with the bros.

In the process of Making Ty Welcome, I wished I could get to know the bros better. Ty often told me things about them that he learned from football or the gym, usually having to do with women. It seemed Jackson had nearly as many liaisons as Ty; mostly they were pretty California girls. Deck was a player but lately was interested in some woman named Melissa. Kyle was the dark horse: his liaisons were apparently trashy, rough, adventurous women who had been around the block. Or several blocks. He was always telling the other guys about some fracas he was having and he was exultant about makeup sex, which implied some sort of previous quarrel. And, Ty informed me, Kyle hinted about rough sex.

I asked Ty what he meant by that. "Well, it started with Jackson bragging he had everything available for what a woman might want. Condoms, KY, vibrator, love beads, incense, candles, bubble bath."

"No whipped cream?"

"That too."

"Well supplied for any occasion. A bordello would be envious. But what about Kyle and his hint?"

"Kyle told Jackson he should add blindfolds and handcuffs to his stash. Think he goes that route."

I could certainly understand why so many women liked Jackson. Aside from his good looks, he had a sunny personality and always seemed happy. Deck had a tough exterior, but I was learning he was a sweet guy on the inside.

Kyle was the enigma—cool and controlled but always with an edge. Mysterious, brooding, dangerous. His eyes always looked like he knew a secret. He was bluntly spoken. A bad-boy persona is a magnet for all women, not just bad girls. And gay men feel that magnetic attraction, believe you me.

I looked forward to seeing the bros whenever I could. Because...brag brag...

My team is hot!

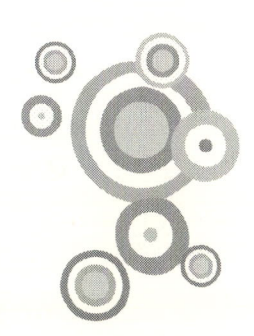

Boys And Basketball And Bromancing

When I had Ty by my side, life was to be enjoyed.

Josh was away on a military training in Nevada, and Anne wondered if Ty could possibly see Tommy again.

"He's moping, he misses his father," she explained. "I think it would be good for him to be around a man he worships like Ty."

I replied, "Ty always misses his nieces and nephews, and he's starved for some kid attention. I have an idea."

So that Sunday we took Tommy to Six Flags Magic Mountain, which left Anne free to have a spa day with Amy. Tommy and I had both been before, but it was Ty's first visit. He was the biggest little boy of all, loving every moment and enjoying all of Tommy's favorite rides.

On the way home, Tommy fell asleep in the back seat while Ty and I chatted. I asked, "Was that fun? Did it make you want to have a little boy of your own?"

"Honestly? Yeah. I could have fun with a son. Teach him how to play baseball, how to ride a bike. Or a horse. A little boy would be great."

"What if you had a girl?"

"My own precious princess?" He smiled at the thought.

"She'd be daddy's little girl and have you wrapped around her finger. I feel sorry for her though."

"Why?"

"I can only imagine your daughter at age sixteen and going on her first date. You'd be there at the door holding a horsewhip, and if the poor boy was smart, he'd hightail it out of there!"

"No need for that. I'm a reasonable man. I'd take him aside for a little man-to-man talk."

"What would you say?"

"I'd tell him in a nice, polite, friendly tone that if he laid a finger on my little girl, he'd be a soprano before the clock struck twelve."

"Definitely reasonable. For an overprotective maniac dad. Could this possibly have anything to do with what you were like as a teenage boy?"

"Every father in Oklahoma shoulda locked up his daughter when I was around. I know exactly what's on a teenage boy's mind."

"And in your case still is!" As we laughed, I looked at him, curious what he would say. "What if you had a little boy who was gay?"

"No problem. I'd say if you grow up to be like your Uncle Martin, you'll be a great man."

THUD!

That's the sound of me.

Falling hard.

Taking up the generous offer of the grateful CEO, we went to the Lakers game and enjoyed it from the VIP box. Ty had a fantastic time talking basketball with other people there, and as usual he charmed them all. It was a foreign language to me, but I managed to not mention a touchdown or third base. The CEO was particularly taken with Ty.

I felt rather big-headed when the CEO described my work. "Your friend Martin here," he announced, "saved my company. Productivity was down, morale was low, the company was losing money, and we didn't know why. At a meeting of business leaders, I heard someone recommend Martin as the man who could find a solution. So I hired him, and he sailed right in and somehow got the employees to let their hair down and tell him what was really going on."

Is it my sincere eyes that get people to talk to me?

"He discovered the staff felt like they were drowning in paperwork but were too scared to complain because of a new manager who had instituted a new system. Martin came up with a much better system that slashed the bureaucracy in half. That brought productivity and morale up for sure. After I fired that idiot manager, I offered Martin the job. But he turned me down."

"I wasn't sure if you wanted me as the idiot or the manager," I joked.

He and Ty politely chuckled. "And that's not all. Martin got suspicious and dug deep into the accounts. He hired a forensic auditor, and together they proved the deputy finance director was embezzling from us. Right under our noses—no wonder we were losing money. Everything got sorted out, and now my company is doing great." The CEO clapped me on the shoulder and said, "Martin is the best. I can hardly thank him enough." I was gratified to see Ty looking at me with even more respect.

We took a selfie at the game, and the photo radiated Ty's adoration of sports and my, well, adoration of Ty. Another time maybe I could arrange for him to go with the bros as they would all enjoy it.

The bros. They were always friendly, and I made up my mind to see them more often and get to know them better. Mere happenstance that they all were extremely good-looking hot hunks. Purely coincidental. Sheer random chance.

An opportunity presented itself. I had taken on a consulting job with a wealthy entrepreneur in Palm Springs. He told me he "hated, detested, and despised" videoconferencing and wondered if I would be willing to see him in person. I told him I rarely traveled for work.

"Can I make a suggestion to tempt you into traveling to meet me?" The following week had a holiday weekend. He owned a beach villa at Laguna and suggested if I would be willing to meet him there on the Friday, I could then have the use of the villa for the holiday weekend and have friends join me. He would not be staying, as he had a trip to San Francisco scheduled. He told me his staff would make everything ready for my friends.

"Is that enough of an incentive to travel to see me in person?"

"It certainly is. That is incredibly generous."

"Anything to escape a video meeting."

And with that, I invited Ty, Kyle, Jackson, and Deck to join me. Touch football was off that weekend because of the holiday, and they happily accepted.

Boys And Basketball And Bromancing

My in-person meeting with the entrepreneur was highly successful. He left late Friday afternoon and I awaited the bros who, even with holiday traffic, arrived not long after in the early evening.

It was a splendid beach villa to be sure. They each got their own guest room, and my client's staff had left everything perfect for us, with plenty of food, drinks, towels—everything needed. The staff told me to simply turn off the lights, turn on the alarm, walk out, leave the key in the dropbox, and they would clean it all up on Tuesday. What a deal!

When they arrived, the first thing Jackson did was throw off his shirt and shorts and jump into the pool in his underwear. Was it lecherous that I liked the slightly transparent tighty-whities? *Not transparent enough!*

We had a nice seafood dinner and cocktails at a posh restaurant in town. Deck, mindful of his bodybuilding diet, had the plainest fish along with a salad. We stayed up that night shooting the breeze.

The next morning I was up first, and I put on the coffee. I prepared all the fixings for breakfast so I could make it to order when each guy appeared. Waffles, French toast, bacon, ham, eggs, hash browns, fruit, pastries—whatever these hungry guys wanted. Deck, ever attentive to his diet, had an egg-whites-only omelet and a fruit-yogurt smoothie. Seemed he was following Miss Doretha's suggestions.

Did I object that they wandered down with no shirts and in their underwear? Did I object to their tousled bed hair? Did I object to all that testosterone surrounding me?

Are you crazy? Objection overruled!

That day we explored Laguna Niguel, buying gifts for friends. I bought a pair of colorful sunglasses for Amy. Deck had that woman Melissa he was getting interested in, and I helped him choose a decorated starfish ornament. Ty bought a nice picture frame, saying he had a photo to put in it. In the afternoon we lazed around the pool at the villa, napping in the sun.

Saturday night I was planning to cook dinner, but they insisted I relax, and we ordered pizza. Deck made himself a large salad, including several chopped hard-boiled eggs. He said, "Tomorrow I can have a cheat day."

After that, I could sense something was on their minds. I decided they were being polite and didn't want to offend me by saying they wanted to go out, so I made it easy for them.

"Why don't you guys go check out the bars in Huntington Beach or Newport Beach?"

They brightened up but Jackson said, "You don't want to go?"

Actually I did want to hang out with them, but it didn't feel right. I would be a fifth wheel. I didn't belong with the bros in that situation.

"Meat markets aren't my scene, but thanks anyway. Try not to break too many hearts. And guys, if you hook up with a woman, go to her place. It wouldn't be appropriate to bring a stranger here because it's not my villa. You understand?"

"Sure thing," said Kyle. "Anyway, the only date Jackson and Deck will find is their own thumb and four fingers. Can they bring those?"

They pushed and shoved like junior high kids and went on their way.

Later that evening I was watching *Saturday Night Live.* Jackson and Deck came in, apparently not finding a hookup. They ended up planting themselves beside me on the couch in their underwear.

Someone mentioned a meat market? Prime Grade-A Beef to my left and right. I'll buy!

I heard Ty come in around three a.m. Kyle returned in the morning.

At breakfast, Ty bragged, "That little beach bunny hopped right into my arms. I surfed her turf, believe me. Jackson, what's that the surfer dudes say?"

"Cowabunga!"

From Kyle, not a single detail. We had visual details, however. He had a huge hickey on his neck, and later on the beach we saw others on his thigh and on his chest. And he had a row of bright-red scratches down his back.

They got into a game of volleyball with some other dudes on the beach. I took photos, and some women sitting nearby started chatting with me. They were curious about the guys, and I assumed they wanted to meet them. When I offered to introduce them, they said it wasn't actually the bros they were interested in, it was *me*. They were fascinated about a group of hunky straight guys with a gay man and what it was about the gay man that made us friends.

Oh. Could my friendship with the bros be considered slightly unusual?

In the game, Jackson and Deck made a great setup for Ty to smash a spectacular spike. He looked to see if I had been watching him, and I gave him a big thumbs-up. He smiled and gave a chin-up nod of acknowledgment, and I could see he was also checking out the women with me. They noticed I was giving him special attention, and so I had to tell about our being neighbors and how I knew the others. Not just tell. I admit it, I shamelessly bragged.

    The women took off. Shortly afterward the guys finished their game and came over, throwing themselves down beside me to tease me.

    Ty: "You sneaky devil, Martin. You're the only one here who talked to a gal today. There were five cute gals with ya."

    Jackson: "Tell us your secret, lover boy."

    Kyle: "I'm stuck with these losers, and you get all the action."

    Deck: "We should hang out with you more often."

    I totally agree with Deck.

    We were flopped on the couches and armchairs later in the afternoon. Ty was watching a documentary about a crime investigation. I was mildly surprised to see Deck doodling and making sketches. He told me, "My favorite subject in high school was art." Go figure. Jackson was strumming a guitar he had brought. I could certainly picture him on the beach playing the guitar and attracting hordes of women like a magnet. Yet another trick Miss Jenn could tease him about.

    I told them I was going for a walk. I went to my room to fetch my flip-flops and when I got to the iron scrollwork gate at the entrance of the villa, Kyle was waiting for me. "I'll walk with you, okay?"

I was surprised, but I said, "Sure."

We didn't say anything as we meandered and strolled down the beach road. The only sounds other than the waves were my flip-flops flip-flopping and an occasional vehicle.

Some way down the road, he broke the silence. "Why didn't you go to the bar with us last night?"

I didn't want to say it was because I felt I would be out of place. I answered, "I thought it would be more fun for you without me there. You could be bros and check out the girls."

"We thought maybe you were mad at us or something."

It hadn't occurred to me they might take my refusal that way. "No, that's not it. I just didn't want you to feel like you had to entertain me when you were wanting to meet girls."

"We wouldn't have felt like that. It doesn't matter to us that you wouldn't check out the girls. We like your company. Next time will you go with us?"

They like my company. "Okay. If you're sure."

"I'm sure. *We* are sure."

We walked on at a leisurely pace. He spoke again. "Ty says it's a good thing he's going to the gym. Otherwise all the food you cook would turn him into a fat blob."

"That boy can put it away. I don't set out silverware, I just hand him a shovel."

"You're not letting him take advantage of you?"

I turned in surprise. "What?"

"It seems like too good a deal. You do all the work, he gets the benefit."

"But I love to cook. Cooking for one is a chore. Cooking for two is fun."

"Does he at least help with cleanup?"

"Always."

"Amy and I were wondering if you were getting a raw deal."

"No. I like cooking and I like spending time with him. And it was my own idea anyway."

He stopped. "Are you spending time with him because you like him, or because you *like* him?" No mistaking the emphasis.

I didn't want to get into a discussion or reveal how strong my feelings were. With Amy, I would only go so far as to admit to having a crush. With everyone else, I sent off strong privacy vibes that this was not up for discussion.

I turned away from him and started walking again. "I like Ty. He's a good neighbor."

"I like Ty too. But don't let him take advantage of you." And after another few steps, "We wouldn't want you to get your feelings hurt."

I stayed silent.

"Don't get me wrong. Ty has nothing but respect for you. You can tell by the way he hangs on your approval for everything. Just don't get in too deep."

It appears I am right that Ty often seeks my approval.

I remained silent. Several yards farther on, he said, "We're all glad you teamed us up for touch football. It's fun, and we like it when you come to watch. Come more often. Bring Amy and anybody."

"Okay, I will."

Still farther, "It was really nice you invited us here for the weekend. You could have just had Ty by himself. We appreciate you included us."

I was being churlish. He had led the conversation and was making an effort with me. I should speak more. Smiling at him, I said, "I've been wanting a chance to get to know you guys for longer than just at a party or a game. It means a lot to me that you welcomed Ty to the gym and you're all together on the football team. And I love that you're here and I can spend time with you." I gave him a sideways glance. "I don't know much about you, Kyle. Mostly that you were friends with Amy in university. Tell me what makes you tick."

He was like a tightly wound watch in some ways. What would he say?

"The million-dollar question. A lot of women try to find out, hoping they'll figure me out and then try to change me. Good luck with that. Like most guys, I like sports and women and cars. I like hanging out with friends. My job is a bit stressful; I think you know I run an investment fund."

"Did you have other jobs before that?"

"I started at a car rental company, and then I worked for a mortgage company. In fact, that's where I met Jackson. Amy doesn't even know this one: there was a time I worked nights as a bouncer at a strip club."

Maybe this is where he found an affinity for rougher, more adventurous women.

"I could see you doing that. You're a built guy."

"I was a swimmer in school, but I also did martial arts and boxing."

Teasing him, I said, "You might want to start hitting the punching bag again, you're losing your combat readiness. Last night's opponent seems to have successfully attacked you with her vacuum mouth and steel-tipped talons."

He touched the hickey on his neck, laughed, and said, "She was, um, enthusiastic."

"Marking her territory."

"That's okay. In return I invaded some of hers."

And both were victors in their war games. I said, "I'm curious about something. Did you and Amy ever have, you know, a time together in university?"

"We had a drunken fling once. Just once. But she said it was too weird with a friend, so it never happened again. She'll kill me for telling you, and then kill you just for knowing. So don't say anything."

We had come back to the villa. He turned to me. "Remember what I said about Ty, will you?"

He stepped close. Too close. He put his hand to the back of my neck. He was just a few inches from my face. He was staring me right in the eyes. Anyone observing us would think we were about to kiss.

What is this?

I held my breath, mesmerized. It was so…erotic. Unsettling. Disturbing. This was the edge I had sensed in Kyle.

Staring. Daring? Finally he quirked his little secret smile. "Nice talking to you."

And then he moved, not looking back as he went in.

I let out my breath.

That was unexpected. Disquieting.

Dangerous.

Boys And Basketball And Bromancing

This time I insisted on cooking dinner. I announced, "Deck can have a cheat day, and I'm going to help him cheat so much, he'll be branded with the letter A for food adultery!" The client's staff had left a huge amount of food for us, but I still had to send Jackson and Kyle to the market for a few other items. I put Ty and Deck to work peeling potatoes.

For appetizers we had a choice of soft pretzels with pub-style cheesy beer dip—went over like gangbusters—and chips with onion, dill, or ranch dip. Dinner for these big eaters included pork loin roast and/or spicy southern fried chicken. (They all chose the "and" from the "and/or.") We also feasted on scalloped potatoes, a rich pea salad, and freshly grilled asparagus with hollandaise sauce.

During all the preparation, the guys were hanging around, intently watching me at work in the kitchen, fascinated by my speed and confidence. So I decided I should put on a show with dessert. I made crème brûlée, and using a chef torch, barely caramelized the top layer of sugar. At that point I wanted to impress, so I doused one of them in cognac, did a quick flamboyant flambé as if it was the most important step, and impressed the hell out of the guys. I let them each flambé their own, and they were so proud of themselves for being sous-chefs.

After dinner and dessert, Deck moaned, "That was so good. Why did we order pizza last night when we could have had something like this? I could cheat like this every day, I don't care if I get fat."

Jackson moaned along with him, "Ty, let's trade. You move to my apartment, and I'll live next door to Martin. I want that deal you got."

StraightForward

Kyle shot me a knowing look.

Ty said, "Uh-uh. If you try that, we'll be havin' the Gunfight at the Not OK Corral."

They wouldn't let me lift a finger after that. Kyle took the lead, and they cleaned everything up. We had a late-night swim in the pool, me enjoying the eye candy as always. In that respect, I had a sweet tooth. *Sweet cornea? Sweet retina?*

Laying in bed that night, I had a think. I mused on the idea that for a gay man, friends are family. Ty was my good friend already, and the bros were starting to feel like good friends too. Were they my family? They seemed comfortable with me, even wandering around in their underwear. Kyle had made it a point to make sure I knew I should have gone with them to the bar, that no one had a problem with me being around.

I was not a bro. Was I their token gay friend? Was that my status?

For a gay man, it is always a nervous situation relating to straight men. If you touch or hug them, will they think you're coming on to them? Ty hugged me, but he hugged everybody. If you flirt, even subtly, will they back off? If you don't touch and don't flirt but you stare, will they be uncomfortable?

And how do you relate to them if you don't like sports very much and you don't have women to talk about or some other bro topic? Would they be weirded out if you mentioned a boyfriend? I realized this was putting all straight guys in the same broad generalization, but a lot of men were just like the bros.

Yet I felt comfortable with them. Was I having a group bromance?

Boys And Basketball And Bromancing

And I had a think about Kyle. That was such an unsettling moment. He wasn't flirting or coming on to me. It felt like...a dare. Daring me to see where I would go or what I would do. He was a flame. Was I a naive moth?

Something occurred to me. Kyle said they wouldn't want me to get my feelings hurt. Colleen the breakfast visitor said she hoped Ty didn't break my heart. Amy said unrequited love sucks and I'd get hurt. Should I take a hint?

The next day, Monday, was the holiday. We lazed around the pool, then cleaned up and headed out in the early afternoon to beat some of the holiday traffic. Ty rode with me, and the others went with Kyle in his SUV. As we were leaving, the bros thanked me for inviting them, for cooking, for a relaxing time.

Back at home sweet home, Ty said, "That was real kind of ya to include the guys. They told me they like you a lot." He looked at me. "As long as you remember I'm Number One. Ya hear?" And he gave me an extra long hug.

Sigh.

Not long afterward, Amy visited, and while I was making lunch, she commented on my lack of attention toward her. "I'm lucky you deigned to spend time with me today. I never see you anymore, you're always chained to Ty. Where is he anyway? Usually he's over here waiting for you to cook him something and wait on him hand and foot. If you had any peacock feathers, you'd be fanning him."

"He does not act like that. Right now he's with Josh. They've taken Tommy and some of his little friends on a hike."

"Oh, that's right. When Josh got back from his training, Anne mentioned something about that."

"He likes helping with the kids."

"Ty's nice with kids, I'll give him that much. Too bad he isn't nice to women."

"What do you mean? He's always polite and tips his hat and says 'howdy, ma'am' and all that."

"Oh, please. He treats women like sex objects, and you know it. He thinks he's God's gift to women."

Thinking of Natasha and Colleen and the multiple overhearings, I commented, "According to some women who have...enjoyed his company, he apparently *is* a gift from God."

"Hmph. There's only one thing he wants."

"Well, he's straightforward and upfront about what he does not want. He's crystal clear that he doesn't want a relationship. And you might not have considered that they treat him like a sex object just as much. Two-way street."

"Relationship? With Ty? A woman deluded enough to fall for his line needs to be told he is definitely not marriage material." She gave me a considering look. "Speaking of not marriage material, just exactly how would you describe *your* relationship with Ty?"

I didn't even have to think about it. "Also straightforward."

She looked puzzled. "How so?"

"He's straight and I'm forward!"

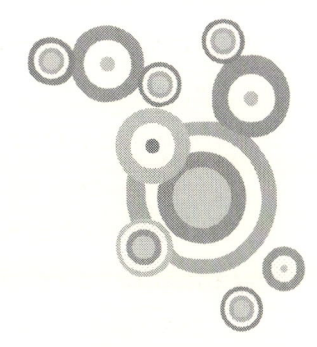

Makeover

In Ty's living room, he was pacing while I sat on the couch. "I don't get it. This gal at work hasn't even noticed me."

I was amused. For once, a woman wasn't throwing herself at him. He was not used to that. "The first woman in the world who resisted you. Call the newspapers!"

"Ha ha."

In this case, an attractive woman in the office down the hall had caught his attention. He had smiled and said howdy a number of times. He normally would have received an enthusiastic response, leading to a date, leading to the bedroom. From her—nothing. And it was driving him bonkers.

Ty grumbled, "She barely says hello and keeps on workin'."

"The nerve of her to concentrate on why she's there in the first place."

"Yeah, buddy, give me a bad time. Kick me when I'm down. I thought y'all would have an idea. I thought you were the Consultant Who Finds Solutions. I don't know what to do."

"Look for another lady? You don't exactly have a shortage of applicants for the position."

"I want to go out with this one."

"What's so special about this one?" *Aside from the fact that she isn't giving you the time of day, which has completely flummoxed you.* "Don't tell me," I said. "Curvaceous and blonde?"

He nodded.

I mused. "Hmm. She seems to be entirely work-focused. The problem is she only ever sees you in the workplace, where she won't think about anything else. To get her attention, she'll have to see you in another venue or situation away from the office."

"Try to meet her outside the office? But if I can't even get her to say more than hello, how am I gonna do that?"

"Do you and your office crowd go out to lunch or anything like that?"

"Not usually. We have a cafeteria that we go to." He thought for a moment. "But we do have a big annual city awards ceremony comin' up in some fancy hotel ballroom that everybody is s'posed to go to. That reminds me, I've been meanin' to ask ya. Do ya have a black tie I could borrow?"

"Black tie? Show me the invitation."

He retrieved it from the refrigerator door, where he had attached it with a magnet. He brought the magnet, a rodeo rider on a bucking bronco, over for me to admire. "I got this here at the National Finals Rodeo. My favorite event. I go every year."

I looked at the invitation. "Well, this event is formal. Black tie means you have to wear a tuxedo with black tie."

"Like at a prom? With a ruffly shirt?"

"Ruffly shirt not necessary, but you have the idea. I don't imagine you have a tuxedo, do you?"

"No. Hell, do I have to rent one?"

"I have an idea about that. Ty, if you want this woman to take notice, it's time to up your game. We're going to call in the experts. I'm getting my measuring tape, and we'll call in an expert for the tuxedo too."

It didn't take long for the Misses Vanessa, Jenn, Penelope, and Doretha to show up with bags of paraphernalia once they heard it was the cowboy who needed help.

"Ooo, sugar, you have come to the right people."

"We are going to turn you into a scrumpalicious treat for that stuck-up bitch."

"Who does Miss Thing imagine she is anyway? Not paying attention to our special man."

"Cowboy, she will be throwing herself at your feet and saying 'Take me, I'm yours!'"

Their fashion theme this time featured satin beautician smocks in lovely pastel versions of their usual signature colors. Miss Vanessa was accoutred in pale heliotrope, Miss Jenn in ashes of roses pink. Miss Penelope twirled to show off her Della Robbia blue, while Miss Doretha posed in eau de nil green. Along the scalloped neckline, their names were embroidered in elegant gold cursive script.

Miss Vanessa patted her hair. "I hope you noticed we all wore our left Tina Turner wigs just for you."

They giggled with delight that Ty remembered their wacky conversation from before when he cheekily replied, "And I wore my left testicle in your honor."

He started helping them with their numerous bags. "Y'all didn't have to go to this trouble—"

Miss Doretha interrupted, "Ooo, honey, what do you think we do all the time? Sit around and play chess? Makeovers are our specialty. We love makeovers. We *live* for makeovers! Those guys on *Queer Eye* are amateurs compared to us."

Ty gulped and said, "Makeover?"

Miss Vanessa took charge. "Complete. If she's not noticing you now, she must have blinders on. By the time we're done with you, her panties will be so wet, she'll need a mop. Miss Jenn, start heating up the wax. Miss Penelope, start whipping up some Specials. He's gonna need one."

"Wax?!"

She went on like a brigadier general, "Martin, get the broom and dustpan out for when we cut his hair. Miss Doretha, get out the body groomers, razor, and scissors."

Ty may as well have tried to bottle a tornado when he said, "Really, ladies, you didn't have to bring all this—"

Miss Vanessa barked out in best drill-sergeant style, "Cowboy, take off your clothes!" Headlights again. Noticing his wide eyes, she said, "Oh, don't get your boxers in a twist. You can keep them on, we won't look at your precious love rod. We've all seen one before. Miss Jenn has seen so many up close and personal, she's guest speaker next week at the urologist convention."

"Dirtbag!"

Ty looked a little wary but started slowly unbuttoning his shirt.

Makeover

Miss Doretha reassured him, "Don't worry, cowboy, we're not going to stuff dollar bills in your jockstrap. Not that we wouldn't in the right situation, but you're safe."

Miss Vanessa started pawing through her voluminous handbag. "Now I know I brought my industrial-strength tweezers. I am itching to get my hands on his eyebrows."

Miss Doretha informed him, "She thinks she's one badass brotherplucker."

Miss Jenn snarkily said, "And not just his eyebrows either."

Medusa would be jealous of the paralyzing look and voice Miss Vanessa directed at Miss Jenn. "Stick to your waxworks, Madame Tussaud." Turning to Ty, "Pay no attention, cowboy. What little mind she has wanders into dark, scary regions."

I had brought in the broom and quietly told Ty, "Relax, you're safe. They talk like this all the time. And really, you'll be amazed with how you end up."

"They're not gonna put makeup on me, are they?"

"No. It sounds like a big production, but they're just going to trim and style your hair and make it so this woman really notices you. Go along with it, let them have fun. This will be the highlight of their year. They love this. They *live* for this." *Just like he lets me have my depraved fun when he goes skinny-dipping.*

Miss Penelope handed Ty a Special and said, "Drink up, stud. The show is about to begin."

They went into well-practiced action. It was a sight to see. They put a facial masque on—"just to bring out that lovely sun-kissed tone"—and while that was setting, Miss Vanessa tweezed and plucked, Miss Doretha and Miss Penelope were doing a mani/pedi, and Miss Jenn was trimming his hair.

"Girl, what do you think? Thin it out in the back?"

"Close your eyes, sugar. I have to use my special comb and work on those pretty eyelashes. Oh my, they are long and thick and luscious."

"Like other things farther south. Mm mm *mmm*!"

"Oops, hold still, honey. You have to excuse Miss Doretha. She gets excited if she sees a pickle, so you can imagine what the thought of other things farther south makes her do."

They finished the first part, and Ty was sent to wash off any masque residue after they peeled it. Miss Vanessa then got to work with her electric razor, very carefully deciding just how much stubble to leave. She and the ladies calculated like a NASA formula while Ty stoically tolerated their efforts.

I went to get refreshments: pink champagne, Brie and crackers, and toast points with pâté. When I returned, Ty was standing and looking like the demons of hell were tormenting him. Understandable. Miss Doretha and Miss Vanessa were using the body grooming razors.

I asked, "How's it going?"

Miss Doretha said, "He has fine blond hair, easy. We're manscaping and reducing the leg hair and arm hair. We'll make the chest hair look perfect, and we'll get rid of what little back hair he has."

"Y'all always talk about someone like he isn't there?" Ty said. "And I don't see why you have to manscape or whatever."

Miss Doretha patiently explained, "Because you have to have just the right amount of body hair, cowpoke. Too little and you look like a plucked chicken. Too much and you look like Guido."

"Who's Guido?"

I said, "Think of a hairy guy with a gold necklace."

"Manscape just right," said Miss Doretha, "and you look sexy and manly. We are taking the opportunity to do just that."

I noticed that the ladies were also taking the opportunity of running their hands all over his body "to check if we got everything." Miss Vanessa's braille method was back in action!

Ty grumbled, "I don't see why this is necessary. I'll have my tuxedo on."

"We are hoping," said Miss Jenn, "that after all this work, Miss Thing stuck-up office bitch will end up in that den of iniquity upstairs and that you most certainly will *not* be in a tuxedo and that you most certainly will *yes* be displaying your manly manhood in all its natural unclothed charms."

He had to agree with that idea, after he figured out what she said. "Me too!"

Miss Vanessa announced, "It's time to wax your back. Oh dear god, he's probably scared. A little wax and a little yank, and he'll screech like a Valley girl at a hairspray sale."

"Y'all can see I'm right here."

Miss Doretha said, "Of course we can see you, hot stuff. You standing there in those sexy boxers revs up our motors, so we have to act like you're our very own Ken doll to play with and treat you like a mannequin. But we keep hoping something or other will flop out. Oops, stand still." Ty was looking down at himself, alarmed, but decided he was safe.

When they started waxing, he didn't screech but he did shout god*dam*mit a few times. After the third time, Miss Doretha asked him if she could kiss it and make it better, and there was deathly silence from then on.

Ty decided to break the silence. "Y'all ...do y'all..."

"What, cowboy? Spit it out."

"Do y'all have boyfriends?"

Miss Vanessa answered. "Well now, that depends. If you're talking about ten minutes in a dark alley, Miss Jenn has them every night—"

"Tart!"

"—but if you're talking about someone steady, well we've had our moments. But alas, it's hard to keep a guy after a certain age and under such, shall we say, nontraditional circumstances."

Miss Doretha said, "What she's trying to say is that old drag queens have a hard time finding guys. And that's why we're so bitchy and twitchy."

"Sugar," said Miss Penelope, tiptoeing her fingers up his shoulder, "we're just dying to know about you and your girlfriends. Tell all!"

"I don't know what to tell you. I've had a few girlfriends, like in high school and college, but mostly I like to stay independent."

"That's what Martin said. I hate it when he's always right. We hate you, Martin! Do you have a long-lost love? A high school sweetheart you wish you had stayed with?"

"My high school sweetheart? We broke up, and she got married to my best friend a year after graduation. They have three kids now."

"Your best friend?!" hollered Miss Vanessa. "This is like 'Jessie's Girl' or something. Do you even talk to him? Or her? I'd scratch her eyes out!" So like Miss Vanessa to thrive on the soap opera.

"Y'all think it was somethin' dramatic, but I was best man at the weddin' and wished them well."

"Oh. Tell us about your first time. You know, the *first* time."

"Y'all mean my first time goin' on a date?"

Miss Doretha was never one to mince words. "No, something far more exciting. The first time you stuck your big dick into a woman's whatzit!"

"Losin' my virginity? Y'all don't need to hear about that."

"Yes we do!" chorused five voices.

"Sugar, we live vicariously," urged Miss Doretha. "We want to hear about the lucky lady who first got to experience the glory of you."

"I don't know about me bein' glorious."

"With you, glorious, notorious, and...and...historious."

"You ignorant cow, historious is not a word."

"Who are you calling an ignorant cow, Elsie?"

Ty butted in, playing peacemaker. "Ladies, why are all y'all so mean to each other?"

"Think nothing of it, big boy. Get back to the historious story. Do you even remember her name?"

I could see his mischievous look. He was going to tease them. "Laurie Elkins. I was a junior, she was a sophomore. We were in my daddy's car—"

"No! Not the back seat!" exclaimed Miss Jenn melodramatically.

Miss Vanessa said, "Not everyone loses their cherry in the fitting room at the thrift store like you."

"Shrew!"

"We were at Lover's Lookout by the lake, and somehow we ended up in the back seat, and somehow our clothes came off, and before I knew it, she was on my lap and...well..."

"Don't stop now!"

"I got a little excited that night. By the fifth time, I calmed down."

They were beside themselves!

"The fifth time! Ooo, he's like a love machine, like a mechanical bull. Laurie Elkins never had it so good with the so-called best friend."

Miss Jenn said, "There. Waxing all done."

"Thank god for small favors," said Ty.

"And now it's time to shave your balls."

"YOU ARE NOT SHAVING MY BALLS!"

"Spoil sport," said Miss Doretha.

"All right," acquiesced Miss Jenn. "We'll let you take care of that yourself. But be sure you do it. Take your time, don't want to hurt those precious golden globes."

"Why do I have to do that? I thought I was supposed to be natural."

"It's so much nicer and cleaner. A partner appreciates it. And there's one big advantage."

Miss Doretha vamped. "It's what porn stars do. It makes you look bigger."

"I'm fine in that department."

"Don't we all know it!"

They sent him off to the shower to get rid of any wax streaks and loose hairs and to freshen up. We cleaned everything, the ladies bickering as usual and making bitchy twitchy comments accusing the others of having their hands all over Ty.

"He is the finest of fine men. I vote we tie him up and take advantage of him and ravish him completely!"

"In your dreams, hussy."

"You'd better believe it! And if you think for one second that I'm a hussy and you're not, that's the volcano calling the hurricane disruptive."

Ty returned wearing a towel and looking marvelous. The manscaping was indeed just right. I thought if the office woman could see him like that, she'd hump him in his revolving chair. His soapy masculine scent...this never failed. My pheromones were having a parade!

Miss Jenn worked diligently to style his hair, artfully achieving that natural look of slightly unkempt and windblown. Hard work to make it look that natural.

I got a text and announced, "Amy will be here in five minutes."

"Amy? Why is she comin'?" asked Ty.

"She has the tuxedo."

Miss Jenn said, "I hope she chose the right one. We need to show off these hard muscles and this fine physique. It better be form-fitting and tight."

Ty said, "I don't like it tight."

"Sugar, I bet you never *once* said *that* to a girlfriend."

Ty rushed off to throw on shirt and shorts. Amy arrived shortly thereafter, carrying several different tuxedo bags. She greeted everyone.

"I have some options here," she said. "Where's the victim?" Ty returned from his bedroom just then, and she greeted him with, "I'm not sure what kind of miracle you're expecting. It's not easy to make a silk purse out of a sow's ear."

"And hello to you too, your highness."

Before they got into their usual battle, I interrupted and said, "I gave her your measurements, and Amy brought several possible tuxedos and shoes from the theatre collection." I pointedly said, for Ty's benefit, "That's *very nice* of you, Amy, to go to *all that work*."

"Thanks, Amy," he said, taking the hint. "But what on earth are they gonna do without you at the theatre if Natasha's finale dress gets stuck in the scenery? They'll need your claws to get it loose."

Amy turned to us and said, "Children should be seen and not heard." She considered Ty as she walked around him and then unerringly chose one of the bags. She held it up and said, "This one. Martin, you'd better help him. He can't even manage to tie his own shoelaces properly let alone figure out a cummerbund."

"Let's get this monkey suit on, Martin."

We went into his bedroom, and I helped Ty with the unfamiliar cummerbund, studs, and bow tie. I returned to the living room, where the ladies were telling Amy about their latest wig creations. I said, "He's ready."

Ty walked in and, to make a cliché come true, five jaws dropped.

He was perfection.

Amy had chosen exactly the right tuxedo style for his body type, with just enough shoulder padding and a flawless lapel line to emphasize his V torso. And the work the ladies did—the combination of the carefully considered haircut and style, tweezed eyebrows, exact stubble, glowing masqued skin, finely manicured fingernails—together with the tux, elevated Ty from a very good-looking man to a sensational vision of handsome masculinity.

I was certainly dazzled.

Miss Penelope started the applause, and the ladies rushed over to ooo and ahh. Ty puffed out his chest and peacocked for their benefit.

Even Amy could not fail to appreciate his beauty. "You clean up pretty good. Who'd have thought? I hope this office lady appreciates it."

Miss Penelope said, "Girlfriend, she's gonna cream. I'm feelin' all runny inside, and I don't even have the right equipment!"

Ty and I helped the ladies and Amy carry things to their cars.

"Thank you for the makeover, ladies, and for the tux, Amy. I 'preciate all this special effort."

"Don't forget to shave your balls," reminded Miss Jenn, making Amy stifle a snort in surprise.

Ty said, "Y'all come back now, ya hear?" which set the ladies to giggling. When we went back into his house, he said, "Well? What do ya think?"

"You look stunning, Ty. I can't believe it. I didn't think there was a way to make you look more handsome than you already are, and they did it. You know, not every man can look equally great in cowboy duds and a tux. You do!"

Ty basked in my gushiness and took a moment to admire himself in the mirror. "Bond. James Bond."

"Double-Oh-Seven, was the story about Laurie Elkins true?"

"Oh, hell no. I was just makin' it up to tease the ladies."

I was curious. "So what was the real first time?"

"When I lost my virginity? Happened so fast, I coulda blinked and missed it. I was kinda advanced for my age and hit puberty early, and I was already gettin' attention from girls. It was the summer I was fourteen, and there was an older gal who lived on the next door farm, and we were out walkin'. All of a sudden she grabbed me and pulled me behind a haystack, yanked my pants down, said 'Holy hell' when she saw my dick, and we went at it. Happened way too fast."

"Too exciting for the Oklahoma farm boy's first."

"Since then the Oklahoma farm boy has had a helluva lotta practice. Now he takes his sweet time."

Well, the makeover/tux operation was a complete success. Ty went to the awards dinner, and the office woman immediately noticed him, unknown whether she creamed herself at that moment. She ended up in the den of iniquity that night, where she also got to appreciate the manscaping and waxed back—aside from the other special wonders Ty had to offer, with which he took his sweet time.

A few days later, Ty was sunbathing by the pool au naturel —much to my delight—and I noticed the balls had been shaved. And he did look—much to my further delight—bigger. Was it wanton that I seemed to be finding reasons to frequently go out and offer him lemonade, iced tea, beer, snacks?

But like all his conquests, this office woman lasted no time whatsoever, and he moved on to new infatuations. He explained, "She was nice, but I decided a workplace thing isn't a good idea after all. I had a workplace dalliance back in Oklahoma that turned out bad." He didn't explain.

As for the story of his losing his virginity, I still wasn't sure I'd heard the real truth. He liked teasing me too!

As Simple As That

Odd.

Ty parked in the driveway at an odd time, before he would normally get home from the gym. Ordinarily I would hear him get out of his pickup, go into his place, and then shortly after hit the pool for his usual swim. But I didn't hear his pickup door slam.

I thought he must be texting on his phone and that's why he hadn't gotten out yet. I continued with my work, and a few minutes later registered a slam. I heard him clomping up the steps in his heavy boots. He stopped and didn't go into his house. I thought about it and realized the steps were slow, dragging, heavy. Usually he bounded two at a time.

Odd.

I waited a few moments, listening to see if he would go into his house. But he didn't. I went to the front window to look, and he was standing there. Head down. Slumped. Twisting his hat in his hands.

Very odd.

I opened my door and said, "Ty?"

He didn't answer. He walked with the weight of the world on his shoulders into my house and stood staring at the floor. Breathing a bit heavily, I thought.

"Ty? Are you okay?"

He didn't answer. I closed the door and moved to face him.

"Is something wrong, Ty?"

His breathing quickened.

"Ty?"

"I had a shitty day at work."

And when I looked more closely into his face, I was shocked to see tears on his cheeks. *What on earth?*

He turned away, putting his hat carefully on the table. He didn't want me to see the tears.

I didn't know what to do. I stepped toward him, turning him and looking at him with concern. I put my hands on his shoulders. His arms were stiff at his sides.

He suddenly gave a choking sob and grabbed me so tightly I could hardly breathe. He wept silently in my arms. I didn't know what to think. This was the last thing I ever expected from a stereotypical tough man who had likely been raised—wrongly—with the idea that men don't cry.

What could have happened? What could be making him cry?

He wouldn't let go of me. I said, "It's all right, Ty. Let it all out."

Eventually he subsided, but he was still sniffing. I reached for a tissue and made him blow his nose. I sat him down on the couch and waited as he attempted to contain himself.

Finally I said, "Tell me."

And in bits and pieces punctuated by throat clearing, he told me everything I hadn't known about his job—finally I was getting the whole story—and what had happened to trigger his huge upset.

Ty worked for the Department of Homeland Security in a federal initiative mandated to help state and local governments. He was assigned to the City of Los Angeles in a unit that focused on combating child trafficking. His unit worked closely with others focusing on child abuse and child pornography.

He had been vague about his job because they were instructed to be discreet and to not reveal details. "We gotta keep a low profile because we work undercover sometimes," he explained. "Some of those times you thought I was out at the bars, I was on undercover surveillance or a reconnaissance, watchin' suspected traffickers or known sex offenders, keepin' an eye on things." Much of his work time was spent looking at social media accounts, tracking financial information, searching for clues on the dark web.

He had become interested in law enforcement when he had a chance to work with a sheriff in Oklahoma. "I'd be one of the apprentice policemen who'd go to schools and give 'stranger danger' talks. I thought this was real important for kids." The sheriff had noticed Ty had a strong empathy for kids and said he should focus on law enforcement for child welfare. After getting his criminal justice degree and attending the police academy, he had worked in Oklahoma City in a similar unit, then transferred here.

Now I knew what he had shown that stalker woman to make her go away and never return: his badge. And I also understood his vague description that he "dealt with traffic and certain population demographics." Traffickers and sex offenders. I even realized his longish hair was to help his undercover occasions by not having a haircut that screamed "cop."

Ty got up to pace as he told the story. "Early this mornin' the police got a tip from a woman who said she had seen somethin' suspicious at a neighbor's house when she got up in the middle of the night to get a drink'a water. She glimpsed a young girl in the window of her neighbor's house. Naked. Usually the curtains were always closed. As far as she knew, he was a single man, and she got worried about the young girl bein' there, let alone the fact she was naked."

The house owner's name had been flagged in the system as being of interest to the child trafficking unit because of a previous sex offender investigation in another state. Once the police let them know about the tip, Ty and his unit took over. His particular unit included his partners Laura and Steve and was headed by Deputy Chief Williams.

"Now this neighbor lady was kinda dingy, and we didn't really know if she was reliable. Last year she called the police sayin' she saw someone in her house in the middle of the night when she got up to go to the bathroom. She wasn't wearin' her glasses, and it turned out she'd seen herself in the mirror!

"This time she didn't have her glasses on neither and said all the girl was wearin' was a necklace. We weren't sure what to think, but it seemed like she was tellin' the truth.

"So we set up a close surveillance operation on his house lookin' for evidence of a girl bein' there. The man put his garbage bins out for collection, so Steve acted like a homeless man and went and looked through the garbage like he was searchin' for food or somethin'. He saw some bloody rags and discarded dog food cans. And there was a girl's scrunchie buried deep down; he almost missed it. We checked with the neighbor lady, and she said she had never seen or heard a dog there. And this made us think the 'necklace' the lady saw was a dog collar, and that he was feedin' the girl dog food. But we couldn't be sure because he mighta had an indoor dog that the old lady never saw."

He continued his story while he paced. A deputy district attorney and a judge were alerted to be on standby for a search warrant. Laura went to talk to the man and look for further evidence.

The man was belligerent, demanding the police stop harassing him. She asked questions about his activities, his job, anything she could to keep him talking so she could look around the living room. One of the first things she noticed was the absence of a dog.

"Laura told us about it after. She decided to more directly confront him. She said, 'We've been looking through your trash,' and the man put up a fuss. 'That's an invasion of my privacy.' Laura came right back at 'im and said 'Trash left in public on a public curb can be looked at by anybody whether it's the trash collector, a homeless bum, a neighbor. Or the police.'

"And then she went on the attack. 'Why did we find a little girl's scrunchie?' The man kinda spluttered and said, 'Anyone could've put that into my trash. You planted it.' Laura said, 'Except we've been watching since the moment you brought it out, and the whole thing is on camera.' 'Oh yeah' says the man. 'I forgot. My cousin visited with her little girl, and she left it by accident.' And Laura said, 'Is that so?'

"And then all of a sudden, Laura abruptly stopped and said, 'What's that noise?' The man said, 'I don't hear any noise' and Laura said, 'I hear something through the furnace vent.' The man said, 'Oh, it's an old furnace, it clanks. I didn't hear anything.'

"Well, Laura knew she had heard chains clinkin' through the vent. And chains don't move by themselves. She pretended she had received a text and she said to the perp, 'I have to answer this text, they urgently need my advice. Just a moment.' She called us and used our code word. She said to us on the phone, 'Hi, in answer to your question, in my judgment it's necessary to go ahead. I've...heard all I need to, it's time to throw off the...chains. It won't work to...deny the reality.' Well, that word 'judgment' was her signal to get the warrant from the judge. And she also signaled us by usin' very slight pauses before important words. She heard chains and the perp tried to deny it.

"Because of all the factors—the old lady seein' the girl, the perp's previous investigation, the scrunchie, the bloody rags and dog food without a dog, and his denial about the scrunchie and the sound of the chains—we got the judge to immediately grant us a telephonic search warrant for probable cause, that we suspected a girl was bein' held captive and in danger. So we went into the house."

He stopped pacing and closed his eyes. I waited for him to continue.

"It was the most awful thing I've ever seen in my entire life. We found her in the basement. A thirteen-year-old girl. Shackles on her ankles and wrists, chained to the wall. Filthy, her hair was all ratty. There was shit and piss in the corner, it was horrible. Dog food and water in bowls. The bloody rags came from her havin' her period. There was a hose he'd use to wash her."

He sat and put his head in his hands. "She...she cowered in the corner, 'fraid of us, screamin' because she thought we were men comin' to use her. My partner Laura had to calm her down."

He started breathing heavily again. "She had whip marks on her back, and there was a bloody broomstick that he had used to...to..." He covered his face. I could barely hear him as he spoke.

"This world is fucked up, Martin. How can men like that exist? How can a monster like that hide among us and we didn't know? I got mad. I couldn't help it. I...kinda tripped the man so that he landed facedown in the shit. And I mighta rubbed his face in it. He'll claim police brutality, but my partners will say he tried to attack me and it was self defense. It's not right, I shouldn'ta done it. But that man deserves life in prison."

I murmured sounds that I was listening, but I didn't know what else to do except let him talk it out.

"At least we rescued that girl. Child Services will take care of her, but she's gonna be scarred for life, Martin. How many more monsters are out there? I never want to see anything like that ever again."

"You did a good thing. You saved that girl."

I took care of him like a child. I made him go wash his face. He said he wasn't hungry, but I fixed comfort food, grilled cheese sandwiches and tomato soup. He managed to eat, though not nearly as much as he normally did. We sat quietly on the sofa and watched a game show on TV. He seemed exhausted.

After a while he spoke again. "Sorry 'bout all the drama, Martin. I just had a hard time with it. Seein' a kid like that... It rips the heart right outta ya. It destroys your soul. It's been a shitty day."

"It's better to let it out."

"It's good you know what I do now. I wanted to tell you from the start, but they ask us to keep quiet."

"I understand, Ty. I have so much respect and admiration for you and for what you're doing. You're saving kids! Ty, you're amazing."

He looked at me shamefacedly. "I'm sorry I cried. Like a girl. Like a god damn crybaby." He looked away and asked quietly, "Am I less of a man in your eyes?"

No no no no no. For someone raised as he was, I knew this was a huge deal to him. "Oh, Ty, you're not less of a man. You're more of a man! It takes a big man to do what you do, and a bigger man to have feelings so strong about justice and about making a better world that he gives it his all. And it takes the biggest man of all to let his feelings be known, to show how much he cares. I can't tell you how much respect I have for you."

"You don't look down on me?"

"No! I look up to you. You are the greatest guy I know."

He seemed to be relieved. "Thanks, buddy. I 'preciate you bein' here for me." He gave a huge yawn. "I'm so tired right now. I can't hardly keep my eyes open." The emotions of the day had drained him completely.

I wouldn't let him go home. He made no protest as I took him to my guest room. He undressed and I tucked him into bed like a child. I waited quietly, and within a minute or two he fell asleep.

    I reached for the lamp and paused to look at his handsome face, less troubled and more calm as he slept.

    This good man with the vibrant, vivid personality? This good man with the colorful language and lusty habits? This good man who loves kids so much that he made it his profession to save endangered children? This good man who trusted me enough to let his tough facade slip and to cry in my arms?

    Was this the moment?

    Was this the moment I stepped from mad infatuated crush into head-over-heels?

    I turned off the lamp and slipped out, quietly closing the door.

    I love him.

    As simple as that.

Two Things I Learned

In the morning I fixed Ty a good breakfast. He went to work, but because he still felt upset from the previous day, his deputy chief let him come home early. He spent the afternoon and evening with me, and I served up an extra-special dinner. This time he ate more heartily. He felt better, he said, so I let him go to his own house with the promise he would come back if he got upset again.

A few days later, Ty invited me to visit him at work. He had decided, since I knew all about it now, he wanted his colleagues to meet me. We were to have lunch with them and then he would give me a tour of their police headquarters. In the building cafeteria, he introduced me when we all sat down together.

"Martin, this is Deputy Chief Williams," except in his Southern accent it sounded like "Deppity," "And this is Laura and Steve." Deputy Chief Williams was a gruff-looking man with jowls and a gut; Laura was short, wearing heels to compensate, and had a trim, stylish haircut. Steve had a heavy five o'clock shadow and a full head of wavy hair. I later learned he was from an Italian American family and his name was actually Stefano.

"I invited Martin cuz you wanted us to update our contact forms, and I want him to be my emergency contact. He needs to know where I work and what I do, so I told him 'bout our operation."

I told his chief and partners, "I applaud everything you're doing. I totally understand the need for discretion."

Deputy Chief Williams said, "In a better world, we wouldn't have this problem. But we do, so we've got to solve it." He brought out a file with a form and asked me to sign it. One thing jumped out at me. In the form Ty had filled out, he had written my name, and in the slot for "Relationship to Employee," there was something I didn't expect. Not neighbor, not acquaintance, not guy next door, not someone I know, not helpful friend, not even friend.

Best friend.

I felt a rush of warmth.

Best friend!

The food in the dull, institutional cafeteria was not tasty, but I had a nice time chatting. Deputy Chief Williams had good stories to tell. I loved Laura; she was friendly and seemed rather competent. She told a few funny anecdotes about the practical jokes they played on Ty as the newcomer. Ty laughed good-naturedly along with them.

Steve started affably talking to me while Ty was conversing with the deputy chief and Laura. He moved his chair closer and put his arm around the back of the chair. Definitely not gay, just being friendly as he chatted. While Ty was carrying on his conversation with the others, he was carefully focused on me and Steve. I noticed he was frowning.

Two Things I Learned

As soon as he could, Ty interrupted us to say it was time for the office tour. I thanked the others and said I hoped I would see them again soon. Ty showed me around, and I found the most interesting part was the sophisticated computer operations center. It was rather impressive compared to the other basic areas, as it had huge screens showing real-time operations just like a movie. When we arrived at Ty's cubicle, there wasn't much decoration. I saw there was a photo of his family. And beside it was a photo of us together, the selfie we took at the Lakers game. It was in the frame he had bought when we were at the beach villa.

This on top of calling me his best friend.

Would it be embarrassing if I swooned in front of everyone?

When he walked me to the front entrance, he finally asked what was on his mind. "What was all that with Steve?"

"What do you mean?"

"I didn't like it that he was practically climbin' all over you. He was tellin' you all about himself, right?"

"Yes, he did tell me about himself."

"He was tryin' to get my goat, tryin' to make himself look all important."

"Or maybe he just wanted to be nice to your friend."

"Deppity Chief Williams is a good boss, and Laura is the perfect partner—she's great. But Steve? I didn't like him actin' like that."

Steve trying to get Ty's goat? Clearly the goat got gotten.

I learned two things from the lunch. I learned that Ty was a little bit jealous regarding his best friend Martin. He didn't like it when others tried to steal my attention.

Best friend? Swoon!

And I learned that Laura was a sharply observant woman. During the lunch, Ty was telling Oklahoma stories. I was watching him with a smile, still in a swirl over being noted as his best friend. And then I noticed Laura looking at me. She had a look of compassion.

Laura knew. She knew how I felt about Ty. And she felt compassion for the gay man who so obviously loved the straight man.

No Biz Like Showbiz

Amy told me her theatre group was going to see a Broadway national tour of the musical *Oklahoma* and asked me to go with her. When I told Ty about it, he said, "I wanna see that. If anyone should see a show called *Oklahoma*, it's someone from Oklahoma, right?"

"It's a musical. Are you sure you would like it?"

"I'm not a heathen. I've seen a musical before. I saw the movie *Grease*."

Amy was distinctly cool to the idea, but Natasha said Ty could sit with her, so it was arranged.

When we arrived at the Pantages Theatre, Amy told Ty, "You do know you have to take off your cowboy hat in the theatre?"

"Of course I know. You must think I'm some neanderthal."

"That would be an insult to neanderthals."

"You're just waitin' for me to take my hat off to *you*. You can keep waitin'."

I sat with Amy in the row behind Ty and Natasha. She stopped grumbling about Ty, and we thoroughly enjoyed the show, Amy paying particular attention to the costumes. I wasn't sure how Ty would like it, but he seemed enchanted with this classic, charming musical. I realized he had probably never seen a musical live onstage before. As it turned out, he loved it!

No surprise that he ended up with Natasha that night. I teased him the next day that as he had seen her more than once, maybe they should get engaged and I could help plan the wedding.

He said, "She has some rich guy givin' her the eye. I'm just the scratch when she has an itch."

"She seems to itch a lot."

"Good thing I happen to excel at scratchin'." He observed, "You know in the musical, where that Ado Annie gal sings 'I Cain't Say No.'? Natasha cain't say no neither."

And who could blame her?

Ty had another brush with showbiz. He came home from the gym hopping with excitement. He told me a woman had come up to him in the workout room and said, "I like your look. I think you have something that would look great on camera. Come see me at my film studio," and had handed him a business card.

The card was embossed on good-quality stock, so it seemed legitimate. I asked, "Are you going to see her?"

"Heck yeah! This could be my big break in Hollywood."

I was a little suspicious because her office was in the Valley, not in Century City or Beverly Hills. I looked it up online, but the website only gave an address and phone number in North Hollywood. I told him, "Whatever you do, don't sign a single thing. Promise me."

He got all duded up for his visit to her office. I wished him luck and reminded him not to sign anything.

He returned a few hours later and came in saying, "I can't believe what just happened."

He had gone to the studio in Van Nuys. The rep had greeted him enthusiastically and said, "You have just the right look. Let's go to my office, and I can tell you about our work at the studio." They had walked down the hallway, and he looked through the inset door windows to see into the studios. He was shocked to see two naked women making out in front of a camera. The second studio had a hetero couple going at it. The third one had a guy playing with himself.

It was a porn studio! I should have known. The adult entertainment industry was centered in the Valley.

I started laughing, and Ty said, "Shut up. It's not funny. That woman brought me into her office, and I was speechless. Big break in Hollywood, my ass. She said somethin' like, 'We do high-quality films here. You'll get a medical test and have a screen test. You do not have to agree to show your face on screen if you don't want to. If you're willing to do gay films, we have many opportunities for that.' They wanted to promote me as a sex-starved Southern boy."

I started laughing again. "Sex is the very last thing you're starved for."

"And then she asked how many inches and was I cut or uncut. Then she wanted me to take off my duds and show her!"

I couldn't stop laughing. At the same time, I was mildly surprised that Ty seemed to know that cut or uncut meant circumcised or not. But of course he dealt with sex traffickers, so he knew the score.

He looked indignant. "Stop laughin'. Shut up. She asked me if I had any questions, and I said 'Ma'am, thank ya kindly for your offer, but I have to say no. What I got to share is shared with one person at a time and not on screen.' I kinda stomped out, but I did stop to watch the two women for a little while. They were hot."

I teased, "This is a wild radical guess, but I have the idea it was not your face that had something she thought would be great on camera."

He looked sheepish. "I think those gym shorts I wear, she saw my dick swingin' and liked the package."

It was true, I love seeing him wear those shorts. "Well, sex-starved Southern boy, you could have put your best skills to use." I started laughing again.

"Shut up. And don't you dare tell Amy. She'll laugh her fool head off and never let me hear the end of it!"

A Better Understanding

Four good friends from Oklahoma were arriving at LAX on the redeye flight early Saturday morning. Ty was happy to see "home folks."

Ty had said, "Buddy, I need a huge favor." And he arranged with me that Fred and Rex would stay in my two guestrooms, while Cody and Billy would stay in his two. He asked me to prepare breakfast for their early Saturday arrival, and he would make pancakes, his one actual culinary specialty, on Sunday morning. They would be out and about for lunch and dinner, and they would depart Sunday evening.

I asked, "Why so short a visit?"

Farmers all, they couldn't stay away from home very long and so could come only for a fast weekend visit. Friends would feed the animals, but it was hard to do all four farms for any extended time. Hence just enough of a short visit to see Ty and his new life in the big city.

He asked for suggestions of where he could take them. After discussion, we developed a possible itinerary: drive through Beverly Hills on the way to Venice boardwalk, see the Hollywood sign, admire the Dolly Parton and Johnny Cash stars on the Walk of Fame, and attend a game at UCLA. For Sunday: visit Universal

Studios and Malibu. Then they'd have to catch their evening return redeye flight.

I figured they would be big guys like Ty, and I was right. No doubt they had played football with him in high school. Their Oklahoma accents were stronger, and they had cowboy hats too. I fixed an enormous breakfast of four-egg bacon and gruyère omelets, spicy sausages, stuffed hash browns, cinnamon rolls, all served with coffee and freshly squeezed orange juice.

Ty of course introduced me. Through breakfast, they looked at me curiously but didn't say much to me. One time, Fred—I think—said, "Got any ketchup, Marty?" Ty immediately corrected him with "Martin," and I thought I heard two of them snicker.

We got them set up in the guest rooms, and I showed them where everything was in the bathrooms. Fred and Rex hardly said a word beyond, "These the towels?" And then they were on their way.

"See ya later, buddy!" shouted Ty.

"Have fun!" I called from the porch.

They were using my car because Ty's pickup wouldn't seat everybody. I heard Billy—I think—ask as he was getting into the front seat, "How long ya known him?"

They were late coming back from the game, and I was already up in my room. They sat on the deck drinking beers and talking. I could hear the clink of beer bottles and heard them going in and out to get more from the refrigerator. It was a warm night, and with the window open, their voices were easily heard.

I was about to close the window when I heard one of them say in a loathsome singsong tone and heavy Oklahoma redneck accent, "Shee-it. Thought he was gonna give us that there keesh crap and dainty crossants for breakfast."

"Fags love that kinda stuff."

I froze.

"Marty's not good enough. Has to be Maarrrtttiiin." In that same horrible singsong tone.

"He walks and talks funny."

"You would too if you sucked cock and got your hairy butt fucked," at which they laughed in a nasty way.

"How can anyone stand to be around a faggot like that?"

"I was scared he was gonna touch me. I mighta got AIDS or somethin'. I was ready to beat the shit outta that queer if he tried."

"Better lock your door tonight, he might try to sneak in."

I could not believe I was hearing this. In my own home. It wasn't like I hadn't heard hurtful words before, but this was painful.

All of my insecurities from high school came back.

All of my doubts and fears.

All of the times I had tried to be friends and been rejected.

All of the times I hated myself.

I should have shouted at them. I should have stormed out, thrown their suitcases in the pool, and locked the door.

I heard them make other remarks, but I couldn't move. I couldn't breathe. I laid down on my bed with a huge lump in my throat. They were hateful, hurtful words.

StraightForward

But it was not the words, painful as they were, that broke my spirit.

It was the silence.

Ty had not said anything. Not a word in my defense, not a word to support me, not a word even to say be quiet.

Silence.

I was utterly crushed.

———

I didn't sleep, heartsick over what had happened. I stared at the ceiling torturing myself. I heard them get up in the morning. I heard Ty making breakfast, bringing them pancakes out onto the deck.

I would dehydrate if I didn't drink some water and get something to eat. I went downstairs quietly, but not quietly enough.

Ty yelled from outside, "Buddy, you there? You got any more orange juice?"

I slammed the pitcher on the counter in my kitchen, and I heard them go silent.

One of the guys said, "What bug crawled up his ass?"

Snickers again.

Ty came to the back door, carrying a plate of pancakes. His head slightly tilted as he looked at me.

"Buddy, you all right?"

I said nothing and went up the stairs. He followed and from the bottom of the stairs, he said, "Buddy, you okay? Is somethin' wrong?"

I gritted my teeth and said, "I didn't sleep."

"Did those boys snore too loud? Sorry 'bout that. We're headin' out soon, see ya when I get back. Thanks for everything."

I closed my door. I heard Fred and Rex get their stuff from their rooms.

Did anyone bother to thank the faggot host? Did they think I would try to kiss them goodbye? Did they think my gay germs would contaminate them?

After they left, I went into a frenzy of cleaning. I cleaned the deck, my kitchen, the guest rooms, the bathrooms. I tried to scrub away any trace of their visit. As if I could scrub away their bigotry.

When I was exhausted, I threw myself on my bed. I could not get the lump in my throat to go away.

With a heartbreak I'd never felt before, I despaired.

I had meant to lock my back door, but I finally had fallen asleep, exhausted physically and emotionally.

I woke up when I heard Ty knock and come in. He said, "Martin, you here?" He waited a moment, and then from the bottom of the stairs, he yelled, "Martin, you up there?"

I kept my voice as even as I could. "I'm tired."

"Oh." He sounded a little uncertain as he said, "Thanks for everything, buddy. I owe ya. I'm puttin' your car keys on the table. Can I take ya to dinner tomorrow as a thank you?"

I didn't answer.

He was tentative and a little worried as he said, "Okay. We'll talk tomorrow. Get a good night's sleep."

I didn't answer.

"Night, buddy!"

I didn't answer.

"Buddy?"

He waited nearly a minute and then left, shutting my back door behind him.

I went down to lock it.

Amy tried calling me, late as we usually did. I didn't answer. She texted me: "You must be busy. Talk to you tomorrow."

The next morning, I heard Ty leaving for work. I went down and tried to do some of my own work, hardly able to concentrate.

That evening, he went swimming as usual. Later he knocked on my door and rattled it as he tried to open it. Usually we left doors unlocked if we were both around, so he had to have been surprised. He knocked on the door again, saying, "Martin? You there?" He called up to my window. "Martin?"

He paced on the deck, he knocked again.

Then the texts started. First from him: "Martin, are you okay? You're not answering."

And I continued not answering.

He must have texted Kyle, who texted Amy, who texted me.

"Ty thinks you're sick. Are you okay?"

I tersely replied: "Busy and tired."

They must have texted back and forth, because Amy soon wrote: "Are you sick? If you need anything, Ty can go get it."

I reiterated: "Busy and tired."

After a few minutes, she wrote: "Martin?" And then she put a row of "?????"

A Better Understanding

But I didn't answer.

Ty texted directly: "Buddy, are you sick? You need anything, I can go get it."

I heard Ty pacing on the deck again. I didn't get any more texts or knocks on the door.

On Tuesday, he went to work but left a note under my door.

"Buddy, is something wrong? Talk to me!"

He had youth club basketball that night, but as soon as he got back, he didn't swim as usual but went straight to my back door, knocking again.

"Martin, you there? Is something wrong? Where are you? What's goin' on?"

He went around to the front and rang my doorbell.

He called out. "Martin, I'm worried. Martin?"

The texts came pouring in from Kyle and Amy: "What's wrong? Are you still sick? Ty says you're not acting right. He thinks something is wrong."

And not long after, Kyle and Amy showed up and rang my doorbell. I was standing behind the door but didn't answer.

Amy said loudly, "Martin! Something is clearly wrong. If you don't answer the door, I'm calling the police."

I cracked open the door, but didn't let them in.

Amy gasped. "Martin, you look terrible. What's wrong? Do you need to go to the doctor?"

"No."

Kyle glanced to his left, and I knew Ty had to be at his door listening. Kyle said, "Ty is really worried about you. You haven't answered your door or talked to him."

"I don't want to talk to him. I actually would like to be left alone."

And I firmly closed the door, loudly turning the deadbolt. I don't know why I was so rude to people who cared about me. And I didn't want Ty to come out.

I heard Kyle say, "Damn." And to Ty he said, "He's mad at you. Did you do some asshole thing?"

"Mad? At me? For what?"

I heard Amy say, "His eyes are all red. Like he's been crying. Did something happen between you two?"

"No! I have no idea. He hasn't talked to me since...my Oklahoma friends were here. Somethin' musta happened. I don't know what it coulda been."

Kyle said, "Better give him time to get over it."

Amy mused, "He wants to be left alone. Let's give him space."

They left. When Amy got home, she texted again: "Martin, is there something you need to talk about? Call me. Please."

Kyle texted: "Do you need me to talk to that asshole Ty about something? Call me."

Even Jackson chimed in: "Kyle says Ty did something. Do you need me?"

These friends cared about me. But my despair made me act in a rude and unforgivable manner.

Ty texted: "Buddy, whatever it is we can talk about it. Please let me in so we can talk."

A Better Understanding

Ty texted: "Martin, no problem is so big we can't talk about it. Please let me in."

Ty texted: "You're not acting like you. What did I do that made you so mad?"

Then he started pacing on the deck. I looked out the window. He was still in his basketball clothes and pacing back and forth, back and forth.

He came to my back door and started knocking.

"Martin, let me in! I'm not leavin' till you talk to me and tell me why you're mad at me! Whatever it is, I'll make it right. But you gotta talk to me!" He started pounding. "I'll pound on this door all night if I have to. We can talk, but you gotta let me in! Martin, I'm not budgin' from here until you tell me why you're actin' like this! Goddammit, give a man a chance to make whatever it is right!"

Better to have it out and be done with him. I unlocked the door and stepped back into my living room. He threw open the door and followed me. I still had my back to him.

"Martin, did somethin' happen when my friends were here? You haven't spoken to me since Sunday. Will you please tell me why you're mad at me?"

I turned around. The look of concern and worry on his handsome face made me ashamed at how I'd been acting.

We stared at each other. I couldn't help it. I couldn't hate him.

He suddenly moved and grabbed my shoulders. I was stiff and resistant, but he held on. "Martin, I've been worried sick about you. Talk to me. Please. We can work it out."

I moved away and sat at the table. In a flat voice, without looking at him, I told him exactly what I had overheard. I didn't spare any details. He didn't say anything. When I finished, I turned to look at him. He had a grim, forbidding look on his face.

"I'm gonna kill those fuckers."

And we had come to the crux of my deep unhappiness.

"Ty, you could have said that then. But you didn't say anything. Nothing! Not a single word. I am feeling like the lowest piece of shit in the world because you didn't say anything! You've broken my heart, Ty. You have *broken my heart.*" Tears were brimming in my eyes.

He had a stunned look. "Buddy, I wasn't there!"

I must have looked like I didn't believe him.

"Buddy, I wasn't there when they were talkin' that shit. I was inside talkin' to my mama on the phone. She called me late because my brother's wife went into labor two weeks early, and she was givin' me the news."

In the back of my memory, I vaguely remembered hearing sometime after that horrible conversation Ty saying, "You boys okay? Need any more beer?" Like he was sticking his head out the back door.

It hadn't registered, I was so upset.

"Buddy, believe me I wasn't there. Do you think I would have let them talk like that? About my best friend? How could you think that of me? You're breakin' *my* heart! That you think I'd let someone treat my friend that way?"

I burst into tears. I felt so guilty that I had doubted him, but they were also tears of relief that he had not done what I thought he had. I should have known better. He had stuck up for me at the youth club; I should have known he would do the same here.

He was hugging me. It was his turn to comfort me.

"I'm sorry," I choked out. "I'm so sorry, Ty. I should have known you wouldn't be like that."

"Martin, please don't ever act this way again. You can always talk to me. I don't ever want you to close your door to me like that."

"I'm sorry I misunderstood. Will you forgive me?"

He hugged me harder. "Will you forgive me for them behavin' that way? I'll deal with those ignorant rednecks later. Those bastards'll hear from me."

I sniffled and said, "I was horrible to you and the others. They must be mad at me."

"No sir. They been just as worried."

"I'll text them right now."

"Buddy, you look right peaked. You hungry?"

The relief of learning Ty had not been part of that horrible verbal gay-bashing made me realize I was lightheaded and weak. The proverbial weight off the shoulders is a real thing.

"Starving. I haven't eaten a thing."

"You text those guys." And this time it was him who made the comfort food. He made—what else?—pancakes.

I texted Amy and Kyle and Jackson: "I am so sorry I acted like that. It was a big misunderstanding. We've talked and everything is fine. I'll tell you about it later. Please forgive me for being unforgivably rude. I love you for caring about me. Thank you."

From Amy: "I am so glad you worked it out. I was really worried about you. I love you."

From Kyle: "We were worried. Glad you worked it all out. Ty better treat you right!"

From Jackson: "Anytime you need us, Martin. You're the best."

Ty was putting the pancakes on the plate. I hugged him from behind and said, "I'm sorry I misunderstood. I feel better now."

"You'll feel even better with some grade-A pancakes. Let's eat!"

We talked into the night with an important, deep conversation.

"Buddy, you know I'm real sorry about all this. But I'm wonderin'. You know those guys are just idiots who oughta know better but don't. But you let 'em get to you. Why not just brush it aside? It wasn't worth your time."

"Ty, you've never had to deal with this kind of thing. When you were growing up, you were popular and handsome. You were the star athlete and the king of the school. Nobody bothered you. But for a gay boy feeling all alone, it's hard."

"Did some asshole beat you up in high school?"

"No, that never happened to me. But it certainly has happened to others."

"And you felt all alone?"

"Ty, it hurt to be called a faggot the first time when I was a freshman in high school, and it hurt just as much this last weekend. I don't know how to explain it to you. The prom king never had someone write nasty words on his locker. He never had a group of guys hurry out of the shower after PE class when he walked in. The most popular guy in school never had someone calling him sissy and queer and making fun of him. The star athlete was never the last one to be picked for a team. The golden boy was never the last to be picked as a lab partner in science."

"That's not right, buddy. That's horrible."

"And it's a reality for a lot of lonely gay teenagers who don't know why they feel like they do, and there's no one to help them find their way. Teachers don't notice. Or worse, pretend they don't notice. It's super difficult to come out to friends or to your parents. You're alone. You don't belong. No one accepts you."

"Martin, after all these years, you know ya have friends who accept you. Look at the bros. They accept you, they don't make fun of you. You're not alone."

"That's just it, Ty. How can I explain it? Even when a group of guys is cool, I feel like I'm not one of them. I'm not one of the boys; I've never been one of the boys. I'm not a bro and never have been. I don't know what it's like to be hanging out with a group of guys. I don't know what it's like to be on a sports team. Even when I'm with all of you, I am not really one of you. I still feel on the outside. Still excluded. Still not one of the boys."

He stood up and paced while he thought. Then he turned a chair around to face me, and sat straddling the chair.

"It's true, Martin. You're not one of the boys."

I looked down, feeling sad and excluded again.

"Look at me, Martin." Reluctantly I did. "You're not one of the boys because you're one of a kind. You're unique and special. Bein' one of the boys is nothin' compared to bein' one of a kind. I don't want anybody else to be like you. I want my one-of-a-kind best friend to stay that way. Just as he is. And he'll never be alone because he always has me."

Oh gosh.

A tear slipped from my eye. He reached over and wiped it off my face with his thumb.

"Martin, we have a one-of-a-kind best friendship. You understand?"

"Yes. Thank you, Ty. You make me feel better."

"That's what I like to hear. Are we straight?" And then we both laughed at the unintended double meaning.

I said, "Is everything straightened out now?" and we giggled. It became a one-upper.

He said, "I had to tell you straight-up."

"Glad you were straight with me."

"I'm a straight shooter."

"Had a hard time keeping a straight face."

"Keep it on the straight and narrow."

"Got it straight from the horse's mouth."

"At least you didn't say horse's ass!" And we laughed. It felt good.

He said, "I'm still hungry." So I made ham sandwiches. A half for me and two and a half for him.

"Mm. Pancakes and ham sandwiches," said Ty as he chewed. "Nutrition at its finest." He regarded me thoughtfully. "Martin, it sounds like high school was a hard time for ya. Is that why you hated Ohio so much?"

"It was awful. High school was a pressure cooker."

"I feel ya. But it's been better since then, right?"

"Later was better. University and starting my career were good. But even then, you can still be excluded. I was never invited to a frat party. I am sure there were times I did not get a job because I'm gay. Nothing was overt, but there were times I should have been the one chosen."

He was paying close attention. I elaborated. "Ty, you can't possibly know. Gay men have to be careful around straight men. If you accidentally brush up against them, will they think you're making a pass? If you invite them, however innocently, to an event, will they think you're hitting on them? If you look at them the wrong way, will they think you're flirting?"

"I guess I understand all that."

I do think our whole conversation was giving Ty some idea of the struggles a gay man goes through.

He said, "I guess from a straight man point of view, we wonder why a gay man doesn't see the beauty of a woman. There's nothin' more excitin' to me than a beautiful woman."

"Women are beautiful, and I can appreciate that. I just don't want to sleep with them."

"Maybe that's it. Maybe straight men don't get why a gay guy doesn't get all hot and bothered over a great rack, or a curvy ass, or that soft skin or sexy voice. I go wild."

"And that's your natural libido, your sex drive. Well, sex overdrive in your case. My libido doesn't work that way."

"Maybe gay men feel like a woman feels."

"From a different viewpoint, but something like that."

"Huh. And the sight of a pussy waitin' for ya to fill 'er up doesn't do anything for ya at all?"

"That would be a no."

"Drives me crazy. I see that, and I'm hard as a rock and ready to take the plunge."

After that slightly bawdy interlude, we cleaned up. Ty rinsed his plate and put it in the dishwasher then said, "Got somethin' else to tell ya, buddy. I hope you won't look down on me when you hear it." He seemed very serious.

As we sat at the table again, I asked, "What?"

"There was a time when I was in high school that I'm sorry to say I was kinda like Fred and them. I was mean to a kid for bein' different."

"Was he gay?"

"No. He was an exchange student from Martinique. His name was Philippe, and he spoke French. He came to our school mostly to get better with his English."

"Was it because he spoke French that you thought he was different?"

"He was exotic lookin' and real handsome. And maybe he was kinda European-actin', and a person coulda thought he was a little on the feminine side. He was gettin' so much attention, and I didn't like that. I thought all the attention should be on me. And I took it into my head to pick on him. I was an asshole. I made fun of his French accent, I bumped into him in the hall makin' him drop his books, I turned my back on him when he was talkin' to us, I'd interrupt him in class. I'd call him Frenchy and a lot worse names."

"That doesn't sound like you at all."

"I was an immature asshole who thought I was big man on campus, and I figured nobody would say a word. And I kept doin' worse and worse things until one day I dumped his tray all over him in the cafeteria in front'a everybody, and I pretended it was his fault that he bumped into me. And socked him in the jaw. The shit hit the fan. All the things I'd been doin' came to the attention of the principal, who was thinkin' about expellin' me. My mama and daddy had to come down to the school to talk to him. My folks and the coach convinced him to let me stay if I did what my mama suggested should be my community service. For a community of two, me and Philippe."

"What did they say?"

"You gotta understand that my mama and daddy were strict and religious, but they lived their lives without judgin' anybody, like lotsa other Oklahoma folks might do. They strongly believed in love thy neighbor and the golden rule and judge not lest ye be judged and that kinda thing. My mama said I had to learn my lesson. Buddy, my mama and daddy said some hard things. My mama started off by sayin' everybody is a child of God and should be accepted for exactly what they are."

Ty had told me that before.

"She said, 'That boy is all alone in a foreign country, learnin' the language. He doesn't know anybody. He's gotta be missin' his mama. And you come along and make life a misery for him.'

"And my daddy said, 'Do you think we raised our youngest to be an ignorant redneck fool? To judge somebody for where they come from or the way they look or the way they talk or act?'

"And then my daddy said..." Ty looked down at the table and clenched his fist. "This is hard for me, buddy. He said 'Your life has taken a wrong turn with this kinda behavior, son. You gonna fix things? Sure would like it if you did somethin' to make us proud.'"

141

When Ty turned to look at me, I could see how painful this still was, even years later. Though he had been a teenager, a young adult, when this took place, I sensed the hurt of a child when Ty said, "I felt so diminished in his eyes. I spent a long time after that tryin' to make my daddy proud."

I didn't know how best to respond to that, so I went back to the incident. "Did the principal expel you?"

"The principal agreed to what my mama said I should do for my community service. I had to sit with Philippe at lunch every day. I had to invite him and make sure he had the best seat at all my football and basketball games. He had to come over to my house every Saturday, and I had to spend time with him and help him with his English, and he'd have lunch or dinner with my family."

"And what happened?"

"I resented it at first. But then bit by bit, I got to know Philippe real good. Once he got a better handle on his English, I found out he was a smart guy and had so many interestin' things to say. My mama and daddy and brothers all thought he was terrific. My daddy said he had a real big heart."

Ty had mentioned something about big hearts before too.

"He was a great guy, and I didn't see that until my mama made me find out. We spent all that time together and pretty soon, he came over most days. He became one'a my best friends. I was sad when he went back to Martinique."

"Do you still keep in touch?"

"We do. He's married now and has kids. One time I went to the Caribbean to visit and stayed for a while. I love his family, his kids are so dang cute. They call me Oncle Ty-Ty." He smiled at the thought of the kids. "Martin, my mama taught me the most valuable life lesson: to accept people exactly the way they are. I want you to see that I'm not like that, how those guys were actin'. I don't want you to be ashamed of havin' me as your friend. I 'preciate you for everything you are, and I love ya just the way you are. You got that real big heart. I love ya, buddy, I really do."

"Ty, if everybody acted like they did in high school, the world would be one giant mess. Thank you for telling me about all that; I can see it was a watershed moment for you. Your mama sounds like a remarkable woman. Maybe one day I'll get to meet her?"

"I'd love to have you meet my mama. She's a great lady. And meet my brothers too."

I teased, "Maybe I could hear some more things about you. What else would your mama have to say?"

"Thank the lord she doesn't know the half. If she knew about how many women I've been with, she'd lock me up!"

"Don't you think she knows already?"

"Well. I guess mamas know everything. Maybe she pretends not to." Looking at me, he took on a serious expression. He seemed to be making up his mind about whether to speak. "Buddy? We gotta talk about somethin' else. We've been havin' a real serious talk tonight, and I think it's time. No more pretendin'."

He started to say something but stopped, got up, and went to look out the window. He fussed with the curtain and appeared to be trying to decide exactly what he wanted to say and how to say it. Finally he spoke in the most serious tone I'd ever heard from him.

"Martin. I'm thinkin'...you...got feelin's..." He turned to face me directly, taking a deep breath. "...for me."

And our watershed moment was upon us.

He waited to see if I said anything. I remained silent.

"That's okay if you do. Y'are what y'are, ya feel what ya feel."

He paused again for a moment to see how I would react and then went on.

"What I want to say is you got feelin's, and I got feelin's too, but not those kinda feelin's. I got feelin's for the man who I can depend on, the man I can tell anything and not get judged, the man I can go to when I'm down. But I can't have sexual feelin's for ya. I'm not wired that way. And I completely understand that's the way you are. I just can't reciprocate it that way."

I could only quietly say, "I know."

He moved to sit beside me again at the table. "Martin, I can't be your boyfriend. But I can be and I am your best friend, and you're mine. You are the bestest best friend I ever had. Nobody gets me like you do. Nobody understands so well where I'm comin' from. I feel such a strong connection with you. Since the day we met."

"I feel that connection too."

"So can you understand what I'm sayin'? I love ya, buddy. For everything you are. And I think maybe you love me back but different?"

Again he seemed to be waiting. What else could I do but admit it?

"Yes."

"But you understand I can't hop into bed with you."

"Yes, I've always known that. You don't have to worry about that."

A Better Understanding

"If it's too hard for you, I'll make it easier and move out."

"NO!" The vehemence of my outburst surprised him. "Ty, I understand everything. Yes, I understand you can't reciprocate, and yes, I know you can't be my boyfriend. I get it." But I didn't want to sound unhappy after all we had shared. So I said with a big smile, "And I totally get that being your best friend is an honor and a wonder and the nicest thing that's ever happened to me."

"Oh, buddy!" He jumped up from the chair to give me a hug and then abruptly let go. "Does it bother you when I hug you? Should I stop?"

"No no no no. Please keep hugging and be just exactly as you are. I won't take it to think you're a boyfriend. I won't take it to mean anything other than you're my best friend."

"Bestest best friend."

"Bestest best friend."

He looked a little relieved at having gotten that difficult subject in the open. He took on his mischievous look. "I can't blame ya for likin' me that way, Martin. I do got a few likeable things about me."

I had to smile at him. "Lord knows you do." I exaggeratedly mimicked him, "Y'are what y'are."

"I don't talk like that."

"Y'all do!" I teased. "If you helped Philippe with his English, does he sound like this?" I made a huge burlesque of his accent. "Goldurn, by cracky, I think I'll set a spell in the rocker on the front porch and whittle and spit. Anybody got a chaw 'a terbakky?"

He laughed so hard. "Guess I'd better go get my whittlin' knife and spittoon. Buddy, it's late, and I'll head home. I'm real glad we had this serious talk."

"Me too."

"You're not mad at me for talkin' about feelin's?"

I heaved a big dramatic sigh. "I love my best friend for exactly how he is. I accept that he's straight. Nobody's perfect."

He laughed and said, "*You* are, buddy. You're my one-of-a-kind perfect best friend." He hugged me once again and said in my ear, "I'm real sorry it was a bad few days. I hope you feel better now. That's my mission, to make you feel better."

"I do. Thank you."

"Night, Martin. Love ya, buddy."

I sat for a long time after he left thinking about all we had said.

Like so many other gay men before me, I had to come to terms with a straight man not being able to reciprocate my feelings in that way. I was lucky compared to those who got painfully rejected. Or even violently rejected.

Gay men often have straight women who are accepting friends. But for a gay man to have accepting and caring straight male friends, and in my case a straight best friend, felt so… healing. It can make up for a lot of previous unhappiness.

The painful episode with those Oklahoma guys hurt me.

But it was this Oklahoma guy who was healing me.

Our misunderstanding led to a better understanding between us. And most importantly, now we both understood what has become the essential part of my life.

Oh yes. Martin's got feelin's for Ty.

Such A Nice Thing To Do

The next day, Ty began the Make Martin Feel Better Project. The first salvo came when my cellphone rang and I saw an area code I didn't recognize. I thought maybe it was a telemarketer, but I answered in case it might be work related.

"Hello."

"This Martin?" The heavy drawl put me on guard, and I froze. "This is Cody, from last week? Can I talk to you?"

What now? I tersely said, "Yes."

"I'm callin' with the other guys too. Can I put you on speaker?" Without waiting for my answer, I heard a click followed by greetings from the others.

He said a bit stiffly, "Martin, we're callin' to say thank you for hostin' us last weekend. We 'preciate you welcomed us and let us stay at your place and cooked for us and everything. Thanks."

I heard a chorus of thanks from the other guys. Then there was a pause. I waited in case there was more, but they were suddenly quiet.

I finally spoke with a drop-dead tone. "Goodbye." As I was about to end the call, I heard Cody say, "Wait."

I didn't reply, and he said again, "Wait. Uh, Martin? We wanna 'pologize for the things we said. You heard us talkin', and we're sorry about that."

"Sorry I heard you. But not sorry you said some homophobic bullshit, right?"

"Wait! We're sorry for what we said. It weren't called for."

I heard the other guys saying, "Sorry, Martin" and "We 'pologize."

"Ty made you do this, didn't he?"

Fred—I think—said, "He called us at two fuckin' a.m. and ripped us a new asshole. He said we were idiots and we were spewin' shit from the wrong end. He said he'd fly back to Oklahoma and whup us if we didn't make it right with you."

"So you're doing this because of Ty, not because of me. You don't really care; you just don't want him to be mad."

"Don't hang up!" yelled Rex. "Ty told us a lotta things 'bout you and everything you done for him. He explained us some stuff about gay men. 'Bout how hard it is for a gay guy growin' up and feelin' alone. Stuff we didn't ever know."

Ty had really listened.

Fred said, "We ain't got no gay guys around here. You're like the first one we ever been around."

"Oh, you have them there all right. But they're hiding because of bigoted homophobia from guys like you."

Rex carried on, "We're gonna do better 'bout that. We promise. Ty made us see stuff we didn't really ever think 'bout. And we understand a lot more, and we're ashamed cuz we know we shouldn'ta called you names and trash-talked. We know we were shitty. Now we wanna make it right."

Cody said, "You didn't deserve that kinda treatment. We do know better. We 'preciate you and hope you'll accept our apology."

I was silent for a long time. I heard one of them cough. It wasn't perfect, but at least there was the possibility there might be four less bigots in the world. Finally I said, "Okay."

Cody sounded relieved. "Sorry we troubled ya, Martin."

The one who hadn't yet spoken, Billy, said, "Ty's changed a lot."

I asked, "What do you mean?"

"Bein' around you, he's changed. He's..."

Rex filled in, "More grown-up."

Billy agreed, "More grown-up, yeah. I think he's grown into someone better, like a better version'a hisself."

Fred said, "He used to be rowdy and wild. He was a hell-raiser, and truth be told, he was an arrogant asshole sometimes. Reckless drivin' in his pickup, drinkin' too much cheap booze, and gettin' into too many stupid fights. And he chased a lotta women."

"That is the one part that definitely *hasn't* changed," I said, and they laughed. This seemed to break the ice.

Cody said, "He's a horny horndog!" in something I guessed was Oklahoma redneck lingo.

Rex confessed, "If you wanna know the truth, we're jealous of you."

You are?

"He made it clear your friendship was mighty important to 'im. Won't tell ya everything he said, but I can tell ya one thing. He said you're the best best friend he's ever had."

He is telling other people about our connection?

"He cares a heap for ya. That made us a little jealous, cuz we used to be his best friends."

"You're still his best friends. His best Oklahoma friends."

"Thanks for givin' us a chance to talk, Martin," said Billy. "We learned our lesson."

I had a sneaking suspicion. I asked, "Did Ty threaten to tell his mama?"

They burst out laughing, and Fred said, "Him whuppin' our ass is nothin'. But facin' his mama?"

Rex declared, "His mama scares the bejesus outta us. I'd rather face the Lord on Judgment Day than her!"

Billy said, "Thanks again, Martin. We hope ya won't look down on us. Please."

Well. Four less bigots was something to aim for.

"We can agree to start over."

The second salvo came. Kyle's name was on my phone screen. I answered and said, "Hi Kyle, what's up?"

"Don't cook dinner. Ty and Jackson and Deck and I are going to First Down, and we want you to join us."

"You guys aren't going to the gym?"

"No, this is something more important we have to do."

"Oh. Okay, I guess."

"One of the reasons, Deck needs some advice, and Ty said you're the Consultant Who Finds the Solutions. Jackson will pick you up at six thirty, and we'll all meet there."

"Okay?" I said a bit tentatively. "There's more reasons?"

But he didn't answer.

Such A Nice Thing To Do

This was strange. If anything, I thought Ty would just come over and ask me whatever Declan needed.

Jackson picked me up at six thirty, and I was a little taken aback when he bounded around to open the car door for me. He was wearing a super-tight t-shirt that showed off his physique in a yummy way.

I commented, "You look like you've been working out a lot, Jackson. That t-shirt is too small for those guns on your arms."

He flexed a little, which I enjoyed, and said, "Yeah, Deck and I work out every day. Kyle and Ty join us most days."

On the way he chitchatted about work and the touch football team and plans for a trip with a cousin to Lake Tahoe.

I said, "So you guys like First Down. I've never been."

"It's your typical sports bar. You can watch football or whatever and the food is good."

When we arrived, the others were waiting for us in the parking lot, and almost before we came to a halt, Kyle was there to open my door. This was weird. What was going on with these guys? Ty and Deck had super-tight t-shirts on too, and Kyle was in a pec-hugging tank top. Hmm. Ty, as usual, had his cowboy hat on.

"Hey, buddy!" said Ty and gave me his trademark big hug. Kyle and Deck gave me man-hugs with heavy slaps on my back. A person could get a bruise. Ty hurried us along, "Come on y'all, I'm starvin'."

Inside it was about half full, mostly jock types, but there were some women too. A basketball game was on the big screen TV. Ty held my chair—hmm—and as we were seated, a waitress came over with menus.

"Darlin', am I glad to see you." Ty flashed that beautiful grin and she smiled, but you could tell she was used to guys hitting on her. "You got some big guys here, and we could eat everything in the kitchen. You've seen all of us before, but this here is our good friend Martin."

I could see her regarding me, curious why I was in a sports bar with them. I was wondering too, and why he was making a big deal. We ordered and when the food came, I could see why the guys liked First Down. The portions were enormous. I had only ordered hamburger and fries, and I couldn't finish it. I ended up giving Jackson half of my hamburger, and Kyle finished the fries.

We talked about everyday things, and they had a running commentary on the basketball game. Midway through the meal, Ty got up. "I have to make a phone call, back in a minute."

As he went off, I turned to Deck. "Kyle said you need my advice? What's going on?"

Deck suddenly looked reluctant. "We don't have to talk about that right now."

Kyle and Jackson were mean. They said, "He's pussy-whipped," and "He's cock-blocked."

Deck said, "I can't talk with these guys here."

It's so typical for straight guys to shut down and not express an emotion for fear of being ridiculed. Horrors! Feelings!

I said, "Uh-uh. I won't let you get away with not talking. Leave these two little boys out of it." Giving them a shut-up look, I said, "No bro stupidity here. Got it?" I turned back to Deck. "It's about a woman, isn't it? Is this about Melissa?"

He still looked a trifle hesitant in front of the others but finally he said, "I've been seeing Melissa, and she's driving me

Such A Nice Thing To Do

crazy. We go out and I think she likes me, and I really really like her. When I drop her off at the end of a date, I think she'll invite me in. But it's a good-night kiss and that's it. She flirts and then backs off, and I can't seem to get anywhere with her."

"Sounds like a cocktease to me," said Kyle.

Deck looked murderously at him. "She's not like that!"

I made a zip-lips motion at Kyle. "Deck, you're probably used to women falling into bed with you pretty quick, right?"

"Well. Yeah. I guess."

Kyle whooped. "His cock is a heat-seeking missile!"

"He's a Wham Bam Thank You Ma'am machine," teased Jackson.

Enough! I turned to Kyle and Jackson, "You guys are no help at all. If you aren't quiet, I'll stick a pin in your life-size inflatable dolls, and then we'll see who needs advice." This set them laughing, and they acquiesced.

I turned back to Deck. "And once you've had your conquest, do you lose interest in the woman after that? You see them maybe one more time and then move on?"

Deck looked surprised. "Yeah. That's right. I lose interest."

"But Melissa you've seen how many times?"

"Oh. We've gone out way over a dozen times. Twenty times?"

Kyle and Jackson looked at each other but didn't say anything after I held a warning hand up.

"Where do you take her on a date?"

"We go to dinner, like, we've been here to First Down. And we've seen a few movies. A few days ago we saw an action movie. I took her to a basketball game one time."

"I see. Let me ask about Melissa. Is she a direct, in-your-face woman who speaks her mind, or is she sweet and cute, or is she career-minded, or what?"

His face lit up. "She is so sweet."

"Is she a girly-girl?"

He had a starry-eyed look on his face. "She's so much a girly-girl. Maybe that's what I like about her the most. She's a real princess. She's like so soft and feminine and wears pink a lot, and it's always a dress, and she waits for me to hold her chair and stuff like that. She told me she reads romance novels and the Hallmark channel is her favorite. And she likes it when I hold her hand when we're walking." He ducked his head. "But she must not like me very much if that's all she wants."

"Oh, on the contrary."

The guys snapped up a bit.

"You think she likes him?" asked Jackson.

"Think about it. Every other woman leaps into bed with Deck, and then what happens? He loses interest right away. Melissa is smart. She's playing hard to get. She's keeping Deck interested because she's making him chase her. More than a dozen dates? And the other women got maybe one or two? And he's still hot after her? Melissa is a very smart cookie."

"Oh," said the guys.

"And Deck. The way you describe her—honestly she doesn't really want First Down or a basketball game or an action movie. That's all sporty stuff that you like. She sounds quite nice because so far she's gone totally with what *you* want. Sports stuff is your style and what you like. But now it's time to focus on *her*. She wants romance. Like in her romance novels and Hallmark movies.

She wants to be the princess swept off her feet by Prince Charming. If you rode up on a white horse, she would swoon."

"So what should I do?" Kyle and Jackson were also closely listening.

"Organize a super-romantic date. Tell her she should dress up, but don't tell her what you plan. Keep her in suspense. On the day of the date, send her flowers. Put one of your drawings with the flowers—that would be utterly sensational. Then you show up in a sharp-looking suit. And your Jeep won't do. You'll have to borrow a car, or even better splurge and rent a Jaguar or some flashy style. Take her to the most elegant restaurant with candles and soft lighting and a pretty view. Talk to her, ask her questions, *listen* to her. Look into her eyes. Focus entirely on her. Nothing about sports or work. For god's sake, not one word about other women or past girlfriends. Laser focus on *her*."

"Damn! After all that, even I'd go to bed with you!" said Kyle.

"Deck, one more thing. She'll love a date like that, with such a handsome guy as her Prince Charming. But you'll screw it up if you make her think you only want to get laid. That's still only about you. Forget the bedroom and take it slow. Just focus right now only on what will make her happy."

Deck was looking thoughtful. "I can do that."

"She knows that the best way to keep you interested is to let you chase her. But you haven't figured out—until now, anyway—that this chase involves romance. Now you know."

"Do you have a good idea for a restaurant to take her to?"

"I think maybe the Sky High restaurant. It has a great view, and they have that soft-lighting atmosphere so you can see the city lights better."

He asked, "Is all this effort maybe too much?"

"Up to now, it's been too many sporty things for you. It's her turn, and you have to get her attention big time before she gives up. Make a grand gesture. Go big or go home."

Kyle, blunt as ever, "Shit or get off the pot."

"Deck, later it will be a mix of what you both like to do. But for right now, try this."

"Me as Prince Charming?"

"You as Prince Charming."

"I can do that. I'm gonna try."

Jackson said, "Ty was right that Martin has good advice."

Like an actor on a cue, Ty came back in. "Okay, guys, up and at 'em. We're goin' to another place. Guys, I texted you the address."

The guys fought—literally arm-wrestled—over who I was to ride with to the next place. Deck won, and so I rode with him in his Jeep. But he wouldn't reveal where we were going. On the way he said, "Thanks again for your advice. I can't wait to see how she'll react."

"I swear to you she'll melt. Her buff, good-looking boyfriend showering her with attention? Guaranteed!"

"I'm not her boyfriend."

"After so many dates, she probably thinks you are and is waiting for you to man up and admit it. Can you do that?"

"Boyfriend?" He didn't answer but was thoughtful.

When we pulled up to Locker Room, the others were already there. Kyle again swooped in to open my door.

I looked at them askance and asked, "You guys do know, despite its name, that this is not a sports bar?"

Kyle answered, "Yeah, it's a gay bar. No big deal."

Ty said, "Fair's fair. Y'all went with us to a sports bar, so we decided it was fair to go with y'all to a gay bar. You gotta have some fun too, buddy."

"Have any of you ever been to a gay bar?" Blank looks all around. Not that I expected anyone to admit it in front of the others if they had. "I didn't think so. Does it make you nervous?"

"No big deal," echoed Ty.

"Look. It's a bar like other bars. Usually nicer decorations, maybe twinkle lights and all that. Better music, dancing, good food."

"Will it be all men?"

"Maybe. Mostly. But there will be women too."

Jackson nearly jumped in the air. "Oh!"

"Jackson?"

It dawned on him. "Ohhh. You mean they're..."

"Lesbians. You can say it."

Kyle got all excited. "Maybe some lesbians will start making out in front of us. That's so hot."

What is it about straight men that two women making out or having sex gets them all hot and bothered?

I continued, "And be careful. Some of the ladies might not be ladies."

"Ohhhh. How do you know?"

"Check the hands. Usually they'll hide their Adam's apple."

"You mean like Miss Jenn and the drag queens?"

"Maybe not quite as outrageous," I said.

Deck asked, "Will the drinks be like all fruity and shit?"

I smiled. "No. But if you want a pink umbrella, you can ask for one." We laughed at the thought of hulky Deck asking for a pink umbrella. The bartender would probably faint.

"Are those men in there gonna hit on us?"

"Look. You guys gotta understand. Four handsome, strapping wet dreams walking in? Catnip in a cat sanctuary! Yes, they will try to hit on you, and you just have to say 'Sorry, not interested. I'm straight.' Don't get bent out of shape, don't get mad, don't take it as a slur on your masculinity. Believe me, there'll be some totally macho gay dudes—more macho than you, believe it or not—so you might understand there could be confusion."

Ty said, "No problem, buddy. We can handle it."

"We can go to another bar. I don't mind at all."

"No sir. We want you to have fun."

Oh yes. This could be very fun.

Not surprisingly, every eye turned toward us when we walked in. Even the people who were dancing turned to look. I could understand why. On the walls were giant posters of jock types: a shirtless football player holding a football, black greasepaint under his eyes; a wrestler with his singlet half off; a swimmer in a teeny Speedo; a nearly naked athlete by a set of lockers, wearing a jockstrap and boasting a big package. My four handsome dudes in their tight shirts looked like the vision made real. I felt rather smug that they were with me. The guys tried to play off the attention, but I could see they were wary.

Such A Nice Thing To Do

I said, "Now you guys see how some women feel in a straight bar." We found a table and the guys tried not to catch anybody's eye. "Guys. Relax. Don't worry, I'll protect your virginity."

Kyle said, "Jackson's not a virgin anymore. His ten-inch dildo took care of that." The guys all laughed as Jackson punched Kyle.

Jackson retorted, "Seven more inches than you," and Kyle returned the punch.

A twink waiter flounced up. "Hello there, big boys. What can I get for you?" He gave Ty the proverbial undress-him-with-his-eyes look and said, "Besides my phone number for this cool drink of water?" Deck started to frown, but I looked firmly at him and told the waiter, remembering the drinks we'd had at First Down, "Three draft beers, a whiskey straight up for the cowboy, and a Campari Orange for me."

"Well aren't you Miss Bossypants? If your super-hot-strong-silent-type bodyguards need any special attention, I'm eager and ready to please." He winked at Ty and flounced off toward the bar.

I was never surprised that Ty always got attention no matter where we went. Even with how gorgeous the other guys were, it was always Ty who attracted attention. His charisma never failed.

"Ty. Do you remember in that diner we went to where that woman gave you her phone number and bought you dessert?"

"Sure do. She was a dang hot little thing."

"Okay, so boys, the same thing might happen here. Some guy might give you his phone number or buy you a drink. Just smile."

Jackson was bouncing a bit in his seat and looking around. "This music is really good. And this place is way nicer than First Down. There's some hot chicks in here."

"Jackson?"

"Yeah, I know."

Kyle: "Gay men have it lucky. They can just hook up with each other and go fuck and then forget about it the next day."

This wasn't the first time I'd ever heard that. Straight guys do seem envious of how easy it appears for gay men to hook up for casual sex.

Deck: "I'm kinda jealous of that. We have to work for it."

Kyle: "Like Deck has to try harder now with Melissa."

Jackson: "You have to tell them you love them and bow and kowtow."

Kyle: "And all we really only want to do is have sex. Forget all that other stuff."

Ty: "Don't know what y'all are goin' on about. I never have to work at it. I have to fight 'em off." They razzed him, and he joked, "Back in Oklahoma, I could be romantical sometimes. I'd stop in at the gas station and buy 'em a corn dog and jojos and a Slurpee."

"Fine wining and dining indeed," I said. "Well, this bar is full of good-looking men who might get a lucky hookup. But as everyone can see, you're the handsomest men in here. Which makes me the lucky one. Hey, I like making everyone jealous!"

The guys smiled as Jackson kept bouncing. Whitney Houston's song summed up his entire body language: "I Wanna Dance With Somebody!"

A biker-type dude in a leather vest with no shirt wasted no time coming over. He had several tattoos and a porn 'stache. He whapped Jackson on the shoulder and said, "Hi, handsome. Why don't you haul that sweet ass out here and dance with me. You can twerk right here," grabbing and stroking his crotch.

The guys were taken aback. I stood up and said, "What's your name?"

"Geoff."

I smiled. "Geoff." Then I frowned and my tone hardened. "Back off."

"Why should I? What, this one's your special sweetheart?"

Trying to be reasonable, I said, "Geoff. These guys are straight."

"Oh. So you're like their little pet gay, huh? Do they take turns getting blowjobs when the others aren't looking?"

Kyle started getting up, but I put my hand on his shoulder and pushed him down. I was so angry. I had assured the guys they would be fine in here, and now this stupidity. I advanced on Geoff.

"You need to shut up! These guys are my good friends, and they should be able to come here without you making them feel uncomfortable. I told them everything would be cool, and now you're ruining it."

The biker dude stared at me, and I gave him a sharp four-fingered poke. I wasn't shouting, but I was speaking firmly and clearly. People were looking at us.

"It's totally out of their comfort zone because they're straight. But they came anyway. To keep me company. To cheer me up. To make me feel better after a hard week." I sensed Ty was now standing behind me. "They didn't have to do that, but they're such good guys, they've made an effort to be here to make me feel more special."

I was hot under the collar and gave him another sharp poke. "Do you like it if straight guys make fun of your gay friends? No, you don't! I told them they would be fine in here. So stop being an idiot who's making an asshole of himself and apologize *right now*!"

The biker dude had the grace to step back and look a little guilty. "Sorry." He glanced at the guys. "Sorry, you guys. I get it. You're good guys to be with your friend."

"Damn right they are!"

He looked again at me and gave a tentative smile. "But you can't blame a fellow for trying." Gesturing toward Jackson, "This guy over here looks like he wants to dance."

"Jackson would *love* to dance. If you asked him *respectfully*, he might say yes."

The biker dude stepped closer to Jackson and said in a hopeful tone, "Sorry for what I said before. Jackson, would you like to dance?"

I had to give him a little credit for being brave enough after our confrontation. Jackson looked mortified and eager at the same time.

"Jackson, it's perfectly okay if you want to get up and dance. You've been bouncing like a pogo stick since we got here. So go ahead. No one will think anything of it other than you like to dance. We know you're straight."

Kyle broke the tension a little bit saying, "He's the biggest pussy hound in the city."

Jackson looked at me, and I made a motion with my hands. "Go ahead, have fun." I pointed to Geoff. "And you. Hands off the merchandise. If I see you grope his ass even once, I will be out there to kick yours!"

Geoff raised his hands. "Like a nun."

I motioned again, and they headed to the dance floor, Jackson already dancing on the way. I turned back. Kyle and Deck and Ty were staring at me.

Deck said in wonder, "You little tiger," and Kyle added, "Don't mess with mofo Martin." They high-fived me, still looking at me like they couldn't believe my outburst.

The waiter had arrived with the drinks. He fanned himself and said to me, "My hero! Let me tell you, that put a twinkle in my winkle. I thought these other guys here were the rough-tough-buff-can't-get-enough ones. But *you!*" He fanned himself again and said to the others, "Attention all you super hot hunks at the table, I heard what Macho Man here with the balls of steel said. You guys are way cool for being here to support your friend. Drinks on the house."

Ty said, "Thanks, buddy."

The waiter gave him a flirtatious look as he was leaving and said, "Leave your phone number if you want to play Ride 'Em Cowboy in ways you never knew." Ty looked a little bemused as we laughed.

Kyle looked at me and said, "So you figured it out?"

"About your good deed for the day? About making me part of the group and making me feel better after a bad week? You guys are about as transparent as a porn star's nightie." I looked at them with affection. "Thank you. I love you for it." I turned and looked at Ty, who I knew had masterminded the whole thing. With the start of a little tear in my eye, I whispered, "I love you for it." I could see this was getting too touchy-feely for them. "Okay, okay, I know. Straight guys don't like all this mushy talk because it's about feelings. You guys have them, but you don't like to admit it. Drink up!"

They relaxed, and I turned to look at Jackson and Geoff. Jackson was blissfully dancing up a storm. I saw Geoff turn and say something to a group of guys, and they all turned to look at us. Then they all told someone else, and they went on to others, all of them turning to look. The news was spreading fast about my coterie of friends. Ty and the guys—completely oblivious. By the time the dance was over, the whole bar was aware of the situation.

The dance ended and Jackson came bounding over to sit down and take a drink of his beer. He said, "This music is so great! Hey, that Geoff guy told me that a lot of the chicks in here tonight are straight chicks. It's more fun for them in a gay bar because they don't get hit on all the time."

The boys perked up considerably and looked at me. I agreed, "Yeah, that can happen." They started looking around to check out the ladies. By this time, the gossip had spread around the bar, and sure enough three cute women came over.

"Hi!" said a perky blonde. "We heard you guys are here especially to be with your friend." The second one said, "That's so cool." She smiled winningly at the guys. The third one leaned in toward them. "You guys wanna dance?"

Kyle, Jackson, and Deck jumped up and happily went out on the floor, with everyone in the bar watching. I turned to Ty and

Such A Nice Thing To Do

said, "Thank you for this special effort to make me feel better. You are simply the greatest."

"Anything for my good buddy. For my best friend." He leaned closer to give me a huge hug. Ty put his arm around the back of my chair. I could see others were noticing our closeness.

I really felt good.

I felt accepted.

While the guys were dancing, a nice-looking man came over and approached Ty. "Hi. I noticed you when you came in. Would you like to dance?"

Ty, ever-charming, said, "Thank ya kindly, sir. I'm here with my friend and want to hang with him. I can't dance to this kinda music anyway. I need some good ol' country-western. Why don't y'all sit down and join us for a drink?"

He signaled the attentive waiter, who sashayed over and said to the man, "A word to the wise. Don't try to steal the Marlboro Man away from his friend. He may look quiet, but he's ferocious!"

Ty popped out with, "Yeah. He's silent but violent!"

We all laughed. Clever Ty, coming up with that on the spot.

The man asked for a beer. As the waiter walked away, he sashayed his hips at Ty, who just laughed.

We chatted for a while with the man, whose name was Glenn, and then Ty got up to use the restroom. I said to him, "Do you need me to be a bodyguard?" Ty laughed and said, "It's fine. I'm a big boy." As he walked toward the restroom, I was not surprised to see two or three other guys nonchalantly follow him to try to take a look. Jackson, Kyle, and Deck came rushing over to chug from their beers and hurried back to the floor to flirt with the girls.

Glenn looked at me. "You're so lucky."

"Why?"

"I don't have any straight friends who would come with me to a gay bar. In fact, I actually hardly have any straight friends."

"I guess I am lucky at that."

"No, it's pretty special. Everyone here is talking about it. It's really quite wonderful, I hope you know that. To have that kind of loyalty, you must be a good guy."

Oh gosh. I was starting to feel gooey inside.

I smiled. "Thanks."

This brought to mind our beach villa trip and how, while the guys played volleyball, the women sitting near me were very curious about how we were all friends. Maybe my relationship with all of them was more unusual than I thought.

"And your cowboy friend. Omigod. He is smokin' hot!"

"He's my best friend," I bragged.

"Friends with benefits?" Glenn asked hopefully.

"Not that lucky."

"Oh." He looked at the dance floor. "I just had an idea." He got up. "Thanks for the beer. Have a good time."

The guys came back to sit with me. Kyle said, "Those women are fun!"

"Did you get their phone numbers?"

"Of course. Deck won't use his because he has big plans for Melissa, thanks to you. Maybe Ty can use it."

Ty returned, and I said "Escaped with your virginity intact?"

"Maybe I did need y'all as a bodyguard. I had to use the stall to protect myself. One of 'em knocked on the stall door and said 'Need a hand?' I guess I'm a chick magnet around women and a dick magnet in the john."

"Always so popular."

A country-western song started, not at all like what had been playing. I looked over at the DJ, and I spotted Glenn. He gave me two thumbs-up. Ty leaped up. "Now there's some music I like! Come on, Martin, let's go dance a boot-scootin' boogie!" He dragged me to the floor to start a line dance, grabbing Glenn and Geoff along the way to join us. Jackson, Kyle, and Deck bounded over to their lady friends to bring them to the floor. Everyone was watching as Ty was smiling and leading the way with gusto. He shouted, "Come on, all y'all!" He had such charisma that it wasn't a minute before everyone in bar rushed to join in. It was so fun. At the end, everyone applauded. Ty yelled "Yee-ha!" and threw his hat, and the crowd laughed.

As we went back to the table, we saw a woman storming in and looking around to find someone. I was surprised to see it was Amy. When she spotted us, it was the Furies from Hell swooping in. She marched straight toward us, pushing one guy out of the way, and grabbed Ty by the arm.

"You motherfucker! What are you doing here? In a gay bar! Are you here to make fun of Martin? Are you trying to take the gay guy out and taunt him? Look but don't touch? You know perfectly well how he feels about you! How could you do this? How could you be such a shithead when he has been nothing but great to you! You are really out of line, Ty!"

The guys had been shocked into silence, but then started to protest. I interrupted. "Amy, no no no. It's not like that. They brought me here to hang out because they want *me* to have fun." She sharply looked at me. "They chose this place just for me. They dressed especially for me. Ty and the guys have done something very nice entirely *for me*. Really."

Amy turned to glare at Ty. He reached for her elbow, but she tried to resist. "Amy, c'mere. C'mere." He pulled her toward him, looked straight in her eyes and said, "Amy. I would never. Ever. Do anything to hurt Martin. He's the best friend a guy could have. Understand me? Never. Ever."

She looked at me and at the guys and then back at Ty. The fight went out of her, and she slumped a little bit. "Kyle, get a chair. Deck, go get Amy a drink." He looked at me.

I said, "White wine."

"Jackson, help with her coat. Amy, you come sit here by Martin." The guys scurried to follow his instructions. He said quietly, "I guess Natasha must've told ya?"

"When you called Natasha to ask if she knew a gay bar anywhere, she was in the costume shop, and I heard her. I asked her what all that was about, and she told me it was you calling and it had something to do with Martin. And he was so upset this week before. And you make fun of me all the time, and I thought you were making fun of him now. And I...I jumped to the wrong conclusion."

"Ya did. But now ya know. You gotta have more faith in me, Amy. I know we give each other shit all the time, but that's just funnin'. For important stuff, you gotta have faith. Understand?"

Such A Nice Thing To Do

After a moment, they nodded at each other. It felt a bit like them making a pact for my sake.

"I'm very sorry, Ty. Guys, I apologize."

Jackson said, "No problem, Amy. I'm really glad we came here. This place is great! Why didn't anybody tell us a gay bar was so fun?"

"Jackson," I said, "The welcome mat will always be out for a hunk like you. For your own safety, wear a chastity jockstrap!"

Soon Amy's good humor was restored, and later I noticed she was treating Ty with a slightly nicer attitude. The guys danced constantly with the women and on the dance floor were frequently surrounded by admiring men. When one particularly high-energy song came on, all of us jumped up to dance, even Ty. A bunch of gay men took off their shirts. Much to the delight of the crowd, my guys whipped theirs off, generating a round of wolf-whistles. Twirling their shirts high in the air, they looked like they were having a blast. Many a boat was floated that night, including mine!

I took a moment to thank Amy for being the damsel in shining armor come to rescue the knight in distress. She said, "I'm still embarrassed. I can't get over it."

"Over what?"

"*Ty* made this all happen. It was a nice thing to do."

"Are you suggesting there's hope for him yet?"

"It must be your influence," was all she would admit to.

Their détente didn't last long, however. We were slowly getting ready to go, and Jackson commented, "We should do this again. Hanging out with just us guys is fun."

"Great," said Amy. "Either I'm invisible, or you think I'm a guy."

Jackson protested, "No, I didn't mean it like that." He floundered with, "I meant the original idea of the bros going out tonight."

Ty had his mischievous look, knowing perfectly well he was poking the beehive when he said, "You know that sayin', Amy. Bros before Hos." Somehow he always knew just which button to push to get a rise.

Amy hotly retorted, "So that means I'm a ho?" She hit the table with her palm. "I hate that phrase. It's demeaning to women."

Deck came to Ty's defense. "He didn't call you that. Anyway, is it actually seriously meant to put down women? I think it's just a rhyming word to be funny."

"I realize the rhyme was used to make it funny. But isn't there a better way to say your guy friends are important without making women sound like prostitutes?"

Ty pressed the point. "What should we say? Somethin' lame like 'Pals before Gals'?" I thought Ty was again rather clever to come up with this on the spot.

"It's not lame if it says what you mean without insulting half the population."

Jackson added his two cents. "Women have their own rhymes like 'Sisters before Misters.'"

Kyle stirred the pot. "Or 'Chicks before Dicks.'"

Amy said, "Ha! Dicks is a good description for *some* people here."

Such A Nice Thing To Do

Deck had been using his phone to look things up. "Seems like women have a lot more mottos with funny anatomy references."

He had our attention.

"'Dolls before Balls,' 'Venus before Penis,' and here's a funny one: 'Flaps before Chaps.'"

As we laughed and Amy rolled her eyes, Ty looked puzzled. "I get the flaps part. But chaps? You mean like what cowboys wear? I think I like flaps *and* chaps."

We cracked up even more. Kyle finally explained, "Chaps is what Brits call guys."

Ty laughed loudest, saying "Hell's bells, how's a cowboy s'posed to know what British people call things?"

Amy didn't miss an opportunity to pick on him. "You're right. English seems to be a difficult foreign language for you."

Ty shot right back. "Ha ha ha. Or maybe I should say *ho ho ho?*" Amy looked like a cartoon character with steam coming out her ears!

I peeked over Deck's shoulder, looking at the mottoes he had found on his phone. "There's another rhyming motto that doesn't insult any gender and fits exactly what this group prefers." This time it was me who had the attention. "Nudes before Prudes."

We drank to that.

Ty peeked at Deck's phone as well and, nodding toward Amy, whispered to me, "Think I should mention 'Nuts before Sluts'?"

"No!" I exploded, laughing. Amy looked at us suspiciously, and Ty pretended total innocence.

As we were leaving, Amy said, "Be right with you, I have to use the facilities."

Ty, seemingly on a button-pushing frenzy, instantly came out with, "Make it snappy, Flappy!"

Flipping him off, she retorted, "Up yours, Chappy!"

The guys 'fought' over who would take me home, but Ty put his cowboy boot down and he won. Of course we lived at the same address, so it was obvious I should ride with him. But it felt heartwarming to have them mock-fight over me anyway.

Back at home, we stood on the porch, and I said sincerely to Ty, "I can't thank you enough for planning this night. You made me feel very special."

"Martin, you are a helluva lot more than special. You're one of a kind!" As he hugged me his cheek touched mine. A first! "Good-night, buddy. Sleep tight, don't let the bedbugs bite."

My eyes watering, I stood and watched him go into his house. I touched my cheek. I knew it could never be more than that, no matter how much I might fantasize.

But I also knew that Ty loved me. Not like he would love a woman. But he loved me as much as he could love another man. Not like a boyfriend, but like a one-of-a-kind best friend.

Glenn was right. I'm a lucky guy.

Kyle called the next day to ask if I'd had a fun time. I thanked him and said, "Usually a gay bar doesn't have that much drama. Sorry about that."

"Is that what they mean about drama queens?"

"Something like that. Did you ask that perky blonde out?"

Such A Nice Thing To Do

"Been there, done that. Went to her place last night afterward."

"Fast work, you bad boy."

We chatted a bit more. And then ten minutes after he called, it was Jackson on the line.

"I had such a great time! That DJ had killer music and it was super fun. We told Alex and Jake from the football team about it, and now they want to go too. Can we go next weekend? Do you have time?"

"Sure. But you know, you don't need me. You can go anytime."

"No way. We need you as bodyguard."

I teased, "You need little old me to protect you from all those big, bad gay men wanting to jump your bones?"

"That Geoff guy gave me his business card. He's not really a biker, he's an insurance agent."

"Go figure." Teasing him a little bit more, "Jackson, you can tell me. Are you ready to leap into bed with Geoff?"

"No way. If we see him at Locker Room, I'll dance with him. That's okay. But you're my special gay friend. It would feel like cheating if I paid more attention to him."

I sort of got his illogic. Maybe I was a pet gay after all. I teased again. "I'll be mad if he slips you the tongue when you kiss him."

"No way!" I could feel his blush through the phone. I loved making Jackson blush.

The day after that, the doorbell rang, and a sumptuous bouquet of flowers was delivered. The card said, "A million thanks from Prince Charming."

I called Declan to thank him. "You didn't have to send me flowers just because I gave you some advice."

Deck replied, "Thanks for the advice, but the flowers weren't only for that."

"Oh?"

"More than that. I took Melissa on the big date last night."

"That was fast."

"I did every single thing you told me to do. It was fun to keep it secret until evening, because she kept texting to ask me where we were going. I didn't give in, I kept her in complete suspense. I wouldn't say anything other than 'dress elegantly.' She liked the flowers, but she especially loved the drawing I made of her. She about died when she saw the Jaguar, and then at Sky High it was like she'd gone to heaven."

"And?"

"I did just what you said. I didn't say a word about sports or fitness or the guys. I asked her lots of questions about her and the things she liked. I had no idea. She has so many cool things she's interested in, I didn't even know."

"Good. And?"

"I took her for a walk on Rodeo Drive, and she loved looking at the store windows and talking about dresses and jewelry and stuff."

"A genius idea, Deck."

"And when we were walking...I hope it's okay to talk to you about this? I can't talk to the guys about this stuff, they just want to give me shit."

It always seems that straight guys can talk more easily to gay guys about feelings than to their bros or to women. "That's just bro bs. So you were walking and...?"

"When we were walking, we held hands like she always wants to, and I don't know, Martin. It felt different. Like I didn't ever want to let go."

"That is incredibly romantic!"

"Martin, I paid attention to what you told me. I realized I was treating women like they were a piece of ass for my convenience. It was hard for me, but I made up my mind before I picked her up that I was not going to take it for granted that I should get laid. And I wouldn't expect it. I concentrated on her, and I told myself that if all she wanted was a kiss good-night, that was fine."

"So?"

"When we got to her house, I thought it would be an ordinary good-night kiss. And I was absolutely ready for that and wasn't going to expect more. But when we kissed, that felt different too. I can't explain it. I felt a little dizzy."

"And?"

"She invited me inside. We sat on her couch and talked some more and kissed and cuddled. She sat on my lap, and I put my arms around her, and I wanted to just protect her and never let her go. It was...I could hardly breathe some of the time. I was holding her in my arms, and I got to thinking about how I would feel if some other guy was holding her and the thought of that made me want to fucking kill anybody who tried. I've never felt like that. And so I...asked her if she wanted to be my girlfriend. And she said yes!"

"Wow!"

"We agreed we're exclusive."

"Deck, you really do have a tender romantic heart hidden by all those muscles. I am so hap—"

"That's not all," he interrupted.

I waited.

"I...spent the night."

Well well well.

"I can't stop thinking about it. I can't even say what was so powerful about...it. I think for the first time I learned the difference between sex and making love. For the first time, it wasn't about getting my rocks off. It was about making her happy. And that made me more happy."

"Bravo."

"I've never felt like this, Martin. Am I falling in love?"

"It certainly sounds like it to me. I practically fell in love with her myself just hearing all this. I'm happy for you, Deck, you're such a good guy. A real Prince Charming! I hope I can meet Melissa sometime."

"You will for sure. This morning I told her about us taking you to First Down and the Locker Room. She thought that was great, and she wants to meet you. She thought all my friends were just other bodybuilders; she was surprised I have friends of other, uh, persuasions. Martin, I didn't tell her about you giving me advice and stuff. Can we keep that secret?"

Such A Nice Thing To Do

"Of course. I would love to meet Melissa. Congratulations, Deck."

"And now you know why I sent flowers. I mean it, Martin. A million thanks!"

Over the coming weeks, it started to be a regular thing where we would all get together. Alex and Jake from touch football joined us sometimes, and they were cool guys. Big jocks like the others, good-natured, a few years younger. Usually we'd go to First Down, sometimes to Locker Room. At Locker Room, I still got a kick out of showing up with my hunky jock entourage and making everyone envious.

I even persuaded Amy to join us a few times, and Ty kept up his barrage of "giving her shit." She would get so mad at him, and he would just grin and egg her on even more. She'd huff at me and swear she would never go with us again, but whenever I invited her, she never turned me down.

I did have to clear something up with Ty during this time. Shortly after our big talk and better understanding, he started wearing his board shorts to swim and suntan. Not skinny-dipping, not buck nekkid. I finally realized he was doing this because he thought I would be tempted or be sad or bothered by the sight. If anything, Martin the voyeur wanted to see!

I finally brought it up. "Ty, you really don't have to do this."
"Do what?"
"Wear your swimsuit instead of skinny-dipping. I know you're trying to be sensitive and thoughtful about how I might

feel, but a cowboy should know it's a little late to shut the barn door after the horse—so to speak—has already bolted."

"Oh. Seein' the goods, you won't get all..."

"I will not turn into a lovelorn slavering beast and attack you. I will be the same as before. I want you to do what you've always done." I teased him, "Imagine Ty with a tan line? Utter catastrophe."

"Damn right. I hate that!" And with that, he threw off his board shorts, and we were back to our previous situation.

Jackson made me come with him to Locker Room a few times by ourselves. He said he wanted to be my wingman. I said that was useless because nobody would even notice I was there if he was beside me. Jackson had a blast dancing and meeting people. Still the biggest pussy hound, he definitely had the attention of the straight chicks who happened to be there. Not to mention admiring gay men.

We all met Melissa, a petite and delightful sweetheart. Of course any girl would look petite next to Deck. I threatened Kyle and Jackson beforehand with death if they made rude bro remarks when we met her. They were on best behavior and even looked a little jealous of how happy Deck seemed to be. Was he ever besotted with her! At the end, they did slip in a few teasing comments about Prince Charming.

Ty said afterward, "She has you wrapped around her sweet little finger."

Kyle, always unfiltered, said, "Pussy-whipped."

It didn't surprise any of us that two months later they moved in together. I love it when the consultant comes up with a good solution.

One weekend, I organized the guys and told them to wear jeans. I gave the bros cheap cowboy hats and flannel shirts.

"Oh gosh, I seem to have bought shirts a size too small. They'll be a little tight. You might have to undo a few buttons." *Okay, by now you know my Machiavellian ways. Perv-vasive and perv-sistent!*

Ty already had his own duds, of course. I dragged them all to a honky-tonk country-western bar named How Dee Do. I said to Ty, "Fair's fair once again. Sports bar, gay bar, and now just for you, a honky-tonk." He was delighted. And I have to say we had a blast line-dancing and enjoying how adept some of the Texas two-steppers were as they pretzeled and did other fancy dance moves.

They had a half-hour of karaoke, and I was totally surprised when Ty stepped up and sang "The Gambler." His whiskey-baritone voice was pleasant, and as usual his charismatic charm got him a huge round of applause. Yet another thing to adore about him!

Jackson had mentioned wingman. In some ways, I functioned like that for them. At all three of our hangouts, there were women who were clearly interested in the guys. There were several occasions when a woman pegged me as the gay friend, and she subtly asked me questions to suss out the guys. I always assured the women they were great guys and safe. It's interesting how straight women will rely on the gay guy to watch out for them.

And it worked another way too. At How Dee Do, a woman approached Kyle, who seemed enamored. She was the hard type that Tammy Wynette sang about, the "painted up, powdered up" kind. I instantly knew she was a hot mess. A guy in a wife-beater jealously watched her talking to Kyle and looked ready to confront him. I whispered to Kyle, "Lose her, she's trouble." He looked startled but took my advice and extricated himself from a potential disaster.

    I liked the guys so much. When I was with my hunky jocks, I was starting to sense what it was like to be a bro. A novel experience.

    True, I'm not one of the boys. But that no longer mattered quite as much. Why? Because Ty thinks I'm one of a kind. And that makes all the difference.

    Ty's determined effort to Make Martin Feel Better, to help me feel like I belonged, was something Amy was right about.

    Such a *nice* thing to do.

Pool Party (Guest Appearance By Dr. Ruth Martin)

The guys were over after touch football for a bro pool party. I decided on a Tex-Mex food theme because that was Ty's favorite. At his request, I especially made the "best guac I ever had."

I started with mini-tacos and ten different fillings to choose from. They devoured everything in sight. Alex and Jake had not yet experienced a meal I had cooked.

Alex said, "Thanks for lunch, Martin." Jake added, "Those were really tasty."

Kyle corrected them, "That wasn't lunch, guys. That was the foreplay, right Martin?"

"I've never heard anybody refer quite that way to appetizers before," I said, laughing. "Digest for a while and then we'll get to the—"

Kyle butted in, "—the intercourse!"

"Ha ha. The main course."

Deck said, "You guys will see. Kyle is right—the way Martin cooks, you'll have a food orgasm."

They were relaxing and drinking Coronas and tequila. Let's just say yours truly was in hog heaven with all those hunks sitting around the pool with their shirts off.

As usual they talked about sports, the gym, their jobs, and —what else?— women. Who they were banging, other guys who were jealous of them, which women they had their eyes on next. They often got into graphic detail, and I could certainly admire their lusty energy. I was pleased with Deck, who was discreet and never said one word about what he and Melissa did in bed, a true gentleman.

They discussed boobs endlessly, but I noticed that the one thing they seemed to shy away from talking about was going down on women. Though Ty did proclaim, "I love goin' down on women. They give ya a better blowjob after."

As I was listening, I went into a bit of a reverie wondering what each of them was like in bed. For all his size, I decided Deck was the most tender. Alex and Jake, a bit younger, liked quantity more than quality. Any way they could get it, wham bam. I decided Jackson had the best dance moves, so he had the best thrust factor. I thought it was Kyle who was the most adventurous, maybe fifty shades of grey. I'd have to think about that. *Is it kinky to be picturing my friends in bed?*

Kyle turned to me and said, "What about you, Martin? You got a fuckbuddy you haven't told us about?"

I popped out of my reverie. That sly guy Kyle. Oblivious though straight guys might be, all of them had to know I had a thing for Ty. However, I always sent off strong vibes that I did not want to discuss myself, and they shied away from saying anything. Was this Kyle trying to lead me into revealing stronger feelings? Time to squelch this.

Pool Party (Guest Appearance By Dr. Ruth Martin)

"A fuckbuddy? Why? Are you offering?" Which of course set them to laughing. I said in a loud stage whisper, "Shall we take this upstairs?" They hooted at Kyle, and Jackson high-fived me. I went on, "Any story I could tell would be boring compared to this rabbit warren. It's a wonder one of your body parts hasn't fallen off from overuse." I smiled innocently at Kyle. "Like Kyle's right hand might fall off?" That got them laughing again.

I don't know why I was talking like this. Maybe I felt relaxed with them. Or maybe it was the vodka Ty had spiked my Campari Orange with.

Jackson asked, "Martin, when did you know you were gay?" The other guys sat up to pay attention to this new topic.

I countered with, "When did you know you were straight?"

He looked a little startled. "I always knew. I never had to think about it. I just am."

"And the same with me. I just am, but it took me a long time to figure that out. I knew but I didn't know, if that makes sense. Even as young as eight years old, I knew somehow I was different from the other boys. I just didn't know why. It took me years to finally come to understand myself."

"Did you ever like women?" asked Alex.

"I went on dates thinking that was what I was supposed to do. Don't get me wrong, I love women and have lots of women as friends. But I finally realized they weren't doing it for me that way."

"Did you ever have sex with a woman?" asked Jake.

This is getting fun, time to play. Again I countered, "Have any of you ever had sex with a man?"

The shocked looks on their faces!

I laughed and said, "I know you wouldn't admit it in front of your bros if you had. No men? Not even when you were drunk and horny? When you were freshmen in high school, I bet you had circle jerks."

They chortled, and suddenly the ever-unfiltered Kyle got defiant and announced, "I had an experience with a guy once." Everyone looked at him in surprise. "I was in junior high, and my friend Bobby came over, and we were watching porn and we started jerking off. And then he put his hand on me and started doing me. I froze, I didn't know what to do. It was just weird. I finally moved his hand away. Never had anything else like that, and we never talked about it afterward."

"What happened to Bobby?"

"He got married and has kids."

"Two horny teenage guys starting to experience sexuality, so they explored. It happens all the time; it was nothing. Yet Bobby and Kyle did not end up having to join the Rainbow Club in high school, did they?" They chuckled. I wanted to make a point. I turned to Kyle and asked, "Was it hard for you just now to say anything about that in front of these guys?"

"I thought you guys would give me shit. But then I thought, fuck it."

"See? Kyle's experience was a nothing blip. Yet it took bravery to even say that much in front of his bros. Imagine how hard it is for a gay man to finally come out, to tell his family and friends."

They nodded, getting the point.

Pool Party (Guest Appearance By Dr. Ruth Martin)

And then I could see the wheels turning. Uh-oh, here it comes. *Another unwritten rule is that sooner or later, straight guys will ask a gay man...*

"Martin, how do gay men know who's going to do...what?"

I just loved playing the guys. "You mean, like what goes where? Didn't anyone teach you the birds and bees? You don't know about your choice of door one, two, or three?" They looked puzzled. "Mouth, ass, or pussy!"

The looks on their faces!

I had never really talked so blatantly with them, only listened, and they didn't know whether to be shocked or delighted at a Martin they hadn't expected.

"It's utterly tragic," I bemoaned. "Gay men only get doors one and two. However, what can be done with those doors..." *Here comes the next question.*

"But how do you like know who's going to...?"

Ooo, I love being a little outrageous. In a comical voice, I carried on. "Who's the pitcher and who's the catcher? Who hides the hot dog in the bun? Who puts the pee-pee in the poop chute? Who launches the rectum rocket? Who's the poker and who's the pokee?"

They cracked up!

Straight guys are so funny. They are dying of curiosity, but they have to get up the guts—and maybe had to be a little drunk—to ask. And in front of other guys, they cannot act like they're eager to know. But once you get going, they want to know *everything.*

"When you're with a woman, who decides what you'll do? I don't think you have a board meeting and vote. You feel it as you go along; you do what feels right in the moment. When you're with a woman, how do you decide whether it's doggystyle or she's on top riding like a cowgirl?"

"Love them cowgirls! Giddy up!" yelled Ty and we laughed.

"It's the same with gay men. We feel it as we go along."

"But I thought gay guys were either a top or a bottom," said Jackson.

"Well, eventually guys might decide they prefer one or the other. Some are what's called versatile." And oh so innocently, "You know, versatile like Kyle and the girlfriend with the strap-on dildo." This set them off completely. They all high-fived me this time, even Kyle.

Hmm. Entirely possible I wasn't far off the mark. And right on cue, here comes the next question. The one with an answer they were burning to know but equally dreading to hear.

"Martin. Does it...like...hurt?"

You could just feel their butts clench at the thought. But I had to play some more. "What does? Door one, two, or three?"

"No! I mean...you know..."

Back to the comical voice. "Oh. When the fudge gets packed, you want to know if there's an owie?" *Keep' em laughing.* "Well, if you really want to know. Think about when you go for a checkup and Dr. Jellyfinger examines your prostate. Ouch, you say when he sticks that skinny finger in. That feels weird, get it outta there! Imagine some guy with a dick like a baseball bat trying to poke his way inside. Hurts like hell!"

They were squirming and practically crossing their legs at the thought.

I began to elaborate. "Unless..."

Pool Party (Guest Appearance By Dr. Ruth Martin)

"Unless what?"

"Unless you make yourself ready. Let me ask this. When you're with a woman and she's dry and not ready, that can be painful?"

"Yeah."

Feeling like Dr. Ruth, I said, "So it takes lots of patience and lube and finger-stretching and foreplay to get ready. Just like sometimes with a woman you have to get her ready. But once you do, then you can have some fun, and you understand what all the fuss is about." They were still looking squeamish at the thought of a man doing that to them.

Time for some more fun.

"There's one more thing about all that. You guys know that women have a G-spot?"

"I hit it every time," bragged Jake.

"Your women are all faking it, like on pornos," razzed Alex, and he made moaning sounds like a bad porn actress. At which Jake pushed him into the pool.

I said, "Gosh, it sounds like the two of you get together to watch porn like Kyle and his junior high friend Bobby. Do you give each other a hand?"

"No!" yelled Alex as he pulled Jake into the pool.

I continued. "Guys have their own kind of G-spot too. Have any of you, in your wild orgies that you keep bragging about, ever had a woman who stuck her finger inside you?"

Now that put them into looking around at each other. Not surprisingly, it was Kyle who spoke up again. "My ex Jessica was pretty uninhibited. When she gave me blowjobs, she stuck her finger inside and was stroking me."

"And?"

"I came so hard I thought my balls would fall off."

The guys were intently listening to this exciting information.

"She hit your prostate. The same place Dr. Jellyfinger checked. The P-spot. Gay men take advantage of this, and you could too. Try it sometime. Just make sure you're clean down there."

Kyle said, "Well, aren't you going to ask us?"

"Ask what?"

He turned to the other guys. "Martin told us about booty business. Shouldn't we tell him what a pussy feels like?" Turning back to me, "Curious? Would you like to know?"

Okay. Gay men want to know everything too. "I'm listening. Tell me all about it. This meeting of the Society of Amateur Gynecologists come to order. The Professors of Pussyology will now elaborate. The Victors of the Vagina will extol the glories of door number three. The Heroes of the Hoo-Ha will proclaim their triumphs!"

Uh-oh, listen to that. Maybe Ty put more vodka in the Campari Orange than I thought.

They had to think about it, stumped as to how to adequately describe it.

Jackson finally ventured: "Kinda hot and squishy?"

Maybe all the food and sex metaphors earlier had influenced Alex, who said, "Like sticking it in warm custard."

I'll never be able to look a flan in the eye again.

Jake was literal: "Feels like the soft part of the roof of your mouth."

Deck was figurative: "Like sweet surrender."

Pool Party (Guest Appearance By Dr. Ruth Martin)

Ty became eloquent on one of his favorite subjects: "It's a Pleasure Island. A slippery slide, all smooth and silky. When I die, I want it to be at the moment my dick is inside a pussy, cuz then I'm already halfway to heaven."

Kyle: "Like an ass, only not as tight." *Leave it to Kyle to conclude on that blunt note.*

Jackson said, "I'm not done finding out about gay men. We never get to hear this stuff. Speaking of asses, is it true that gay men always look at a man's butt first?"

"Actually, they say that's where a woman looks first. But yes, gay men like to look at butts. And everything else! We get off on lots of things. Like when a man wears a loose pair of gray sweatpants, it's a huge turn-on with what's swinging around."

"Kind of the opposite when a woman wears tight pants," commented Kyle. "When we can check out the camel toe."

"Oh," I grimaced at the thought. "And it's a free pass for gay men when we're in the showers or standing at the urinal. You've all been in that situation, and you look at other guys and what they've got to offer."

"We do not," said Alex, as he and Jake hoisted themselves out of the pool and dried off.

"Yes you do. It's subconscious. All men do that. It's about comparing. You've all seen each other in the shower at the gym. I am positive you all know, to the exact centimeter, what everyone has on display." They couldn't look at each other.

Ty made us all laugh when he said, pointing to himself, "They for sure know who's the horse in the stable!"

I went on, "Gym showers give gay men an extra buzz. Especially those that are size queens."

"What's that?"

"A gay man who obsesses about big dicks. A size queen wants king-size."

"Sounds like Miss Doretha," said Ty, which made everyone laugh.

I asked the guys, "Where do you look first?"

Alex said, "I'm an ass man myself. Baby got back and I get going."

Ty put in, "Lips can set me off. Just thinkin' about the fun stuff that could happen."

Kyle said, "This might sound weird. Some women have really sexy feet. When they wear open-toed high heels with all those straps and their toenails are polished..."

"Oh yeah," said Deck. "I like that a lot."

"It's not weird at all," I said. "It's such a common turn-on, that's why they have so many porn videos where the women wear high heels while they're having sex. Isn't that right, Ty?"

He laughed, knowing I was also secretly making a reference to his porn studio escapade.

"Y'all know it doesn't happen that way in real life."

"Speak for yourself," said Kyle.

"Oh ho!" I exclaimed. "So it seems Kyle's ladies not only wear high heels in bed, they're also—let's see—in full makeup, wigs, and jewelry, are never having their period, are always shaved down there, and both of them climax at exactly the same time. So realistic."

The bros laughed, with Kyle joking, "Isn't that the way with everybody?" and Jackson asking, "How do you know so much about straight porn?"

Pool Party (Guest Appearance By Dr. Ruth Martin)

"Meanwhile," I informed them, "back on the topic of who looks at what, all the women I know think men always look at boobs first. And I'll tell you why. Let's have an eye exam." Turning to Jake, I asked, "Jake, without thinking, what was the color of your last girlfriend's eyes?"

"Blue? I think."

"Epic fail! You don't know because your eyes were always a little further south. Women think men can't look at anything but their boobs. If you guys want to impress a woman, make sure to mention her eyes so she knows you looked north sometimes."

Kyle was slyly looking at me. He said, "Let's have another eye exam. Martin, without looking, what color are Ty's eyes?"

Kyle is such a trouble-monger. I answered instantly, "Oh, he has beautiful hazel eyes. And a dazzling smile. That's what you first notice about Ty." To confound any plans he may have had for me to confess being sweet on Ty, I immediately continued, "Kyle and Jackson have blue eyes, Deck has eyes so dark they're almost black, and Jake and Alex have brown eyes." *So there!*

Jackson asked, "What do you like to look at first?"

"I happen to be a chest man. Kyle here has the treasure chest." With his swimmer's build, he popped his chest out to show off. "And we already know from Miss Jenn who has the perfect booty." *And the perfect blush.* "Jake and Alex have guns for days, and Deck could be a bodybuilder fitness model."

"Really?" asked Deck.

Before I could turn to him, Ty jumped up and said, "As for me, we already know mine's the biggest dick!"

Oh so true!

191

They started laughing and teasing each other about dicks. I heard Jackson say that his nickname in high school was Beer Can. *NTMI: Never Too Much Information.*

I stood up and ever so ingenuously said, "Well, I have a measuring tape. You guys could whip 'em out, and we can have a contest?"

They practically fell out of their chairs laughing.

"So much junk here we could hold a garage sale. Time for the main course. Who's ready for Texas T-bone steaks, Tex-Mex ranch potatoes, fiesta avocado tomato salad, and jalapeño cornbread?" Not a surprise that they all were.

After they demolished the meal, I announced, "Half a cow gave her life for you hungry carnivores." I had fixed two steaks for each of them.

Alex said, "Those were the best steaks I've ever had."

Jake added, "Kyle and Deck were right."

Jackson smiled at me. "You're such a fantastic cook, Martin. You'll make someone a good husband someday. Oops." He had accidentally dropped his fork and knelt to pick it up.

So of course I said, "Are you proposing?" The guys laughed because it did look a bit like a marriage proposal situation. "Are we supposed to take this upstairs, too? If I have to keep going upstairs every time one of you makes an indecent proposal, I'll be worn out." And right on cue, they laughed. I felt "on" with the guys. *If there's one thing gay men learn quickly in high school, it's to make the jocks laugh so they don't pick on you.*

I went back into my house to get churros with caramel rum sauce, and Kyle followed me to get another drink. On his way back out, he paused at the door and said, "Martin, you know what I think?"

Pool Party (Guest Appearance By Dr. Ruth Martin)

"Yes?"

"You really need a fuckbuddy."

I stared dumbfounded as he went out while Ty and Jackson came in.

Ty had heard Kyle and frowned in his direction. "He oughta mind his own damn business."

Jackson asked, "Hey Martin, can I say something?"

Setting aside my surprise at Kyle's statement and Ty's reaction, I said, "Sure, what's up."

"I just want to say I'm glad you feel comfortable enough with us now to talk about all that stuff. Thanks!" And with that observant statement, he hugged me.

Is it pervy that I was enjoying bare-chested Jackson, smelling of pool chlorine, giving me a hug?

He spotted the dessert. "Are those churros? I love those." Grabbing the tray from the counter, he took them out to the other guys.

Ty smiled at me while he went to get himself another beer from the refrigerator. "God damn, Martin, I gotta say you surprised the hell outta all of us. Buddy, you're somethin' else!" And I got a hug from bare-chested Ty as well.

Okay, my new perv is to get bare-chested hugs whenever possible. Heir-apparent of Machiavelli will now make a sordid plan for more pool parties.

At the door Ty said, "And one more thing. In the gym I got eyes, and I can see what's on offer. Mine *is* the biggest. Nine stars on a good day, baby!" He winked at me and left.

OM...Gracious!

StraightForward

What Happens In Vegas

For Ty's birthday, I came up with a perfect present. I organized the gang for a short trip to Las Vegas to see the last day of the USA National Finals Rodeo. He was super-excited. It would be Ty, me, Kyle, Jackson, Deck, and Melissa. Unfortunately, Melissa sprained her ankle the day before, so she decided she would stay at home and her sister would help her. She insisted Deck go without her but did make him promise not to go to a strip club no matter what Ty wanted. Deck said he would see a magic show.

On Saturday morning, the Bros had touch football, and then we took an afternoon flight from Burbank. At the airport in Las Vegas, we had the surprise of running into some of Ty's friends from college days, and he was delighted at this unexpected reunion.

My schedule for Saturday evening: have dinner, do a little gambling, and then on the dot at midnight—in a secret plan that the others knew but Ty did not—we'd celebrate with cake and champagne. Sunday schedule: see the exciting final rounds of the rodeo and return to LA that evening.

What Happens In Vegas

However, when we arrived at the hotel to check in, my plans went awry. I had reserved three suites, the original plan being that I would share with Ty, Kyle with Jackson, and the third was for Deck and Melissa. Now without Melissa, Deck had the suite to himself. And that was a circumstance soon to be changed.

Ty said, "Buddy, would you mind if we switched things up? I'd like to have that single for me. I got plans to find me a little filly tonight to celebrate my birthday with a bang. You know what I mean. I wonder if I could be by myself there, and you could share with Deck? If it's okay, I'm gonna meet those college friends for dinner, and we're goin' to a strip show. And then I'm ropin' me a heifer! I need some nookie from a cookie! I'm gonna bring her back to my stabbin' cabin and get into my birthday suit just for her!"

Hiding my disappointment, I gave a bright smile and said, "Whatever the birthday boy wants."

Kyle had been laughing during Ty's little comedy, but then he looked at me with a slight frown of concern. He instantly said, "Birthday boy, go do your thing. Jackson, you share the suite with Deck and you go to the magic show with him. I'll share with Martin, and we'll go to dinner and gamble. I'm in a mood to win!"

Ty went off happily, saying, "See you boys tomorrow for some good ol' rodeo!"

Kyle and I strolled past the beautiful fountains at the Bellagio then went in to play the slot machines. Kyle played blackjack and won a small chunk of money, so he treated for dinner.

    Over dessert he said, "Martin, sorry Ty screwed up the plan for midnight cake and champagne."

    "He didn't know. He and whatever lady he finds can enjoy it when they stumble in at god knows what time."

    "And...I think you were looking forward to being in the hotel room together with him."

    It was true. I had been anticipating the excitement of being in the same room with him in the bed next to mine. I couldn't deny it, so I didn't say anything to refute it. Instead I breezily said, "I'm happy to share with you. Ty can get his jollies, and tomorrow we'll have a great time at the rodeo."

    "Well, sorry it didn't quite work out."

    "We're having an adventure. It's fine."

    He looked at me with that same little frown of concern. "We worry about you."

    I was about to take a drink but set my glass back down.

    "Jackson and Deck and I get worried that Ty is taking advantage of your feelings."

    I looked away.

    "Martin, it's no secret how you feel. We see the way you watch him every moment. I know Ty wouldn't want to hurt you, but sometimes it seems like you're giving and he's taking."

    Kyle waited, and when I didn't reply, he continued. "It's obvious you're important to each other, but we think it's a little lopsided emotionally. You want to give him everything, but he can't give you everything back. God knows we'd be happy for you if Ty decided he could swing that way. But that's not gonna happen. You know that?"

"I know," I answered quietly.

"We worry maybe you're hurting inside. Are you really, truly all right, Martin? We've even talked about looking for a gay guy at the gym to introduce you to. We think it would be better for you not to depend on Ty so much. Would you let us do that?"

I stared at my water glass.

"If we introduce you to someone, will you push him away? Actually, Ty wants your attention so much, will *he* push him away?"

"No."

"So we can introduce you?" And ever blunt, "Can we fix you up with a fuckbuddy?"

I said, "It's not like what you're suggesting. Ty and I completely understand where we're at. We have a...beautiful and caring friendship. It's not him taking. He gives to me. He spends time with me, he does things for me. We're there for each other."

He considered for a moment. "As long as you know we're there for you too."

"Thank you."

"You hold yourself back, Martin. You know you do."

"I know."

He tried to lighten his tone. "You have a lot of secrets, Martin. We hear more about Jackson's latest girlfriend's tits than we hear about you."

I smiled. "He does have a lot to say about that. Them. Those." And it should come as no surprise that I held myself back, pushed the feelings inside their box, and brightly said, "Speaking of tits, there's an impressive pair sitting at the end of the bar."

"I noticed."

"That redhead has been staring at you for the last thirty minutes and sending signals a blind man could read. Go say hello. To both of her."

He laughed at that old Groucho Marx line.

"Go make her day. I'll head back to the suite."

"You sure?"

"Yes. One thing, though. I don't think that shade of red exists in nature. And I don't think her bazooms were as nature provided either!"

Later, Deck and Jackson stopped by my suite to say the magic show was wonderful.

"Where's Kyle?"

"He's making the acquaintance of someone who, shall we say, does not plan to join a nunnery. I think if she could have thrown him on top of the bar and had her way with him then and there, she would have."

They made bro approval sounds then looked at each other for a moment.

Jackson asked, "Are you upset? About dinner, and the cake and champagne?"

To forestall any possible litany of "We are worried about you," I said, "No. He can have fun the way he wants on his birthday. I just hope his 'little filly' likes German chocolate cake with coconut-pecan frosting."

They laughed. "Thanks for organizing all this, Martin," said Deck. "I have to go call Melissa."

"Goodnight guys. Be ready to rock and roll for the rodeo!"

I watched TV for a while and then went to bed, leaving the curtains open so I could see the lights of the city. I thought about dinner with Kyle. Of all the guys, he was still the most enigmatic to me. There was much more to his cool mysterious persona than I yet knew. I'd have to think about it.

Close to midnight, I was awakened by the arrival of Kyle and his redhead. They stumbled in, tipsy, and didn't turn on the lights. Either the giggling redhead didn't see I was there, or she was oblivious.

But Kyle knew I was there.

What is this? I thought he'd have gone to her place for his escapade. But he brought her here?

He's done it on purpose. What's going on?

They were by his bed, and Kyle said, "Ready for a good time, Lacee?"

She had already started undressing. "I've been ready since nine o'clock, kiddo." She revealed a nice figure, with upslung tits that clearly had silicone help. Kyle took off his shirt but did not remove any other clothes.

What is Kyle doing?

I stayed still. With the ambient light from the window, I could see everything pretty clearly. I could hardly breathe.

Kyle looked directly at me.

He knows I'm watching. He was expecting it!

And he went at it.

They had a long period of kissing. Then he started on her boobs, sucking and pinching. He threw her onto the bed, pushed her legs apart, and started pleasuring her with his tongue and fingers. But his eyes were still on me as she squirmed and made whimpering sounds.

What was this? Was he an exhibitionist who enjoyed the attention? Was this some kind of pity voyeurism because he felt sorry for me? Or was it like Amy had accused in the bar, making fun of the gay guy, taunting him with look but don't touch?

I couldn't help it. I could not bring myself to turn over or shut my eyes. I had been feeling lonely and vulnerable and craving. I started using my hand, not caring that Kyle saw me.

"Like it?" he asked. Though Lacee answered with a little scream, I knew the question was for me.

I do like it.

It was one of my fantasies come true, watching one of my guys in action. I didn't care if it was pity voyeurism; I was enthralled. I only wished he was completely naked too. He must be planning to get her off, and then he would take his turn.

She orgasmed, squealing her approval. Then he abruptly stood. I stopped my hand.

"Time to go, Lacee."

He wasn't going to undress and get off himself?

"You don't want—"

"No. Time to go."

Lacee got up, wobbling as she dressed. When she went to door, all she said was, "Good-night..." and then seemed to have to think about his name, "...kiddo." She let herself out.

Kyle went to the bathroom, and I could hear the shower. I was still in shock from him doing all that in front of me, let alone wondering why he didn't take his own pleasure. The shower ended, and I heard him brushing his teeth.

When he came out of the bathroom he was naked. He was hard, his long cock pointing straight out like an arrow. This brought me right back to full attention! He moved toward my bed.

He spoke in a hot, dangerous voice, "Enjoy the show?" And he threw the cover off and got into my bed beside me.

I hastily scooted so I was sitting up. "What are you doing?"

He moved so he had his shoulder tight against mine. "What do you think I'm doing?"

I hardly knew what to think.

"Remember I told you about my junior high friend Bobby? And I said that was the only time I'd ever had an experience with a man?"

I remembered.

"Guess what? I lied."

He put his hand on my cock. I tried to pull away in reaction, but he wouldn't let go and started moving his thumb up and down in a most distracting way.

"Bobby and I were fuckbuddies all through high school. Yeah, we had girls all the time, the swim team groupies. But every Monday night we had a 'study session.' We studied, all right. Each other."

I was speechless.

"He never knew our senior year I was fucking his mom too. Like mother, like son."

He kept that slow maddening thumb going.

"I'm not gay, Martin. But I like having options whenever I feel like it. And I feel like it now. He was my fuckbuddy then. Guess who's my new fuckbuddy now?"

And then he suddenly moved, straddling me. His massive chest and shoulders were right there for me to appreciate.

He fixed me with those piercing blue eyes. "Don't worry about Ty. He'll never know. It's not like you're cheating on him. If he can have fun next door banging some babe, you can have fun fucking with me here."

I tried to move, but he leaned down, his mouth close to mine.

"If it makes you nervous, we won't fuck—this time—but we can do lots of other things."

"But—"

"Shut up. Time to study, Martin."

And he proceeded to shut me up most effectively.

Kyle turned out to be, shall we say, a brilliant scholar!

He was no stranger to another man's body and was vigorously aggressive. I hadn't been with a man since I had met Ty. I had a lot of pent-up sexual energy that he let me expend in a most exhilarating way.

Afterward in the shower together, he said, "Ty will never know about this. Or Amy either. What happens in Vegas stays in Vegas."

"Yes." I could still barely speak.

"And Martin? We'll 'study' again when we feel like it. We're fuckbuddies now."

I toweled off first and returned to my bed. Back under the covers, I closed my eyes when I heard him coming out of the bathroom. He got into his bed.

After a minute, I risked it and peeked. He was on his side, looking fixedly at me with those compelling eyes. We stared at each other for an unbearably long time.

I couldn't stand it. I closed my eyes. I heard him turn over. *Did this really just happen?*

In the morning, I was on tenterhooks. He acted as if nothing had gone on. Was this going to be an "I was drunk, I can't remember a thing" moment? We joined the others for breakfast, and I caught him looking at me. He raised his eyebrows and gave me that little secretive smile. He remembered, all right.

Dangerous!

Ty said, "Thanks for the cake and champagne in the hotel room, buddy. That was real thoughtful."

We all wished him happy birthday, and he went on to gloat about his evening. "The strip show was somethin' else. What those gals did to that pole was astoundin'! And the little gal I brought back to the hotel, she was like ridin' a bronco, she was all over the place. She did some astoundin' things to my pole too!"

Kyle and the bronco gal have much in common.

I was finding it difficult to focus. "Seems like your bronco gal had her cake and ate it too. I hope she enjoyed herself."

"Oh yeah. You can be damn sure a lotta enjoyment was had."

Definitely sure for all parties concerned.

We went on to watch the real bronco-riding. I have to say it was much more fun than I thought it would be. We all had a grand time. Ty was beside himself with excitement, giving us running and knowledgeable commentary throughout.

In the stands, I was squeezed by Ty on one side and Kyle on the other. I was hyper-aware of Kyle's shoulder against mine, the same way it had been the night before. I tried to look from the side of my eyes without turning my head to see the expression on his face. He seemed unconcerned.

Nothing had changed in my feelings toward Ty. He was always Number One. But I was having those morning-after-uneasy-about-what-happened-did-I-do-something-stupid feelings. I knew Ty would be mad if he found out Kyle and I had a fling. He would think Kyle was trying to move in on his territory and become Number One instead of him.

Kyle was perfectly correct, though, that if Ty could have fun, I could as well. What's good for the gander is good for the other gander too. Or something like that.

Look at me. A gay man stuck literally between two hot straight guys and worried about cheating when there was no official boyfriend relationship to be seen. Go figure.

Kyle was a most pleasant diversion, but I was uneasy about his intentions.

Oh, yes. Kyle and I have unfinished business.

The next day back at home, Ty came in after his usual gym workout and swim in the pool.

"Hello, Ty. Amy sent this birthday gift over to you."

"A gift? From *Amy?*" He opened the small package, and it turned out to be a miniature toy derringer. The card said, "So you can have a matched pair."

I had to laugh. When he had brazenly bragged about his "pistol", she had smacked him back, calling it a "derringer".

"God damn that girl. I'm gettin' her good when I see her!"

Oh yes. Ty and Amy have unfinished business, too.

That week Ty stayed after dinner every evening and spent time with me, giving me lots of attention. He seemed extra complimentary about the meals and wanted to watch shows I liked on TV. One night we instead had a rather heartfelt conversation about life in general. Isn't that what best friends do? I wasn't complaining. But it was odd he had stayed longer every single night.

Finally I said, "Fess up, Ty. Is there some reason you've been spending every evening with me?"

He looked contrite. "At the gym, those boys lit into me. Deck said it was rude I went runnin' out on you guys with my college friends. He said I ruined your plans about cake and champagne at midnight. Jackson told me I was outta line. They told me I needed to make it up to you for screwin' up your plans."

"What did Kyle say?"

"He just said, 'What happens in Vegas stays in Vegas.'" Ty looked at me a little hangdog. "Buddy, are ya mad at me?"

"They shouldn't have said one word. It's much more important to me that you had fun on your birthday. It was random chance you ran into friends you hadn't seen in so long, and I'm glad you caught up with them. And you didn't know about the midnight celebration."

"Buddy, I never want ya to be mad at me. If I ever hurt your feelin's, ya gotta say somethin'."

"You're the best," I said sincerely. And on top of that, this week he had been making a sacrifice—for my sake—of something vastly important to his own well-being. So I brought that up. "Can I ask you something? You've been off sex duty, so to speak. You haven't been with a woman all week. Are your balls turning blue?"

"God damn, I'm at full mast and ready to sail."

"You've spent a lot of extra time with me, thanks. But now you'd better take care of business. Surely there must be some women somewhere who have blue..."

"Clits?"

We snickered. "Go show a woman a good time."

And that night he certainly did. Four good times. No one was singing the blues anymore!

Exquisite Torture

In an effort to really show he was giving me attention, Ty went all out for my birthday and bought us tickets for a four-day cruise from Los Angeles to Cabo San Lucas and back.

He knew it wasn't a good idea to spring something like this as a surprise, so he told me in advance. That way I could organize taking Friday and Monday off, which he had to do as well. Plus he wanted us to be prepared with the right clothes and such.

I looked at the itinerary and cruise information. "Ty, you booked these at a travel agency, right?"

"Yeah, they were real helpful. The gal I talked to was nice."

"And what did you tell her?"

"I told her I wanted to go with my friend Martin and have a special time just for the two of us. I wanted to celebrate how much you mean to me."

I paused a little too long.

He said, "Why are you askin'?"

Better to get it over with. "Ty, this is a...gay cruise." I expected some sort of explosion or exclamation or a goddammit at least. But he surprised me.

"Really? I just wanted somethin' short and easy to fit our schedule."

"I think when you told her about me and a special time and how much I mean to you, she assumed a gay couple and booked it accordingly."

"I don't care. You want me to go back and change it?"

"You don't want to change? It won't bother you?"

"Should it bother me? Can't be any different than goin' to a gay bar, right?"

Well... "You do know you'll get a lot of attention?"

"No problem. You'll be there to protect my virginity. And if they think you're my boyfriend, they can just be jealous."

They will indeed be jealous, and I don't mind one little bit. "Okay. If you're sure. It's a wonderful present."

"It'll be fun."

And that was a totally inadequate word for what transpired.

As for how much I mean to him—oh my my!

I made sure we were well prepared with the right clothes. I also took time to explain about bears, cubs, twinks, twunks, daddies, otters, leather queens, and such. He asked if it would be all men, and I said no, there would be women too. Lesbians. Straight couples would be there simply to have fun. And I said we would see female crew and performers.

"Hot damn!"

"But you can't go there, Ty. There are strict rules about fraternizing between crew and passengers. They could get fired and might be blacklisted from working in the cruise industry. You can't do that to them."

"Oh. Guess I'll have to be a good ottercub or daddybear or twinktwunk or whatever I am."

We boarded the crowded cruise ship. Already he was getting some admiring stares. I was worried about whether he would become uncomfortable and just want to stay in the cabin all the time. Was I going to spend the whole trip being bodyguard and fending off horny gay men who thought he was up for grabs?

The cabin. Kyle was right that I had been excited at the thought of sharing a hotel room with Ty in Las Vegas, which, alas, had not come to be. Sharing a cabin with Ty? I was *very* excited about that.

And when we got there, I didn't know whether to kiss or castigate the travel agency. It had one double bed. They had assumed we were a couple. Thinking Ty would rather have separate beds, I discreetly asked the steward if there was a cabin with twins, but none were available. All in all, I loved the swankiness of the cabin, including a private balcony. Maybe Ty would want to suntan buck nekkid there, which I would not dream of perv-enting—oops, preventing.

Ty didn't seem to be bothered at all. He was excited to get unpacked and see the ship. Ever organized, I informed him my towels would be the ones on the right, and I would sleep on the right side of the bed.

"Why's that?" he asked.

"Because I'm always right," I joked.

"Ha ha. Let's go check out the ship."

Trepidation after trepidation after trepidation. The attention he was already getting. The cabin together. The double bed. Was I going to be in a state of near hysteria this whole trip?

We took a good perambulation around the ship, with many men turning to look at Ty as we passed. He was all smiles and said howdy to everyone.

At lunch, we went to the more casual dining salon. This one had a buffet; it wasn't formal like the captain's dining room. No gloved or bow-tied waiters here. We decided to share a table with whoever came along. A rather suave, overly tanned man in his early forties sat with us. Gold necklace, gold bracelet, gold watch, diamond ring, expensive sunglasses, perfectly tailored clothes, perfect Italian leather shoes. His name was Hayden, and he was a smooth conversationalist. Ty cheerfully chatted away. I could see Hayden looking askance at the two of us. He had to be wondering what was going on.

Ty got up to get seconds at the buffet. As soon as he was out of earshot, Hayden dropped the suave act and said, "Why did you bring a straight man?"

I was instantly on my high horse. The nerve! "What makes you so sure?"

"You've heard of gaydar, dearie. Straightdar works too."

"Why shouldn't he be here? Is it any of your business?"

"I get it. He's somebody you hired. Gay for pay? An escort? How else would *you* get a man like that?"

Well now, you can imagine this didn't go over very well. *Dilemma: how could I explain to Ty why Hayden had an oyster fork stuck in his eye? Guess I'd better not.*

"Is that," I asked in a drop-dead tone dripping with venom, "what you think?"

"He's certainly attractive; I can see you're getting your money's worth. Surely he'll take a better offer from me."

I leaned closer and smiled ever so cattily. "You vicious queen. You can go fuck yourself, because you're the only one on this ship who would stoop that low. For the record, he paid for the tickets. For my birthday. And when I blow out the candles on my cake, my wish will be for you to fall overboard. Feel free to go to hell. *Dearie*."

He nonchalantly got up and collected his latest model cellphone off the table. Ty returned with a loaded plate as he was moving away, and Hayden said, "See you later. I hope."

As Ty sat, he inquired, "How come he left?"

"Just so you know, there are some men who need to have a wooden stake hammered into their heart. Stay far away from that one."

I continued to seethe while Ty continued to eat his way through thirds plus two desserts.

The first event was the Dog Tag T-Dance. Ty had seen many men without shirts, so he went shirtless and wore his board shorts and flip-flops. And his cowboy hat.

I asked, "No Speedos?"

"Wouldn't be caught dead."

"Are you sure about the hat?"

"Keeps the sun off my face."

And of course in that multitude of men, Ty was the only one with a cowboy hat on. Instantly noticeable, instantly recognizable, instantly memorable, instantly the center of attention.

I explained that a red dog tag meant no go, yellow meant maybe, and green meant available. "Do you want a red one?"

"Heck no, nobody'll talk to me. I'll take a yellow."

"You have no idea what you're letting yourself in for. Even if you had red, they'd still hit on you. Yellow, you'll be swarmed. Green, there would be a line outside our cabin door and all the way to the main deck."

"Are you takin' a green?" Interestingly, he looked slightly vexed at that idea.

"Oh, I'll wear yellow. It's more mysterious."

"Don't worry. I'll tell everybody I'm with you. Do you want me to pretend to be your boyfriend?"

Thinking about that malevolent Hayden, I said, "They might see through that. And it wouldn't stop them anyway."

"Got no respect? If they're gonna be like that, I'm puttin' my arm around you and givin' you all my attention."

That sounded great, but Hayden would probably try to knife me when I wasn't looking.

At the T-Dance, Ty's wonderful masculine good looks and charisma would have been enough to get attention. The cowboy hat, his Southern accent, and the yellow dog tag brought a huge circle of admirers as we greeted and met people.

Everyone was nice and chatted with me, but I was not the attraction, Ty was. At one point, Ty casually put his arm around me. I wasn't sure what to think about that. Was he putting on a show for the onlookers?

I caught the looks even if Ty was oblivious. If they hadn't yet figured out Ty was straight, they had to be wondering what magic tricks I played in bed to keep someone like him interested in the likes of me. And if they had cottoned on to him being straight, they were wondering what magic tricks I played to have his attention like that.

Envy or disbelief.

I admit it. I was getting a kick out of lording it ever so smugly over the envious ones. *Ha! Take that!* As for the disbelievers, it made me wonder what's so bad about me they think he wouldn't like me?

If someone was getting a little too friendly with Ty, I pointedly found a way to remind that someone of my presence. This was weird. Around women, he could flirt all he wanted and I didn't bat an eye. But around other gay men, my ire was on fire!

Territorial, thy name is Martin.

In other words: Bitch, he's mine!

Security Council meetings at the UN are a breeze compared to the sexual politics of a gay event.

A man with a clipboard came through the crowd saying to certain men, "Hi. Could you come with me? We have something special planned."

Ty looked at me when he got asked, and I shrugged. Ty said, "Here goes nothin'" and went off with the man.

I actually relaxed a lot at that moment and enjoyed visiting with the men near me. I could take the time to enjoy the eye candy of hunky, fit gay men in their Speedos.

All became clear. An underwear/swimwear fashion show commenced, with men from the crowd having been selected to model. Of course the rep had picked tall, handsome, sexy Ty. I was pretty sure Ty would point-blank refuse to wear a Speedo or a jockstrap, so I wondered what they would put him in.

When Ty came on, he was in a pair of tight boxer briefs, the kind with a contoured pouch in front to make the family jewels into the crown jewels. *That* looked enormous.

And when he hung his cowboy hat on the pouch and flexed, the crowd went wild.

When he came off the stage, he bounded toward me and gave me his usual exuberant hug. Well, I do recognize the highly remote possibility that I might have looked just an eensy-teensy-weensy bit self-satisfied that the other men saw him hugging me. Okay, I was smug as a teenage boy getting laid for the first time. *Ha! Take that!*

I said, "Congrats, supermodel. You got a huge round of applause."

"That was fun. I get to keep these if I wear 'em for a little while around the deck today. And we get to have a bottle'a champagne at dinner."

We wandered and said hello and howdy. And every set of eyes was glued to you-know-what. Ty looked fairly amused. As for me, I'm sure my expression said I-know-what-the-you-know-what-actually-looks-like. *Ha! Take that!*

Frequently, men offered Ty a drink. I was halfheartedly included with "Oh, and your friend too. What's your name again?" I wanted to throw the drink in their face. *Ha! Take that!*

We went up to the infamous Dick Deck where men could sunbathe naked. I wondered if skinny-dipper Ty would shuck the enhancing boxers, but it seemed that his fondness for nude sunbathing only applied in the privacy of our pool. We found a pair of lounge chairs, and I reveled in slathering suntan lotion all over him and more so when he did the same for me. And I may possibly have reveled an eensy-teensy-weensy bit in the envious looks I was getting.

Okay, they wanted to slap that superior expression off my face. *Martin! Take that!*

Ty said, "This is a nice place for a moonlight stroll under the stars. I could see bringin' a gal up here."

I said, "This is the place to get a blowjob after dark."

"And I repeat, I could see bringin' a gal up here. But don't worry, I value my life. I won't come up here unless you're here to protect me."

"I'm glad you appreciate the danger."

I had to turn over on the lounge chair so the crowd wouldn't see the evidence of what I thought about being on the Dick Deck at midnight with Ty. I'm the dangerous one!

In the formal dining room, we sat by ourselves for dinner. This was much nicer, with chandeliers, wall sconces, tablecloths, and tuxedoed waiters. He insisted he didn't want to share a table because he wanted to concentrate on me for my birthday. *Swoon!* Using the voucher he had for champagne, we had a merry round of toasts to each other and proceeded to get sloshed.

"You havin' fun, buddy?"

Let's see. I have my obsession all to myself, a whole bunch of gay men are envious of me, I'm sharing a cabin and a bed with him tonight, and Hayden is not around to spoil my good time. Does cloud nine in hog heaven give you the right idea?

"It's wonderful you did this, Ty. You are the man of my—of everyone's dreams."

"All for you, buddy."

A husband and wife couple stopped by and told Ty they had noticed him in the fashion show. Dottie and Paul were quite pleasant and said they hoped to see us around. As they left, Dottie turned to give Ty an inflammatory look.

I said, "It figures. The one straight female passenger on the boat finds you."

"What's their story?"

"Who knows. They probably think a gay cruise is a lot more fun than playing bingo on some cruise with a crowd of octogenarians. Or it could be they're bisexual, or it's a marriage of convenience. Maybe she's looking for another lesbian, or he's on the prowl for a gay hookup."

"That look she gave me would set fire to the prairie after a rainstorm. I think she has her eye on me."

"As does every other person on the boat."

"That was kinda fun at first, but it gets a little much after awhile. I'm not the only one to see. Have to say there's some real good-lookin' men on this cruise. You gotta be lovin' the eye candy."

My tipsiness led me to say, "I only have eyes for you."

He played with his champagne glass and wouldn't look at me directly when he said, "You lookin' to get laid on the cruise? Want me to step aside?"

"I'm looking to have a good time with my bestest best friend. And that's it."

He smiled at me and winked.

A hot cowboy plus too much champagne would make anybody swoon, right?

Exquisite Torture

That night we enjoyed a show in the theatre. A comedienne warmed the crowd up, and a group of young performers gave a sprightly show of Broadway standards and dance numbers. On the way back to our cabin, I was tipsy enough to hold his arm down the corridor. And he didn't object because no one was around.

Okay, this is getting out of hand. I may need to be sent to swoon rehab.

Back in the cabin, I took the first shower, and he went after. When he came out, he had on a pair of well-worn striped boxers, apparently his version of pj's. And when he crawled into bed, I realized this was going to be torture. If I brushed up against him, would he think I was making a pass? If I got hard being so near him, would he get upset? If *he* got hard in the middle of the night—which most men do three times a night while sleeping, the statistics say—how would I feel about feeling what I might feel?

Now I knew what is meant by exquisite torture. It was exquisite to share a bed with him but torture to not be able to do anything. Oh, how I wanted to touch. But I should not, could not, would not violate his trust. It would destroy his trust in me if I touched him inappropriately when he didn't want that. Looking was fine. Hugging was fine. But trying to kiss him or feel him or grope him, that was not fine. I would have to be in control to keep his trust.

Ty faced me, and we had a bedroom tête-à-tête.

Seriously, one step closer to swoon rehab.

"You're an amazing man, Ty. A straight guy who goes on a gay cruise for his gay friend. This is the best birthday present I've ever gotten."

217

"Anything for you, buddy. And really, it doesn't scare me to be around all these gay guys. They are what they are, I am what I am. Doesn't change a thing."

"Did you like being in the fashion show?"

"That was real fun. You think they all noticed the country cowboy?"

"Especially where he hung his hat."

"Is this where someone makes a joke about well-hung?"

I had something on my mind. Well, other than *that*. "You know that Hayden man we met at lunch? He's bad news. And I think he'll try to smarm his way into being around you tomorrow. Will you avoid him, please?"

"Is Martin jealous?" he teased.

"He's a snake. He thinks he could offer you money to have sex with him."

Ty was silent.

Uh-oh. Is he offended?

Then Ty said, "How much?"

"What?!"

He laughed uproariously. "The look on your face could crack a diamond. Gotcha there, buddy!"

"You are terrible."

He was gleefully enjoying his joke.

"So will you please avoid him?"

"No problem. Didn't like him much anyway."

We talked about the events of the day and about a few of the people we had met. Pretty soon, he started dozing and fell asleep.

Exquisite Torture

Me? No chance I would fall asleep. I was hyper-cognizant of his body so close to me. I felt his warmth. I smelled his manly scent. I heard his regular breathing. I looked at his beautiful face in repose. It took all my self-control to not lean over and kiss and taste his skin. Maybe I could just stare at him all night. But that would drive me crazier and make it worse.

So I turned over to face away from him, hoping I could get him off my mind and fall asleep.

He was very warm, like I think most athletes are.

Mmmm. Heavenly.

I had to stay still because I was completely aware *that* was near my leg. He was taller than me, so it wasn't right by my ass. But it was plenty close. This kind of excitement could give a person apoplexy.

All that body heat and the events of the day finally lulled me into sleep. Even though it was exquisite torture, I could get used to this.

We arrived in Cabo San Lucas and went ashore to see the sights. We strolled through the picturesque old town, laughing at the little kids playing barefoot in the streets. We enjoyed authentic Mexican food and spent time at the beach where we had fun jet skiing, and Ty even tried parasailing.

That evening was the White Party theme night. For Ty, I had rented a beautiful white cowboy outfit with silver embroidery, and the white cowboy hat and belt had silver stars. Wow, did he look good. I had a sharp-looking white blazer outfit, and I matched Ty in that I had a belt with an elegant silver star too. Let nobody doubt who was with who!

As usual, he had a lot of attention, but tonight I felt slightly more relaxed about that. Maybe because I knew I had him all to myself in the cabin.

That relaxation ended, however, when we went to the lounge. Green leather upholstered furniture, wood paneling, faux antique lamps with soft lighting, and round tables with wooden chairs gave a warm ambience. It was comfortable in an understated way. I had gone to the bar to get us a drink, and when I came back Ty was starting a poker game with several men. Including Hayden, who looked at me triumphantly and spitefully.

I was fit to be tied. I whispered in Ty's ear, "What about avoiding him?"

"Don't you worry 'bout that. He's gonna get his comeuppance in Texas Five Card Hold'em." I remembered Ty had sung a karaoke version of "The Gambler." Maybe he had some skills I didn't know about.

Paul and Dottie, dressed in matching white sailor outfits, also came by. They lingered to watch. Dottie caught Ty's eye, and I saw him give her a smile.

I sat sullenly nearby, mad at Ty for being around Hayden, infuriated with Hayden for being a threat. Then in a petulant huff —hissy fit is what Ty would call it—I stormed off to the pool area and watched some water acrobats giving a splendid exhibition. Which I didn't actually enjoy because I was in such a state.

After an hour of sulking, I went back to the lounge. Ty, Hayden and the other poker players were gone. Where could Ty be? I looked around that part of the deck and couldn't find him, so I gave up and went back to the cabin.

Where I found his cowboy hat on the doorknob in the universal signal of the roommate being occupied with bedroom matters.

If I was fit to be tied before, now I was *enraged!*

Had that snake Hayden gotten him completely drunk and tricked him into a fling in the cabin? Had he offered him such a huge sum of money that Ty gave in? The mere thought of another man having what I couldn't have sent me raging up and down the corridor, twisting the hat, and inwardly cursing.

Should I go in and throw that asshole out?

What if, despite my warnings, there was a female crew member who was breaking the rules with him? He might think he could get away with it, not realizing cameras kept watch on the corridors. The security officers were no doubt this moment watching me pace and thinking I was yet another gay man whose boyfriend was cheating on him.

I had just about made up my mind to interrupt when I heard the door open. I waited to see who came out.

Paul and Dottie.

They hurriedly left, not even looking my way. I went in, and Ty was out on our little balcony looking at the ocean.

"Hey buddy," he said as if an emotional earthquake had not just roiled my life.

I threw the cowboy hat at him, and he looked surprised. I glared. "What were they doing here?"

"Paul and Dottie? They stopped by for a chat."

"Why was the cowboy hat on the doorknob?"

"It was? Oh, I get it. She was playin' with it and tryin' it on, and she musta put it on the doorknob after that. I think she thought they were gonna get lucky."

"They?"

"They wanted a threesome. They come on these cruises to find a man who Paul likes and who she can enjoy too. I told 'em no thanks, three's a crowd." He looked at me. "You were gettin' upset out there?"

"I thought that awful Hayden had talked you into something."

"Oh, I made some money off him."

"What?!"

Ty laughed and said, "You were thinkin' he was in here payin' to get at the goods? Well, buddy, that's never gonna happen. He got his comeuppance, I told ya. I won twenty-four hundred dollars off him in the poker game." Ty flashed the cash at me. "Look, Martin. If I was gonna get paid for foolin' around with a guy, the richest man on earth couldn't afford it." He came over and put his hands on my shoulders. "Sorry you got all upset. We okay?"

"I was stupid. I'm sorry." I sat on the bed feeling embarrassed.

"You got jealous. You're not the only man who's ever let his dick do his thinkin' for him. I've been in trouble way too many times for lettin' the wrong head make decisions. Gotta admit I'm surprised it was in-control-Martin this time and not me. Wooee, that's a first." He sat by me, put his arm around me, and pulled me closer. "You're human, buddy. I admit I got a little jealous when some good-lookin' men were around at the dog tag thing. I don't like the idea of you goin' off with just any guy. So I guess it's natural you should get jealous when some man comes on too strong to me." He stood up. "We good?"

"We're good."

Then his thoughts went to his other favorite subject besides sex. "Can we order room service? Let's use up some'a this money I won." And we pigged out on gourmet hamburgers and french fries and milkshakes.

In bed that night, after he fell asleep, I was torn. Amy and Kyle and the guys worried that I was getting too emotionally invested in Ty. After tonight's upheaval, I had to admit they could be right. On the other hand, my emotional investment was fulfilling me with the closest friendship I'd ever had.

He was a prize I would never give up.

On Sunday the ship embarked for the return to LA. Ty played horseshoes with a group of admiring men and scored a bunch of ringers. As he said, "A cowboy oughta win at horseshoes, don'tcha think?" We enjoyed sunning on the Dick Deck. We met a lot of great guys and happily did not catch sight of Hayden, Paul, or Dottie. In the evening we loved the dance show, with Ty whistling for the stunningly beautiful female dancers.

That night in bed...our last night together like that. I wondered if I could convince him to do another cruise. But if it was a straight cruise, he'd want separate cabins so he could enjoy his women. Maybe we could do another kind of trip somewhere. But it was the same problem, because he'd want to meet women and bring them back to his own hotel room. This gay cruise, despite some blips, turned out to have some pretty marvelous benefits for me. And it might be my only chance for a long time to be like this. I should appreciate it.

Ty had done this *for me.* A thought occurred as we were in bed and having good-night talk.

"Ty? You knew it all along, didn't you? You knew this was a gay cruise when you booked it. It wasn't an accident."

"Ya caught me, buddy. Yep, I told the travel lady I wanted you to have a great experience."

"I think you had more fun than anybody."

"Sure did have fun. Let's do it again next year."

No argument whatsoever.

When he fell asleep, ever so softly and quietly, I turned to face him.

I wouldn't offend him or make him angry by touching his dick or being inappropriate in a way he didn't want. I would be in-control-Martin out of respect for him.

But I could damn well take advantage of being so close to him.

I lay awake for a long time, savoring his handsome face, wallowing in our proximity. I finally fell asleep, my head near his shoulder. Did I even once entertain the notion of moving farther away when I felt a certain something brush against my leg?

You know the answer to that.

After all...

I'm human.

Only The Best For Martin

Bodybuilding Fitness Contest!

The gym was sponsoring it, and Deck had decided to enter. The bros, Ty, Amy, and I arrived at the venue, which was crowded with spectators. I think the place was a boxing gym they'd rented for the occasion and set up for a show. An unglamorous raised stage featured a backdrop with a bodybuilder and a trophy in silhouette. Those who arrived early grabbed the folding chairs near the front; everyone else stood at the sides or in the back.

Melissa had come with a group of her friends. She spotted us and came over to say hi. She looked delectable, wearing a lovely sundress and giving us her sweet smile.

"Nice dress," said Amy.

"Thank you all for coming. It means a lot to Deck that you're here to support him."

"Wouldn't miss it," said Ty.

"It's you who got him interested in this, Martin."

"Me?"

"You told Deck one time that he could be a fitness model. And for some reason, he always says that whatever Martin tells you to do, you should. That got him thinking, and he put all his effort toward it. You'll be impressed when you see him in his posing trunks." She returned to her friends.

Ty sniffed. "Can you guys smell that? I think the contestants used every bottle of coconut oil they could find. I'm gaggin'."

The aficionados in the crowd were intent and shouted their approval as the competition began. I have to say there were some mighty fine specimens among the contestants, some in Speedos and some in the briefest of posing thongs. Amy and I were appreciative, to say the least.

Ty looked bored. I asked him, "Not enjoying this?"

"It's a sausage fest. I prefer sushi."

In the next section of the program, it was female bodybuilders, and he perked up. "God damn. They got more muscles than I do."

Amy commented, "Look how stylish the women's bikinis and high heels are."

Ty asked, "Could you see yourself wearin' somethin' like that?"

"I wouldn't dare to wear that in front of you. It would enflame your senses."

"Or put the fire out," he countered.

"What about a posing thong? Can you picture yourself in that?"

"You gotta be kiddin'! That looks so—" He stopped.

"So gay?" I finished.

"Well, yeah."

"I could say this whole bodybuilding thing feels homoerotic to me."

"I'm not goin' there. Those posin' thongs are ridiculous, your butt cheeks are hangin' out. My junk would be too much for one of those things anyway."

"If you were to add a lot of padding," said Amy.

"Which, by the way," I added, "some of them have."

"I wouldn't need one anyway. I'd use my cowboy hat to cover up the goods."

"What?"

"Cuz I happen to have a nice hook to hang it on."

While Amy huffed, Ty winked to remind me of the cruise fashion show.

When Deck appeared, we screamed and hollered and carried on, Ty using his fingers to whistle loudly. Deck was bronzed and confident, and for a man with a massive frame, appeared rather graceful as he made his poses. And did he look sensational in his posing trunks. Amy and I turned to each other and said, "Wow!" Even Ty appeared to be impressed.

At the end, Deck won an award for Best Debut. In the bodybuilding world, that was quite good.

Afterward the contestants, seemingly unconcerned with how little they were wearing, greeted their friends in the crowd. Kyle and Jackson had disappeared briefly and returned with a hot bodybuilder in tow. Oh ho. The plan to introduce me to someone was now in play.

"We wanted to introduce you. Martin, this is Francisco. He's from Spain but lives here in LA now."

This was one of the contestants who had worn the briefest of posing pouches, amply filled. I was mesmerized by his glorious chest. I noticed he had won a first place medal, conveniently hanging between his pecs, so I hurriedly said, pointing to the medal, "Congratulations on your win."

"You were watching me? Gracias. Did you notice these?" He had a lilting Spanish accent. He flexed his biceps and invited me and Amy to test them. Rock hard. Amy was not at all discreetly ogling him and enjoying it. Kyle and Jackson were looking expectant, and Ty—oh. Ty was not looking happy.

Francisco said, "Give me your phone, Mar-teen, for a selfie together." I handed him the phone, and he took the photo.

Ty turned to Amy and said in an annoyed tone, "Want me to take your picture with that dickhead? I gotta tell ya, though, droolin's not a good look for ya, babe."

She snapped out of her ogling stare.

Instead of giving the phone back, Francisco dialed a number. "There. I called my phone. Now I have your number, and you have mine. Give me a call."

Kyle said, "He will."

"Adios," said Francisco, and he went off to greet some other admirers.

"Well?" asked Jackson. "What do you think?"

"So blatantly obvious. Like that wasn't a setup or what."

Deck came up. Ty, pointing toward Francisco, asked him, "You know that Spanish guy?"

"Francisco? Yeah, he works really hard at the gym. Maybe a little arrogant."

"He's gay?"

"As that famous three-peso bill."

"He's too full of himself." Turning to me, he said, "I don't think you should call him. He's not good enough for you. I don't like that guy."

Kyle looked at me knowingly. He leaned in and whispered, like a ringside announcer, "And he pushes him away!"

We lavished praise on Deck. He proudly told us, "A fitness photographer took my number. He wants to use me in his next shoot." He smiled at me in thanks.

A few days later, Ty asked, "Did that guy ever call you?"

"Which guy?"

"That Spanish guy with too many muscles and a love affair with his mirror."

"Francisco? We talked a couple of times."

Ty raised his eyebrows.

"Nothing went on."

He hmphed skeptically.

Ty was not the only curious one. Kyle and Jackson pestered me daily to see what was happening. I assured them they had done a fine job of playing matchmaker and said we'd let things take their course.

Ty had gone to youth club basketball on Tuesday evening as usual, and Francisco dropped by for a visit. We were friendly with each other, let's say. Nothing serious. Francisco wanted to be a Spanish conquistador, but this Montezuma's halls remained unconquered. He pretended my house was too hot and took off his shirt. All so that he could proudly show off his muscles, inviting me to touch. Miss Vanessa's braille system back in action. I did find out that biceps are not the only rock-hard thing Francisco had to show off. *My hand slipped, I swear!*

We were having a drink, shirt and propriety restored, when Ty returned home and came over, knocking on the open back door before he stepped in.

"Buddy, whatcha doin'? Oh." He spotted Francisco and instantly lost his smile.

"Hi, Ty. Do you remember Francisco?"

"Hola," said Francisco charmingly.

"Hello," said Ty not charmingly.

"Francisco came over for a drink. Would you like to join us?"

"No sir. I just came over to say good-night." He couldn't get out of there fast enough.

The next morning, Ty was having coffee on the deck before he went to work, and I went out to say hi.

He looked at me unsmilingly. "Well? Is this the walk of shame?"

I smiled at him, thinking he was joking. "I believe the map shows the walk of shame leading directly from your front door down both sides of the street."

"Maybe so. I got nothin' to hide." He waited and then pressed me. "Well? Did he stay and flex all night for you? While lookin' in the mirror?"

Ty was jealous! "Actually, he left fifteen minutes after you."

"Oh." He turned back to his coffee. "Good."

"What is this? You can have every woman in town come through your revolving door, but I need a permission slip from you to see a guy?"

"No, 'course not. If you meet a guy who's actually good for ya, I don't have a problem with that, I won't say nothin'. You got your needs like I got mine. But that one's *not* good enough for ya. I don't like that guy."

I put my hand on his shoulder. "Yes, Dad."

He hmphed, but he put his hand on top of mine.

Later, Jackson informed me, "Ty told us to stop pushing Francisco toward you. He really doesn't like that guy. Kyle told Ty to let you choose who you want and to stop interfering, but Ty was having none of it. He told us if we were playing matchmaker to do a better job. He said only the best for Martin."

Protective and slightly possessive Ty. As ever, the problem was that "only the best for Martin"...was Ty!

StraightForward

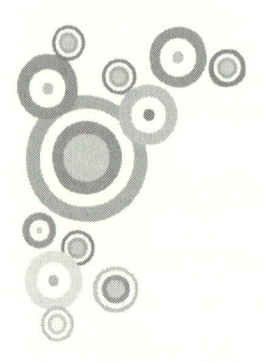

Go Big Or Go Home

Deck called me to express his appreciation for having suggested he could be a fitness model. I had casually tossed out the remark at our pool party, but I had meant it. He said the photographer had done a first shoot with him and was already selling images. He told Deck he would do well and to expect to make some money.

"You worked extremely hard in the gym to bring your body to this point, Deck. Super dedication!"

"Your ideas are brilliant, Martin. You know, Melissa still talks about our big romantic date to Sky High."

"But it was you who did all the work—until the dawn's early light, I seem to remember," I teased. "What are you and Melissa up to today?"

"We're going to her friend's gender reveal party."

"Watch out—a woman goes to that kind of party, and she'll want a baby of her own."

"That's sort of why I called you."

"You want me to help her make a baby?"

He laughed. "I think I have that part handled, thanks. I need your help with an idea because I want to take the next step that could lead to that."

"Oh?"

"I bought a ring, Martin. I'm going to propose."

I gasped. "Deck, that's fabulous!"

"I pay attention to everything you say. You said something at First Down that gave me an idea of how I should go about it. I need to do an over-the-top proposal. Go big or go home." He reminded me of what I had said and wondered if I could help him.

Oh, yes. I certainly can.

It was a Saturday afternoon. Deck, saying he had an errand, left the house where he and Melissa lived together. Melissa's sister was in on all the plans, and the next step of the plot commenced when she arrived to visit Melissa. She brought a pretty pink Cinderella-style dress for Melissa to look at, concocting some sort of story about suggesting it to a friend as a bridesmaid dress for an upcoming wedding. She asked Melissa to please model it for her to see if she liked it—all a ploy to make sure Melissa wasn't in bathrobe and curlers or something.

Deck's plan began. He first had a box of chocolates delivered to Melissa with a message: "Sweets to the sweet." It was signed "P.C." We later found out from Melissa's sister that she said, "This must be a mistake. I don't know anyone with the initials P.C."

Ten minutes later, a bouquet of flowers arrived with a message: "To the flower of my heart. P.C." Melissa wondered if somebody was stalking her.

Ten minutes later, a bottle of champagne was delivered. The message: "A toast to the perfect woman. P.C." Melissa told her sister, "This is making me nervous. Should I call the police?"

The second the door closed on the champagne delivery guy, family and friends surreptitiously crept from around the streetcorner to positions on the front lawn. Once everyone was in place, a brass quartet played a fanfare. Neighbors started coming out to see what was going on. Three kids on bicycles stopped in the street.

The quartet played the fanfare once again, and Melissa, in the lovely pink dress, peeked out the door with her sister behind her. Melissa came out, clearly bewildered by the presence of the group.

"What's going on?"

And once again, the fanfare.

We heard the clopping of hooves, and Deck, dressed in a princely costume, rode up on a white horse. Oh so romantic! Melissa brought her hands to her face, and a huge smile appeared. The onlookers bowed and curtsied. Even the three kids got into it.

Leaping from the horse, he dashed to the steps, and bowed, the fanfare ending right at that moment.

"My lady Melissa. I've searched the world for the perfect woman, and I've finally found her. Your Prince Charming begs your leave to ask..." Kneeling in the classic proposal pose, he pulled out a ring box and opened it. "Will you marry me?"

With a squeal of delight, Melissa shouted *"Yes!"*

While all of us cheered and whooped and applauded, neighbors included, Deck picked that sweet girl up as easily as if she was a feather pillow. Holding her tight in his strong arms, he dipped her till her head was nearly at the ground and gave her a glorious movie-star kiss.

Was that romantic! I noticed the kids had an "ewwww" look on their faces, but they liked the horse.

The bros formed an archway using prop swords crossed overhead, while the ladies tossed flower petals. Deck carried Melissa through the archway to the horse as the quartet played another fanfare and the happy couple rode off into the sunset together. Well, almost. They rode a block away to the horse trailer rented from the nearby equestrian school. The kids raced after them on their bikes, and as the newlyweds walked back to the house hand in hand, the kids were circling around them like cartoon lovebirds. We broke out the champagne, brought by Kyle in his SUV, and celebrated.

In our conversation at First Down, I had said, *"She wants romance. Like in her romance novels and Hallmark movies. She wants to be the princess swept off her feet by Prince Charming. If you rode up on a white horse, she would swoon."* I helped with the logistics, such as hiring the quartet, finding the equestrian school nearby, and arranging with Amy for the costumes and prop swords. Deck had actually come up with the nitty-gritty details of what he would say and do. He had learned to be a romantic guy, all for the woman he loved. I knew I had a hand in helping him learn to express those feelings, helping him go big or go home. The big-muscled man certainly went big!

And Hallmark? You can just go home.

StraightForward

Advice To The Lovelorn (Guest Appearance By Dear Abby Martin)

I asked Ty, "Would you be all right having dinner elsewhere tonight? Jackson called, and he seems anxious to see me about something. I thought maybe he could have dinner with me."

"No problem, buddy. I can go to the diner."

"The greasy spoon diner?"

"Yessir. I'm cravin' one'a those roast beef sandwiches they put open on a plate and drown it in gravy."

"That should earn the diner a Michelin star."

"I guess. Whatever that is. So why does Jackson need to see you?"

"I'm not sure. He sounded nervous."

"I think maybe he wants to talk to you about playin' on the other team."

"Another touch football team?"

"Martin. The *other team*. I got eyes. He's been spendin' a heckuva lotta time at Locker Room. Kyle and Deck noticed too."

"And if he has a reason to be there other than the music and dancing?"

Advice To The Lovelorn (Guest Appearance By Dear Abby Martin)

"If he wants to start likin' guys, that's fine by me. He can fly right at it. You already know how I feel 'bout that."

"I don't know if that's the case with Jackson."

"Think you're about to find out tonight. Think he's gonna need ya to hold his hand and help him, buddy."

"Oh. Will you guys stay quiet and let him figure it out?"

" 'Course we will. If the subject comes up, you tell him we got his back. Just like I always got yours."

Is it any wonder why I feel the way I do about this man?

For dinner, we started with wine and an elegantly presented bruschetta platter. Then, along with Caesar salad—homemade dressing, of course—we had Fettucine Martin, my own version of the pasta with a rich white sauce including chicken, buttermilk, sour cream, garlic, parmesan, and a host of secret ingredients. Colonel Sanders' eleven herbs and spices are like a dash of salt compared to my concoction. Jackson managed to inhale three large portions, rivaling Ty in his eating capacity. Gotta fuel all those muscles. For dessert we had gelato—yes, homemade—and cappuccino.

During the meal I bided my time, waiting for him to reveal why he needed to see me. Jackson showed me the photos of all his latest women: Susie, Carmen, Jasmina, Elle, Ebony, Samantha...*Gosh, he nearly rivals Ty in the bedroom as well as at the dining table.* With this litany of women, I was seriously doubting Ty's assumption.

"You appear to be dating half the female population of California."

"Oh, that's only this month." He scrolled to another photo. "Here's another one I just met."

"Yet another one? Jackson meeting another woman is like adding grains of sand to the beach."

"Ha ha, you must think I add by the truckload. Here's another one, she's really great. She's Colleen from Thousand Oaks, and she works in a pharmacy. I like her a lot."

Uh-oh. When I saw her photo, I knew she was the nice woman I talked to on the deck after she had spent the night with Ty. She was the one who hoped Ty wouldn't break my heart. Was Colleen destined to go out with all my hot straight friends?

"Did you meet her at the pharmacy?"

Slightly embarrassed, he answered, "No, I met her in the produce section at Ralphs. She helped me choose which melons to buy."

I burst into laughter. "Miss Jenn totally has you pegged! Well, if it works, why not?" I wasn't about to reveal Colleen's history. Let the past remain there.

He excused himself to use the bathroom while I started clearing things from dinner. When he returned, he came up behind me at the dishwasher and put his hand on my shoulder to get my attention.

"Martin, answer me honestly. Do you think I'm gay?"

Startled at his abrupt question, I nearly dropped the plate I was holding. It took me a moment to respond. "Do I think you're gay? No."

"What makes you so sure?"

"Other than the three thousand, seven hundred and seventy-three photos I just looked at? There's nothing to make me think that."

Advice To The Lovelorn (Guest Appearance By Dear Abby Martin)

"It was only three thousand, seven hundred and seventy-two." He was maintaining his sense of humor. Good. "Not even bi?" he asked.

"Not even that either. But it doesn't matter what I think. What do you think?"

"I have a problem, and I don't know what to do. You know I go dancing all the time at Locker Room."

"Which does not make you gay."

"Today one of the guys from there, Brad, called and asked me on a date."

This could be a crisis for Jackson. Think how hard it is for an actual gay man to admit it and come out; it's an utter consternation for a straight man if he is perceived as gay by other men. Yikes! But it does depend on how secure the man is. Ty and Kyle would laugh it off if anybody foolishly said such a thing about them. But Jackson?

"He didn't just say let's go for a drink?"

"No. He said, 'I want to take you on a hot date.'"

"How do you feel about that?"

"I don't know how to feel about that. I couldn't think what to say, and I didn't want to hurt his feelings."

"Always better to be kind."

"So I stalled and told him I was busy tonight. Martin, at Locker Room, men flirt with me a lot. Like, all the time."

"I can imagine."

"Am I sending out vibes I don't know I'm sending out? Do *they* think I'm gay?"

"Jackson, if you get hit on by a lot of gay men, it doesn't mean you're gay. It means you're attractive. Ty gets hit on all the time."

"But is there something about me that they see and I don't? Sometimes I guess I flirt back a little. Is that what makes them think I'm gay?"

"You're imagining too much. What actually is happening is they think you're a hot guy who's friendly and nice. They feel safe flirting with you. You won't punch them in the nose or something. It happens you're naturally flirtatious, and you flirt back. You're just being your usual self in a different environment. No big deal."

I had finished loading the dishes and went to sit at the table. I thought he might join me, but he leaned with both hands on the kitchen counter.

His real inner turmoil finally surfaced. "What if I've been... wondering..." he took a deep breath, "what it might be like to be with a man? What if I'm tempted to go on the date with Brad? Does *that* mean I might be gay?"

Feeling a bit like Dear Abby giving advice to the lovelorn, I spoke calmly and matter-of-factly to put him at ease. "Curiosity is normal, whether you're six years old wanting to play doctor with the neighbor girl. Or twenty-eight years old wanting to play doctor with the pharmacist."

He laughed and relaxed his posture. At least he was not freaking out.

I went on, "Gay men, like me, are curious what it's like to be with a woman. It certainly does not mean there's a hetero Martin lurking inside. It just means I'm curious. Straight men can be curious what it's like to be with another man."

Jackson was outwardly maintaining his sense of humor when he said, "I guess it would be like trying some new video game, getting used to a different joystick."

Advice To The Lovelorn (Guest Appearance By Dear Abby Martin)

But I could see he was inwardly still fretting. "Look, Jackson. To me it's obvious you're straight. Clearly the biggest pussy hound in the city likes women. So when you ask me if I think you're gay, I think not. But only you can really say what's going on inside your libido. Maybe being around so many flirtatious men at Locker Room leads you to speculate. Maybe you're becoming what's called bi-curious." I shook my head skeptically. "I don't know if I see it as more than that, if at all."

"What should I do? Should I go on the date? To see if I like it? What if it turns out I'm bi? What do I tell Kyle and our friends?"

"Jackson, first of all, you don't have to tell anybody one single thing. Only if you choose to. Second of all, you see how our friends treat me. They'll be more than cool. They'll have your back. Guaranteed."

"Even Kyle?"

"Especially Kyle." *No doubt about that.* "And third, there's no rush about dating. No race, no deadline, no pressure. Maybe later, if you remain curious, you could try dating a man."

He sat beside me at the table but was silent.

To make him feel better I said, "I know one thing about Brad and the other guys flirting with you at Locker Room. They clearly have sensational taste in men."

Jackson smiled gratefully. "Thanks."

"Tell me about this bold man Brad."

He showed me a photo. Brad bore a startlingly strong resemblance to Jackson, curly blond hair and all, though not quite as muscular. A person might well think they were brothers. I couldn't blame Jackson for potentially being attracted to someone as hot as, well, himself. But it seemed almost like incest!

"He's devastatingly handsome. Like you. In fact, too much like you. Wouldn't it be like dating yourself? A little narcissistic? On his part too."

"I never thought about that."

"A hot date with Brad could give a whole new meaning to the phrase 'go fuck yourself.'"

He laughed, and trying to get him to feel more settled, I said, "Look. I understand that you're flustered. You get hit on a lot, and now you're anxious that people think you're gay. Brad is just trying to see if he could get lucky. None of this means you're gay.

"Here's what you do. Tell Brad you can go to dinner. Tell him, nicely, it isn't a date. But you do want to be friends. Just say you aren't interested in dating men. You can make a little joke and say, 'Sorry, Brad, you don't have the right equipment for a hot date. I like women.' If the proper moment comes up, maybe he could tell you what it was like for him when he first wanted to explore."

"Okay. That sounds good."

"No matter what, I'm here whenever you need to talk."

"Thank you, Martin. I appreciate your advice. Thanks for the wonderful dinner too." He reached over and hugged me. Jeanne Phillips, who took over from her mother as Dear Abby, gets money, recognition, and admiration for her column, but I got a hug from Jackson. Worth it!

Ty brought home an accomplice for nighttime shenanigans, so I didn't talk to him until the next morning. He asked how things went with Jackson.

Advice To The Lovelorn (Guest Appearance By Dear Abby Martin)

"Was I right? Is he gonna start likin' men now?"

"The other way around. A lot of men flirt with him at Locker Room, and he's feeling worried about that."

"Is that all? Lotsa gay men flirt with me, like on the cruise. I don't pay that no nevermind."

I smiled at his quaint expression.

"Anyway, I'm tellin' ya. Gay men flirtin' with me won't ever get me interested in other men's ugly dicks. Much as I tend to 'preciate the beauty of the goods I got."

I envisioned the gots he goods. The good he gots. The. Goods. He's. Got. *Whew! See what the mere thought does to me?*

Back on track. "Please just stay quiet, and let's allow Jackson to come to whatever realization when he's ready."

"Sure thing. Bet he liked dinner."

"Maybe as much as you liked your roast beef sandwich smothered in gravy."

"It was fine. And the spuds, green beans, sliced cukes in vinegar water, and cherry pie too. What'd you guys have?"

"Nothing nearly as appetizing as that."

"I know better. He got the tastiest meal and the wisest advice."

"I saved some Fettucine Martin for your lunch."

"Buddy, you're the best." And because some things are more important than others, he asked, "What are we havin' for dinner tonight?"

As for me, maybe in the future if Jeanne Phillips retires, you can send your lovelorn questions to: Dear Abby Martin!

Touché

For Amy's birthday, Ty did indeed get her good. Amy hosted the party at her place, and the bros were there plus Melissa. Natasha and the theatre group also attended.

The drag queens delighted the eye with their as-usual unusual outfits. Their common fashion theme tonight, bird prints, indicated a sale at the fabric store. Perhaps the most tasteful was Miss Vanessa, wearing a black silk dress decorated with exquisite hummingbirds in iridescent colors. Hot pink flamingos embellished Miss Jenn, and oversized toucans made Miss Doretha a riot of color. Miss Penelope, however, stole the show with cartoon-style pelicans featuring huge droopy pouches placed exactly where they needed to be for the most comic effect on her bosoms.

Anne and Josh showed up, having gotten a babysitter for Tommy. I could see the drag queens giving Josh the eye, but his uptight, military posture and the presence of Anne made them behave in a mildly proper way.

Not proper with Ty and the bros, though. They were all over them with their usual lascivious comments.

Miss Jenn: "Jackson, I can't make up my mind what I like better, your big blue eyes, your big white smile, your big sweet ass cheeks, or your big thick—"

Jackson: "Thank you, Miss Jenn."

Miss Penelope: "Kyle, if you feel the urge, I'd be happy to let you have your wicked way with me, throwing me up against the wall, undressing me first with your eyes and then with your hot hands, and then you can bend me over and—"

Kyle: "Thank you, Miss Penelope. Could you make me one of your Specials?"

Miss Vanessa: "I do declare, Declan—ooo, I like the way that rolls off my tongue, declare Declan—that your biceps are as big as my thighs."

Miss Jenn: "You ignorant slut, unlike your thighs, they aren't referred to as Thunder Biceps."

Miss Vanessa: "Slag! As I was saying, your beautiful sweet Melissa here is too petite and too skinny—bitch!—to enjoy you properly. You need a big girl to take care of that big, giant, mouthwatering—"

Melissa: "Thank you, Miss Vanessa."

Miss Doretha: "Cowboy, I thought about wearing a saddle tonight."

Ty: "A saddle?"

Miss Doretha: "So you could hop on and ride me till kingdom come. Or maybe the saddle should go on you! After all, you're hung like a—"

Ty and me: "*Thank* you, Miss Doretha."

Ty had told us to be ready because he had a special surprise for Amy. When I brought out the cake I had baked—a yummy poppyseed cake with cream cheese frosting, all from scratch need you ask—Ty disappeared. We sang "Happy Birthday" to Amy, and she blew out the candles while we clapped.

    Ty came back in carrying a small speaker connected to his phone. He started some loud music, and everyone turned toward the doorway. In walked a hunky man in a spectacular cowboy outfit. Ty had hired a stripper!

    The drag queens hooted and hollered while the bros were laughing hysterically. Even Josh was smiling. Amy was blushing furiously while Kyle made her sit in a chair in the middle of the room. Ty was gleeful. Amy had an "I can't believe this" smile as the spectacle progressed.

    The stripper was good. He went through his moves, and man was he sexy. He worked Amy, bumping his crotch in her face, shaking his butt, doing body rolls, taking off his clothes item by item. The drag queens whistled and yelled, "Take it off!"

    The cowboy got down to only his hat and a pair of chaps without jeans. In his final move, he whipped off the chaps to reveal a jockstrap with a waistband that said Giddy Up! We all applauded while Amy just kept smiling, shaking her head.

    The cowboy took a bow, using his hat to cover his crotch. He pointed at Ty and blew Amy a kiss. The drag queens all tried to grope him on the way out.

    Ty turned the music off and went to Amy.

    She said, "You fucker. I can't believe you did that. You are in so much trouble."

    He gloated and said, "You loved it. Martin, you loved it didn't you? Ladies, did you love it?"

Miss Vanessa said, "We sure did, sugar. Only thing better is if you had done it yourself."

Amy pointed her finger at Ty and said, "The shit has hit the fan. You are asking for it." Then changed to her middle finger.

"Bring it on, birthday gal."

When Ty grinned at me and winked, I said, "Touché!"

Nightmare

    Ty and I had a lovely dinner together. I made grilled salmon with lemon-butter sauce, potatoes au gratin, steamed broccoli, and a warm bacon salad. As always, he wanted seconds and thirds. We were on the deck by the pool, his usual beer in his hand, me with my Campari Orange. It felt so nice to be relaxing and chatting. The evening was pleasant, perfect.

    "It's way better weather here than in Oklahoma. Right now it's like hell there, so hot and humid, flies and mosquitoes and chiggers everywhere. Roadkill armadillos for decoration. But I do say it's got the sky and the sunsets. That's the best of Oklahoma. Beautiful."

    "Do you miss it?"

    "No sir, I like it here fine. It's harvest time there right now. Mama and my brothers are workin' night and day, it's their busiest time. Sometimes hardly any sleep. And this is a time when money is tight, waitin' for the harvest profit to come in. I offered to send money to Mama, but she said they got it covered, thank you anyway."

    "What a good guy you are."

"Yes sir. Thanks for a great dinner as usual, Martin. Time to hit the hay, busy day tomorrow. Night buddy, love ya."

Love ya right back.

The next day, I was still feeling the glow of the lovely night we had together. If I wistfully sighed one more time, I would turn into an ingenue in a Regency romance. So pleasant to daydream about.

Until the daydream became a terrifying nightmare.

I was busy that afternoon with my consultant projects when the telephone rang.

"Martin, this is Deputy Chief Williams. There's an emergency, we need you right away. We've had a serious incident. Ty's been hurt."

"Hurt?"

"He has a gunshot injury, and the hospital needs your consent on some procedures. You're Ty's emergency contact, and you're the person who has to make medical decisions when he's incapacitated."

"Incapacitated?" I was starting to panic.

"He's unconscious, son. He's fightin' for his life."

My world came crashing down.

"Laura is on her way and will be at your place in about ten minutes to bring you to Cedars-Sinai. We'll get you here fast."

I couldn't panic. Ty needed me. I rigidly brought myself under control. I had to think what to do. I rushed to be ready for Laura. I had the presence of mind to grab my phone charger—I would have to call Ty's mama as soon as I knew what was happening.

I called Amy to ask her to meet me at the hospital. She promised to call Kyle and the guys. I heard the siren and rushed to jump into Laura's police car. She screeched away from the curb, siren and lights going.

"Laura, what happened? Is Ty going to—" I couldn't say it.

She could see I was starting to panic and grabbed my hand. "Hold on, Martin. They're working on him. Deputy Chief Williams said all he knows so far is that they'll have to do surgery. They're life-flighting a specialist from the naval hospital in San Diego."

"He was shot?"

"Yes. Bad situation. We had an Amber Alert this morning that a young boy was snatched near a school by a man in a white van. LAPD was scrambling to look for it and got a tip that a woman had seen a van of that description being pulled into a garage. The owner of the property had been flagged by our team as a suspicious individual because he had previously been cited for loitering near a school playground. So our unit took the lead, with LAPD as backup.

"The guys and I rushed to the scene, but no sirens, because a SWAT team was on its way. We parked and hid behind our car, waiting for them to arrive when the garage door started opening. It looked like the perp was going to make a run for it in a second vehicle. So we had to take action.

"We ran to the garage as the perp was about to push the boy into the car. We had our guns out and told him to freeze, but he had a gun too, and he grabbed the boy around the neck, pointing the gun at his head.

Nightmare

"Ty said something like, 'You got nowhere to run. Let the boy go.' And the perp said, 'If I can't have him, nobody can have him.' Right then we heard the SWAT team sirens, and the man was distracted. The boy kicked him and got loose and started running away. The man pointed his gun, and just as he was shooting, Ty dove in front of the boy, taking the bullet."

"Oh, god."

"Ty saved that little boy's life. Steve shot the kidnapper, who died at the scene. We were wearing our bulletproof vests, but it was a freak thing. As he was diving, Ty had his arm raised, and the bullet went through his armpit. The SWAT team paramedic immediately started helping him. Ty was swearing and then he passed out, I think from blood loss, and they couldn't revive him. They rushed him to Cedars-Sinai, and they've been working on him. That's all I know, Martin. I hope to god he's all right. He saved that little boy by jumping in front of that bullet. He's a hero."

"People can survive gunshot wounds, right? He's gotta be all right."

"This one is apparently serious. That's all I know."

"He has to be all right!"

She looked at me with sympathy and compassion. "I know what you're feeling, Martin. We'll hope for the best."

We arrived at Cedars-Sinai emergency and rushed in. Steve, looking completely distraught, hurried toward us. Deputy Chief Williams, grim but contained, told me what he knew.

"Martin, we're waiting for Dr. Jordan. She said the specialist surgeon from San Diego will arrive at any moment. The hospital administrator said you'll have to sign some forms, I don't know what."

It was torture waiting for the doctor. We waited. We waited.

Laura told me, "We've been in these situations with other colleagues. It's best to try to remain calm so that you can be clearheaded and help Ty." Again that look of compassion. "I know, Martin. It's hard."

Amy came rushing in, looking upset. I leaped up and she hugged me, saying, "Oh, honey. Have faith, Martin, he'll make it. He's tough."

Kyle, Jackson, and Deck arrived straight from the gym, still in their workout gear. I explained everything that had happened so far to all of them.

We waited. We waited.

In a moment when I was less panicked, I decided that Ty's mama needed to get here, even if we didn't know for sure all the details of what was happening. I called her and started by introducing myself.

"Martin, I know exactly who you are. Ty has said so very many good things about you. I'm Emmaline."

I hesitated.

She asked, "Has something happened? It's about my sweet boy, isn't it?"

I dreaded giving her the bad news, but she accepted it with remarkable calm. I felt myself calming while talking to her. I had remembered Ty's conversation about the harvest and it being a difficult time with so much to get done and little money while waiting for the profit. I went into efficient Consultant Who

Nightmare

Finds the Solutions mode and took care of everything. I booked the redeye flight for Emmaline and reserved a hotel room close to the hospital. I called Cody to ask him to take Emmaline to the airport and help ease the way, as she had never flown before. He would tell the other guys and help in any way he could.

I spoke with Ty's team, and I found out the reason Steve was so distraught. He had never killed anyone. Plus, he felt guilty that he couldn't have done more to prevent Ty being shot. Laura assured him that it happened so fast, there was nothing anybody could have done. When Steve went to the restroom, she told me that it was standard practice that Steve would go on paid administrative leave while they investigated the incident. He would see a psychologist. She said that in the earlier part of her career, she had a partner who was injured on duty, and she had felt very guilty. She said the psychologist helped her a lot. "And when Ty comes out of this—and he will come out of this, Martin—he should see the psychologist too. It helps."

We waited. We waited.

At last Dr. Jordan came out, followed by a hospital administrator. Dr. Jordan, a slim Asian woman with jet-black hair in a severe bun, looked worried but adopted a calm bedside manner when she came up to me. I stood to speak with her.

"Martin? I'm Dr. Jordan, the lead physician. This is Miss Beecher. Let me update you. Do you want everyone to hear this?"

The others had gathered around us. I said, "Yes, absolutely."

"This is the situation. We've stabilized Ty as well as we can at the moment, and we've quickly but carefully evaluated what needs to be done. Ty has remained unconscious. We've taken him to the surgical suite and are prepping him now.

"The specialist surgeon, Commander Markworth, has an expertise in extreme trauma cases. He's reviewed the results of our tests and is scrubbing up at this moment. Two of our top neurologists on staff will assist. With me so far?"

"Yes. Neurologists—why?"

"I'll get to that. The bullet entered Ty at an unusual angle through his armpit. We think it may have struck the edge of the Kevlar vest which significantly diminished its force. It passed through muscle, nicked the liver, and collapsed a lung. These are problems, but the easier ones for us to deal with. We have intubated Ty for the procedure, and when we repair the lung, we expect it will reinflate and we can remove the ventilator. We can repair the torn muscles and liver, and we must do so because there is internal bleeding. With me?"

"Yes. There's a harder problem?"

"It's important that we remove the bullet as soon as we can. It can lead to infection, which leads to sepsis, which leads to septic shock, and that would be dire. The bullet has lodged near the spine. We aren't sure if it caused any damage to the spine, but it has certainly impacted a number of nerves. This is why the neurologists are necessary. We're worried that it may have affected his mobility. A good sign is that his arms and legs respond to stimuli. This shows the nerves are working. But where the nerves are located presents difficulties. One mistake could result in a partial paralysis."

I started shaking. Kyle put his arms around me from behind and said, "Easy, Martin." Amy held my hand.

"Martin, I will be honest. This is a difficult surgery and will take hours. As I said, some things are easier to repair, but the removal of the bullet and dealing with the attendant nerve damage is risky. Highly risky."

She gave me a kind but firm look. "Martin, we have every hope the surgery will go well. But I must tell you that he will still be unconscious, in a coma. We don't know for how long. We will repair what we can inside, but his body is in a fight to repair itself. I have to tell you that there is the grim possibility that he will not wake up from the coma."

My world was crashing down again. Kyle tightened his hold on me. "Easy. Easy."

"Because your name is on his medical consent form, Miss Beecher is here to get your signature that you consent to this highly risky surgery and that you understand the risk of paralysis."

I shakily said, "I understand."

"And in the case that he does not wake up from his coma, we must ask you what the wishes are. You can tell us to keep trying everything we can, or you can sign what is called a Do Not Resuscitate form, where we keep him comfortable but do not take extraordinary measures to keep him alive."

I looked at her and at Miss Beecher, who was holding a clipboard with the forms. Amy and Jackson were looking at me to see what I would say. Deputy Chief Williams had a neutral face.

I stood more firmly. "I consent to the surgery. As for...the other, he's young, he's strong, he will fight. Please keep trying to do everything that you possibly can."

Miss Beecher started marking places on the form for me to sign. Dr. Jordan said, "I concur. If we have to revisit this later, we can."

Amy and Jackson looked at the form with me to make sure it said what I wanted, and I signed it.

My friends decided they would take turns waiting with me, with Jackson up first. Kyle and Amy would go to my house to collect a change of clothes, make sure everything was secure, and bring me my laptop so that I could contact my clients to put my work on hold. Amy would contact Anne and Josh and Natasha. Kyle would call the youth club director, Coach Jones, and the touch football guys to let them know what was happening.

Deputy Chief Williams took Laura and Steve back to the unit "to deal with fallout" and for Steve to see the psychologist on an emergency basis.

Miss Beecher took us to the surgical suite waiting area. I called Emmaline. She was already at Oklahoma City airport with Cody. I updated them with the news, trying to make it a little more palatable so that she wouldn't endlessly worry on the flight. Again she accepted it with grace and calm.

She said, "I'm prayin' for my sweet boy. God will take care of us."

They were calling for boarding already, so I said I would see her when she arrived.

We waited. We waited.

Jackson constantly reassured me and even held my hand when I started to panic again.

Nightmare

Amy arrived to take his place. I tried to briefly get my mind off my fear by quickly emailing my current clients to explain the situation.

I paced. Amy brought me coffee. I paced some more. Friends were calling and texting and Amy answered for me, saying, "Martin will get back to you. He's a little stressed right now." She begged me to please lay down on the seats to take a nap. She would instantly wake me if any news came. I tried, but the seats were too uncomfortable, and I couldn't sleep anyway. In my head I kept hearing, "one mistake...partial paralysis...the grim possibility he might not wake up from the coma..." over and over.

Ty! Fight! Survive! Don't leave me!

Kyle arrived to take Amy's place. She hugged me goodbye and said, "Try to keep up your spirits, Martin. You're right. Ty is young and strong. He'll fight."

The surgery had been in progress for several hours. Surely they would be finished soon. I was getting more tense by the minute waiting for Dr. Jordan to reappear.

As it was so late, we were the only ones left in the waiting area. All other surgeries had been completed, and those who had been waiting had spoken to the doctors and left.

Kyle was across from me and looking at me intently. "Martin, doing okay?" He took a deep breath. "Amy and I talked, and she asked me to speak with you because she was afraid she'd cry. Martin, we want to say we hope the surgery will be successful. But are you prepared if—"

"I can't think about that. I can't."

"We're here for you. You never have to go through this alone. We're here."

"I can't lose him, Kyle. I just can't. I'm not ready for that."

"No one is ever ready."

"I don't know what I'll do…if…" I flung myself out of my chair and leaned against the wall, standing and crying.

Kyle followed and turned me around and hugged me close. He said, "Cry it all out, Martin. Let it all out. He loves you too."

I finally stopped crying and stood there holding onto him. I smiled tentatively. I felt better for having let my bottled-up emotions out. I was still very scared, but I knew had to face it.

Just as we started back to the seats, Dr. Jordan came in, followed by a tall, stocky man with a military buzzcut and a forceful mien. I clutched Kyle's arm. She said, "Martin, this is Commander Markworth who led the surgery."

"Hello, Martin and—?"

"Kyle."

I was holding my breath, steeling myself.

"First, we feel the surgery has gone well." I let out a huge sigh of relief. "It was difficult, I'll admit, but the neurosurgeons here are top of the line. Ty is being moved to the ICU, where he will remain until we feel he can go to a regular room. Right now, one of the neurosurgeons is with him and observing him."

"What happens now?"

"Without getting too technical, we were able to repair the internal bleeding, torn muscles, and lung. It's beginning to reinflate, so we think the ventilator can soon be removed. His breathing is good, blood pressure and heart rate are good. The fact that he is so fit helped. The bullet was within millimeters of the spine, and we removed it—that was tricky, I can say—and it appears the spine is undamaged."

Dr. Jordan said, "He says tricky, but I can tell you that it was a seriously difficult operation. Commander Markworth did a brilliant job."

"What about the effects of the nerve damage and the coma?"

"His arm and both legs appear stiff but respond to reflex stimulation," Dr. Jordan said. "This is good. He will require physical therapy in the future. But that's some time off."

Commander Markworth continued, "He'll still be in coma for some time. From my trauma experience in the past, I would say it will be at least a few days before he comes out of it. His body has experienced a huge trauma, and to fight the pain and to repair itself, it will put itself in the best situation to achieve that."

"But he will wake up?"

The doctors looked at each other, and Dr. Jordan answered. "It's hard for doctors to make an ironclad promise in such situations. I will say that it is my feeling he will, partly because he's young and strong as you said. But now only time will tell."

"I concur," said Commander Markworth. "No promises, but I have every hope. By the way, Dr. Jordan told me the circumstances. That young man is a hero."

The nurse came out to take us to the ICU waiting area. Though many of our friends were asleep by now, we texted everyone with an update.

Deck and Melissa arrived near three a.m. to take over for Kyle. At that point, Ty had been in the hospital just over twelve hours. Deck had kindly offered to take the late shift. He and Melissa brought food and were as sweet as always. They were with me when a tired Dr. Jordan came out to say that the ventilator would be removed.

Laura brought Emmaline straight from the airport. I had texted Laura what was happening so she could reassure Ty's mother on the way. When Emmaline arrived, she gave me a hug and took my face in her hands.

"Hello, Martin, you dear man." She looked closely at me. "Oh, I can see you're worried and fearful. Please be calm. Right now my boy is struggling. But all will be well. I'm a woman of faith, and I can tell you God will answer our prayers."

She had gray hairs mixed in her blonde strands. Her features were strong, resolute. She had some lines and wrinkles, and kind eyes and smile. Her skin was tanned from farm work, and her hands were rough. I looked closely. I could see Ty in her features. I thought her a strong woman, a bit like a pioneer woman who could stare the elements in the face and deal with whatever happened, come what may. Salt of the earth. A Mother Earth. She projected such an even-tempered demeanor, I felt calmer just being with her.

She met Dr. Jordan and Commander Markworth, and they told us Ty's vital signs were excellent. The neurosurgeons reported that it seemed his extremities could move, but stiffly. His level of movement and the requirements for physical therapy would have to wait until he awakened. They were sure at least one arm and one leg would require therapy. The commander

Nightmare

would return to San Diego now, as the surgery had been his job. Now the recovery phase would be led by Dr. Jordan.

My main fear was about Ty coming out of the coma. The physical therapy part did not worry me, as he was so athletic and I thought he would do well. But the coma—*I'm scared.*

They would observe him, and if his vital signs remained good, they would move him out of the ICU and into his own room.

Emmaline said, "Thank you, doctors, for taking care of my boy. Now we will leave it in God's hands."

I asked Laura if she would take Emmaline to the hotel to get her checked in and settled and then bring her back. We were in a waiting game.

Some hours later, in the evening, Dr. Jordan decided to move Ty to his own private room, and finally we got to see him. I hated seeing him hooked up to a monitor, and with an oxygen line, IV, and catheter. His chest and shoulder were swathed in bandages. He looked like he was sleeping peacefully, however.

Dr. Jordan regarded me and, without needing to ask, had the hospital set up a cot for me in the room. I would be sleeping there.

Emmaline had to be tired from the redeye flight and the stress. I encouraged her to go back to the hotel. She serenely agreed, saying, "I can leave Ty in God's hands and your hands."

Emmaline spent the next day sitting with her son. We talked, and I learned a lot about the life of the farm, her other sons. I told her about myself, my work. I sometimes got onto my laptop to answer emails.

There were times when we were quiet and the only ones there with him. I saw her clasping her hands with her eyes closed. She was praying.

She told me, "It helps me to pray, Martin. It helps to calm my fears and settle my soul. I have faith that God will hear our prayers. Try it, you'll feel better."

I persuaded Emmaline to go back to the hotel again when she was tired. It was quite near, she could come back quickly at any time. I would not be leaving.

For two days, Ty's condition remained much the same. Vital signs were good, but he did not wake up.

And then Ty had a setback.

In his coma over the past couple of days, he frequently twitched, and it did appear that the affected arm and both legs could move, albeit stiffly. But then he quieted and became morbidly still. The neurosurgeons came back. They said he still responded to stimuli, but they admitted to being worried as to how immobile he had become compared to his constant twitching activity before.

Emmaline went back to the hotel that night as I assured her I would be on watch. Jackson had offered to spend the wee hours of the morning with me, and he suggested I sleep on the cot while he stayed awake. I napped a little bit, but just couldn't sleep while I was so worried.

Jackson said, "Kyle's my best friend. But we don't have the closeness that you and Ty have. I wish we were closer. You and Ty are, like, inseparable."

I regarded him curiously. "Jackson. Do you think you ever had feelings for Kyle?"

"Oh, god no. That would be a useless thing to do. He's straight." He looked mortified. "I'm sorry, Martin, I shouldn't have said that. I know how it must be difficult for you."

I pretended to be bewildered, looking back and forth from Ty to Jackson. "What? You mean Ty...is straight?"

It felt good to laugh after all the tension. We were so tired we were silly, and just looking at each other set us to laughing again. It helped to let out the stress.

Finally Jackson said, "I love Kyle—as a friend—but he's too complicated."

"That he is."

And dangerous.

It was quiet in the hospital room, with the only sounds the beep of the monitor and ambient noise from the hallway. Emmaline and I were each sitting in the utilitarian chairs provided in the room, our thoughts to ourselves. She would be heading to the hotel soon, and I would be with Ty during the night.

Emmaline was calm and very much in control of her emotions. Outside I rigidly appeared composed, but inside I was still a blubbering mess.

She startled me when she spoke without looking at me. "Ty is my youngest, my baby. We spoiled him a bit. He was always a rascal, always gettin' into mischief, always comin' home with scrapes and bruises and cuts, always a ruckus. A spankin', bein' sent to his room without dinner, washin' his mouth out with soap.

None of that worked. If there was a way to get into trouble, he found it."

"He was a handful."

"And then some. Later when he was in high school, he was a decent student, very good athlete. But he still got into some serious shenanigans. More than once his coach and I had to talk the principal out of kickin' him out."

I didn't tell her I knew about the situation with the exchange student, Philippe.

She sighed. "He and his daddy didn't see eye to eye. Lord, they had some arguments. After his graduation, Ty didn't seem to have any ambition. He'd hellcat around, and his daddy and I didn't know how to get him to find a goal in life. It seemed like his only goal was to party and get into ruckuses and spend time with trashy women. His brothers tried to talk sense into him, but it just went on."

I was fascinated listening to this history of a Ty I hadn't known.

"One day, he had a serious incident. He was tipsy, and he drove his pickup into a telephone pole. Thank God no one got hurt. We had an old justice of the peace who could've—maybe should've—thrown the book at him. Instead he assigned Ty to a strict community service: he had to help the sheriff's office. And the sheriff was a former drill sergeant who wouldn't put up with any nonsense from Ty. And from that, Ty got an interest in law enforcement, and he applied to college. That crusty old justice of the peace knew what he was doin'."

She sighed again. "It still wasn't easy. He'd attend for a while, and then he'd stop. He'd play ball—he was always a good

Nightmare

athlete—but even that didn't keep him there all the time. He went to the Caribbean for six months, stayin' with a friend. He seemed to be in a kind of limbo. He and his daddy started arguin' again, and Ty rebelled. His daddy would say, 'What are you doin' with your life, son?' and Ty said, 'I'm livin' it, Daddy. The way I want to.'"

She clasped her hands. "I prayed all the time, hopin' he would find his way. And that he and his daddy could reconcile. Finally Ty seemed to make up his mind to move ahead. He went back to college and applied himself and finished his courses. He started workin' in law enforcement and seemed like he was showin' us he was gettin' ahead in life. He and his daddy started talkin' regular again; his daddy was a lot happier with Ty. All of us were in a happier situation.

"But then his daddy got sick. And one day he had a heart attack. That good man passed away two hours before Ty could get there. Ty was grief-stricken."

"Poor Ty. I think he was always seeking his daddy's approval, always wanting his daddy to be proud of him?"

She nodded at me. "You understand him real good, Martin. He got a little belligerent again, not as bad as before, but it made me and his brothers worry that he'd slip back into his bad habits. One day he got into a terrible fight at his office, a ridiculous fistfight in the corridor. He and some other officer fightin' over a woman there, the kinda woman who thrives on drama like that. They could've fired all of them. But they gave him a chance. Take a transfer or be fired. Ty took the job here in LA."

She regarded me with a calm, understanding look. "And that's when he met you. Ty talked to me about everything. I know you were a real good influence on him. You introduced him to nice people, your friends became his friends, you broadened his horizons, you made him do that youth club project, you found him a touch football team. From day one, you've been the finest of neighbors and the finest of friends."

I had tears welling in my eyes. She put her hand to my cheek. "You been real good to my boy. Good to him and good for him. And the family thanks you for it. We thank God you came into his life."

Emmaline took my hands. I couldn't look away from her calm eyes.

"Martin, everybody is a child of God, and everybody should be accepted for exactly what they are. I know, Martin. I *know* how you feel about my boy. You're pinin' for him, and he can't return that in the way you want. Someday he'll meet the right woman and settle down. But I want you to know somethin' from me. I want you to know that if my boy had...other inclinations..." She paused.

She looked lovingly at me.

"You would be the man I'd want him to marry. I'd be right proud of that."

I had been trying so hard these past days to maintain control. I lost it. I burst into tears, sobbing uncontrollably. She hugged me like she was my own mama, and she let me weep, saying, "It's all right, sweetheart." I cried out my loss at not having Ty in the way I wanted and cried out my fear that we would lose him. She kept patting me, saying, "It'll be all right."

Finally I calmed down, still sniffling. "Martin, I've been prayin', and I hope He answers my prayers and Ty comes back to us. But if God decides Ty has to go to heaven, we'll grieve. Then we'll pick ourselves up and move on. No matter what happens, I hope you will always love Ty and always be his best friend. And I sincerely hope that one day you'll find the right man who'll see you for the fine person you are and will love you in the way you need. I pray for that too."

After giving me a final hug and then wiping a tear from my face, she stood and said, "I'll go to the hotel now and pray and sleep a bit. I'll be back later."

I thought about all his mama had to say. She was that proverbial pillar of strength, calm and focused. It was her own child fighting to survive, yet she had taken time to show care and worry for my well-being. As the Bible would say, a woman to be admired and praised.

The nurse had come in to check on her patient. Ty was breathing strongly. The monitor beeped in steady reassurance.

It was well after midnight. I closed the door behind the nurse as she left. This was the first time I'd actually been alone with Ty, as there had always been others there—Emmaline, the friends, Steve and Laura, the deputy chief. I had asked the friends not to be with me tonight; they had done enough.

Now I was alone with Ty.

I went to the end of the bed and looked longingly at the man I loved.

I understood a lot more after what Emmaline had told me. Why he got started in law enforcement and the job incident that brought him to LA, why he constantly sought my approval, almost as a replacement for what he missed from his father.

I thought of how much we had done for each other. How much we meant to each other. How in his own way he cared for me. How in his own way he loved me.

I spoke.

"God, are You there?"

Am I crazy, talking out loud?

"God, are You listening? You and I don't know each other very well, but Emmaline says You'll listen. I don't know much about praying; can we just talk?

"Can I ask You something? Could You please give Ty back to us? Let him come back. Please! He has so much to live for. Think of all his family and friends who need him. Think of all the kids he can help in the future—that's really the most important. He has so much he has yet to do."

I spoke more softly. "And I don't mean to be selfish. Lots of people need Ty. But please bring him back. For me."

Now I was whispering. "I don't have to tell You why, do I? You already know, don't You?"

I didn't know what else to say.

"I guess when you finish praying, you're supposed to say Amen. But I'll just say Aman. A Man. *This* man. Please give *this* man back to us. Thanks for listening."

Strangely, I felt a little better. Maybe Emmaline had the right idea.

I moved closer. I reached over and brushed a strand of his blond hair away from his face then bent over and kissed him on the forehead. I looked at his eyes, trying to will them to open. I put my hand to his cheek. It was soft and had a bit of stubble. I wanted to kiss his lips, but I just couldn't take advantage in that way.

I sat and took his hand into both of mine. I caressed it, feeling the rough calluses, the little hairs near his wrist. I turned his hand over and kissed his palm.

Could he hear me? Would he hear me and understand deep down inside?

"Ty. Come back to us. Please wake up for us. Please don't go. *Please don't go.* We need you. *I* need you. Come back to us." I held his hand to my cheek. "You are the best man I know. Please don't go, I need you, Ty. I need you."

The tears began, my feelings overwhelming me. I held his hand tight against my face. I kept repeating "I need you" over and over.

I finally subsided. I tenderly gave his cheek a good-night kiss and remained sitting by his side, holding his hand.

I had fallen asleep sitting by the bed. When I woke up, the first glimmers of sun were shining. My head was resting on my crossed arms, near Ty's hand.

I tenderly took his hand once again.

And then I felt his hand give mine a squeeze.

I looked up, hope flaring.

His eyes were open.

He was looking at me.

"Goddammit! Feels like a bull kicked me. There any water, buddy?"

I leaped up, joy flooding through me. "Oh, thank god! Thank god you came back!" I rang the buzzer for the nurse and got him some water.

He said, "I'm tired. Damn, it hurts!"

When the nurse came in, I said "He's awake!" And a scurry of doctors and nurses took over. There were several tests and doctorly discussions. I held his hand every moment I could.

Though it was early in the morning, I called everyone to tell them the news. Emmaline came hurrying in and rushed to kiss Ty, saying, "My sweet boy." Only for Emmaline would I let go of Ty's hand.

Dr. Jordan started to explain to Ty the medical details of what had happened. He was tired and not grasping everything, and he fell asleep. Later the deputy chief would fill him in on the police details, and I would fill him in on everything else.

Dr. Jordan spoke to me and Emmaline. She said, "This is a significant step forward. We must be watchful for any signs of infection or sepsis. I think I can say from our tests today that his prognosis is excellent. It will be a long road to complete recovery, but every sign is good."

Emmaline and I were thrilled.

Dr. Jordan continued, "We'll keep him here for at least a week. There will be more tests, but as I say, the signs are good. He will need constant care at home for a long period of time after that."

Emmaline asked, "Should I bring him home to Oklahoma?"

Dr. Jordan said, "No, that would not be advised. We'll need him here for regular visits and to keep a close eye on him."

I spoke up. "He'll stay with me. I will take excellent care of Ty."

Dr. Jordan had seen my devotion. She looked satisfied and said, "That would be an ideal solution."

Emmaline put her hands to my face and said, "How can we ever thank you, dear Martin?"

When Dr. Jordan left, Emmaline said, "I know all will be well. Martin, I can go home now. Could I kindly ask you to get me a ticket for tomorrow? I'll stay with Ty today and see him again tomorrow before I leave, if you can arrange that? My other boys need me back at the farm. It's our busy time."

"Yes, I'll take care of the ticket and arrangements right now."

She looked at me for a moment. And then, almost like she knew I'd had my midnight conversation, she said, "God heard our prayers, Martin."

Amy persuaded me to go home for a short time while Emmaline was with Ty. At home I watered the plants, dealt with the mail, gathered up clothes and other things I needed. Jackson volunteered to take me back to the hospital.

Ty was dozing but woke up when I came back in for the night. Emmaline had left to go to the hotel to pack.

"Buddy, how ya doin'?"

"Me? I want to know how you're doing!"

"I need a whiskey, and a blonde with big boobs would be okay too. The whiskey first."

"Now I know you're on the mend."

"Buddy, Mama told me somethin'. She said you were with me every single moment here, you never once left my side while I was asleep. I can't thank ya enough. You're always there for me."

"Always, Ty."

He was starting to doze off again. He said, "When I was asleep for so long, I was dreamin'. You were in my dream, and ya kept sayin' you needed me." He was drifting. "You needed me."

I tenderly took his hand. "Always, Ty."

But he had fallen asleep.

I gently brushed the hair from his forehead, where I gave him a soft good-night kiss.

One final conversation to be had at the end of this day.

"God, are You there? It's Martin again. Remember me, we talked last night? You maybe don't get enough credit, so please know You've done something wonderful. If there's anyone who can especially appreciate Your efforts, it's me. You're the ultimate Consultant Who Finds Solutions. On behalf of all the kids Ty will be helping in the future, I want to say thanks for giving him back to us. He will do great things, I promise. You'll see!

"And God? I was kind of selfish before and mentioned myself? I hope You won't hold that against me. You see, that wonderful day I met Ty, the first words he said to me directly when he shouted at me out the door were 'I need ya, buddy'.

"Well, I've learned something crystal clear from this whole hospital experience. The need goes the other way. So much the other way."

Always

All ways

Ty.

"And one last thing. You know Ty says goddammit a lot. Sorry about that, he doesn't mean anything by it. That's just his way of talking. Thank You for overlooking it.

"I'll try to be a better friend and talk with You more often. Thanks again for giving him back and thanks for listening."

Aman.

The King Holds Audiences

Emmaline left the next day with my assurance that I would take excellent care of her "sweet boy." I promised we would have video calls every day with her and her sons. Deck took her to LAX airport, and I had arranged for Cody to pick her up in Oklahoma City. I met Ty's brothers during the first video call, all handsome men with stronger Oklahoma accents than Ty's. One of them was chewing tobacco and using a spit cup. They were hearty men, not nearly as charismatic as their baby brother, but appealing.

Ty was a popular patient. The visits from the female nurses (and one gay nurse) picked up considerably. "Just want to see if he needs anything." Dr. Jordan wanted Ty to try to walk at least to the bathroom, even if it was extremely slow and difficult. I think the nurses had arguments over whose turn it was to help. Dr. Jordan had some suspicions of the nurse competition, so she assigned a male nurse to help him—except he was the one I thought was gay, so someone still had some enjoyment with bathroom duty.

Presents kept coming in. The youth club sent a photo of the team holding a huge sign saying Get Well Coach Ty. Coach

The King Holds Audiences

Jones and the touch football league sent a football-shaped balloon and flowers. Amy's theatre sent a photo of the whole cast, with Natasha leading the way blowing him a kiss, along with a bag of chocolate kisses.

His unit members took turns visiting. He always enjoyed seeing Laura, and after I had told him how Steve had been at the hospital constantly while Ty was in emergency, he was more cordial. Laura revealed that during the follow-up investigation, forensic tech specialists had examined the footage from their body cams and calculated the trajectory of the perp's bullet. If Ty had not leaped in, it would have hit the child in the head.

Steve said, "We all admire you, Ty. That was a brave thing to do."

Who wouldn't admire a man like that? *Who wouldn't love a man like that?*

The bros came over, which suddenly triggered a raft of extra attention and visits from the nurses. I know the boys got some new phone numbers! When Kyle and Jackson started teasing Ty about naughty nurses and hospital gowns and such, he laughed a lot, even though it sometimes hurt. Dr. Jordan told me, "Laughter is a good medicine. Tell them to stop by often." I always enjoyed their visits.

Josh and Anne brought Tommy. Ty was beyond delighted and made Tommy sit beside him on the bed. They said that Amy was busy with final dress rehearsals but would visit when she could. Anne had brought along a children's storybook, and Ty and the thrilled Tommy read it aloud together while Josh and Anne visited with me. Then I took Tommy on a walk to show him the hospital while Josh and Anne had a chat with Ty.

Ty reveled in the attention of the constant visits. He was a bit like a king having audiences in his court.

But then...

The day the drag queens came to visit is one Cedars-Sinai hospital will not soon forget!

They came sashaying down the hall in a drag-queenly royal procession. It was a scream. They were dressed in over-the-top candy striper outfits—sequins included, to be sure—and were wearing oversized double-ponytail wigs. They gave little twinkle finger waves, greeting every staff member, patient, and visitor in the hallway. Those not confined to bed came to the doorways, wondering what was going on.

When they arrived at Ty's room, it was hysterical. The look on his face!

Miss Vanessa: "Cowboy, why are you all alone in that bed? I think you need company for a little personalized health care. Is the problem a pulled groin? Is it because you haven't pulled it enough? I can help."

Miss Penelope: "We brought a gift perfect for someone like you." It was a large doll in a nurse outfit holding a sign saying Nurse Nancy Says Get Well Soon. Miss Penelope told Ty to watch as she raised the doll's arms. That brought the skirt up, and it turned out to be an inflatable sex doll!

Miss Jenn, ever interested in fashion: "That hospital gown is so unbecoming. No sequins, no feathers—horrible. And it looks much too warm. I'll rip it off your hot body and give you a refreshing sponge bath. With my tongue."

Just then a rather handsome and sturdy male orderly came in to adjust the monitor. He took one look at the spectacle in front of him and came to a halt.

Miss Doretha: "Oh sugar, don't let us stop you. You look like you could use some help. Need some assistance with catheter removal? Does the urologist need an extra hand for hernia checks? Oh, I'm feeling faint, can you give me mouth-to-mouth resuscitation?"

He beat a hasty retreat.

They were wonderful fun, regaling Ty with merry stories about the latest parties they had been to, their recent makeovers and such.

Miss Penelope: "I wonder if the plastic surgeon is around? I could talk to him about sculpting my magnificent breasts."

Miss Vanessa: "He would need military-grade foam in a cast-iron bra to bring those droopy tits up."

Miss Penelope: "Fishwife!"

Miss Doretha: "Cowboy, I had an idea to make you rich. We could sell dildos based on your too-big-for-your-britches endowment. I'd be happy to take extensive measurements and make the mold. We could call it—drum roll, please—The Tytanic!"

Miss Jenn: "Don't be surprised by our outfits. I always wanted to be a candy striper when I was younger."

Miss Vanessa: "You mean when doctors were bloodletting and using leeches."

Miss Jenn: "Harlot! Cowboy, don't you have a nice lollipop you'd like to share with your very own candy striper? I could suck it for you."

Dr. Jordan arrived.

Miss Vanessa: "Oh, Dr. Jordan. You're so cute. Take good care of our precious cowboy here."

Miss Penelope: "He needs to get back into the saddle."

Miss Doretha: "He needs to be riding someone...something every day."

Miss Jenn: "We want him to live up to that famous saying about the horse you rode in on."

Dr. Jordan drily said, "I'll do my best."

The ladies were leaving in a flurry of goodbyes and elaborately thrown kisses and promises of home-cooked meals with special attention to "dessert." The handsome orderly came back and stood stock still again.

Miss Doretha: "Oh sugar, I just love you strong, silent types." She growled like a tiger at him. "Watch out, I might bite. Except in important, sensitive places!"

As the ladies flounced out, Dr. Jordan and the orderly shook their heads while Ty and I laughed. The drag queens paraded down the hall, royally waving two fingers and blowing kisses.

Ty: "God damn that Amy! She sent them here."

When Amy showed up that evening, he accused her of doing just that, purposely sending the queens to visit.

She replied innocently with a sunny smile, "I have no idea what you're talking about. I'm sure they came simply to offer solace and succor."

Ty said, "Suck somethin'. They have only one thing on their minds."

The King Holds Audiences

Amy turned to give me a little wink.

She had brought Ty a gift, an old-fashioned erotic paperback she had found in a used bookstore. It was entitled *The Cowboy and the Schoolmarm*, and the cover featured a cowboy with his shirt off, a terrified schoolmarm, a leering outlaw, and a blowsy saloon tramp. We giggled like kids finding their older brother's porn magazines. I read some of it aloud in my burlesque Oklahoma accent which made it funnier:

> The cowboy brazenly ripped her calico dress from neck to waist, revealing her bosom inside a tight bodice, which barely covered her ample, heaving, rounded breasts. The schoolmarm said, "What do you want with me, you brute?" and the cowboy replied, "You might be the schoolteacher, but I'm gonna teach you what makes the Wild West *wild*".

We laughed so hysterically—at both the purple prose and my accent—that the nurse came to check on us. I hid the book under Ty's blanket. When she had left, Ty pointed to the bodice on the schoolmarm. "What's that thing called again?"

"It's called a bodice," Amy explained. "And in romance novels, a bodice is usually ripped off on the way to a passionate encounter."

"Sounds good to me. I think every woman should wear a bodice. The rippin' part's the best."

"It figures a dirty-minded cowboy like you would enjoy that idea."

279

"Speakin' of rippin', is Natasha havin' a conniption about her fast costume changes? The zipper sticks, or she can't get her fishnet stockin's or her bra off fast enough? I can help her practice."

Amy said, "In the theatre the costume helper is called a dresser. In your case, you could be the undresser."

"Damn right! When you gonna do a show with a nude scene? I could design the costumes for that."

They were enjoying their back-and-forth but all with good humor this time. When Amy got up to leave, she dropped her mock-snarky tone and spoke warmly as she took his hand. "It's good to see you recovering so well, Ty. See you at Martin's when you get to go home." After she left, he looked bemused.

I asked, "I may be mistaken, but between candy stripers and dirty books, did somebody's balls nearly get busted today?"

"No sir. I oughta put that girl over my knee and give her a good spankin'. She'd love it!"

And so would he.

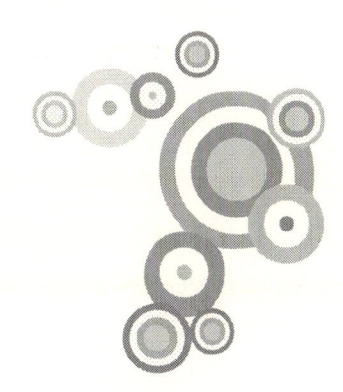

Isn't That Love?

His home convalescence began. It would be some time before he could be on his own at all. I moved him into my house, ensconcing him in the guest room on first floor.

Ty had multiple physical issues. He could not raise his right arm above shoulder level, and it was weak. It would take therapy to get it back to normal, and to be able to play basketball and football again. His right leg could barely move. His left leg was better but stiff. His legs would require much more extensive therapy, which the doctors were certain would result in a return to normal. But it would take time.

He needed my help to struggle to the bathroom. He could manage toilet business on his own, but I had to help him back to the bed or couch. Showering required my assistance at first, especially to make sure he didn't fall, and I brought in a shower seat. For the few times I did help him shower, it was a test of my willpower to not get excited by everything. Like before, when he smelled so fresh and clean, my pheromones were rioting. Soon he could manage on his own. *Rats. I was quite enjoying shower duty.*

At first, he would sleep a lot. That was the time I could do my consultant work. I resumed a few projects that were not overly time-consuming.

Also during this time when he was more frequently sleeping, I reached out to the friends who had stood by me during the crisis times in the hospital. I wholeheartedly thanked them for coming to my rescue and simply for being there. Amy, Jackson, and Deck all spoke lovingly and made me feel as cared for as I was trying to make Ty feel.

That sweetheart Melissa sent a card I treasured. I kept it on my bedroom dresser. It had a picture of a bubbly, fizzy glass of champagne.

> Dear Martin,
> I've decided everyone should have an effervescent gay man in their lives. Your devotion and love for Ty is something we all admire and remark upon. It is not only Ty who is lucky to have you, WE are lucky to have you.
> XOXO
> Melissa

Curiously, it was Kyle who had the biggest reaction to my heartfelt thank you. He came to visit, and while Ty was sleeping, we sat by the pool. Ty could call out to us if he needed something.

"Martin, of course we had to help you be with Ty. It was terrible for him, but don't you know you're important to us too? We'd never let you go through that trauma alone. Being with you is the least we could do."

Isn't That Love?

I started to reply, but he kept going. "Ty better appreciate all you do for him. He'd better not take you for granted. We tell him that if he isn't good to you, he'll answer to us. You're not just anybody. You're important."

That made me feel good. "Thank you, Kyle—"

At that moment Ty called out, "Martin, you out there?"

"Be right in," I yelled back and started to get up.

Kyle grabbed my arm and fixed me with his intense scary look. "You and me, Martin. You know what I'm talking about."

We stared at each other for a long fraught moment.

I gave a quick nod.

"We'll see each other soon," he said as he let me go. We went inside for him to greet Ty.

"You guys have a nice visit out there while I was sawin' logs?"

"We did," I said.

"We had a lot to catch up on," said Kyle. "Martin is going to help me with a study project." He gave me that intense look again.

What was it about him that made my heart beat faster? Unfinished business!

Ty under my care: I coddled him, I babied him, I waited on him hand and foot. I made all his favorite foods, kept him entertained. I loved this chance to give him my full attention. And have his full attention on me!

When Ty watched sports on television, I was nearby and did some work then, responding to him when he made a remark. I was amused at the times he yelled and cussed at the screen as if the referees could hear him.

We grew even closer. When we watched shows together, there were a few lovely times he would take my hand and pat it and hold it for a minute, not saying anything. This was a big step for Ty. He wouldn't do that in public, but at home he could. I didn't say anything; I just let it be and enjoyed the moment.

One time on the couch as we were watching a movie, he said, "My back hurts." He turned himself and laid down with his head in my lap. I was a bit surprised but he just kept watching TV.

Did I dare?

I touched his hair.

He didn't react at all.

I let my fingers stroke his hair.

He closed his eyes. I put my hand on his chest and could feel his heart beating. I started to pull my hand away, but he put his hand on top of mine to stay.

Sigh.

I turned the volume down and switched the table lamp off. The only light was from the flickering images on the TV screen. Finally he did fall asleep.

This was such a lovely moment. I craved his affection like a drug. *What would it be like to have this all the time? What would it be like to have him touch me in the same way? What would it be like—*

I had to stop my reverie. I could have this moment but wouldn't get more. To even have this much was lucky.

Isn't That Love?

I let my special man sleep, my fingers in his hair, my hand to his heart.

But like always, it was my heart in his hands.

I was content. I had never been so content. Ty seemed quite content too, especially given the physical challenges he had. I was happy to be devoted to his care. We laughed, we joked, we teased, we shared everything about ourselves, we told deep dark secrets. I was so happy.

When he was content, I was content.

When I was happy, he was happy.

Isn't that love?

Not that it was always sunshine and roses. He would get frustrated at his physical limitations and snap, and that's when I always involved others to cheer him up. We had video chats with the family and Oklahoma friends. The bros and other friends frequently visited, and that laughter was excellent medicine for Ty.

We had to visit Cedars-Sinai every week, and that involved some doing to get in and out of the car. He was starting to move a little better, and Dr. Jordan said, "You're doing well. I think physical therapy will definitely begin to have some effect now. We'll be sending a home therapist to you."

"Deppity" Chief Williams came to visit early on and told Ty the city had given him a disability payment and pension. Later he could return to work if he recovered well enough. All costs of his convalescence were covered, and he presented me with a check to get started. I had protested it wasn't necessary, but he said, "You can't be expected to pay for expenses. You taking care of Ty is the best thing for him—much better than any nurse we'd hire."

Steve and Laura also came by. Ty was far more cordial toward Steve, who had gone back to modified work but was still seeing the psychologist to deal with the trauma of shooting someone.

I asked the psychologist to visit Ty just in case. I left them alone to talk, and later on her way out, she told me she thought he was doing well. He didn't seem to need her help, though she would be happy to come back anytime. It seemed Ty was more worried about Steve than himself.

Amy was quite busy with the theatre season, but she did visit when she could. Their usual battle continued, Amy and Ty giving each other as good as they got, but it was more good-natured. One time Ty brought out the inflatable doll and said, "I'm bored lookin' at this nurse outfit. You got somethin' else?" She said, "I just might," and a few days later she showed up to dress the doll in a schoolmarm outfit with a bodice like on the cover of the book. She put a sign saying, I Can Teach You a Thing or Two! Let 'Er Rip!

And after every visit, I noticed Ty looking at *The Cowboy and the Schoolmarm* and the newly costumed inflatable doll with a thoughtful expression.

Naughty Nurse

It was time to begin physical therapy. As promised, Cedars-Sinai arranged for a home therapist who would visit three times a week.

The doorbell rang, and standing there was Nicholas. My height, trim and fit, impeccable beard and haircut. Lovely eyes and smile.

Wow! I could feel an unmistakable spark as we looked at each other. Electric was not the right word to describe it. Nuclear would be closer.

As I brought Nicholas over to meet Ty, there was no reason to think he was anything other than straight. But everything in me said Nicholas had felt the spark too. I was sure of it.

Nicholas was friendly but businesslike. He took Ty through his first exercises, explaining everything carefully and thoroughly. On a few of the exercises, Ty would need my help, and Nicholas gave me good instructions. One time, to show me how a particular move should be practiced, he had to put his hand on top of mine. I almost jumped at the electric energy.

He was good with Ty, pushing him. He was smart. He could see that Ty responded best to a bro challenge, sort of a competition. I was impressed. And wondering. And, I can't deny, excited.

When he was leaving, Nicholas handed me his card and said to please call if anything was needed and that he would see me on Wednesday.

"Looking forward to it," I replied.

Nicholas left, and when I turned, Ty was giving me a wicked look.

I asked, "What?"

He mimicked, "Looking forward to it."

I blushed. I know I did.

"Goddammit. I was hopin' I'd get Naughty Nurse Nancy, and instead *you* get Naughty Nurse Nicholas. God damn!"

"What are you talking about?"

"You gotta be kiddin' me! The two of you were eye-fuckin' each other through that whole thing. I got pregnant just bein' the innocent bystander."

I blushed more than Jackson.

"I may be a country cowboy, but I got eyes," he said, spouting his favorite line.

"Well, turn your overheated imagination off. As you can see, he's utterly professional. He won't have anything to do with a patient. Or the patient's helper."

"Maybe so. But when my therapy ends, I can just imagine what kinda therapy he has in store for you. Lawdy, you practically jumped outta your skin when he 'accidentally' touched you. I oughta report the two of you for indecent exposure of your dirty minds."

"Would you like me to ask Dr. Jordan to send us a different therapist?"

"No sir. I thought he did a real good job. Gimme that card." He entered Nicholas's phone number in his contacts. "Here. Gimme your phone."

I should not have fallen for it. He entered the contact in my phone, but I was still discombobulated and didn't notice he kept typing. Looking at me mischievously, he sent a text.

"What did you just do?" I snatched the phone to look.

He had texted Nicholas: "This is Martin. Ty enjoyed your session very much. Your hands are sooooo nice. See you on Wednesday."

"I'm going to kill you."

"Now he has your number. You should thank me."

"Nothing will come of it. He's too professional."

"Professionally top notch, yessir. Yeah, he's good." Ty looked at me meaningfully again. "But is he good enough? We'll see."

Of course I had to call Amy and tell her all about it. She said, "Martin, I haven't heard you this giddy about someone since the day Ty moved in."

"Well, nothing will happen while Ty is his patient."

I can't lie. I looked forward to seeing Nicholas, and it became apparent that Nicholas was indeed interested but trying not to show it. He would remain professional. Ty teased me mercilessly and said my mind had so many dirty thoughts it needed to be washed out with soap.

Speaking of dirty minds, I couldn't ignore the ever-fascinating topic of Ty's sex life. He might have trouble with his arm and both legs, but other particular appendages were raring to go. He was a lusty guy, and it was only a matter of time before he wanted to get back to business.

We were watching a TV show with a ravishingly hot blonde, and he said, "Goddammit, she makes me horny." He joked, "Where's that inflatable doll?"

To be honest, I had always been willing to be Naughty Nurse Martin and help Ty out in such ways too. But we could never go there.

So I soon asked Natasha to visit. How to put this delicately? As Ty might say, there were ways to have a happy ending that didn't require he be as agile as a gymnast. I was sure Natasha would figure this out.

As they were chatting, I pretended they were distracting me and said I had to go over to Ty's house for peace and quiet to get my consultant work done, and could Natasha please keep him entertained.

Well, she certainly did. Of course I knew what to expect, and I knew Ty was perfectly aware of what I was doing, and I knew that he knew that I knew...You get the picture. Later, after Natasha had left, he said, "Can we put Natasha on the physical therapy payroll? *All* my body parts need therapy. And she's a specialist. That gal is a superstar at everything she does." He winked at me and said, "Wooee, she plumb wore me out." And he added with a smile, "Nobody gets me like you do, buddy."

I completely coddled Ty, but not in the matter of his exercises. If he relentlessly teased me about Nicholas, in return I relentlessly pushed him on his exercises. If he tried to slack off, I threatened him. "If you don't get to work, no more tacos for you. No more Coronas!"

"You're worse than any coach I ever had. All right, I'll do my exercises."

He was progressing so well in his recovery, I knew he would soon be allowed to return to his own house. He no longer needed constant attendance but still needed help sometimes with exercises, and he could not yet return to work. When Nicholas told him it was time, I think Ty and I both felt a little regret. We had bonded so much more closely while he stayed in my house, it was hard to let go of the physical proximity we had gotten used to. But it was time to let go.

I still cooked and entertained him constantly. It soon felt like it was much the same, as we spent a lot of time together in each other's houses.

Magically, I always seemed to be around when Nicholas came for physical therapy sessions. Ty was without mercy and teased me to distraction.

Back in his own house, he had the privacy he needed. I had Jackson come over and introduce Ty to the wonders of Tinder. And did that explode into flames! The women could come to his house because he couldn't go out to the bars just yet.

I teased him and said we could put on his Tinder profile: "Medical Emergency: Uncontrollable Swelling Between Legs" or "Nymphomaniac Required for Endurance Test" or "Expert at Fitting Big Things into Small Places."

"You're just a laugh riot," was his answer.

The parade of willing women started, and Ty was soon making up for lost time. And from the open-window overhearings, it seemed there was plenty of lost time that had to be made up for.

That was surely his favorite therapy of all.

One day, with that mischievous look in his eye, he suggested to Nicholas that we should go out to lunch so that Nicholas could observe him getting in and out of the car by himself and how he was doing while out and about. Nicholas could show him things he should improve on. Nicholas agreed, saying it was a good idea. I said to him later, "You are so obvious. You want it to seem like a date."

And Ty replied, "You should thank me. Lawdy, it's gonna be miserable. With all the attention anybody's gonna give me, it'll be like I'm the invisible man."

The lunch was wonderful. Nicholas relaxed to the point of being able to converse about things other than physical therapy requirements. He told us about his hobbies, such as restoring old furniture pieces and surfing. We learned he grew up in Delaware but moved to LA for the weather and for surfing. I commented, "You should meet our friend Jackson, he's a surfer too."

Contrary to his claim of being invisible, Ty was at his most charming and talkative, making little jokes and funny remarks. Then he started asking questions, and it soon became apparent that he had begun interrogating Nicholas, albeit in a fairly charming way. I think Nicholas knew what was going on, but he answered everything in an easygoing manner.

When we got home, Ty said, "Well? You should thank me. That was a good idea."

"Thank you. It was fun. Even when you were the Gestapo wringing information out of him. I'm surprised you didn't bring a pair of pliers to rip out his fingernails. I was afraid you'd ask the waiter to bring a bucket of water so you could waterboard him."

"Somebody has to do the dirty work."

"You're like the dad who sits in the back of a station wagon when the girl goes on a date."

Now we could have expeditions. I took Ty to the youth club, where he could coach from the sidelines, even if he couldn't run up and down the court yet. On Saturdays we went to touch football, where he could see his friends and enjoy the games. Sometimes we went to First Down. When Jackson wanted us to go with him to Locker Room, Ty said I should go with Jackson but he would stay home so that Jackson could "explore his feelings." I reminded Ty to be quiet about this with the others, and he said, "Pussy? Dick? A sheep in the barn? Who cares, let 'im find out what he wants."

It was around this time that the Martin project started up again. Kyle, Jackson, and Deck decided to be worried again about whether I was getting too invested in Ty and whether he was unintentionally taking emotional advantage of me, blah blah blah. So they started introducing me to guys from the gym again, somewhat to Ty's displeasure. They would introduce me to guys at First Down, to a friend of one of the touch football players, to

Coach Jones' cousin, for god's sake. And for each and every one, Ty was adamant. "Nope. Not good enough. Only the best for Martin."

Deck and Melissa invited us to their place for dinner, and it just so happened—not coincidentally—that one of Melissa's coworkers was there as well. Ty said, "He's not horrible. But not good enough."

Natasha even got in on the act, inviting us to the theatre to meet a guest performer. The actor was quite warm and funny in his role, and when we went backstage, he seemed rather fun. He talked about his career and upcoming projects. But I could see Ty took an instant dislike to him.

After we left, he said, "That guy is only out for himself. He'd stab you the moment you turned your back, and he'd wipe the blade on your costume. I don't like that guy."

And to Natasha, "Not good enough. Only the best for Martin." And he invited her over to remind her repeatedly in his bedroom.

Jackson, on hearing about these incidents, was diplomatic and said, "Ty is a little overprotective. He just wants the best for you."

Kyle was not at all diplomatic. "Protective? He is *possessive*, and he gets jealous at the thought of you giving attention to someone else!"

Planting Seeds (Guest Appearance By Gardener Martin)

With Ty back in his own house again, I turned my thoughts to his future. I asked him if he wanted to get back to the unit, and he was ambivalent. I invited Laura over, asking her to find a way to bring up the topic. As it was perfect weather, they sat outside by the pool. I was glad she had dressed in t-shirt and jeans, as I thought Ty would be more relaxed than if she was in her work pantsuit and heels. I could overhear parts of the conversation. She encouraged him to not be afraid to talk to the psychologist. She said there was a high burnout rate among those who worked on issues of child abuse, child pornography, and child trafficking because it wore a person's soul down. She herself would be asking to transfer to another area soon. There would be no questions asked if he wanted something else.

But what could that something else be? It was time for the Consultant Who Finds Solutions/Bestest Best Friend to plant some seeds and let the garden grow.

Ty had worked well with the at-risk teenagers at the youth club. They were tough boys, and even though they were in rough personal situations, he brooked no excuses and made them rise to his standard of sportsmanship and conduct.

With Nicholas' secret approval, I organized the whole thing with the youth club director and with the help of my CEO client who had a Lakers connection. We got a raft of donated tickets to a Lakers game, and the director asked Ty if he would take the teenagers on a field trip to see it. He said he hoped they would have good behavior, but they sometimes acted out and he couldn't be sure how it would go. Would he be up for that, given the challenges?

Ty was more than happy to be in charge. As his physical abilities were better, I didn't push to go. I would let him be and see what happened.

The teenagers had become used to me being around to help during his convalescence when Ty was there to coach from the sidelines. When I wasn't at the bus for the field trip, they wondered, "Where's that Martin guy?"

I heard later from the youth club director that when the students learned I 'couldn't' be there to help, they immediately stepped up to the plate—*wrong sports metaphor for a basketball game. Stepped up to the free-throw line?*—and vied for the chance to help Ty as he negotiated the bus and the many stairs at the arena. Ty had reminded all of them to exhibit good manners: say thank you for the tickets when my client stopped by to greet them at the game, let other people go first, say sir and ma'am if an adult spoke to them.

The boys were thrilled to pieces. When my client stopped by their seats, he told Ty, who had always impressed him, to bring them up to the VIP box after. The boys got to meet a few of the

Planting Seeds (Guest Appearance By Gardener Martin)

players. They were beyond excited and exhibited the best behavior ever.

I congratulated Coach Ty on the success of the field trip and how well the teens had behaved. He said what every teacher and coach knows, "Ya get whatcha expect."

For the second seed, again with Nicholas' secret approval, I carefully stage-managed Anne, Tommy, and Tommy's teacher Ms. Meyer.

Anne called Ty, saying that Tommy wanted to bring Uncle Ty to his school for show-and-tell.

"Show-and-tell? I thought kids brought their pet guinea pigs."

"He wants to show off his cowboy Uncle Ty."

"Well, whatever he wants."

He wore his best cowboy hat, red shirt with black Western embroidery, boots, and black jeans with a huge, gaudy belt buckle. He would be the showiest show-and-tell ever. I ordered a lariat online to be delivered express because he wanted to show a roping trick. He practiced by the pool, and it was nice to see that his arm had progressed so well.

I did go along with him this time because I was taking no chances. The gardener has to tend the roses more than other flowers, and this particular rose would get prize-winning care from Gardener Martin. I had priorities.

I reminded Ty that at school, he had to watch his language. He said, "Goddammit, you don't have to tell me that. I got a motherfuckin' brain cell or two!"

Tommy's teacher, a young and seven-months-pregnant Ms. Meyer, welcomed us. We gave each other a subtle look, as she had graciously acquiesced to all of my plans. We met the kids in the commons area they shared with other classes.

Tommy proudly introduced his Uncle Ty. A few of the children knew him from Tommy's birthday party, and he waved to them and said howdy. He answered the usual questions: Where's your pistols, and where did you park the horse?

"Mister Ty, what's that belt thing?"

For all I knew, he might have won the gaudy belt buckle in a mechanical bull riding contest at some Oklahoma City country dive. Ty answered, "Darlin', I won this ropin' in an amateur contest."

"What's ropin'?"

"My daddy raised a few cattle, so I had to know how to use a rope. One day this little dogie, a baby calf, was tryin' to run away. Let me show you." He brought out his lariat, and the kids sat up in excitement.

"Tommy, will you be my little dogie? When I say go, you start runnin' around the room." Ty shouted "Go!" Not exactly a subtle Lord Laurence Olivier, he declaimed, "Oh no! The little dogie is escapin', I gotta lasso him! Don't let him git away!"

He twirled his lariat, threw it, and plop! He neatly caught Tommy in the loop and pulled him back.

Planting Seeds (Guest Appearance By Gardener Martin)

Pandemonium! Every kid wanted to be the little dogie. Ms. Meyer wisely intervened and said, "No more lassoing. It's time for recess."

One little boy asked, "Mister Ty, will you come to the playground with us?"

Ty answered, "Sure will. Recess is my favorite subject."

The kids clamored and dragged him off to the playground. He played and romped with the kids, pushing them on the swing, catching them on the slide, riding the merry-go-round. Some of the kids played "lassoin' the little dogie" with an imaginary rope. It was pretty funny to see the teeter-totter with Ty on one end and five kids on the other. I took a cute photo.

And now for the next part. Ms. Meyer and I made a good team, and the plot was about to take a twist. When we went back in, Ms. Meyer said, "After recess, I always read a story to the children."

Ty said, "Okay if we stay and listen too?"

She was the Meryl Streep of Oak Grove Elementary when she suddenly said, "Oh," and grabbed her pregnant bump. "Oh!" We looked at her with concern, and she said, "Oh, dear. I feel a little queasy. Martin, will you walk with me to the nurse? Ty, could I trouble you to read the story to the children? My aide Gracie is here. She can help you if needed."

It didn't occur to Ty to wonder why the aide couldn't read the story. He said, "Hot da—I mean, love to! Martin, you tend to Miz Meyer. Come on, kids."

Ms. Meyer and I went out the commons doorway and immediately skulked out of sight to listen.

I think Ms. Meyer may have usually read the story with the kids in their chairs, but Ty led them to an area of the commons with several beanbags. He took off his hat and settled them all around him, kids draped all over him, clutching his arms and legs. One little girl had her thumb in her mouth.

He began. "Once upon a time..."

It was a fairy tale clearly intended to teach children about diversity. It featured a dragon and a unicorn who wanted to be friends, but the other magical creatures said, "You can't be friends, you're different." And the dragon said, "It's good that we're different." And the unicorn said, "Being diverse is what makes our friendship more special." And as a result, all the magical creatures became friends with each other.

The little girl popped her thumb out and asked, "Mister Ty, what does 'diverse' mean?"

By this time, Ms. Meyer and I were blatantly looking around the edge of the door, eager to hear how Ty would answer.

"Darlin', that is a *wonderful* question. Diverse means different. And that's good. When each person—or dragon or unicorn—is different, they're special. And can be a friend. And if dragons and unicorns can be diverse and be friends with all the magical creatures, then people can be diverse and be friends with everybody. My mama taught me that everybody should be appreciated for exactly what they are. We have to value the specialness of each person. I wonder, do we have any special kids here? Let's see."

Ty pointed to each child and said, "You're special. And you're special. And you're special," all the way around the circle. The kids were giggling.

Planting Seeds (Guest Appearance By Gardener Martin)

He stood, putting his hand above his eyes and elaborately looked around the room. "Are there any diverse special kids around here? Stand up and wave your hand if you're a special kid so I can see you!" Every child leaped up and waved a hand, still giggling.

"Let's have a special kids group hug!"

I took a photo of that lovely moment when all the special kids—including that big kid Ty—were hugging.

Ms. Meyer said, "I have never seen someone so at ease with children."

Ty spotted her and asked, "Miz Meyer, would it be all right if we stayed longer and helped out?"

"That would be wonderful, Ty."

Ms. Meyer and I looked at each other. I was unable to disguise my triumphant look.

We ended up staying the whole afternoon, helping with spelling tests and sundry other second grade tasks. I noticed he was making sure to help every student, and just as he did as Coach Ty, he often said, "Great job!" and "Good work!" and "You did it!"

When the school day was ending, Ty high-fived every child like he did at basketball and praised each one. The kids clutched him en masse in another group hug and begged him to come back. Ty promised he would come again. Ms. Meyer and I looked at each other, and she gave me silent applause.

Gardener Martin had planted this seed oh so very well.

As for human magical creatures, I know one dragon and one unicorn who value the specialness of each other so much, it's like a fairy tale come true.

StraightForward

The Beautiful Heart Of A Beautiful Man

I lassoed—that is, roped—Josh and Ms. Meyer in on the next plan. It seemed there was to be an afternoon field day at the school, where each child brought a parent for fun games. However, I found out from Ms. Meyer that there was one little girl with a single mom who simply could not get off work. The school often found surrogate parents for such occasions, and so I put Josh and Ms. Meyer to work.

When Josh picked Tommy up after school, Ms. Meyer and the little girl, Nini, were nearby. Josh said loudly, in the same sort of overacting style Ty had, "Tommy, your Uncle Ty is so sad. He found out we're having a field day, and he said it sounds like fun, and he wishes he could come. But he can't."

Tommy asked, "Why can't he come?"

"He doesn't have a kid to bring him."

Tommy fell right into the plan. "Let's find a kid who needs someone!"

Ms. Meyer chimed in, saying, "Nini, did you tell me your mother couldn't come to field day?"

Tommy marched up to Nini and said, "If I share my Uncle Ty with you, will you invite him to field day?"

The Beautiful Heart Of A Beautiful Man

Nini agreed, Ms. Meyer organized it with the mom, and all was set.

For the field day, the kids could wear special costumes with their parent if they wanted. Josh and Tommy planned to be in superhero outfits. Well, what Nini wanted was to wear her tutu. And she wanted Ty to wear one too. She put her second grade foot down, and that was that. The tutu was mandatory, nonnegotiable.

Ms. Meyer called to explain, worried that Ty would want to opt out. He didn't hesitate. Not for one second would he let a little girl down.

"Where can I find me a tutu?" he asked.

I didn't dare borrow from Amy for fear she would use it, no matter the good cause, to find a way to tease Ty. So I asked Miss Vanessa, saying I needed it for a costume party. What she sent was the gaudiest, most multi-layered tutu ever known to man. The sparkle factory had to have gone into overtime to produce this. It was the prima donna of all tutus—except this prima donna was a cowboy.

I did not attend, though it killed me not to go. I did not want to appear to be forcing everything. I had put it in motion, but I wanted Ty to come to a realization himself.

Josh reported the whole thing to me in a phone call afterward. When Ty showed up in the tutu, holding Nini's hand, the other parents were amused, especially the dads. But when word got around about the situation, they were highly approving.

He was a hoot. Ty easily became the crowd favorite while the parents were playing games with the kids. Straight men are usually oblivious, but even Josh noticed how the single moms (and one gay dad) were paying lots of extra attention to Ty.

Josh reported a dynamic moment. He told me that when the organized games had ended, the kids were free to play while the parents had a break. The kids were at the age of "Ewwww boy germs, ewwww girl germs" so they played separately. The girls were jumping rope, and the boys were playing keep away. However, one little boy wanted to jump rope. The other little boys were making fun of him, and he was starting to cry. His mother was at a loss what to do and so was trying to get him to play keep away.

I felt a pang as Josh told this. It struck a chord with me and would probably do the same with a lot of other gay men. In our childhoods it was so common to be teased for sometimes wanting to be with the girls and not exclusively with boys.

It seems Ty had immediately sized up the situation. He went over and said, "Hey little buddy, I want to jump rope, but I need your help. Will you show me?" He took the little boy over to where the girls were playing, and Ty and the boy started jumping rope together. Everybody watched as the little girls turning the long rope were laughing in delight at Ty. With his still slightly compromised legs, he could only jump eight times before getting tangled up. The little boy got in and jumped seventeen times, and the girls applauded. Josh saw what was going on and joined them. And then a few other dads did too, enthralling their little girls. This engendered a rush of little boys abandoning keep away. Soon they were all merrily jumping like mad. I praised Josh for joining in.

The Beautiful Heart Of A Beautiful Man

Similarly, when the kids were gender separated and playing foursquare, Ty didn't wait to see if there was a teasing issue. Ty joined the girls group, which triggered a few moms to join the boys group, and then it mushroomed to become a mixed event of fierce foursquare fun.

He had taught a great lesson in inclusivity. Ms. Meyer later told me that the parents were in awe of Ty. One of them had asked her if Ty was a teacher.

Way, way ahead of you on that.

I wasn't surprised to also learn from Ms. Meyer that several single moms (and one gay dad) were angling for information.

Josh said, "Ty was great. That little girl Nini was the proudest kid on the playground because she had Mister Ty. Tommy was happy he had shared, but he did feel the need to remind his friends, 'That's *my* Uncle Ty.'"

Josh sent me a video of Ty romping in his tutu, and it was hilarious with it bouncing up and down as he jumped rope. Josh explained, "I'm not showing Anne, because she would show Amy. And you and I both know Amy would find a way to tease Ty." Using some military-speak he said, "I'm not giving Amy a tactical advantage. But I knew you would want to see it."

Ty in his tutu was too, too funny. Oh, what a wonderful man!

As for Ty, "That was real fun. I loved recess as a kid, and I still love it now. Plus I got a few phone numbers from some'a them single moms. They came to school, so I'm gonna be the one to give 'em an education."

I told him he was a superstar for taking Nini, for being a good sport with the tutu, and especially for how he helped that little boy. He said, "I'm not standin' by when a kid needs to be included. I learned that lesson a long time ago. You know all about that. Do you think that little boy might turn out to be gay?"

"Just because he wanted to jump rope? Oh, I don't think so. What is important is that all those children learned to be kinder and inclusive. You taught a valuable lesson." I put a little emphasis on the word "taught."

Martin, Martin.

You've put your heart in.

How does your garden grow?

The seeds were planted. We would see.

I had no scruples, however, about throwing in one little tease about the tutu, telling him I would be happy to set it up so that he and Natasha could do *Swan Lake.* If he needed to borrow a sock to stuff in his tights, I would be happy to loan one.

"Ha ha, aren't you the funny one. I have no need for *that*. You know, why do all those ballet guys seem to be well-endowed? What's that all about?"

I explained the concept of a dance belt keeping the balls snug, making it smooth in front, and how this emphasized the crotch. "It's similar to the idea of a cup like you wore in baseball, but it's fabric like a jockstrap. Bet you never thought baseball players and ballet dancers had any such thing in common."

"So it's all costume trickery. Yeah, I've been fooled a coupla times by women with a push-up bra. I gotta get ready. I'm meetin' up with one'a those single moms."

"You should wear the tutu so she recognizes you."

"Ha ha."

The Beautiful Heart Of A Beautiful Man

I took a screen capture from the jump rope video to make a marvelous photo. Ty was leaping, and the tutu was flying high. He had a glorious dazzling smile, arms high, sun shining right on his face.

I had a collection of photos in my bedroom. It was clear who was the star of my life. Ty by himself, with me, washing his pickup, with Tommy asleep on the sofa, at the Lakers game, with the bros playing beach volleyball, in the tux, by the pool but not X-rated, in Las Vegas, on the teeter-totter, the special kids group hug, hanging with the bros, at a party. Ty in his tutu took pride of place in the collage. It represented the beautiful heart of a beautiful man.

I loved that photo.

Tu tu adorable.

StraightForward

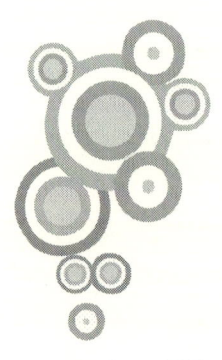

Kid In The Candy Store

One day during a physical therapy session at Ty's house, Nicholas was telling us that his gym was closed for extensive renovations and he would have to find a new place to go. Ty immediately said, "Why don't ya come to my gym? In fact, I've been wantin' to ask ya if I could start workin' out. I miss it. Can we go?"

So they came up with a plan that the next day Nicholas would pick him up, and they would go to the gym to work out. Because Nicholas had to rush off right afterward to meet a patient in Reseda, I would come to the gym to fetch Ty.

The next day when I arrived at the gym, I didn't spot them. I asked one of the staff, and she said to check the locker room.

When I hesitantly walked in, Nicholas had already left. Kyle and Jackson were helping Ty into the showers. He was hobbling! It turned out he had pushed himself quite hard, and at the end, it seemed to have been too much. He had pulled his hamstrings and worried that he had ruined all the progress with his legs. Nicholas had looked him over and said he would be okay. He told him to temper it and work up more gradually to his old level. So at least Ty could continue.

Meanwhile, remember that unwritten law about gay men seeing their straight friends naked?

In the showers, Kyle knew I was ogling. He turned and gave me his dangerous look and secretive smile.

Jackson—beer can indeed. *OM...Gosh!*

And Deck. Dirty, inquiring minds everywhere wondered how petite Melissa handled that particular muscle. *OM...Goodness!*

On the way home, Ty was relentless. "You were a kid in the candy store. Too much to look at."

I could not pretend otherwise. "I admit I enjoyed the view."

He snorted and continued teasing. "Too bad you weren't there to see Nicholas workin' out. He wore a tank top and skimpy ol' shorts. You'da been droolin' over his manly chest, and you'd wanna squeeze his rock-hard biceps. As for his bubble butt—"

"You've been watching too much porn."

"Just sayin'."

He sat back, and we were silent. While I was contemplating the tantalizing vision he had described, Ty was contemplating something else. A few minutes later, he said, "Nicholas is a really good therapist. And a good guy."

I turned to him. "Well. You finally have something nice to say about a guy. Does this mean you like him?"

He thought about it. "Maybe."

"And you'll give me a permission slip?"

"Funny." He looked out the window and then turned back, "I only want the best for my best friend." He looked out the window again. "Kyle yelled at me. I admit I get a little protective sometimes. But if Nicholas takes you away from me, I guess I'll have to get over it." He huffed a deep breath. "Yeah, he might get my approval." Ty was looking down at his knees.

I said, "Don't worry. Nobody will ever take me away from you." I understood my cowboy. All of his overprotective and possessive ways stemmed from not wanting to lose his best friend.

Back at home, the phone calls started shortly thereafter, one after the other.

Jackson: "Nicholas is such a great guy. And he likes surfing! If you decide you don't like him, maybe he could be my first date with a man?"

Me: "I thought you weren't ready for that yet."

Jackson: "Maybe. We'll talk about it."

Kyle: "Finally Ty might be backing off. Nicholas is super cool. We invited him to join touch football."

Deck: "Melissa and I want to invite you and Nicholas over to dinner."

Me: "It hasn't gotten that far yet. Nothing will happen while Ty is his patient."

Amy: "Kyle told me. So Nicholas is turning out to be someone special? Can't wait to meet him!"

Late that night a text from Kyle: "I know you liked the show in the gym. It's time for a trip to Las Vegas. Just the two of us."

What an erotic rush! After a few minutes, I finally texted back: "Maybe. We'll see."

He sent me an emoji with a tongue sticking out.

Still unfinished business.

Yay Team

The touch football season was ending, and as a culmination, all the teams had a final evening tournament, though it was not meant to be a championship and there was no trophy. With eight teams, there were four total games, opponents drawn randomly from a hat. Each game lasted twenty minutes. No overtimes if it ended in a draw. It was all about good fun, not about winning.

There were hot dogs and sodas, and friends came to cheer the teams on. Some fans brought banners and balloons, and occasionally some girlfriends would be cheerleaders. The gay team had rainbow flags.

Ty had been working out regularly at the gym, and had progressed so much it was clear he would soon reach the end of his physical therapy. During his convalescence he didn't get to play football, of course, but we did go to watch the games. Jake had taken over as quarterback. Kyle had indeed invited Nicholas to join the team. I was proud of him, and I was very proud of how welcoming the bros were. For tournament night, Nicholas agreed that Ty could play for ten minutes, and then Jake would take over.

The gang all showed up. Amy, Natasha, and a host of glamorous theatre actresses were well appreciated by the many male spectators and players. Melissa, her sister, and some of their friends were there to lend support for The Bros.

When it was our turn to play, by chance the opposing side was one of the teams with cheerleader friends. Just as Coach Jones was about to blow the whistle, we heard a blast of horn-honking. A car came screeching to a halt on the roadway beside the field.

Out stepped the drag queens! They were dressed in over-the-top cheerleader outfits, complete with pom-poms. They wore giant bouffant 1960s wigs and sported the most enormous boobs ever seen—in 1960s pointy bras, no less. The crowd was laughing hysterically, and the gay supporters hooted. The Bros were just shaking their heads in disbelief.

As it was an adult crowd, they could get away with being risqué. They sashayed their way over to the sidelines and Miss Vanessa grabbed the mic from Coach Jones.

She signaled the other cheerleaders, who were smiling at her, and said, "You there. Move your asses and give the big girls some room. Bitches, we're here to bring it on!"

The ladies hefted their enormous bosoms and took their places while the other cheerleaders, who were good sports, laughed and made "we are not worthy" bows at them. Miss Vanessa waved to Amy, who used portable speakers and a Bluetooth device to start a slow but catchy percussion beat.

They're the Bros with extra muscle
We're the Queens with extra hustle

Yay Team

Now it's time to bust our bustle
Ready Set Go!

Who's gonna win the game tonight?
(Bringing the guys forward)
The Bros! The Bros! The Bros! The Bros!

Who says the Bros are sheer delight?
(Parading around and pointing to themselves)
The Queens! The Queens! The Queens! The Queens!

Who has the strongest arms on the team?
(Bringing Declan forward and making him flex)
Declan! Declan! Declan! Declan!

Who has the nicest ass on the team?
(Bringing Jackson forward and making him twerk with them)
Jackson! Jackson! Jackson! Jackson!

Who has the biggest chest around?
(Bringing Kyle forward and making him show off)
Kyle! Kyle! Kyle! Kyle!

Except Miss Penelope pointed at herself and showed off her boobs in competition. There was much hilarity when her left boob slipped and she tried to push it back into place, but it didn't work. The crowd howled as she grabbed Kyle's hand and put it under her sweater to push, mugging outrageously as to how much she was enjoying it.

Who has the biggest you-know-what?

(Instead of shouting his name, the ladies put two fingers to their mouths in a "naughty, naughty" look. Miss Doretha pointed to Ty, mouthed, "Oh my god!" and fanned herself. He turned a little red, but had a 'what can you say?' smile.)

Who's gonna score on the field tonight?
(Moving the guys back to the field)
The Bros! The Bros! The Bros! The Bros!

Who's gonna score in bed tonight?
(Pointing at each other)
Not you! Not you! Not you! Not you!

Except Natasha raised her hand and waved at Ty!

Who wants the game to start right now?
(Grabbing Coach Jones and moving him forward)
Coach Jones! Coach Jones! Coach Jones! Coach Jones!

Miss Jenn had the crowd make a drumroll on their knees and draw out a long "Yayyyyy." The other ladies gave Coach Jones a sign saying YAY, and then they each grabbed a placard turned blank side toward the crowd.

At a signal from Miss Vanessa, they flipped the placards around to spell out "YAY M-E-A-T!" The crowd laughed hysterically at their many comical attempts to get it right, with misspellings and upside-down letters and arguing with each other. Finally it said "YAY T-E-A-M!"

This reminded me of a funny scene I saw at Amy's theatre in a play called *Vanities*. Natasha had played a Texas cheerleader horrified about a letter-card mishap. I knew who had given the ladies this particular idea.

The crowd gave a huge round of applause while the ladies twerked at them and blew kisses. Then the four of them sat triumphantly in the stands.

Ty made a little finger-pistol shot at Amy, who mirthfully smiled and put her two fingers to her mouth like the "naughty, naughty" pose.

Coach Jones blew the whistle.

Ty played the first ten minutes, and it seemed everyone knew about his months of physical therapy and what had caused it. Not a single member of the opposing team went near him. When he left the field, the crowd gave him a standing ovation, the drag queens shaking their pom-poms. He gave a bright smile and wave.

During the game Miss Jenn got a big laugh when she got all excited and bellowed at the top of her impressively bosomed lungs, "Jackson! Move that sweet beautiful ass down the field!"

The teams tied at the end. Coach Jones thanked everyone for the season, and all the players joined their supporters and enjoyed refreshments.

Amy, Natasha, and the ladies had been hearing about Nicholas for weeks now and were excited to meet him for the first time. I told the drag queens, "You be careful what you say," I pointed at myself, "or this bitch will bring it on."

They were mostly respectful, and he handled all the attention with his usual equanimity. Amy and Natasha were certainly asking a lot of questions. They started out with typical getting-to-know-you inquiries but rapidly moved on to "How many boyfriends have you had?", "What kind of guy is your type?" and then blatantly pushed their agenda with "Martin says you're great company. Can we invite you both over to dinner? Oh, and Ty too."

At one point, Miss Penelope grabbed his hand and said, "You're so cute, Nicholas, my heart is racing. Feel this!" And when she brought his hand to her heart, her boob slipped again.

Miss Vanessa said, "That saggy tit is as limp as your last boyfriend's dick!"

"Vixen!"

Nicholas was a little nonplussed but was very charming about it.

As we were getting ready to leave, they all had to whisper their reactions to me.

Amy: "Honey, he's marvelous. I wish he was straight."

Natasha: "He's a keeper. Tell Ty to call me."

Miss Vanessa: "Ooo, that beard is so sexy. I want me some beard burn right between my thi—"

Me: "*Thank* you, Miss Vanessa."

Miss Doretha: "Under those shorts is a schlong that can't go wrong. I was gonna grab it, but I thought you might bitch-slap me."

Me: "Very considerate. Thank you, Miss Doretha."

Miss Jenn: "What a cute bubble butt. Ooo, I want to take those sweet cheeks in my hands and squeeze—"

Me: "*Thank* you, Miss Jenn."

Miss Penelope: "I wanted to go out there and tackle him."
Me: "It's touch football. No tackles."
Miss Penelope: "Touch? I can touch? Wherever I want? Move *over*, Diana Ross, I'm gonna reach out and touch someone. Sign me up!"

On the way home, Ty was still beaming over the standing ovation. "Just like my high school days." But then he snapped, "God damn that Amy. She put the drag queens up to it."

"The crowd loved them. They were pretty funny, you have to admit."

"Yeah, they were. She's gonna get it." He looked at me. "And you thought I was bad, torturin' information outta Nicholas. Amy and Natasha—"

"—were the Spanish Inquisition. They were curious to finally meet him. They liked him."

"The guys on the team all like him."

"Do you like him?"

I could see he was trying to control a little flare-up of possessiveness. "We'll see."

But he smiled.

Who is the man with the best best friend?

Well Deserved

I was watching TV with Ty in my house when I got a phone call. I answered, "Hello...Yes, this is Martin." I listened to the caller, sometimes saying "Yes" or "Yes, I can do that," looking at Ty while he spoke. I said, "Yes, I know exactly what I can do. I'll take care of every detail."

When I ended the call, Ty asked, "Who was that?"

"A work thing. Nothing special."

But it's not work, and it is very special.

It was the night of the annual awards dinner, and I was helping Ty get into his tux. I was already in mine, as I was going with him to keep him company.

"Do we really have to go?"

"Yes, Ty. Your deputy chief wants you there to show everyone that you're recovering and doing well. He said it will improve morale."

"If I have to. I hate wearin' this monkey suit."

"But you look glorious in it."

Well Deserved

At the awards dinner in the sumptuous ballroom, we were seated with Laura, Steve, and Deputy Chief Williams. It was a grand affair, with hundreds attending. The food was fine, but the awards did tend to drag on. Ty noticed three tables beside us were empty, each with a reserved sign. He said, "Guess those folks decided not to come. If they didn't have to come, why did I have to?"

Deputy Chief Williams said, "We're glad you're here, Ty. Good for folks to see you up and at 'em." He gave me a subtle nod.

The awards were nearing an end. With another nod from the deputy chief, I got my phone out and sent a text.

The emcee began speaking. "For our final award this evening, it is my honor to introduce the mayor of Los Angeles."

During the applause, the mayor took his time getting to the podium, greeting people along the way. At the same time, a group of people began filling the three reserved tables.

Ty said, "What are those people doin' comin' in at the very end? That's kinda rude." He looked over and did a double-take. "That's Mama! What is Mama doin' here? And my brothers?"

He started to move, but I put my hand on his arm and said, "Don't move. You'll see."

"Cody and Fred and those guys? And there's Amy and Kyle and all those guys? What's goin' on?"

"You'll see. Hush, the mayor is starting to speak."

I had, at the invitation of the deputy chief, organized everything to the last detail. In complete secrecy from Ty, I had organized flights and hotel for Emmaline, his brothers and their families, and the Oklahoma friends. Amy provided all their

319

formalwear from the theatre, even for Ty's nephews and nieces. I had organized all the bros, and Deck had brought Melissa; Amy, resplendent in a strapless floral gown, was there with Anne, Josh, and Tommy; Ms. Meyer with her husband and infant son; Natasha from the theatre; the youth club director and Darius; Coach Jones; Dr. Jordan and Nicholas from Cedars-Sinai; and Commander Dr. Markworth, a striking figure in his naval uniform.

The deputy chief had promised to reserve as many seats as needed, and I had no trouble convincing everyone to attend. I had insisted on utter secrecy to completely surprise Ty.

"What is this, Martin?"

"Hush. Wait."

The mayor stood at the podium and began. "It is the highest calling to offer one's life in the service of others. Today, a child is alive, safe, and healthy, due to the effort of one selfless individual. At great physical cost to himself, this individual exemplifies the motto To Protect and to Serve. His actions are worthy of our highest respect and approbation. His actions do honor to the idea that in serving the greater good, you serve all mankind."

I wasn't watching the mayor; I was watching Ty. His breathing had quickened. Other people around be damned, I put my hand on his.

"That child, alive today, stands as a tribute to the courage one man can show in the face of danger. That child, safe today, will have the chance at a better life. That child, healthy today, is a testament to all that heroes aspire toward.

"As mayor of Los Angeles, I have the privilege of awarding our city's highest honor to this selfless young man for his meritorious conduct and most worthy deed.

"The Medal of Valor for Heroic Conduct in the Line of Duty is awarded to..."

Ty squeezed my hand hard.

"....Dixon Ticonderoga Fields."

A thunderous standing ovation. Ty gave me a quick hug, shook the hand of the deputy chief, rushed to hug Emmaline. He made his way to the stage, where he and the mayor had to wait while the sustained applause carried on for some time.

My hero. I am so proud!

The mayor presented the medal, and invited Ty to speak.

"Howdy, everyone. Golly. Y'all caught me by surprise." The audience chuckled at his Southern accent. "Y'all can call me Ty." The audience laughed, having heard his unusual name. "I hardly know what to say. I see my Oklahoma family is here—what a fantastic surprise, thank you for bein' here. Thank you to all my friends, I'm honored by your presence. Thank you to my unit, they are fine colleagues. And I certainly must give enormous thanks to my doctors, Commander Markworth and Dr. Jordan, for keepin' me alive. A giant shoutout to Nicholas for puttin' me back on my feet."

He looked directly at me. "And a most special thank you to my best friend Martin for every damn thing he has done for me. Love ya so dang much."

He didn't say the ubiquitous "buddy" like he always does. And he said he loved me in front of everyone.

He held up the medal. "I thank you, Mr. Mayor, and the city for this unexpected honor. I am humbled and grateful." He looked out at us. "The life of a child is the most precious thing we hold in our hands. It's our duty to do everything we can to protect this treasure." His voice slightly broke. "I'm glad that I was able to do my part."

Thunderous applause again. He made a beeline to see his mother. I was near enough to hear as Emmaline put her hands to his cheeks.

"You're a hero, my sweet boy. You've done something so good and so honorable. I thank God every day that He kept you alive. I only wish your daddy was here. Your daddy would be so proud—so very, *very* proud—of his son."

I could see how much this affected Ty. He was having a hard time staving off tears. He might cry in front of me, but could never in front of others.

The Oklahoma contingent hugged and greeted him, the nieces and nephews clustering around.

Emmaline turned to give me a loving hug and then, holding my arms, gave me a searching look. She said, "Martin, you look well. You look happier. Are you?"

"I'm the happiest I've ever been," I told her.

I had met Ty's brothers in our video chats, but now Emmaline introduced me in person. They were a bit reserved compared to their outgoing younger brother, but I felt they were good, down-to-earth guys. I could see their resemblance to Ty; what a handsome family. They were heartfelt in their thanks to me for taking care of Ty.

Cody and the other guys—Fred and Rex and Billy—came up to me as well. Cody seemed to be their spokesman. "Martin, we'd like to thank you for startin' over with us. Thank you for makin' sure we were here when you didn't have to do that. It's mighty special to see Ty get this award. Thank you for thinkin' of us." Each shook my hand. Maybe we had four less bigots in the world after all.

During the after-dinner drinks and dessert, Ty made sure to see every one of his family and friends. He radiated with pride when Commander Markworth, Dr. Jordan, and Nicholas told him he was their best patient. His unit team was warmly congratulatory, Steve in particular being sincere in his praise. Coach Jones and the youth club director eagerly shook his hand in congratulations. Darius high-fived him and shouted, "Way to go, Coach Ty!" which made the nearby attendees laugh.

When he got to Anne and Josh, Tommy ran to him. "Uncle Ty!"

"Buddy, I'm so glad you're here. Will you give me a hug?" which Tommy happily provided.

Ty loved holding Ms. Meyer's young infant. She called him a true hero for saving a child, and my ears pricked up when he replied, "Thank you, ma'am. I think you're the hero for what you do every day for kids."

And I also noticed that all the women nearby were perking up for another reason. *What is it about straight women that the sight of a young hunky man holding a baby sets their wombs aflutter?*

The bros had bro-hugs and bro-fist bumps and bro-hand clasping, and it was all too bro-ey for words. They admired the medal and good-naturedly razzed Ty about his unusual name.

Ty had many well-wishers other than friends and family. A society lady with blueish hair intoned, "What a splendid young man you are. Dahling, you simply must attend my next soirée."

Ty said, "Thank ya kindly, ma'am, that sounds wonderful." He turned and whispered to me, "What's a soirée?"

The mayor's assistant, in five-inch stilettoes and a power gown, if such a thing exists, handed him her card and said she'd arrange with him to come to city hall for an official photograph. Then she added, "And please. Call anytime. For example, tonight."

Well, that left no doubt in anyone's mind as to her intentions. However, Natasha was not about to let an interloper interfere in her own plans.

Using her best temptress voice, Natasha said, "Heroes deserve a reward, and I am sure you understand how the reward system works. After all, you are in law enforcement. Good boys have time reduced for good behavior." Cue the seductive look that could launch a thousand ships. "Bad boys who show me bad boy behavior, they just might have to be punished with some particular form of hard labor. And I do mean hard." Glamorous divas promising such rewards—that is, rewards disguised as punishments—outrank power-dressed politicians every time.

Ty was gracious to all who expressed their appreciation. Some gentlemen were sitting quietly at a table, and when they saw a chance to greet Ty, they stood up and came over. Ty was polite as always, saying howdy and shaking hands and thanking them. I admired his good manners as he took time to give them his attention.

"Congratulations on the award, Mr. Fields."

"Thank ya kindly, sir."

"We're pleased to know a real hero; you're an inspiration. I'm Parker, and with me are Dale, Vern, and Jonathan."

"Much appreciated, gentlemen, thank ya kindly."

As Ty turned away to continue meeting other people, Dale asked, "You don't recognize us?"

Ty turned back, puzzled.

In a voice that sounded vaguely familiar, Jonathan said, "What if I asked did you remember to shave your balls?"

I turned sharply to look closely at the men.

Oh. My. Word.

It was the drag queens! None of us had never seen them out of drag before.

Ty couldn't get over it. "Is it really you?"

I had invited them. They had accepted, but when I didn't see them come in with the others, I assumed they had changed their minds because they didn't want to be in such a formal environment. I had not in any way suggested they tone down. Yet here they were in their everyday personas. We were used to seeing them with sparkle and glitz, as larger-than-life spectacles. Now they were pleasant but ordinary.

Ty: "Why aren't all y'all dressed up like usual?"

Jonathan/Miss Jenn: "It's your big night."

Dale/Miss Doretha: "We didn't want to steal any attention."

Parker/Miss Penelope: "We all have jobs and lives where we dress, well, down instead of up."

Vern/Miss Vanessa: "When it's the right moment we transform ourselves." *A transformation like caterpillars to butterflies.* "But for this moment, we didn't want to upstage our friend when he got his award."

Jonathan/Miss Jenn added: "And that's what's most important. Your award. We're proud of you, Ty. We think you're so brave, so courageous."

"Well, now... gents, I got somethin' to say about that. I'm not the only courageous one around. There's other kinds of courage. Like yours."

"Us? Courageous?" Jonathan asked.

As he spoke, he gathered them into a circle, like he did when he coached his basketball players. Without their high heels, Ty towered over them, and they had to look upward at him.

"Yes, you. All y'all have the fortitude and guts to buck society. You got the bravery to live how ya want and love who ya want. I had to be brave just once. You gotta fight against ignorant bigots every single day of your lives. Doesn't that take more bravery, more guts? In my mind, you're the ones with a helluva lotta courage."

The four men gaped at him, eyes glistening at this unexpected show of empathy and support. I was impressed with his maturity.

Parker/Miss Penelope said, "Thank you, Ty. We appreciate you saying that. I hope one day you'll let me introduce you to my wife and kids."

You could have knocked Ty over with a feather. Me too!

He continued, "Oh. I can see you're shocked by that. Let's just say I have an extraordinarily understanding wife."

Vern/Miss Vanessa said, sounding more like what we were used to, "She'd have to be understanding to put up with you."

"Bastard!"

Vern/Miss Vanessa went on, "The rest of us never walked down the aisle. I did have a girlfriend before deciding to, shall we say, express myself."

"Thank you for sharin' that part of your life, gents. Whichever way you choose to be, dressed up or dressed down, I like ya just the way y'are. And I thank you for comin' tonight. I'm honored all y'all are here."

In our times together, the drag queens had only ever given him air kisses and arm clutches and twinkle waves—I think out of consideration that he might be uncomfortable with anything more. This time, Ty stepped forward and gave each of them a warm and caring hug. The four men were visibly affected, Vern/Miss Vanessa tightly closing his eyes as he held on to Ty, Dale/Miss Doretha afterward taking off his glasses and dashing a hand to his cheek.

Remember me telling you that having straight friends who accept you can be so healing?

Miss Jenn/Jonathan brought us to more familiar territory: "So remember, cowboy, you'll always be our special man."

Miss Vanessa/Vern: "Whenever you need a makeover..."

Miss Penelope/Parker: "Or a Miss Penelope Special..."

Miss Doretha/Dale: "Or want to make money with the Tytanics..."

Together they struck a glamorous pose and larger than life was suddenly back on display: "Call on us!" If Natasha ever needed a new glamour pose, they would be a great resource.

And just like that, as if someone had snapped his fingers, they were back to ordinary. They returned to their table. As they went, Miss Jenn/Jonathan couldn't resist and turned back to give us a surreptitious twinkle wave, which made us laugh.

"I can't believe how different they look. Dressed like this, they're so quiet and kinda unassuming."

"Who would have thought?" asked Amy from behind us.

Turning he said, "Hello, Am—hot damn!" For the first time that evening, Ty got a close look at Amy in her stunning gown.

She said, "Congratulations, Ty. Well deserved."

He walked all the way around her in appreciation. "Hot damn! You are a sight. You look beautiful, Amy. Nice dress." Amy and I were both surprised at this rare compliment. Then he teased, "Did you pay another costume designer to help you out?"

Amy looked to the ceiling. "Martin, you're the one who deserves a Medal of Valor for putting up with this impossible creature." Then, in her usual feisty manner, she said, "Ty, much as I enjoy putting you in your place, I think it's time to declare an official truce. I'm going to regret saying this because you'll never let it go and I'll never hear the end of it, but I want to tell you..."

She looked down for a moment, then brought her face up with a smile. "I want to tell you that you are a really terrific guy, and I am so happy you came into our lives." And she surprised him, placing elegantly manicured fingers to his cheek and giving him a kiss on the other one.

He stared after her, dumbfounded, as she walked away, blowing us a kiss.

Finally he spoke. "God damn that girl." He turned to look at me. "She did it, buddy. She busted my balls."

And you're lovin' it.

And then it was my turn. I had been patient, knowing my turn would come. "Ty, I am bursting with pride. I am so proud to have you as my best friend."

"Buddy, you're the bestest best friend. I can't believe you did all this. You kept it secret and got everybody here without me knowin' a thing." Ty hugged me and said in my ear, "The day I met you was the luckiest day of my life. I don't say it often enough. Love ya." Again without the standard "buddy."

One day...

One day he'll tell me he loves me and say my name.

One day.

And to the surprise of the family, the bros, the gentlemen/drag queens, everybody else nearby, and most of all me, he brushed his lips on my cheek. Almost like a quick kiss. In front of everyone.

"Damn!" said Miss Vanessa/Vern from her table. "Wish I could get me some of that."

Breaking News

It was a day full of exciting news. The first bulletin came from Deck and Melissa, who called me in the morning.

Melissa: "Hi, Martin. We want you to be the first friend we tell. We're expecting."

Me: "Wow! Congratulations!"

Melissa: "It's all your fault."

Me: "What?"

Melissa: "Deck finally told me how you helped him with all his romantic plans. So that's why it's all your fault."

Deck: "And that's why we want to ask you something. Since you helped make this happen, will you be godfather for our child?"

Oh gosh, here I am getting all gooey again.

Me: "I would be so honored to be godfather. Thank you."

The second exciting news came from Dr. Jordan. Ty had finished his physical therapy. Dr. Jordan congratulated him on his excellent recovery and said she would not need to see him again. "Nicholas told me you were his hardest-working patient. He was extremely pleased with you. He said Martin was a huge help pushing you to progress."

Ty beamed at her praise. "Nicholas was absolutely the best. Martin just likes to kick my ass."

Mimicking his comment from before, I said, "Somebody has to do the dirty work."

On the way home came the third exciting news, the bulletin I had been patiently waiting for.

I said, "This is fantastic, Ty. You can go back to your normal life as it was. Have you thought about returning to the unit?"

"I've been thinkin' about that. Deppity Chief Williams and I talked. He said I was always welcome, and I could be in any department, not just that one. But I don't know if I really want to go back to law enforcement. Deppity Chief Williams said I would always be in a desk job because of my injury. That doesn't rightly appeal to me. I might have a coupla other possibilities."

I had pushed him toward two different options. I knew which one I really wanted him to do. The seeds had sprouted.

"You do?"

"The youth club director offered me a job. That would be right rewardin' work; I know I could help those boys. But there's somethin' else I might like better."

This is it, the rose is about to bloom!

"You remember when we visited Tommy's school?"

I knew it I knew it I knew it I knew it I knew it! The Consultant Who Finds Solutions/Bestest Best Friend scores big time with this one. The rose is in glorious full bloom. Bette Midler could sing a song about it.

"I liked it. A lot. What do ya think about me..."

"Yes?"

In a rush he said, "About me goin' back to college and gettin' a teacher's certificate? You know I love kids, and when I go to the school, it's been eye-openin' how excited I feel about it. Would they take a country cowboy to be an elementary teacher? I think I could be a teacher." He took a breath and looked at me. "What do you think, Martin?"

He was anxious for my answer. Of all the times he had sought my approval, I knew this was the most important. I could tell he was desperate for me to agree. Oh, how I had longed for this day.

"Ty. That is a brilliant choice. Best idea ever."

He was practically jumping up and down in his seat with excitement. "Really? I'm gonna start lookin' into that right away."

So attuned to Ty's needs, I knew it was a perfect choice for a man who loved kids so much. *And my behind-the-scenes manipulations, my stage management, my planting seeds, will forever remain a secret.*

"I'll tell Deppity Chief Williams I'm gonna pass on the department. I gotta get to work right away on applyin' and startin' courses. I gotta think about what I should be. A classroom teacher like Miz Meyer or a PE teacher or...What's the matter, Martin?"

The thing is, he is finely attuned to me too.

"It just hit me. Your therapy is done, your recovery is done. You won't need me. Will we still see each other as much?" I sounded a bit forlorn as I said a simple "Oh."

"You are batshit crazy. You won't be able to get rid'a me. We'll still see each other all the time. Who do ya think is gonna help me with my homework for my teachin' courses? You're on duty to help, buddy." Then he got a knowing look. "That is, if you can find a moment for little ol' me. I'm gonna be forgotten in a corner. Tossed aside like an old rag."

"What are you talking about?"

"Physical therapy has ended. You know what that means? Nicholaaaaaasss," he sang at me.

I couldn't deny I had been thinking about that.

"You can call him when we get home, Martin."

"No. It has to be him who calls me. It has to be him who decides to move from professional mode to something else."

"He'll call. Bet you anything he'll call tonight."

The round of friend phone calls started up fifteen minutes after we got home. Ty and the bros apparently had been burning up the phone lines. And I thought it was teenage girls who were gossipy.

Jackson: "Nicholas will call. You can tell he's into you. If it doesn't work out, can I call him?"

Kyle: "Ty shocked the hell outta me when he said if Nicholas doesn't call, he'll kick his ass."

Deck: "Remember you and Nicholas have an invitation to dinner with me and Melissa."

That evening, we met the bros at First Down to celebrate Ty's recovery and his career plans. Ty was ebullient as he told the bros about wanting to be an elementary teacher. I thought they might be astonished, but instead Kyle surprised him by saying, "That's a great idea. Amy told me you're a marvel with kids."

Ty was dumbstruck. "Amy said that?"

"Well, she said you should be kept far away from humanity in general, but with kids you're absolutely miraculous. Go for it, bro."

"*Amy* said that. Huh."

Deck carefully said, "Maybe it will end up you being my kid's teacher." And when they turned to look at him in surprise, he revealed to the guys his exciting news, which led to another round of toasts to the first dad in the group.

"Don't worry, Deck," I said. "Uncle Ty and Uncle Jackson and Uncle Kyle would love to babysit. Changing diapers will be fun!" Their mortified looks were priceless. Deck and I cracked up!

This was such a nice evening with the guys, celebrating all this good news. Nevertheless, I was a little distracted and edgy. My phone was on the table beside me, and it was Kyle who said, "Don't worry. He'll call."

The guys focused on me.

I said, "I feel like a schoolgirl waiting for a guy to ask her to the prom."

Ty said, "He has your number. He'll call."

I tried to joke a bit. "You guys have it easy. Women don't need your numbers. They can just look on the restroom wall."

They smiled. Jackson said, "Ty doesn't bother with numbers anymore. He just swipes right on Tinder. Over and over again."

I kept joking to take my mind off my own phone. "It's a wonder his cellphone screen doesn't have a groove worn into it."

We had more drinks, talking about sports and the gym and such. And teasing about women and having babies and them teasing me about guys and lots of lewd comments and jokes and general bullshit and...

Gosh! I feel sort of like...

It had happened so gradually over the last several months. But here I was, fitting in and having fun.

...like a bro! I belong to a group of bros!

And then the phone rang.

Instant attention. I looked. The screen said "Nicholas."

Ty gave me a thumbs-up. The guys were intently watching.

I answered. "Hi Nicholas...Yeah, it's noisy here. We're celebrating Ty's recovery...Ty, he says congratulations on your recovery...Ty says thanks for everything, buddy...Just a second." I stood up, covering the phone, and said, "It's too noisy. I'll step outside."

Jackson said, "You got this, Martin."

Deck fist-bumped me.

Kyle said, "Go for it, bro."

Like he had said to Ty. A bro!

Ty winked at me. "What are ya waitin' for?"

I went outside to continue the conversation.

I came back ten minutes later, and it was as if a new student had walked into a classroom the way they turned to look.

I was walking slowly, deflated. I looked grim and tight-lipped, like I was about to cry. I stopped and threw the phone on the table.

The guys looked at each other.

335

Ty said, "Buddy? You okay?"

Four chairs were shoved back and they stood up, very concerned.

And then I smiled and laughed. "Fooled you! He asked me out to dinner tomorrow night."

They laughed and high-fived me, and we had yet another drink to celebrate. I texted Amy, who texted back, "Way to go, Martin" with a big heart emoji.

The next night, I was pretty excited. The texts came in.

Amy: "Call me the second you get back!"

Kyle: "If you need a threesome, you know who to call."

Deck: "Melissa and I hope it's the most romantic date ever."

Jackson: "I hope it goes great. Ask him if he wants to go to Locker Room with us."

The news had spread, because I got more texts than usual.

Emmaline: "Ty says you met someone he thinks is a good man. I am happy for you, dear Martin. You deserve someone special. Ty also told me his plans for being an elementary teacher. I know very well you had everything to do with that. Thank you from a grateful mama!"

Natasha: "I hope you have a fun date. Does Nicholas like theatre? Tell Ty to call me."

Even Dr. Jordan was in on it: "So obvious this would happen. Nicholas couldn't stop talking about you. Diagnosis: Smitten!"

And what could I say about the text from Miss Vanessa on behalf of the ladies: "Sugar, don't do anything we wouldn't do. And that ain't much. And when you do do it, we want to hear every single dirty, disgusting and delightful detail."

And the second one following: "PS Miss Doretha wants to know how many inches."

I said, "You'd think this was CNN breaking news."

Ty was merciless again. "Just so you know, the porch light will be on when you come home. I'm gonna flick it if you stay out there too long."

And "Or maybe the porch light isn't needed. Am I gonna see you come crawlin' in tomorrow mornin' on the walk of shame?"

And "Do we need to have that little talk? You're gonna be safe, right?"

And "I have some condoms if you need 'em. They're XXL though. In the gym, it looked like Nicholas had it goin' on. He might have the dick o' death."

I said, "Stop! That's absolutely not going to happen. He's taking me to dinner only. I can tell you, he's the type of guy who will take his time. He wants to get to know me away from the therapy situation. You saw how he was so rigidly professional with his work. Very methodical and proper. I think it's the same thing for his personal life. I think he's a little bit old-fashioned and will go slow."

"Well, if he's gonna wait and be all proper and shit and ask my permission for your hand, I'm gonna say what in the hell was he waitin' for."

"So don't get excited. It's a first date, nothing more."

"I can tell you for a fact from my own experience that a lotta people end up in bed on first dates."

"That's because you practically wear a neon sign that says 'I fuck on first dates.'"

"And every other date too. I don't waste any time, buddy. Maybe you should put the move on Nicholas."

"No, that's not going to happen. He's old-fashioned. I know that he will want to make the first move."

Ty looked mischievous. "Does that mean he's the top and you're the bottom?"

I blushed. "We'll find out. But not on the first date."

"Maybe he's into whips and chains. Kyle could loan you a set of handcuffs."

"And you can be quiet right now."

Nicholas arrived to pick me up, holding the door like a gentleman and everything. Ty came out of his house to say hello. I thought Ty might embarrass me, but he was a gentleman too. "Nicholas, thank ya so much again for all the therapy. I feel great." He gave Nicholas his usual big hug and said, "Have a nice time at dinner."

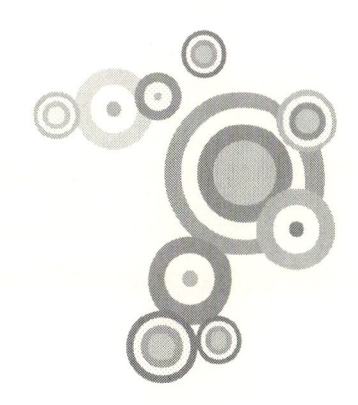

The Door

We had a much more than nice time at dinner. We had a *wonderful* time at dinner. Conversation was so easy and fun. We laughed a lot. Away from work he was more relaxed. And being away from the interrogations of Ty, Amy, and Natasha helped too.

When dinner was finished, I was right. It was dinner only, no double entendre invitations for afterward—all very proper.

When he dropped me off, I had to laugh. The porch light was on. Nicholas walked me to the porch, and we talked for a few more minutes. We set a date to meet again. I wondered what would happen next. I knew I had to let him make the move.

And he did. He took my chin in his hand and gave me a lovely kiss good-night. Such a lovely man.

I went inside, floating on air like Fred Astaire. And there was Ty, sitting on my couch with his arms crossed, like a cliché 1950s dad. I laughed. It was endearing that he waited up for me.

"If you were out there much longer, I was gonna yell, 'Get a room!' Did ya have a good time?"

"Nicky and I had a wonderful time."

"Nicky!" He stood, clapping his hands to his head. "Oh for god's sake, let it at least be Nick!" Continuing on to the kitchen, he said, "I'm glad ya had a good time, buddy."

"We have another date on Friday."

"Another date?" And then he went very quiet and still. He looked away. He abruptly went through the back door to the deck, where he stood looking up at the sky.

I followed and stood looking lovingly at him. *I know what's wrong.* He spoke in a hoarse whisper.

"Am I gonna lose ya now, buddy?" He sounded so bereft. "Goddammit. Didn't know the reality of losin' ya would hit me so hard."

"You're not losing me. Nothing will ever take you away from being my best friend."

"What if ya end up like gettin' married to him or someone else?"

I reiterated, "Nothing will ever take you away from being my best friend."

He looked away and took a few steps toward the pool. "I shoulda asked ya this a long time ago. Do ya get jealous when I'm with a gal?"

"Not the women you bring home for one-night stands. You barely even remember their names the next day."

"But what if I meet someone who I'm interested in? More than for a one-night stand?"

"A two-night stand?"

"You know what I mean. Someone I start goin' on lotsa dates with. Who I might marry?"

"I admit it. I'll be insanely jealous. But I'll be happy for you too."

He turned to me, and he repeated my words back to me. "Nothin' will ever take you away from bein' my one-of-a-kind best friend."

I spoke mock sternly. "But whoever you're interested in has to have my approval. Only the best for Ty!"

He stepped toward me and took both my hands. He stood for a moment, looking at our hands joined together. And then he looked up at me with those beautiful hazel eyes. Oh gosh, I was falling all over again. His eyes brimming, he spoke to me. With love.

"Best friends forever? Promise?"

"Best friends forever. Promise."

A wedding vow of best friendship under the stars in the sky.

He brought his hands to my shoulders, and I thought he would give me a hug. But to my complete surprise, he gently brushed the hair from my forehead. And to my utter ecstasy, he put his hands to my face and brought his lips to mine to give me a sweet, tender, beautiful kiss.

Ohhhh.

Ohhhh.

Thank You, God. Oh, thank You!

He went to stand in his doorway. I walked on stars to my own open door and turned to say good-night.

He said the long-awaited words that filled my heart.

"I love you, Martin."

I looked at him, my heart bursting.

"I love you, Ty."
You are the miracle of my life.
I love you more than you'll ever ever imagine.

Soon.
Soon I would see how things went with Nicholas.
Soon I would become a bigger part of Deck and Melissa's life in my upcoming role as godfather.
Soon I would help Jackson to find himself. Whichever way he went, I would support him every step of the way.
Soon I would take care of unfinished business with Kyle. This was uncharted territory.
Soon I would help Ty get started with his new career. This man who loved kids so much would make a brilliant elementary teacher.
And the hardest thing.
Soon I would have to bring myself to acknowledge the burgeoning interest between Ty and Amy. It was clear they liked each other. Soon he would ask her on a date, I was certain. He'd ask me first if it was okay, and I would say yes. I would be jealous, but I would say yes. On the one hand, I should be delighted that my two closest friends could be happy with each other. But on the other hand, could I help feeling burningly jealous at the thought of Amy sharing a bed with Ty, having the one part of him I could not have? I would have to come to terms with that.
Those feelings will be put in the box never to be revealed.

The townhouse owner called me again to see if everything was good. I assured him the townhouse and property were excellent and I loved living there.

"And how is it with your neighbor?"

"Great. We've ended up being best friends."

"Well, isn't that a treat. You know, when we talked before, I told you he was a nice guy. I had a feeling you'd like him."

If someone had told me that a straight country cowboy and an effervescent gay man would become bestest best friends, that the straight man would be a hero, that the gay man would become the bro of a splendid group of straight men, I wouldn't have believed them.

Yet here we were.

On that first day, when our doors were open and I heard him shout and walked into his life, could I have ever known that my life would be changed so much? That I would become so happy and fulfilled?

Yet here we were.

Some people say that a straight man and a gay man have problems getting along. That such a relationship is fraught with dynamics that other relationships don't have. That there are many things each could not understand about the other.

Yet here we were.

Those doors were open, leading to an entirely *beautiful* friendship. The most caring friendship. The bestest best friendship.

Our story is rather straightforward: it's a love story. A different kind of love story, but love is most assuredly there.

Can anyone else have a story like this?

You might even know the words I'll use to answer. In fact, you might even recall they're the same words you "heard" me "speak" when I began my story. These are the straightforward, exclamation-pointed, upper-cased words for straight men and gay men who are ready to enter a *beautiful* friendship. Come on in, guys, because...

"THE DOOR IS OPEN!"

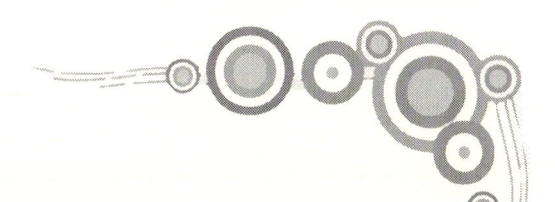

A Note From The Author

This is a work of fiction. All characters and events are fictional. Events that never happened to people that never existed.

Martin Parnell is the pseudonym of a theatre director. He has beautiful friendships with a plethora of exceptional straight guys. His relationship with them is straightforward: they are straight and lord knows he's forward!

Special thanks to my magnificent main cheerleaders and beta readers:
Grant and Nancy

Special thanks for thoughtful comments and extraordinary support:
David B, Enrique, Ian, and Kris R

Special thanks for advice or inspiration or both to:
Baris, Barry, Bojan, Darrell, another David B, the late yet another David B, Erin, Gary, James R, Jim K, John P, Ken, Radovan, Rebecca, Rhett, Stefan, the late Steve J, Steve W, Tim D, Tom B

For their warm encouragement and more inspirations, special thanks go to:
Aaron, Alyssa, Andrew, Anita, Abena, Beth, Brian, Carolyn, Chris B, Chris C, Dan, Debi, Divonsir, Doree, Erich, Fatimah, Fred, Gabriel, Hillary, Jake, James H, Jennifer, Jim I, JoAnne, John M, Judy, Kate, Kelley, Kris K, Kristen, Kurt, Linda, Mark, Megan, Michael, Mimi, Pam, Pat, Pati, Patrick, Paul, Rachelle, Ron, Roxy, Sandy, Sara, Ted S, Therese, Tim G, Tina, Todd, Tom K, Vladan, Will, Zilah

A shoutout to Rachel, girlfriend at the time of one of my special straight guys, who said to me, "Everyone should have an effervescent gay man in their lives!" Aman, Rachel.

StraightForward

A shoutout to Jack Heifner, author of "Vanities", for the football game letter-card mishap inspiration.

Special thanks to Bergmann Graphics and Caldwell Design for their wonderfully eye-pleasing illustration and design of the cover and interior (Tim B and Cassie).

Special thanks to Indigo Editing, Design and More for expert editing, advice and publication management (Kristen, Ali and Vinnie).

Special thanks to Veritas Business Law for warmly supportive legal services (Ted R).

Special thanks for enthusiastic digital marketing and fun emails (with as many exclamation points as I use!) to Books Forward (Rachel and Elysse).

And special thanks to you delightful readers! If you enjoyed this different kind of love story, please leave a review on Amazon and elsewhere. (Please give a warning if you mention spoilers, thanks.)

You can write to the author at: mparnellauthor@gmail.com

Made in the USA
Las Vegas, NV
26 December 2022